Big Girls Love Dope Boys, Too

A Book of Short Stories

Tyanna Presents Authors

Big Girls Love Dope Boys, Too: A Book of Short Stories
Copyright © 2020 by Nikki Rae, Chantel, Asia, TN Jones, & Tyanna
Published by Tyanna Presents
www.tyannapresents1@gmail.com

Jasir and Diandra
A BBW Love Story

Nikki Rae

Synopsis

Diandra Wilson is a single BBW who is about her business. She's focused on her goal of working for herself. Nothing can get her off track... until her best friend, Kira, asks her to do something that she normally wouldn't. Keeping her word to Kira, Diandra's life changes in ways she would never have imagined when she meets Jasir Jones.

Jasir Jones is a twenty-five-year-old dope boy. The only things he's interested in is selling dope, making money, and running through as many women as he can... that is, until he crosses paths with a BBW that he finds extremely attractive. Jasir wouldn't have typically been interested in being with a BBW, but there was something about Diandra that he couldn't shake.

Diandra is from an established, successful family, so dating a dope boy is out of the question. But... will she still feel that way once she meets Jasir, or will she give love a shot with a dope boy? Find out in this drama-filled BBW love story!

Chapter One
Diandra

"Bitch, I love you to death, but your life is beyond boring. You need to get out sometimes. All you do is work and come home. You need to go get you some dick," my best friend, Kira, nagged.

"I like my boring life, thank you very much. That's how you stay out of drama, and the last thing on my mind is getting some dick. Dick doesn't seem to do shit but have y'all bitches tripping and crying over theses sorry ass niggas. Nah, I'm good with that."

"So what? Are you going to die a virgin?"

"I ain't say all of that. All I'm saying is, I'm not in a rush. I have plenty of time to get some dick. Now if you don't mind, I need you to get out so I can get some work done."

"So are you going to come to the party with me or not? It's not like you have shit else tomorrow." Kira pouted.

"Damn, you a pain in my ass, Kira. I'll go just this once. Now get out, please," I said, pushing her towards the door.

"Thank you, bestie. I promise we're going to have a ball," she said before walking out the door.

My name is Diandra Wilson, born and raised in Camden, New Jersey. I was twenty-two with no kids or a man. I worked at TD bank downtown. I'd been working there for a little over a year. I started working at the bank as soon as I finished college. I had my master's degree in business and finance. I planned to work at the bank for another year. I was saving up for my own business. I wasn't sure what kind of business I wanted to open, but I knew I wanted to work for myself and that it would be something in finance.

In my spare time, I made jewelry and sold it online. I was about anything to make money.

My parents were still together. They'd been together since high school. My mother, Teresa, was a wedding planner, and my father, Jacob, owned a car dealership. My parents were pretty down to earth and cool people. I loved my parents with everything in me, but to be honest, I was a daddy's girl. It was nothing that my dad wouldn't do for me, including buying me the new twenty-twenty range rover. My truck was a beauty. It was black and white and fully loaded.

I lived alone in the new apartments that they'd build just six months ago in Centerville. I had a two-bedroom, but one of the rooms I used as an office for the days that I worked from home. I wasn't much of a people's person. I always enjoyed being by myself. I wasn't sure it was because I was an only child, or I just didn't like people. I didn't have any friends besides, Kira. I talked to a few girls from the job, but it was mainly about work related stuff. Kira and I had been friends since grade school. Kira was like my sister. I was only three months older then her. Kira was the total opposite of me and most people didn't understand why the two of us were friends. Kira could be a little wild, but she was as loyal as they came. She always had my back no matter what. Kira just believed in living her best life, and I didn't knock her for it.

✿✿✿✿✿

It was the next day, and I was mad at myself for telling Kira that I would go out with her. I was drained from work and didn't feel like going anywhere, but I was a woman of my word, so backing out wasn't an option. As soon as I got into the house, I laid out my clothes, then took a shower. I then laid down because I needed to take a nap. I hadn't been out in the past six years, so I knew tonight was going to be rough.

I woke up from my nap around eight and started to get dressed. Kira had already texted and said she would be here to pick me up at nine. After brushing my teeth and washing my face, I lotioned down and got dressed. Since it was fall, I decided on a pair of black ripped jeans, a white shirt, making sure to show a little cleavage. I paired it with a red leather jacket and my heeled red leather boots. For a BBW, I considered myself well put together. I was a plus-size woman: size eighteen to be exact. I carried my weight well, plus, I was tall. I was a caramel complexion. When I was a kid, all the kids teased me because I was bigger than everyone in my class, but it didn't bother me not one bit. Ever since I was a little girl, I was confident about my weight. I always loved food. As a matter of fact, I hoped it was going to be some food at this party that Kira was dragging me too because a bitch was starving.

"Damn, bestie. Look at you looking like a snack," Kira said when she walked in my bedroom.

"Thanks, hun. You looking good yourself, but remind me to take my damn key," I said, rolling my eyes.

Kira was pretty and high yellow. She usually always had red hair that fit her complexion perfectly. Tonight, my boo was rocking a denim romper showing off her perky breasts and super big ass. The outfit showed all her curves and was a good look on her.

Against my better judgment, I rode with her instead of taking my own car. I knew how she could get. If it were up to her, Kira would close the place down, and if tonight was one of those nights, I would catch a Lyft home. We pulled up to some club over in Philly and it was packed, which was the first red flag. I wasn't much of a people person, so large crowds were a no-no, and I damn sure wasn't beat for standing in this long ass line. We walked toward the line, and as I was proceeding to the back of the line, Kira Grabbed my arm.

"Girl, where you going? We don't have to stand in that long ass line," she said, walking up to the bouncer. "Hey, Bear," she greeted him.

Bear was tall and chocolate with a lot of muscle and a baldhead. He was kinda cute.

"Wassup, Kira? You looking good as usual," Bear said, taking in Kira's appearance.

"Thanks, Bear. Is Kirk here yet?"

"Yeah, he just got here. He told me to let you in," Bear replied.

We walked into the club, straight to the VIP section. It was a nice crowd in the building, but I was glad to be in a more intimate setting. I didn't even know whose party it was. All I knew was, it was the dude, Kirk's, friend party. Truth be told, tonight would be my first night meeting Kirk. Kirk was one of the niggas Kira was fucking. As soon as we got to the VIP, the waitress took our drink orders. I wasn't a fan of drinking, but when I did drink, I ordered Crown peach.

"So where your little boo at?" I asked, scanning the room.

"Girl, I'm not sure, but let me text him and let him know that I'm here."

A few moments later, two fine ass guys walked into the VIP section, but one particular guy caught my attention. One of them was light-skinned with curly hair and blue eyes, but the one that caught my eye was the tall and chocolate, perfectly built guy. He was dressed to perfection, and I could smell his swag from here. It'd been a long time since I'd even looked at a man like that, but he was just outright gorgeous.

"Hey, baby. Wassup?" the light-skinned guy said to Kira, placing a kiss on her lips.

So it was clear that he was Kirk, but I wanted to know who the other guy was.

"Hey, baby. You looking good as usual. Now let me not be rude. Kirk, this is my best friend, Diandra. And, Diandra, this is my baby, Kirk, that I told you about," Kira introduced.

"Hey, Diandra. It's nice to meet you. This my best friend, Jasir."

"Nice meeting you guys as well," I said.

"I ain't gonna lie. You fine as hell for a big girl," Jasir said, fucking up the mood.

And just like that, I was turned completely off. I hated when guys said stupid shit like that. I hoped he didn't think that was a compliment.

"I would say thank you, but I'm not pleased with your comment. In fact, it was quite insulting. I wasn't aware that big girls had a certain look. How would like if I told you that you fine for a dark-skinned man?"

I swear it was men like him that made me keep my pussy to myself. I couldn't find a man yet that was worthy enough for my jewel. Kira nudged my arm, but I just gave her a look. She knew how my mouth was. I was good people, but I didn't take shit from anybody.

"I'm sorry, Diandra. I didn't mean it like that, but you're right. I shouldn't have said that. It was disrespectful of me. Please forgive me. Can we please start over? My name is Jasir, and I think you're beautiful."

I wanted to stay mad so bad, but he did apologize, and he was cute.

"My name is Diandra, and thank you. You're a handsome man yourself," I stated.

"Damn. I thought you were about to fuck my boy up, but now that that's over, let's party," Kirk said, causing us all to laugh.

Chapter Two
Jasir

"Nigga, will you hurry your slow ass up? You always gotta take forever to get dressed. I told you I had one of my chicks coming through the party tonight, and your ass about to make me late. You worse than females," my boy, Kirk, whined.

"Nigga, shut your bitch ass up. In here sounding like a bitch. You know I like to look good, and that takes time and perfection," I told his ass.

I couldn't wait to meet this Kira broad because lately, that's all I'd been hearing about was this Kira check. Which was unusual. Me and Kirk didn't do the settling down shit. We were block boys, so there was no space for a woman. Don't get me wrong, we got our dicks wet, but all that boyfriend and girlfriend shit was out.

The name is Jasir Jones. I'm twenty-five years old and was raised in Camden, NJ. I was an only child, and for my entire life, I wanted to be a boss. It had to be my way or the highway. Kirk and I had been friends since the first grade. We lived on the same block for most of our lives, up until we wanted more. Since we lived in the hood, we decided to make some fast cash and become dope boys. But like I stated before, I always had to be the boss. So I did whatever I needed to do to become one, and that's what I was: a Boss. Niggas knew not to fuck with me unless they wanted to get laid to rest, and Kirk was no different. We ran shit in this city, and that's how it would remain until we decided to give this shit up.

We got to the party and went straight to the VIP section to go meet up with one of Kirk's chicks. When we got there, the chick Kira was with caught my attention immediately. I was surprised because she wasn't the kind of girl that I would typically be interested, but she was beautiful. We started off on the wrong foot when I told her she was beautiful for a big girl, and she laid my ass out. For some reason, I felt bad and I had to make it right because I wanted to get to know her. So I apologized and asked if we could start over.

After she accepted my apology, the four of just talked and chilled. Eventually, it ended up being just me and her when Kirk and Kira dipped off for a bit. After talking to her, she was cool so far. Her mouth was a little spicy, but I kinda liked it. After the club, the four of us went to the Black Horse Diner. A nigga was hungry as shit. After we left the diner, I dropped Diandra off and took my ass home and went to bed.

It'd been two weeks since I'd met Diandra, and I couldn't seem to get her off my mind. It didn't matter how much I tried to forget about her. I thought about her every day. I was mad at myself for not getting her number. I guess I didn't want to come off as thirsty. To be honest, I never had to do anything to get a woman's attention because women threw themselves at me, and if I wanted to entertain them, I would. But this was different already because for the first time in my life, I was checking for a chick, and a BBW at that. Not that it was anything wrong with being with a BBW. It's just that I never even considered it before, but I guess it was a first time for everything. Remembering that Diandra said she worked at a bank, my black ass decided to pop up at her job and open up an account. I hoped to see her.

I walked into TD bank and scanned the place, but I didn't see Diandra. I still decided to open up an account so I could have an excuse to come back. When I was finished opening my account, I was on my way out the door, and Diandra was on her way in with another woman.

"Hey, Jasir. How are you?" Diandra said.

"I'm good. How are you? And I didn't know you worked at this bank," I lied.

"Yup, this I the one," she replied. "Well, it was nice seeing you. I have to get back to work."

"It was nice to seeing you too. Actually, do you mind if I call you sometime? I would love to take you out," I told her.

"Sure, you can call me, but we'll see about the going out part," she answered.

"Damn, it's like that? It's cool. I'll take your number for now."

After she gave me her number, I called her so she could have my number. I walked away feeling happy as hell. When I left the bank, I decided to go see what Kirk was up to. I hadn't heard from the nigga all day. That was unusual. He must have been up in some pussy. When I got to Kirk's door, I didn't bother knocking. I just pushed in the code and let myself in. I walked to his room and some chick was riding the hell out of that nigga. I just stood there and watched for a few before I let my presence be known.

"Damn, ma, you riding that dick," I said, scaring the shit out of her.

She hopped off kirk's dick so fast, all I could do was laugh. She hurried up and threw the covers over her body that I had already seen. I couldn't lie. She did have a nice body.

"Kirk, hurry up in here. We got business to take care of," I told him before making my way to the kitchen to get something to drink. A few minutes later, the chick walked out the room to leave. She wouldn't look me in the face, so I decided to fuck with her. "Have a good day, ma," I said with a smile.

She just waved at me and walked out the door.

"Damn, nigga. You about to make me change my code. You can't just be walking up in here scaring my women off. I was just about to nut, and thanks to you, I didn't get it. Now I'm about to go hit your moms off and get my nut," Kirk joked.

"Nigga, don't make me lay your ass out in this kitchen. Best friend or not, you better keep your comments to your damn self about my mom," I told him.

"Then I suggest you stop fucking up my nuts and we'll be good," Kirk shot back.

After we were finished bullshitting and talking shit to one another, we headed to take care of some business.

Chapter Three
Diandra

I was surprised to see Jasir leaving my job last week. I'd been working there for a little over a year, and I would have remembered someone as fine as Jasir. Surprisingly, I had fun the night I went to the club with Kira. Chilling with Jasir and Kirk was cool too, after I had to lay his ass out for making that stupid comment. But once we got past that, everything was good, and he seemed pretty cool. I can't lie and say that I didn't think about him every day since the night at the club. I was actually glad that he came to the bank. A few times, I was tempted to call or text him, but I refused to come off as thirsty. Besides, he was the one that asked for my number but still hasn't used it yet.

I was on my way to see my parents. It seemed like forever since I'd seen them with everyone's busy schedule. When I got to my parents' house, as soon as I hit the door, the aroma from whatever my mom was cooking caused my stomach to growl. I was glad she was cooking because I was hungry and was tired of eating out. I used my key, and my dad was sitting in the living room watching TV.

"Hey, Daddy. How are you?" I said, hugging him and placing a kiss on his cheek.

"Hey, Princess. I'm good, baby. How are you?"

"I'm good, Daddy. Just working and taking my online classes."

"That's good, baby. I'm so proud of you. I hope you have time to stay for dinner. Your mother and I would love to chill with you for a few hours."

"Of course, I have time for my two favorite two people. Not to mention, I'm starving." I walked into the kitchen to where my mom was. "Hey, momma."

"Hey, baby. It's about damn time you made your way over here. I almost forgot I had a daughter," my mom said, being extra as usual.

"Well, I didn't forget that I had a mother. I've just been a little busy with work and classes, but I apologize. I promise I won't stay away from y'all this long again," I told her, kissing her on her cheek.

"That's more like it, so anything new going on in your life?" she asked.

"Nothing at all. Same story, different day," I told her honestly.

"Baby, you gotta learn to live. Life is too short to waste, Diandra. Not to mention, I hope to have grandchildren one day, and at the pace you're going, I'll be too old to interact with them."

I thought about what my mom said, and for some reason, Jasir came to mind.

"Mom, I hear what you're saying, but before I have kids, I need to get my career off the ground to support these grandkids that you want so badly. By this time next year, I'll own my business."

"Just don't let time get away from you," she told me.

I sat with my parents for a little over two hours before I decided to go home. As I was walking through my door, my phone buzzed, indicating that I had a text. I knew it couldn't be anyone but Kira. When I looked down at my phone, I was surprised to see that I had a text from Jasir.

Jasir: *Hey, Diandra. I'm sorry I haven't hit you up, but I got caught up and had to go out of town for a minute. But now that I'm back, I wanted to know if you would have dinner with me tomorrow night?*

I couldn't help but to smile at his text. I read the text three times before I responded. I had to play it cool like I wasn't worried about him.

Me: *Hey, wassup, Jasir? It's cool. I've been pretty busy myself, and, sure. I don't mind going to dinner with you.*

Jasir: *A'ight, cool. I look forward to our date. I'll pick you up at six. Just shoot me your address.*

Me: *I look forward to our date as well. I have some work to do, so I have to call it a night. I'll see you tomorrow.*

Jasir: *Cool, do your thing. I'll talk to you tomorrow. Good night, beautiful.*

Me: *Good night, Jasir.*

Once I was done texting Jasir, I did a happy dance. I couldn't believe that I had a date. I had to call Kira and tell her about tomorrow with Jasir.

"Hey, bestie. I didn't expect to hear from you at this hour. I thought your head would be buried in the books," Kira said as soon as she picked up.

"I called to tell you that I have a date tomorrow."

"Girl, shut up. You're lying. Who the hell do you have a date with?" Kira asked excitedly.

"I have a date with Jasir."

"Jasir, who? Are you talking about Kirks' friend Jasir?"

"Yes, Kirk's friend," I told her.

"Oh My God. It's about damn time you going out with a man. I thought you were going to die a virgin," she said with a chuckle.

"Bitch, shut up. It's just dinner. I didn't say shit about fucking. I don't even play those types of games."

"Chile, please. Do you know how many times I was somebody's dessert after dinner on the first date?"

All I could do was shake my head at Kira's statement. I loved my best friend, but my best friend was a little fast ass thot. "Well, I won't be anyone's dessert anytime soon, but I have to go. I'll tell you how my date went tomorrow night."

After we said our goodbyes, we hung up. I took a quick shower and climbed into bed still smiling.

✮✮✮✮✮

The workday had gone pretty fast, and the fact that Jasir and I texted all day made it go even faster. I couldn't wait to see him in a few hours, although I was truly nervous. I had butterflies just at the thought of him, and that had never happened to me until now.

I only had an hour to get ready for my date. I decided to wear something simple yet cute. I laid out my burgundy long-sleeve bodycon dress, and I planned to rock my burgundy and gray leather knee-high boots. Once I was out of the shower, I lotioned and put my clothes on. Not feeling like fooling around with my hair, I put it in a high ponytail and made sure my edges were on point. I threw on some jewelry and perfume, and I was ready to go. I heard my doorbell, and the nerves in my stomach started to do backflips. I hadn't entertained a guy in two years, and the last date that I had never made it to a second date. I had a very low tolerance for men and their bullshit. You had one shot to impress me and give me a reason to keep you around.

I grabbed my gray leather jacket and purse and opened the door. Jasir was looking so good that he caused my jewel to jump. I couldn't understand how a man that I hardly knew could have that kind of effect on me. Jasir was rocking this bad ass burgundy jacket with a pair of burgundy Jordans and some dark blue jeans. His locks were freshly done, and he smelled delicious.

"Damn, Diandra. Excuse my language, but you are sexy as hell," Jasir said.

I just smiled at his comment. He was a little more street than I cared for, but I guess I could sweep that under the rug for now.

"Thanks, Jasir. You're looking handsome yourself."

We walked to his car, and he opened the door to his white twenty-twenty Lamborghini truck. I made a mental note to ask him what type of work he did because most regular nine to five workers wouldn't be able to afford a car like this. I could tell that he had custom work done on this car. The car was extremely nice; nothing that I would ever imagine driving in. He drove blasting nineties R&B until we pulled up to the Capitol Grille restaurant. I'd never been here before, but it looked expensive. We walked into the restaurant looking like a power couple, and I was feeling myself.

"Good evening, Mr. Jones. You can follow me this way," the hostess said.

We followed her to the back, which was a secluded area. When we got to the table, it was a setting for two with candles lit and a bottle of red wine. I felt extremely special. After we ordered, we talked and got to know one another. I finally got up the nerve to ask the million-dollar question that I felt like I already knew the answer to.

"Jasir, what is it that you do for a living?" I asked nervously.

He took a sip of his drink, never taking his eyes off me. "Ma, I'm not going to hold no punches. I'm a boss," he stated.

"A boss at what company?" I asked sarcastically.

"I'm a boss in these streets. I'm a dope boy," he said honestly.

The table fell silent, and I wasn't sure what to say. I knew this was probably my first and last date with Jasir because I just couldn't see myself being with a dope boy. Not to mention, my father would kill him and me. What I look like being a career woman dating a drug dealer?

"You good, Diandra? Wait, let me guess. You're judging me, thinking, why would a woman like you want a dope boy, right?"

"Jasir, I'm not judging you. It's just that, I don't see no reason to go any further. We live two different lifestyles. Not to mention the fact that my parents would never approve of me dealing with a dope boy."

"Look, Diandra. I'm not about to beg you to accept me for who am, but I am going to say this. Your parents don't have to approve of me because I won't be fucking either one of them," Jasir said.

I dropped my mouth open because he didn't have any chill. He said the first thing that came to his mind. It was one of the things that I liked most about him.

Jasir paid the bill, then we headed out. The ride back to my place was quiet. I felt bad for how our date ended. I should have kept my big mouth shut. I guess I was judging him. This was only our first date, and I already told him what my parents wouldn't approve of. We pulled up to my house, and I decided to break the ice.

"Jasir, I'm sorry for the way I spoke to you at dinner. I hardly gave you a chance. I felt like I ruined our date, and I apologize. It's just that, I've never dated a street guy before. If it's not too late, I would like to see you again."

"Yeah, it's cool with me, but don't you want to check with your parents first?" Jasir stated sarcastically.

"You know what? You know my number. I have to go," I said before getting out the car and going into the house.

I was upset at his last comment, and I needed to talk about this, so I called Kira.

"Damn, bestie. Your date over already?" Kira answered the phone on the first ring.

"Well, hello to you, too, and, yes, it's over already. Can you come over? I need to talk."

"Say no more. I'll be right over." Kira was at my place in ten minutes. "Girl, what happened? Did that nigga do something to you?" she asked.

I told her everything from start to finish. Kira just shook her head at my story and gave her opinion. She was the type of friend that would always keep it real and never held any punches. I took in everything that she said, and now I had to decide how much did I care about Jasir being a dope boy. We'd only been on one date, and I wasn't even sure if we would be together. It wasn't like we were talking marriage. What could a few harmless dates do? After talking a little while longer, Kira finally left, and I took my ass to bed. I didn't have to work tomorrow because it was Saturday, and I didn't work on weekends, but I did have some studying to do.

Chapter Four

Jasir

"Nigga, you still ain't hit that yet?" Kirk asked, all up in my business.

"Nah. I keep telling you Diandra not that kind of woman."

"I know you not getting soft on me, bro? You mean to tell me that y'all been kicking it for damn near three months and still haven't fucked or got your dick wet from somebody else? This ain't even you, bro," Kirk stated.

"Just leave it alone and worry about who you fucking," I told Kirk before getting in my car and peeling off. I was headed to go see my mom.

On the ride to my mom's crib, I thought about what Kirk said, and he was right. I was changing, but I wasn't sure that it was for the best. Diandra and I had been dating for three months now, but she still wasn't giving up the pussy. We damn near spent every day together, but she was cracking not a bit. I thought about getting some from elsewhere, but a part of me felt like Diandra was worth the wait. The other part of me felt like it was just pussy, so why did I have to wait? I understood that she was a virgin and shit, but it's not like I was with her to hit and bounce. I was in this for the long road unless she did something to fuck it up.

I haven't really told anyone about me and Diandra, and neither has she. We just wanted to enjoy one another. At first, I didn't think we would work out because I was a dope boy and she was a businesswoman, but since the first night, she hadn't brought it back up.

When I got to my mom's crib, I could smell the fried chicken from the door. I turned my key and walked inside. My stomach instantly growled. I walked in the kitchen where I knew I would find my momma.

"Hey, Momma, wassup? It smells good as hell in here," I told her, placing a kiss on her cheek.

"Hey, son. Have a seat, and I'll fix you a plate. I swear it seems like you can smell my cooking from your house. Every time I cook, here your ass come. It's been damn near three weeks since you been over here, and that ain't you. So who is she? And don't even think about hitting me with that 'I've been busy' shit," she replied.

I found it crazy that my mom knew me so well.

"Mom, how did you know it was a woman?"

"Boy, I raised your ass. That's how I know. Besides, only a woman that a man cares about can keep him away from his momma, especially a momma's boy like yourself," she answered.

All I could do was shake my head. Besides Kirk, my momma was truly my best friend. I don't know what I would do without her.

"Her name is Diandra. We've been dating for about three months. I'm really feeling her, Mom. She's nothing like any other woman that I fucked with. To be honest, we have been together for three months, and we haven't even had sex yet."

"So what you saying is you're in love?"

"Nah, I ain't say all of that. Don't get me wrong, I care about her, but the L-word is a bit much," I replied.

"Boy, please. Who you think you talking to? Your ass is in love rather you know or not. And when the hell have you ever waited three months for some pussy? Let me ask you this, son. Have you fucked anybody else since you been with her?"

I took a deep breath before answering. "Nah, I haven't entertained nobody else," I told her honestly. *Damn, maybe I did love Diandra*, I thought to myself.

"Well, son. I hate to be the barrier of bad news, but your ass is in love. And it's about damn time. I was wondering when your black ass was gonna get tired of pussy hoping and settle down and have some kids." My mom was dragging this a little too far. I hadn't even hit it yet, and she was already talking about kids.

"Mom, slow down. We still getting to know one another."

"Boy, don't tell me to slow down. Bring that girl by here on Saturday so I can meet the woman that got my son's nose open." My mom had jokes tonight, I see.

I wasn't sure if I was ready for the parent meeting just yet, but I knew better than to play with my mom. So I had to get Diandra over here on Saturday.

After chilling with my mom for a few hours, I decided to check on a few sets before meeting up with Diandra.

When I got to Diandra's crib, she was sitting at the kitchen table making jewelry. I respected her hustle. She was about her money and could care less about my money. That was one of the main reasons why I fucked with her so heavy. All the chicks I fucked around with only wanted me for who I was and what I had, but, Diandra? She was about something and wanted more out her life, and I couldn't do anything but respect that.

"Hey, you. How was your visit with your mom?" she asked while hugging me.

"It was straight. She wants to meet you this Saturday."

Diandra's eyes got wide, and I could tell that she was caught off guard. "Your mom wants to meet me?" she asked as if she didn't believe me.

"Yes, baby, she wants to meet you. Are you good with that?"

"Yeah, baby, I'm good with that. I was just surprised to hear you say that. That's all. Are you hungry?" she asked, trying to change the subject.

I didn't say anything else about it since she already agreed to meet her. "Nah, my mom cooked, so I'm still full. But what's up with you?"

"Not much. I've just been here taking a few tests, and when I got finished, I ordered some stuff for my jewelry."

"That's what I love about you. You're always on your shit to become somebody," I stated, not realizing that I just told her that I loved her. *Was my mom right about me being in love?* I thought to myself. The room was silent for a moment, and I didn't expect her to say it back. I didn't even mean to say it.

"Thanks, Jasir. Thanks for noticing," was all she said.

"I notice everything about you," I told her honestly.

I only stayed at her house for a little over an hour. I had a meeting in the morning. I was getting into real-estate, and I had a meeting about my first two properties. I was kinda excited. On the ride home, I thought about everything that my mom said and how I saw myself changing ever since I met Diandra. I didn't think it was a bad thing, but maybe I should slow down and take a step back.

When I got in the house, I took a shower and lit a blunt. I was sitting in my man cave smoking and having a shot, ass naked. I hated clothes, so I was always naked, which was another reason why I hadn't spent the night with Diandra yet. She wasn't ready for all of this, and I didn't want to make her uncomfortable in any type of way. The only thing that we'd done so far was kiss. I mean, kissing was cool, but I was a grown-ass man, and I was ready to get my dick wet. If she wasn't going to give up the ass, it would only be a matter of time before I went elsewhere.

Chapter Five
Diandra

The only thing I could think about all week long was meeting Jasir's mom. I was so nervous. I know we'd been kicking it for a little over three months, but I wasn't aware that we were at the "meeting parents stage." However, how could I say no? I honestly haven't even told my parents about Jasir yet. I knew that after I met his mom that he was going to want to meet parents, and I was scared because I knew they wouldn't approve of Jasir. But it was a good thing I always thought for myself and would only leave him alone if I wanted to. On the other hand, I just wasn't ready to disappoint my parents, especially my dad. I was daddy's little girl, and no man was good enough for me in my daddy's eyes. Especially not a dope boy.

"Girl, what you over there in deep thought about?" Kira asked.

"I'm nervous to meet Jasir's mom," I told her.

"Girl, what you nervous for? You only have a couple of hours, so you need to get your life in order. I mean, what's the worst that could happen? She either gonna like you, or she won't. The only thing that matters is if Jasir likes you or not. I swear your ass be worried about the wrong shit. You need to be worrying about when you gonna buss it open for that nigga before he gives the dick to some other bitch. No offense, but that nigga looks like he got a big dick, and if he's anything like his best friend, he'll know how to use it."

All I could do was shake my head at her crazy ass. But she was right: I was felling Jasir. I think I love him.

"Anyway, let's change the subject. Wassup with you and Kirk?"

"Shit. We just chilling right now, getting our fuck on and hanging out," Kira answered.

"So do you love him?" I asked.

"Honestly, I never really thought about it, but I guess I do love his sexy ass," she replied nonchalantly. "Do your love Jasir?"

"Yeah, I believe so. I've never been in love before, but I know that he gives me butterflies, and I think about him all the time. He's the first guy that I've ever considered giving my virginity too, so I guess I do love him."

"Damn, it's about time, but I'm happy for you, Diandra. Just try not to let fear fuck it up. I like Jasir for you."

I didn't say anything else. I just nodded my head in agreement. Once Kira was finished doing my makeup, it was time to get dressed. Jasir was picking me up in an hour, so I needed to hurry up. Once I was dressed, I looked in the mirror, and I was satisfied with my look. I kept it simple and cute. I decided on jeans, a shirt, and some heels. I wore my hair out in loose curls with some light makeup. Jasir was a very punctual man, and if he said he was going to be here at a certain time, then that's what he meant. When I opened the door, Jasir took in my appearance and bit down on his bottom lip. For some reason, that shit turned me on.

"Damn, you looking good. I hope my momma don't try to steal my girl," Jasir stated.

I wondered was he playing, or if his momma was into females, but I decided not to ask. When we got to his mom's house, the nerves in my stomach were doing backflips. When we got to the door, Jasir pulled out a key and opened it.

We walked in the house, and it was nice as hell in here. I was feeling the décor of the place.

"Hey, Mom, we're here!" Jasir announced as we walked toward the kitchen.

"Boy, stop all that damn yelling in my house. You know I'm in the kitchen," his mom said, causing me to snicker.

"Hey, Mom. This is my girlfriend, Diandra, and, baby, this is my mom, Jamela," he introduced.

"Hi, Ms. Jamela. It's nice to meet you," I told her, holding out my hand.

"It's nice to finally meet you as well, but I don't shake hands. I'm a hugger," she said, leaning in for a hug. "Jasir, I see you went and got you a woman with some meat on her bones."

"Mom, chill."

"Boy, don't come up in here acting all brand new. You know my mouth, and you know I don't bite my tongue. Where do you think you get it from?"

I'd only been there for a few minutes, and I already liked his mom. Jasir just shook his head at her.

"Is there anything that I can help you with?" I asked Ms. Jamela.

"The only thing you can do is have a seat and enjoy yourself. Everything is already done, but I appreciate you for asking."

We all sat down to eat, and the food was looking good. She made some beef ribs, mac and cheese, collard greens, and cornbread. After Jasir said grace, we all dug. The first bite in, I was in food heaven.

"So, Diandra, tell me a little about yourself," Ms. Jamela said.

"For starters, I'm twenty-three, and I'm an only child. My parents have been together since high school. I work at TD bank downtown, but this time next year, I plan to open up my own business. I have my master's in finance and business," I told her.

"Oh, you're businesswoman? I like what I'm hearing so far. So you're okay with Jasir being a drug dealer?" she asked, catching me off guard.

I had to think about how I wanted to answer that before I answered. "Honestly, I don't like the fact that he sells drugs. I think he has the potential to be a great businessman and work for himself legally. So my hope is with growth and maturity and that he will want something better with his life," I answered honestly.

"I like you already. I think you're perfect for my son. You seem to have your head straight and you're going in the right direction. I can see why my son is in love with you, and not to mention that you're a beautiful woman. Do you still live at home with your parents?"

"No, ma'am. I have a two-bedroom apartment. I also sell jewelry on the side so I can save up for my business and a house. I should be straight next year to do both. I'm about my money, so I don't have much of a social life." All I could do was continue to be honest.

I was enjoying the conversation, and I liked his mom. Jasir was stuffing his face just listening, but he didn't say anything. He must have spoken highly of me, or she just knew her son. Because I couldn't ignore the fact that she said that Jasir was in love with me.

"Do you want kids?" she asked.

"At some point, yes, but I would like to get my career off the ground first before I start having kids. I'm still a virgin, so right now, today, it's not on the top of my list."

"Wait, you've never had sex before? Are you waiting for marriage?" she asked as if she was shocked by my revelation.

"No, just the right one," I answered.

"Do you love my son?"

At that moment, my heart was beating fast, and this question was the first one that had me scared to answer. I knew the answer, but saying it out loud would make things more real than I wanted to believe. Not to mention, we'd never said it to one another besides the one time he made the comment about loving my hustle. And I didn't know what to say then. But I guess it was time for the moment of truth.

"Yes. I love Jasir very much," I admitted.

Jasir chocked off his juice that he was drinking, but then his face lit up like a kid in a candy store. "I love you too, Diandra," Jasir said back, causing my heart to flutter.

It was at the moment I knew that Jasir would be my first. I was wearing a smile so big that it was starting to hurt my face. For the rest of the evening, we chilled and talked. We even had a drink. I couldn't believe that I had a boyfriend now. I just needed to introduce him to my parents and get this over with. I learned more about Jasir from his mom, including how he became a dope boy and why. Jasir also shared some shocking news with us both about getting into real estate and him purchasing two properties already. That made me proud and a little more comfortable about introducing him to my parents.

✩✩✩✩✩

Later that night when we left his mom's house, it was about nine o'clock, and I wasn't ready to go home just yet.

"Jasir, why don't we go to your house for a few hours and watch some movies or something?" I suggested.

"A'ight, that's cool."

Jasir turned up the radio and we both sang along to the songs that were playing until we reached his house. This was only my second time over because this was something that I normally didn't do. After all, he always came to my place. When we got there, I started to get nervous because I knew that tonight was the night I wanted to have sex with Jasir. I was typically the one to beat around the bush about anything, but, man, this was a big deal to me. When we walked into the house, it was nice and cozy. It was pretty chilly outside, but it was nice and warm in here.

"Jasir, I had a nice time at your mom's tonight. She's cool as hell."

"Yeah, it turned out better than I thought," he said, and bit down on that damn lip of his again.

I didn't know what it was about him biting his lip that turned me on so much, but I swear I was turned on to the fullest. "So you love the kid, huh?"

His question caught me off guard. "Yeah, I do. Just like you love me," I told him.

Before I knew it, our lips were glued together. We had kissed quite a few times at this point, but none of the kisses felt anything like this kiss. Wasting no time, I started unbuttoning Jasir's shirt. He gave me the eye, but he didn't stop me. Before I knew, we were both naked. Jasir led me to his bedroom and it went down from there.

He gently laid me on the bed, never once breaking our kiss or eye contact. He placed a trail of kisses down my body until he got to my center. He paused and licked his lips before slowly stroking my swollen pearl, causing me to quiver instantly. It was things happening to my body that I never knew was possible.

"Oh my God, Jasirrr, this feels so good." I moaned.

His licks became faster, and my body started to shake. I swear it felt like I was about to piss on myself. I tried to move away from his mouth, but he gripped my legs and pulled me back into his mouth.

"Stop running, and cum in my mouth. I want to taste that sweet nectar." He groaned.

Giving in to his demand, I stopped running and enjoyed the tongue lashing that I was receiving. "Oh my God, Jasir, I'm about to cum!" I moaned in pure ecstasy.

"Yeah, give that sweet shit," Jasir said in between licks. He pulled me further into his mouth and licked my pearl faster, causing me to cum inside of his mouth.

"Oh, fuck, I'm cumming!" I yelled.

Jasir came up and kissed my lips. "Damn, that pussy sweet," he said, kissing me once more. "Are you sure you ready for this?" he asked while stroking his long chocolate thickness.

I just nodded my head yes. Jasir reached over in his drawer and put a condom on. I had never been so nervous and excited at the same time in my life. Never breaking his stare, he kissed me gently before entering my wetness.

I gasped in pain. Jasir asked if I wanted him to stop, but I told him no. He was gentle and attentive to my body. The more he eased in and out of me, the more it started to feel good.

"Oh my God, this pussy feels so fucking good." Jasir groaned. His strokes got faster and a little harder.

"Ahh, Jasir, don't stop." I moaned as it felt like my body was about to explode.

"You ready to cum for me, Diandra?"

It was something about the way he said my name that drove me crazy. "Yes, baby, I'm about to cum." I moaned.

Jasir sped up his strokes and kept saying *"Fuck,"* so I knew he was close to cumming. Hell, I was about to explode my damn self. This was a feeling that I would never forget.

"Fuck, baby, I need you to cum for me because I'm about to cum, ma."

He didn't have to tell me twice because I was right there.

"Oh my God, Jasir, I'm cumming!" I yelled out as my body convulsed. I came so hard that I felt like I was having an out-of-body experience.

"Fuck, I'm cumming too, baby." Jasir groaned as he let his seeds off in the condom. After he came, he collapsed on the bed to catch his breath. Jasir pulled me onto his chest, and I swear it felt like the safest place on earth. "You know from here on out, it's just me and you. I'll kill a nigga just for looking at you. You and this pussy belongs to me," he said in a serious tone.

"And that same rule applies to you. You and that dick belong to me, and I will cut any bitch that try me," I told him.

I couldn't believe that I was no longer a virgin, and I didn't have a single regret. We did it once more before finally falling to sleep.

The next morning, I woke up to breakfast in bed. I didn't even know that he could cook. This was something thing that I could get used to. The more we dated, the more of Jasir's soft side come to surface. He made me some French toast, sausage, and cheese eggs.

"Thanks, baby. This is good. I didn't know you could cook."

"Your man can throw down in the kitchen. Do you see who my momma is? I just don't cook much 'cause I never had a reason to cook before now." I thought that was so sweet. "When you finished eating, get showered and dressed. I want to take you shopping."

"Okay," was all I said before I finished stuffing my face.

For the rest of the day, Jasir and I shopped, ate, and had sex nonstop.

Chapter Six

Jasir

Shit had been going great with me and Diandra. I also learned that baby girl was a little freak. I guess she just needed someone to bring that shit out of her. Well, I was the man for the job. It'd only been a few weeks since I took Diandra's virginity, but we'd been fucking every day as if she'd been getting it in for years. I was surprised that she could handle my dick size 'cause a brother was blessed, and I knew what to do with this blessing.

I'd just picked up Kirk so we could shoot to the dealership because I was ready for a new whip. I pulled up to the dealership and looked around. I saw a few cars that piqued my interest. I walked into the building to holler at my nigga, Jacob. This was the only dealership that I fucked with because he always had the best cars. Not to mention, he did a little side business for me that made both of us some money.

"Hey, Jacob, wassup?"

"Hey, Jasir. What's good with you? It's been a minute since you've here."

"Yeah, I've been a little busy. I got myself a woman now, and, man, she's keeping me busy and out of trouble," I told him, thinking about Diandra.

"You mean to tell me you found a woman that made you want to settle down with? She must be one hell of a woman, and the pussy must be out of this world. I've been knowing your ass for years, and you run through women like they running out of style."

"Yeah, it wasn't something that I was expecting, and you ain't never lied about the pussy being A-I. Baby girl was a virgin when we met."

"Damn, you're a lucky cat. You remind me of myself when I was in high school until I met my wife. She swept me off my feet, and we've been together ever since."

"Hey, Daddy," I heard a familiar voice say.

"Hey, Princess. I forgot that you were coming by," Jacob said.

I turned around and was staring into the face of Diandra. I know I must have heard wrong because I could have sworn I heard her call Jacob, Daddy.

"Hey, baby. What you doing here?" I asked.

Diandra just stood there for a second before answering. "Jasir, this is my dad's dealership," she answered shyly.

Jacob was wearing a face of confusion. "Diandra, how do you know Jasir?" he asked.

Diandra was hesitant to speak because she just stood there. "Daddy, this is my boyfriend," she finally said.

I wasn't expecting what happened next. Jacob punched the shit out of me, catching me off guard. Once I caught my balance, I hit that nigga back. I could hear Diandra screaming, but neither of us didn't stop until Kirk broke us up.

"What the fuck are y'all doing?" Kirk asked.

"This nigga is fucking my daughter!" Jacob barked.

"I didn't know she was your daughter, Jacob, but what you not gonna do is put your fucking hands on me. If it wasn't for the fact that you were my girl's dad, and somebody that I consider my boy, I would have put a bullet in you for that shit you just pulled!" I shot back seriously.

"Diandra, when the fuck did you get a boyfriend? And are you aware that he sells drugs? You can't be with him, Diandra. This shit ends today," Jacob said like he didn't sell drugs too.

"Nigga, what the fuck you mean is she aware that I sell drugs? Is she aware that you sell fucking drugs?" I asked, not meaning to let that slip, but I was pissed.

The room fell silent, and I bounced. I just couldn't stand there another second. I needed some time to myself, and I would deal with this shit later. Kirk was right behind me. I hoped in the car and peeled off. I was driving fast as hell.

"Nigga, pull this shit over. You not about to kill both of our asses because you're mad," Kirk said.

I pulled over and let him drive because at the rate I was going, we would have gotten pulled over by the cops, and I damn sure wasn't in the mood to deal with no cops right now. Kirk drove to Pat's, and we sat at the bar and ordered some wings and Henny. Food and a drink was the only thing that was gonna calm me down right now.

"Now, nigga, what the fuck happened back there?" Kirk asked.

"Nigga, I told you. Diandra is Jacob's daughter, and he not feeling me being with his daughter, so that nigga stole me."

"Damn, that shit is crazy. Sounds like a TV show. And why haven't you met her parents anyway? If she's serious about you, why hasn't she told them about you?" Kirk said, not making the situation any better.

"Look, just change the subject because I need to calm down and deal with that shit when I'm thinking more clearly."

After we finished eating, I dropped Kirk back off to his car and took my ass home. Once I got in the house, I checked with my workers and made sure everybody was straight and told them if they needed anything to hit up Kirk because I wasn't going to be available for the rest of the day. After I sent my text out, I powered off my phone and got in my bed because I needed to sleep this shit off and start over.

✿✿✿✿✿

Somebody banging on my door caused me to jump up out of my sleep and grab my gun. I looked at the clock it was six o'clock. I didn't realize that I'd slept for so long. When I got the door, I looked out the peephole and was shocked to see Diandra on the other side of it. I opened the door, and she looked like she had been crying all day.

"Diandra, what are you doing here?" I asked.

"I'm here because I've been calling and texting you for hours with no response. I know what happened earlier was a mess, but why are you taking it out me?"

"Look, I needed some time, and honestly, Diandra, you're not that innocent in this. For one, why haven't you told your parent's about us? Let me take a guess. You're ashamed of me? Don't want to have to say the words out loud? You don't want anyone to know that you fell for a fucking dope boy?!" I yelled.

Diandra just stood there and stared at me with a look of hurt. "Fuck you, Jasir! I shouldn't have come here," she stated.

"Fuck you too, Diandra, and maybe you shouldn't of come here!" I yelled.

As soon as the words left my mouth, I felt like shit. I had no right to talk to her like that. And as wrong as I knew was, I was being too stubborn to go after her. All of this shit was new to me. Chasing after a woman and meeting parents and shit wasn't my thing because I didn't do relationships. Diandra had a nigga fucked up. I was doing things I never thought I would do, and

I wasn't sure if I liked it or not. I felt like I was getting soft, and that just couldn't happen. After I tried calling Diandra a few times and she didn't answer, I finally decided to take my ass to sleep. Today was just too much for me. Now I remember why the hell I never wanted to be in a relationship. Because a few months of being in one had changed me already. Got me fighting my girl's dad, and just caring about other people's feelings was too much.

Chapter Seven
Diandra

The last two weeks I'd been a wreck with emotions. I couldn't believe that one minute I was having the time of my life and feeling like I was in a relationship with the greatest man ever. Now, I'd been depressed and crying for the past two weeks. I could hardly speak. Not to mention that I hadn't heard from Jasir. My dad and I were not on the greatest terms, and this was the first time that me and my dad had ever had a fallout and not spoken to one another. It was killing me because I was a daddy girl and loved my dad with everything in me. I hated that we were going through this, but he still had no right to talk to me the way he did.

"Diandra, someone out there to see you," one of my coworkers said to me.

I couldn't think of anyone that would be here to see me except Jasir, and as much as I missed him, I just wasn't ready to see him right now. When I got to the front, I was surprised to see my mom. I immediately thought something was wrong.

"Mom, what are you doing here? Is everything okay?"

"Baby, I'm here because I'm sick of this shit between you and your father. This has gone on for way too long. Neither of you hasn't quite told me what was going on, but I know it has something to do with a guy. So I need both of you to be at the house tomorrow at seven," my mom said.

I was no way ready to face my dad right now. I was still on an emotional rollercoaster. Not to mention that I hadn't spoken to Jasir in two weeks. So how the hell was I suppose to get him at my parents' house?

"Mom, I don't think that's a great idea. I'm not ready to see dad, and I don't think he wants to see me right now," I told my mom honestly.

"Diandra, it wasn't a question. I'm telling you to be at the house tomorrow at seven with whoever this mystery man is. Now, I have to go, and I'll see you tomorrow," my mom said before walking out.

I couldn't believe this was happening. For the rest of the day, all I could think about was the conversation I had with my mom.

That day I ran into Jasir at my dad's dealership had been the only thing on my mind. When Jasir stormed off after getting into a fight with my dad, me and my dad got into it pretty bad. My dad had never spoken to me that way before, but it was something that Jasir said about my dad selling drugs that I couldn't get past. Of course, my father denied it, but Jasir didn't come off as a liar. I just knew something wasn't right, but later that night was when my heart felt like it was crushed by a truck. Jasir's words hurt me so badly that even once he called, I couldn't bear to talk to him. When I got home from work, I decided to text Jasir because I didn't know how he was going to react after two weeks of not talking.

Me: *Hi, Jasir. I know you're probably surprised to hear from me, but my mom came up to my job and asked me to bring you to my parents' house so we could all talk. I told her I didn't think it was a great idea, but she insisted.*

After I sent the text, I realized that I didn't send him the address. So I texted him the address, then got in the shower and took a long, hot shower. Today was one of those days that I wished I was a drinker or a weed smoker. When I got out the shower, I threw on some boy shorts and a tank top and made my way to the kitchen to make me something to eat. I decided to make some wings and fries.

Once I was done eating, I made some jewelry and read a few chapters in this book I was reading. I was trying to do anything that kept me busy to help keep my mind off of all the things that could take place tomorrow night. I thought about how I was a virgin all this time, and when I finally gave up the cookie, I became single within two weeks. I couldn't deny that I was missing Jasir like crazy. Jasir's dick game was everything, and I wished he was inside of me right now. Then maybe I wouldn't be so stressed.

✫✫✫✫✫

I had an hour before I had to be at my parents' house, and I still hadn't heard from Jasir. Jasir hurt me with how he talked to me the day I showed up at his door, but I didn't want us to end that way. Over the last two weeks, I realized how much I truly loved Jasir, and I wasn't ready for us to end. After I was dressed, I headed over to my parents', not ready for the conversation that I knew was going to take place. I was tempted to call Jasir, but I didn't want to feel like

I was dick riding. I was sure that he got my text but decided to ignore me. I walked into my parents' house, and my mom and dad were both in the family room.

"Hey, Mom and Dad," I spoke when I walked in.

"Hey, baby," my mom spoke back, but of course my dad was on good bullshit and didn't say anything.

I knew it was a bad idea coming here tonight. It was evident no one was ready to get past this. I didn't bother to say anything else to him because I didn't want to have to be disrespectful.

"Jacob, I know damn well you heard your daughter speak to you. I don't care what the hell you two have going on, but disrespect isn't an option. Especially in this house," my mom said, not dealing with my dad's bullshit tonight.

"Mom, it's okay. He doesn't have to speak if he doesn't want too," I stated.

"Yes, the hell he does have to speak to his only daughter. Diandra, where's this guy that has you and your father in an uproar?"

"I texted him, but I don't think he's going to show up. We haven't spoken since everything happened two weeks ago."

She was about to say something when the doorbell rang. My mom went to answer the door, and I could hear Jasir's voice. For some reason, my heart was pounding. When Jasir walked into the living room, my heart melted, and I no longer wanted to be mad with him.

"Hello," he spoke when he walked in.

"Hi, Jasir," I spoke. I took in his appearance, and, man, he was looking good. All I wanted to do was make love to him right here. What I did know was, I know I didn't want to be without this man.

"I'm not sure what's going on with all of you, but someone needs to tell me what's going on," my mom stated.

"I'll tell you what's going on. This fucking dope boy thinks he's going to be with my daughter, and that's not going to happen."

"Jacob, shouldn't that be Diandra's decision? We raised a bright woman, and I think she's more than capable to make her own relationship choices. Diandra, do you love this man?" my mom asked.

Everyone's eyes were on me waiting for my answer, so now was the time for the moment of truth. "Yes, Mom. I do love Jasir. In fact, I'm in love with him. I didn't tell y'all about him because I was scared of this very thing happening. Dad, I don't want to beef with you. Everyone knows that I'm a daddy's girl. I don't want to hurt you, but I am a grown woman, and I'm the only one that can choose who I decided to be with."

"Jacob, with all due respect, I've known you for a long time, and I think you cool as shit. But I need to be honest with you. I'm in love with your daughter, and I would never do anything to hurt her, or put her in harm's way. I know you're used to me being with a lot of different women, but never have you ever heard me tell you that I loved any of them. Nor, have you ever heard me say that I was in a relationship with any of them. Yes, I sell dope, but that's not what defines me. I treat Diandra like the queen she is."

All I could do was smile because, besides two weeks ago, he'd been nothing but good to me. I walked over to Jasir and grabbed his hand, but he had other plans and kissed my lips.

"Well, Mr. Jasir. I've only known you for a few moments, and I can already see why my daughter loves you. So y'all have my blessing," my mom expressed.

"Thanks, Mrs. Wilson. I appreciate it. I promise to protect your daughter's heart. And now I can see where she gets her beauty from."

"I guess I did overreact a little bit, but this is my world, and to be honest, I would probably never think anyone is good enough for my baby girl. And you're right, I have known you for a long time, and you've never lied to me before. So I all I can do is hope that you don't start. Diandra is a grown woman that's capable of making her decisions, but if you hurt my daughter, I'll kill you myself. That's not a threat, it's a promise," my dad warned.

The meeting started a little rocky but seemed to be turning in the right direction.

"Mom and Dad, thank you for letting me live my own life. Jasir makes me happy."

"You make me happy too, baby."

We sat and talked a little longer during dinner. The only thing I had on my mind besides ripping Jasir's clothes off, was if what he said about my dad selling drugs was true? I just didn't want to ruin the moment and ask right now.

Jasir followed me back to my place. We had somethings we needed to discuss, but right after I needed to get some dick. When we got to my house, we walked in and I thought we were going to talk first, then get it in. But Jasir had other things in mind. I could hardly close the door before he picked me up and carried me to the room. He threw me on the bed and stripped me out of my clothes. Once I was as naked as the day I was born, he started to suck on my nipples, instantly causing me to get wet. Jasir and I sexed one another all night long, forgetting all about talking. He fucked me so good that I forgot what the hell I wanted to talk about.

☆☆☆☆☆

The next morning, I got up and made me and Jasir some breakfast. While I was cooking, someone was pounding on my door. When I opened it, it was Kira. But she was crying and hysterical.

"Kira, what's wrong with you?"

"Me and Kirk. Were out last night and he was shot. I was trying to call you all night long. And they were trying to contact Jasir. Have you seen Jasir?" Kira cried.

"Oh my God, is he okay? And, yes, Jasir is here." I walked into the room and Jasir was sitting up on the bed.

"Babe, who's at the door?"

"Baby, it was Kira. She said that Kirk was shot last night."

Jasir jumped up and ran into the living room. I threw on some clothes because I knew he was going to go to the hospital, and I would be right there with him for support.

"Baby, I have to go to the hospital and check on my boy."

"I'm coming with you," I told him putting on my sneaks.

After making sure everything was turned off, the three of us rode together. I decided to drive so those two could gather their thoughts. We got to the hospital, and Jasir walked to the reception desk to get the room number. Me and Kira stayed behind to give him some privacy.

"Kira, what the hell happened?"

"We had just come out from Outback Steak House, and on the way to the car, we noticed this lady being robbed. So when Kirk tried to stop the guy, he shot Kirk. I'm just so shaken up because Kirk could be dead right now, and then who's going to help me raise our baby?"

I was wearing a look of confusion because I had no idea that she was pregnant. I didn't even know they were that serious to be having a baby. I didn't even think Kira realized that she let that slip.

"Kira, did you just say you were pregnant?"

"Yes. I planned to tell you first thing this morning. I found out yesterday evening, and that's why we were out eating. We were celebrating, and he almost lost his life from trying to do the right thing," Kira cried.

I felt bad for my best friend. I couldn't even imagine how scary that had to be.

"Everything is going to be okay, best friend. Kirk is fine, and you're going to be a mommy. I'm happy for you."

"Thanks, Diandra, and you're going to be an auntie and a God mom. I can't wait to spoil him/her, although I hope it's a boy."

I told Kira how the meeting went last night and about the great makeup sex that we had. I was tired, and since everything was good with Kirk, me and Jasir went back to my house.

Chapter Eight

Jasir

I was happy as hell that my boy was good after being shot. When I first found out that he was shot, I thought we had beef, and I didn't feel like dealing with that shit right now. I was trying to get my real estate businesses off the ground and my surprise for Diandra together. I'd just brought two more properties, giving me a total of four properties now. I owned two houses and two office buildings. Shit was starting to look up for me. I was ready to get out this street game and become straight legit.

Everything was going great between me and Diandra after the meeting at her parents' crib. At first, I wasn't going to go because in my mind, I was done with Diandra after everything that went down with her and her dad Jacob. I was missing her like crazy when we were apart. I hated that she had me open the way she did so soon, but being apart from her and not talking to her for two weeks made me realize how much I loved Diandra. I never thought I'd see the day when I would be ready to give up my player's card and just be with one woman. Diandra was everything you could ask for in a woman, and some. Although my baby was a BBW, I was loving every one of her curves. If something happened with her, I'd probably only date BBW's.

I was on my way to pick Diandra up for work so I could give her my surprise. When I walked into the bank, it was this dude all up in baby's face, but I was about to dead that shit because I didn't play about mine, and Diandra was mine. I planned to make her my wife one of these days. My mom loved Diandra, and that was all I needed, even though I didn't need her approval, but I'm glad that I had it. It was no greater feeling in the world to know that your mom loved the woman that you loved, and vice versa. I walked up and stood next to the guy that was talking to Diandra.

"Hey, baby."

"Hey, baby. I'll be right out," she said, smiling from ear to ear. She already knew I was on my bullshit.

"Okay, my sugar pie. I'll be right over here," I told her, calling her something I'd never called her before. All we both could do was laugh at my comment.

When we got in the car Diandra just shook her at me while laughing. "Nigga, you're a fool. Don't be coming up to my job showing your ass. This is my place of business."

"And you're my place of business. That dude was all up in your face, and I wasn't having that."

"Boy, you're a damn fool. Now what is this surprise that you have for me that you had to drive me and pick me up from work?"

"If I told you, then it wouldn't be a surprise, would it?"

Diandra just rolled her eyes at my sarcastic remark. After driving for twenty minutes, we were finally at the destination.

"Jasir, this building is beautiful. What is it?"

"Just follow me." I walked into the office building. Office room by room, and Diandra was at awe with the building. It had four huge offices inside of it.

"Oh my God, Jasir, this is nice as hell."

"Well, I'm glad that you love it so much because this is your new office building," I told her while passing her the deed to the place. I wanted her to know that I was for real.

"Jasir, I know you're lying. What do you mean this is mine?"

"Just what I said. This is your office building. I told you I would give you the world, and this is just a small start. You deserve this and more. It's nothing sexier than a woman that has her head on her shoulders and goes after what she wants, and you, dear, are that woman. I know that you were saving up to buy your own building, but now you can use that money for something else. And before you try to reject my offer, I need you to know that this is one hundred percent yours, and your name is the only name on the paperwork. And if anything happens between us, this is still yours. I paid it completely off."

"Oh my God, Jasir, this is just too much. I can't believe you brought me a building, but I'm so grateful. Thank you so much, Jasir. I love you so much," Diandra cried.

I knew she would be happy, but I didn't expect her to cry the way she was crying.

"Baby, stop crying, and I love you too. I didn't have anything done to it because I wanted you to be able to decorate your office the way you want.

Now, I would like to pay for it, but you can choose your own décor and furniture."

Without saying another word, Diandra squatted and began to take my pants down. She freed my thickness from my boxers and sucked it into her mouth, causing me to throw my head back. I swear it felt like her mouth was wetter and warmer than normal. My baby was a real freak, and that's just how I liked her. I had the true definition of a lady in the streets, and a freak in the bed. Diandra sucked me dry, making sure not to waste a drop.

"Thanks, babe. This was the nicest thing anyone has ever done for me," she said with a wide smile.

"You're welcome, McNasty. I know one thing. If you keep sucking my dick like that, you gonna have a few office buildings," I told her honestly.

Diandra was sucking my dick like a porn star, and that shit had me wanting to run out to buy her a few more buildings so I could keep feeling this shit. After that nut, my ass was ready for a nap. After we walked around the building, I just listened to her tell me some of her plans for each room with a smile. I was happy that I could put a smile on my woman's face and make her happy.

After we were finished at the office, we went and grabbed something to eat before I dropped her off. I needed to handle some shit in the streets with Kirk. After chilling for a month after he got shot, he was fully recovered and back in these streets. I picked him up from Kira's spot. He damn near moved in ever since he found out that she was pregnant. I was surprised that she could tame that nigga because Kirk was way worse than me when it came to the ladies. Kirk had no problem fucking a different chick every night, but ever since he had been fucking around with Kira, he hadn't been fucking with any other women. I liked Kira for Kirk. Not only did she calm his ass down, she was there every step of the way when he got shot. Kira was there for him every day.

"Damn, nigga. Where the hell you been all day?" Kirk asked as soon as he got in the car.

"Nigga, hello to you, too, and if you must know, I was with my girl. I brought her an office building so she can open her own business."

"Damn, Jasir. Sis got a nigga sprung off that pussy. You out here buying buildings and shit for a woman that's not even your wife."

"Kirk, shut the hell up, and I don't get sprung. I sprains the pussy. Now let's go make this run so I can get you back home with your baby momma. You talking about somebody being sprung. You pretty much moved in with Kira's ass, *and* you knocked her up."

"Nigga, just drive and shut the hell up." Kirk didn't have shit else to say because he knew I was right.

Chapter Nine

Diandra

I was at the mall trying to find Jasir something for our six-month anniversary. I couldn't believe that we'd been together for six months already. Jasir and I have gotten pretty close. It seemed like we'd been together for years. My office was just about finished, and everything was to my liking. I only changed the color in two of the rooms and added furniture. My office sign was just put up today. I decided to call it Diandra's Finance and Credit Solutions. Once I got my foot wet in the business game, I was going to hire a few people to work for me. It took me three months to get everything straight, and I planned to have my grand opening next month. I gave my two weeks' notice to the bank, and they were sad to see me go, but I needed to move on to something better and of my own.

I decided to go into the baby store and pick up something for my Godchild. I already knew I was going to be the Godmother, but Kira and Kirk officially asked me and Jasir to be the Godparents, and we both gladly excepted. They were finding out what they were having tomorrow morning, and they asked us to come along. Kira and Kirk didn't want to know what it was tomorrow because they wanted to have a gender reveal.

I didn't feel like gender reveals were necessary. I felt like they were a waste of money. Whenever the time came for me to have a baby, I would just have a baby shower. I didn't get anything too crazy. I just picked up a few blankets, that I was later going to put the baby's name and date of birth on them once I learned what his or her name would be. After I paid for my items, I left out the store. I still had to figure out what I should get for a man that seemed to already have everything. Jasir already had plenty of jewelry, clothes, and sneakers, but what I didn't see him wear that often was a watch. So maybe I would buy him one. I wasn't expected him to buy me anything because I wasn't even sure if he knew that we'd been together for six months, or if this was something that he would even celebrate. I just felt like this was a girl thing.

I paid for Jasir's watch, then headed to my car. I was about to visit my parents. My dad and I were finally back to normal. Me and my mom were devastated to learn that my dad was involved in some illegal business with Jasir, but, hey? What could we do? When I got to the house, I didn't see my dad in the living room, so my guess was he wasn't home. I knew my mom was in the kitchen because I could smell the food.

"Hey, Mom. It smells good in here. What are you cooking?"

"Hey, baby. I'm making your father some hot and honey glazed ribs, mac and cheese collard greens, and cornbread. I can make a to-go plate, but you can't stay because we're having a date night tonight. And you know what comes after a good meal like that, don't you? I get to be your father's dessert," she said. wearing a wide smile.

"Eww, Mom, that is way too much information, and you can just put me a plate up. I'll pick it up tomorrow."

"Girl, what the hell you ewwing about? Don't act all innocent. Your ass getting fucked now, and from what I can see, Jasir is fucking you pretty well. You're ass been glowing for the past few months, and not to mention that ass and them thighs are getting thicker than they already were."

My mom had me sick to my stomach talking like that. She was always free with her words, but this was too much.

"Mom, have fun tonight. I'm out. But I stopped by because I need you to cater Kira's gender reveal. We find out what she's having tomorrow, so we'll probably do the gender reveal sometime next week."

"Okay, that's fine. I don't have anything booked for that week, but let me know the date as soon as possible."

I kissed my mom on the cheek before heading out the door. I had to hurry home and cook dinner. I asked Jasir to be at my house at eight, and it was almost six already, not leaving me much time.

Jasir just got to the house and the food was smelling good. I made this pasta dish that I saw on Facebook. It was some type of alfredo with shrimp, sausages, and cheese, and I made some garlic bread. I couldn't wait to eat because for some reason, I was super hungry.

"Hey, baby. It's smelling good as hell in here, and you looking good."

"Thanks, baby. You're looking good yourself," I told him, placing a kiss on his lips. I was only wearing a black piece of lingerie, and Jasir couldn't keep his eyes off of me.

"Baby, how the hell am I suppose to enjoy this good looking food when you sitting across from me looking like you want to be fucked?"

"Well, you have to have your dinner first before you can have dessert," I flirted.

Jasir just nodded his head and licked his lips. He knew that would get to me. It was something about the way he licked his lips that turned me on. Right when we finishing up dinner, I pulled out my gift for Jasir and passed it to him.

"Baby, what's this for?"

"Today is our six month anniversary, and I just wanted to get you a little something."

"Oh, wow, babe. It's been six months already? Now I feel bad that I didn't get you anything. Why didn't you say anything?"

"Jasir, I wasn't expecting you to get me anything. I know guys don't usually be into this kinda stuff."

Jasir opened the box and pulled the silver diamond watch out. "Babe, this watch is hot. I see you got a little taste in jewelry."

"I honestly wasn't sure what to get you. I noticed I haven't seen you wear a watch, so that's what I got."

"I don't know why, but I never were into watches, but this is fire, so I'm going to rock it. Thanks, babe. Now excuse me for a minute. I need to use the bathroom."

While Jasir was using the bathroom, I started to clean up the kitchen. I was so glad that he liked his gift. I was so deep in thought that I didn't even hear Jasir walk back into the kitchen. He walked up behind me and startled the hell out of me.

"You scared the hell out of me. I didn't even hear you walk back in here."

"I didn't mean to scare you. But, listen. I love your gift, and I hope you love yours just as much I love mine. Happy sixth-month anniversary babe," Jasir said with a wide smile.

He was always full of surprises. He passed me two jewelry boxes: one long and one square one. I couldn't believe he remembered. Jasir surprised me more and more every day. I opened the first box, and it was a pair of gold earrings with my name in them. The second box had a matching bracelet. I was loving my gift. I kissed Jasir passionately. He then grabbed my hand and took me to my bedroom for a sex session that lasted for more than two hours.

✫✫✫✫✫

Today was the gender reveal party, and Kira and Kirk were excited to find out what they were having, as well as their parents and mine. Kira was like a daughter to my parents, and they felt like they were having their first grandkid. As soon as everyone was finished eating, it was now time for the moment we'd all been waiting for. Jasir and I decided to keep the reveal simple but fun, so, of course, we had to play a joke on our best friends before we actually revealed the sex of the baby. We had one big balloon that they had to pop together. The looks on their face when they popped the balloon was priceless. Pink and blue confetti fell from the balloons along with three pictures two of a boy and one of a girl indicating that they were having triplets.

"Why the hell are there two colors and three pictures?" Kirk asked.

"The two of you are having triplets: one girl and two boys," I lied.

"I can't have three babies! I'm still trying to brace myself about one baby. Are you sure?" Kira asked. They both looked so flustered that I couldn't continue the joke. I just burst out laughing.

"Y'all, let me stop playing. It's just one baby, and here's the real reveal." I laughed as Jasir brought out a pinata and hung it up.

"Damn, y'all almost gave my ass a heart attack," Kirk said, causing everyone to laugh.

"Sorry, but we had to do it and have some fun."

We had the pinata custom made into the shape of a baby. The two of them both started hitting the pinata until the blue Confetti fell out. That's right. I was about to have a Godson.

"Congratulations, y'all! Next up is the baby shower in a few months, and I can't wait to shop for my Godson." I gave both Kira and Kirk a hug.

After we served the cake, we cleaned up and headed home.

Chapter Ten

Jasir

I'd just pulled up to my mom's crib. It'd been two weeks since I saw her. I was so busy with flipping properties and helping Diandra with her business that I didn't have time for shit else. I walked into the house, but I didn't see my mom, so I walked towards her bedroom. I thought I was tripping when I heard moaning but I wasn't. When I got the door, it was cracked and some nigga was fucking the shit out of my mom. I instantly felt sick to my fucking stomach.

"What the fuck," I said out loud.

The moaning came to a stop and my mom yelled from the room, "Who the fuck is in my house?!"

Swallowing the lump that was in my throat I answered, "It's me, Mom."

"Dammit! Jasir, wait in the living room! I'll be right out! Remind me to take my damn key back!" she yelled.

All I could do was shake my head. I thought she was putting some clothes on to come out, and the next thing I knew, I heard moaning again. I walked out and slammed the door. I wasn't sure who the nigga was, but I didn't like his ass already. You just gonna keep fucking my mom knowing that I was here?

About ten minutes later, my mom came and opened the door with a robe on to get me. At that point, I was traumatized and pissed off. I'd never caught my mom fucking, even when my mom and dad were still together.

"Jasir, you can't just be using your key and coming in here when you want. I gave you that key for emergencies," she said, pissing me off even more.

I wasn't sure who the hell she was trying to show off for, but she had me fucked up. I knew it was her place and that I should've knocked, but I had a problem that she was trying to act like she ever told me that before. I'd been using my key and coming in here ever since she and my dad got a divorce and I became the man of the house.

"Mom, I know this is your house and all, but who the hell are you showing off for? You ain't never tell me to knock first, but it's cool. I'll leave your key. It's evident that you got some new nigga up in here blowing your back out. I'm just pissed I had to see that shit, but that's my fault for barging in. I'll holler at you later," I said, putting the keys on the counter.

"Boy, bring your ass back in here. Don't think you too old for me to whoop your ass. I have the key to your shit, too, but I don't just come and use the key whenever I want. And stop acting as if you ain't never seen nobody get fucked before. Jasir, I have needs just like you do. So calm down. Besides, it's no one new."

I looked at her like she was crazy. Now I was really confused because I'd never seen my mom with another man outside of my father, and that was a little over five years ago that they divorced. I turned my ass back around because I wasn't crazy and didn't play any games with my mom.

"Hello, son," I heard a voice say, and when I looked up, I was staring at my dad.

"Dad, what the hell is going on?" I asked, looking at my mom for answers.

"Jasir, me and your father have been seeing one another for the last two months. I didn't tell you because I wasn't sure if we were just having a fling or if we were serious. It turns out that we still have deep feelings for one another and decided to give us another shot."

I stood there speechless not knowing what to say. I knew I needed to get the fuck out of there before I did or said something that I would regret. Me and my dad talked damn near twice a week, and he couldn't tell me like a man that he was back messing around with my mom? I found that shit foul and more so disrespectful.

"Cool. I'm out. Y'all don't owe me shit, but I have to get the fuck out of here," I said before storming out the door.

As soon as I got in the car, the first person I called was Kirk. I needed to vent and get as high as I could get. I linked up with Kirk and told him what the fuck just happened, and that nigga thought the shit was funny. I didn't find shit funny about what I said. I was really in my feelings about this shit. I knew my parents were grown and they could do what they wanted, but I just didn't understand where all this shit was coming from and how long would they have waited if I didn't walk in on their asses. I needed to bust a nut, so I headed to Diandra's to let out some frustrations.

"Baby, what's wrong?" Diandra asked as soon as I walked in her door.

I guess she could tell by the look on my face that something was wrong. I told Diandra what happened at my mom's house and at first, she giggled, but she did agree that they should have at least told me what was going on. I knew once I calmed down I would go back and talk to my mom and find out what the hell was really going on with my parents. This shit was crazy, but they were grown and capable of making their own decisions. So for now, I was going to mind my own business.

Chapter Eleven
Epilogue

Diandra

Here it was, one year later, and me and Jasir were still together and expecting a baby girl in four months. I was so excited when I found out that I was pregnant, but no one was happier than Jasir. Everything was falling in place better than I could imagine. My business was good, and Jasir ended up owning his real estate company, that seemed to be doing more than well. He and Kirk were still dope boys, but they just ran shit from behind the scenes . The two of them went into the real estate business together. They both just wanted to focus on their families. Kira was now a stay at home wife to my Godson, Kirk Jr. Kirk said he didn't want his wife to work right now, but if that was something she wanted to do in the near future, he would be okay with it. You heard right. My best friend was married to Kirk. They had a small, beautiful intimate wedding.

"Hey, baby are you ready?" Jasir asked, breaking me from thoughts.

"Yes, I'm ready."

He kissed me on the lips before leading me downstairs. We got to our destination in no time. The set up was beautiful, and my mother was catering the event. The ceremony was about to start in just a few short moments.

"Who giveth this woman away?" The pastor asked.

"I do," Jasir answered as he gave his mother away to his father.

I still couldn't believe that his parents were getting remarried. But I thought it was the cutest thing, especially since his mom hadn't been with another man since their divorce. The wedding was now over, and it was beautiful. Jasir's mom was a lovely bride, and his father was also a handsome man. It was evident where Jasir got his charming looks from. He was his father's best man, which I also found cute. He was about to give his toast.

"May I have everyone's attention? When my parents first told me they had gotten back together and wanted to get married, I wasn't too happy about it. But I had to understand that when you're in love, marriage is what you do. It took my parents to be a part for five years to realize that they didn't want to be apart from one another, so all you could do is respect that kind of love. Cheers to love and happiness." Everyone clapped their hands at Jasir's speech.

"I just have one more thing to add. As you all know I also found a woman that I can't live without, which is why I decided today was the perfect day to let Diandra Wilson exactly how I feel." Jasir starting walking towards me, and my heart began to race. Once he was standing in front of me, he dropped down on one knee. "Diandra Wilson, you're the love of my life, and I want to love you for the rest of my life, and then some. From the moment I met you, I knew that God loved me because he took the time to make you just for me. Diandra Wilson, will you please make me a happy man and marry me?"

My mouth was hanging open wide, and the tears fell freely. I had to get my emotions in check before I answered Jasir. "Yes, Jasir. I would be honored to be your wife," I cried.

Jasir wiped my tears and kissed me passionately like we were the only two people in the room. For the rest of the day, I just enjoyed my soon-to-be husband. Yup I was a big girl that was in love with a dope boy and not only was he was in love with me but he wanted to marry me.

The End...

Adelynn & Hakeem
A BBW Love Story

Chantel

Synopsis

Who says that big girls can't love a thug? If anything, we love them better.

Adelynn Ready is thick in the thighs and easy on the eyes. In short, she's every man's dream. Still, that doesn't keep her safe in this love game. After she breaks up with her high school sweetheart, things just start spiraling downward. Thinking that love isn't for her, she keeps moving towards her dreams. Then, she bumps into the one and only, Hakeem. It's like love at first sight, but Adelynn isn't sure that she's ready...

Hakeem O'Neal is the king of the streets of Dalton. He has women throwing themselves at him, but he only has eyes for one person: Keisha. That is... until he bumps into Adelynn. Now, he's no longer happy with Keisha, and he wants to venture off into new things. Sparks and hearts race when he and Adelynn come into contact with each other. Could there be something there for them, or will Hakeem continue to do him? Stay tuned as we find out in this BBW love story.

Adelynn

"Rayleigh, how is the schedule looking for today? I got to run out in a minute and get some stuff to finish Theresa's outfit," I stated, checking my emails to make sure I didn't miss anything important.

"You have a meeting with Mrs. George at ten, a meeting with Mira at twelve, Sara at one, and Laura at four. No one has canceled, but Sylvia called and wants to meet tomorrow. So I rescheduled her for tomorrow at one. I can go out and get the stuff you need. You know I don't mind," Ray mentioned, and I just looked at her from over my glasses.

"Now, Ray, you know I like to go because I have to feel the material. You just can't get anything for these women. You know that they are bougie as hell. I appreciate the offer, though.

Hold all my calls. The only person I wanna talk to is my mother. I have to get the day started."

"You got it, boss," she said before walking out.

I couldn't do nothing but shake my head. Ray was a real kind of special, but she was about business, and I think that was why we clicked the way we did.

It was now 8:30, and I had to get it together. My day was full of festivities. Let me introduce myself before I go any further. My name is Adelynn Renee Ready, and I'm twenty-six years old. Born and raised in Dalton, Georgia. I have a daughter named Ashlynn, and she is my everything. She is the reason why I grind the way I did. I am a plus-size queen, and I wouldn't let anyone tell me different. I'm the owner of Thick Gurlz boutique. The reason I started designing clothes was because I was tired of going in stores and only finding stuff for skinny bitches.

I would never forget the day that my mom and I went to the store to find me a cute dress for school. Like, it would always be stuck in my head. That would be something that I would never forget.

"Excuse me. Do y'all have this in a bigger size? All I see in this damn store is clothes for skinny people. Well, as you

can see, we are not all skinny. A lot of us have meat on our bones." My mom hissed.

To say I was embarrassed was an understatement. My mother was a rare breed, though. She said what she meant and meant what she said. She didn't sugar coat it for nobody, and I think that was the reason I was like I was.

"I'm sorry, ma'am, but we don't. The biggest size we have is a five, and from the looks of things, you couldn't get one arm in this." The clerk laughed.

Next thing I knew, my mother had slapped her across the face. She looked like she wanted to say something, but she was still in shock.

"Don't you ever say no shit like that again. I hope y'all don't sell another piece in this bitch. Y'all discriminating on the bigger people. I'm so tired of people thinking they are better than us just because they are skinny. Come on, Adelynn, let's go." My mother grabbed me as we headed out the store.

I was hurt about everything that went down. We didn't find a dress for me, and my mother went into this depression stage. I hated seeing her like that, so I decided to do something about it. When we got back to the house, I went in my room and got my sketch book out. I started designing clothes for us bigger people. I was only nine, but I knew what I wanted to do when I grew up. I designed a lot of things and got good feedback on everything I designed. At the age of twenty-one, I was an owner of my boutique. It was my other baby, and I took pride in what I did. I wanted to set an example for my daughter, since her father skipped out on me. His parents never approved of me, so when I got pregnant, he got ghosted. That was fine, though, because my mother was there every step of the way. I wouldn't trade my daughter for nothing in this world.

"Adelynn!" Ray yelled, taking me from my thoughts. I looked at her ass like she was crazy. Like, who the fuck was she yelling at? "I have been calling you for the last five minutes, but you were in your zone. The only way to get you out is to yell at you. I'm sorry, not sorry. Miss George is here," she rambled.

"My bad, Ray. Please send her in," I requested as I got myself together.

In walked in Miss George and a nice-looking brother. I couldn't say that I'd seen him around here, but he was definitely eye candy. She was holding onto this man like her life depended on it.

"Good morning, guys. Please come in and have a seat. Can I get you guys anything to drink before we get started?" I smiled.

"I'll have a water, please," she replied without evening asking her man.

"Can I get you anything, sir?" I asked, and his eyes said everything.

"Naw, I'm good. Thanks, ma." He smiled and showed his grill.

"Ray, can you please bring Miss George some water?"

"Please call me Keisha."

"Alright, Keisha. Let's get down to business, love. What can I do for you today? I have some designs in these books. If you see anything you like, please let me know. If you don't like anything, I can make you something custom."

"Owwee, this is cute. What you think, baby?"

He didn't look thrilled to be here at all.

As she was looking at pictures, I caught him staring at me. I couldn't say that I didn't like it because I loved it. I saw he was amazed with my curves. I saw how he was scanning my body and licking his lips. A lot of men couldn't deal with me because even though I was big, I knew how to drive you crazy without taking off my clothes.

"Alright, I think I'm going to go with these three. I want this one in black, pink, and red. This one I want in yellow, purple, and white. And lastly, I want this in red, black, and blue," she ordered.

As she was talking, I was trying to write everything down. When I was finished, I walked around to my computer and started typing everything up. She was asking for a lot, but I was gonna deliver no doubt. After giving her the deposit information, her man pulled out his card and gave it to me. Putting it in my hand, there was an electric shock that went through my body.

"Alright, Keisha. Thank you for trusting me to make this for you. I will be in touch with you, and I hope you guys have a nice day. Let me show y'all out."

As I walked them out, I felt a hole being burnt in my back. I knew that he was staring, so I put an extra twist in my walk as I headed to the door. As I held it open for them, her man brushed against me as he walked out. I saw how Keisha looked at me, but she needed to check her man. Not me. As I closed the door, I saw the look Ray was giving me.

"Damn, Adelynn. Why the hell he was on you like that? Keisha acted like she didn't like it either." Ray smirked.

"Girl, you should've saw his ass in the office. His ass was so disrespectful. As long as he don't come in the way of my money, we good," I concluded, walking back into my office.

It was now going on 11:30, and I was starving. I knew that I had an appointment coming at twelve, but a sister was hungry. I called Ray up front and asked her if she could move Mira's and Sara's appointments back a little. When she told me it was done, I closed my computer down and grabbed my purse.

"Ray, I'm going to get something to eat. Do you want anything?"

"No, I'm good. I got some lunch. I'm trying to save a little money," she responded.

I nodded and headed outside. When I made it to my car, I grabbed my phone and dialed my mother to check in. After the phone rang for what felt like forever, she finally answered. "Hey, Mama! How is Ashlynn doing?" I asked, connecting my phone to Bluetooth.

"Chile, she is good. We just got done eating, and she 'bout to get ready for her nap. How is work?" she asked.

"Work is good. I got a new client today, and she wants some of everything. It's gonna take me forever, but I'm up for the job. I'm going to get me something to eat before my next client comes. I got some tea for you when I get home," I added, and she sucked her teeth.

"Really? You just gonna leave it like that? I see how you do. Well, get your work done and hurry home. I'll talk to you when you get here. I'mma try and take a nap, too, with Ashlynn. I love you, baby," she ended before hanging up.

Minutes later, I pulled up to Fatburger and got out. When I made it inside, I locked eyes with that sexy creature from this morning. Lord, this man was everywhere I was, and I didn't mind one bit. Prancing over to the counter, I ordered me a fat burger combo with a large vanilla shake. They gave me my ticket, and I went and had a seat. While waiting, I strolled through emails and Facebook. Nothing interesting, so I logged back out. When they called my number, I grabbed my food and headed back out the door. Making it outside, I looked back in, and ole' boy winked at me. Oh, he was one brave motherfucker!

After getting the day over with, I was ready to head home and lay it down. I couldn't do that because I had so much to do in so little time.

Walking in the house, I was greeted by my daughter and mother. They were two faces that I could never get tired of seeing. These two were my everything.

"Hey, Princess. Hey, Mama. How are my two favorite people doing?" I asked as I placed my bag on the hanger by the door.

"Hey, Mama. I missed you today. How was your day?" For Ashlynn to be three, she was smart as hell.

"It was good. Better now that I see your face. Was you good for grandma today?"

"Nana!" my mother corrected me. She didn't like to be called grandma because she said she *was not* old.

"My bad, Ma." I held up my hands.

"Yes, ma'am. Ain't that right, Nana?"

"You *were* good today. Come on. Let's get you in bed so your mama and I can talk."

"Good night, Mama. I love you." Ashlynn gave me a big hug and a kiss.

"Night, Princess. I love you more."

I got comfortable on the couch, and next thing I knew, I was snoring. Today was very productive, though. I was just glad it was over.

Hakeem (Sticks)

"So, babe. What do you think about the outfits that I got today?" Keisha asked me. Keisha was aggy as hell, but that thing between her legs had a nigga stuck.

"They were nice. I can't wait until I can see you in them," I replied.

I knew that if I didn't answer her, she would bother me until I did. My mind was still stuck on baby girl from this morning. She had curves in all the right places, and I didn't mind lifting the fupa to get to it. Baby girl had a nigga's mind gone. She was light skinned like I liked, and her eyes were hypnotizing. She was everything I liked in my women. A skinny nigga like myself didn't want a skinny bitch because I didn't want our bodies to catch a fire when we fucking. I wanted something that I could hold onto as I hitting it from the back. I was never into skinny bitches, though. Don't get me wrong, they were pretty in the face, but that was it.

Keisha wasn't always big; she was medium when we first met. I had to fatten her up a little. I just didn't like another nigga looking at something that belonged to me. Call me selfish, but I knew how niggas thought. Before I go any further, allow me to introduce myself. The name is Hakeem Neal, but everybody called me sticks. I'm six-four, weighing about one hundred seventy-five pounds. I had Third Street on lock. If you needed drugs, I was the man for you.

Keisha and I had been together for a minute, but it wasn't that serious. I ain't gonna lie. I look at women from time to time, but I always came home to Keisha. I'd cheated, but I kept my bitches under control. I laid the pipe and kept it moving. I didn't know why I did it because Keisha was a freak. Every chance she got, she sucking a nigga's dick. She knew that I loved that sloppy toppy. She was a nigga's rider, though. Keisha was my runner. When I needed shit moved, she'd move that shit for me. No questions asked. Enough about me, though. Let's get back at the matter at hand.

"Babe, I gotta make a run to make sure things are running smoothly. I'll be back later. Don't wait up," I stated before grabbing my keys.

I was hoping that I ran into ole' girl again, but it was no way that was gonna happen. It was almost 10:00 at night. Wishful thinking, I guess. After kissing Keisha, I headed out the door and jumped in my whip. When I made it to Third street, it was quiet; that was the kind of shit I liked. I wasn't with all that loud shit on my block. I tried to keep the Feds out my business. Parking my car, I jumped out and dapped Marco. Marco was my brother from another mother.

"What's going on, nigga?"

"Shit, nigga. Same shit, just different days. What's going on with you? I can't believe Keisha let your ass out," he joked.

"Nigga, fuck you. Keisha don't run shit. How is things over here?"

"Shit gravy over here, bruh. What's on your mind, though?"

I hated how this nigga could see through my ass. "Check this out. So, Keisha and I met with this fashion designer today, and a nigga feel in love," I started, and Marco shook his head. "Bruh, now you know I like my women with the extra meat on their bodies. Baby girl had curves in all the right places. As I scanned her body, she had that fupa like I like. I guess it was some kind of coincidence because I saw her ass again at Fatburger while me and Keisha was eating lunch. I can't get my mind off her ass, though," I ranted.

"Damn, nigga. I see that you got it bad. Where you meet her at, though?"

"Shit, I think her boutique name is Thick Gurlz, I don't even know, man."

"The only person that I know that got a boutique here is Adelynn Ready. Is that her?"

"Hell, I think so. I can't even remember her name; all I can remember is her body."

"Man, I'mma tell you right now. She bougie as fuck. Keep it moving; you don't stand a chance with her," he stated, and I looked at him like he had lost his mind.

"Fuck you mean, 'I don't stand a chance'? You must don't know who the fuck I am. I am Sticks, baby. I can get any bitch that I want. Hell, watch me work. I bet I can get her ass."

With that, I traveled in the house. Everything was in order, and it smelled like Pine Sol and bleach. We weren't like them other traps; we liked to keep our shit clean. I nodded at a couple workers as I moved through the house. When I saw that everything was being handled, I made my way back outside, with Marco on my heels.

"What about Keisha? If you are serious about her, I can set that shit up. But if you gonna play, you might as well not even look her way." He hissed.

"Let me worry about Keisha. She already know her place, so we don't have nothing to worry about. Just set that shit up." I dapped him up and headed to the house.

I was more than sure that Keisha wouldn't be a problem. Hell, I might see if I could juggle both of their asses. That shit didn't sound bad at all. When I made it back to the house, I jumped out the car and made my way inside. Keisha scared the shit out of me sitting in the living room in the dark.

"Damn, girl. What the fuck you sitting in the dark for?" I asked while shutting the door.

"Are you attracted to me anymore?" she asked, and I looked at her ass like she was crazy. Here she goes with that insecure shit.

"What you mean am I attracted to you? If I wasn't, your ass wouldn't be up in this bitch. Get out of your feelings and come to bed."

"No. I be seeing how you be looking at other bitches. I peep all that shit. I just don't say anything because I know who you come home to. I ain't dumb by a long shot, Keem. I notice everything you do. Are you cheating on me? You know what? Don't even answer that. I don't even wanna know." She ended her little rant.

"Keisha, what the fuck you want from me? I'm out here grinding so ya ass don't have to and seem like all you wanna do nowadays is nag. But I think I got what you need," I stated as I pulled my dick out of my pants. "This is all your dick. I don't care if I give it to other bitches from time to time. Can't nobody do this dick like Keisha. Come show him some love." I motioned.

She looked like she didn't want to, but she crawled over to where I was standing. She grabbed my dick while looking me in my eyes. The way her eyes pierced through my soul made my dick harder from the anticipation. She gathered up a lot of saliva in her mouth and spit on the dick. Before the spit could travel down my shaft, she was slurping it up while moaning. Shit kinda threw me off balance. She was sucking my shit like she had some shit to prove. Shit, I already knew that she gave the best head, hands down.

"Aahh, fuck, girl. Suck all this dick." I moaned as I started thrusting my hips.

She gagged at bit, but that didn't stop her. "Fuck you better fuck this throat. You know I live for shit like this," she managed to get out as I fucked her in the mouth like she asked.

Not even five minutes passed and I was cumming hard down her throat. Like the nasty bitch she was, she didn't let one bit go to waste. She licked her lips as she got up off the floor. Shit, my ass was ready for a fucking nap. As she got up, she kissed me and headed to the room. I sat down on the chair and closed my eyes. The thick chick from the boutique came to mind. This shit was gonna be harder than I thought. I just had to have her. Miss pretty was gonna be all mine soon. Just watch.

Adelynn

"Alright, Princess. Be good for Nana. When I get off, I will bring home some ice cream," I said to my daughter.

"I'm always good, Mama. Can you bring me a doll home today?" she asked me, and I nodded.

This little girl had a room full of dolls, but she always had room for more. Hell, to think about it, I was like that when I was younger too. So I knew where she got it from.

"Alright, Mama, I'm out. Do you need me to pick up anything on the way home tonight?"

"Nope. All good here, baby. Have a good day at work. We will see you when you get home," she stated, kissing me on the cheek.

With that, I was out the door. On the way to work, I stopped by Starbucks and got me a caramel Frappe and Lemon slice. I couldn't make it through the day without either one of them.

When I pulled up to the office, I grabbed my bag and coffee. Upon making it inside, Ray had a weird look on her face while she was on the phone. She put her finger up to stop me from going to my office. I sipped on my coffee as I waited for her to get off.

"People just don't know how to shut up when they are on the phone, I see. This lady called about an appointment, then she wanted to tell me her life history. I had to shut that down real quick. Anyways, good morning, boss lady. Let me warn you what you about to walk into. I tried to tell him to wait out here, but he insisted on waiting in your office," she started, and I stopped her.

"Ray, who did you let in my office? Now you know I don't play about people being in my office when I am not here." I was pissed.

"I'm sorry. He was a fine ass brother. He kinda caught me off guard, so that's my bad." She was running behind me talking.

When I made it to my office, I swung the door open. I instantly got pissed. Marco's ass had his feet on my desk.

"Boy, if you don't get your feet off my desk, we gonna have problems. Thank you, Ray. I can take it from here," I mentioned as she was lusting over Marco. I could see it in their eyes that they wanted to rip each other's clothes off.

"Alright. If you need me, I'll be out here at my desk," she ended, walking out, and shutting my door.

"Marco, what are you doing here?" I asked with a frown.

"Still the same feisty ass, Adelynn, I see."

"You better believe it. Ain't never gonna change," I said proudly. "What can I do for you, Marco?"

"Damn, no small talk or catching up? Get right down to it, huh?"

I could see right through his ass. "Nope, I got work to do. As you can see, I am a busy woman. I have a lot of shit to make today, so make it quick."

"I feel you. Anyways, my man, Sticks, wanna get at you," he started, and I cut him off.

"Who the hell is Sticks?" I asked, looking confused.

"He told me that he came up here the other day. He really feeling you."

"The only man I know that came up here the other day was the man with Keisha. If that's who you talking about, that's a no for me. I don't mix pleasure with business," I said. Even though that man was fine!

"It ain't even like that. He's not feeling Keisha the way he feeling you. This is different. I have never seen him like this."

"Like I said, I don't mix pleasure with business. If that's all you came for, you can let yourself out. I got work to do," I ended, walking around to my desk and turning my computer on.

"Still the same ole Adelynn from high school, I see. Well, you have a good day," he replied before walking out my office.

I ain't gonna lie. I couldn't take this stupid smile off my face. I had a client's man that was into me. If I was back in my high school days, I would have took him from her. But I couldn't do that right now. She was one of my biggest clients. As I got my day started, I couldn't keep my mind off this man. Like, everything about him screamed boss. My mind had me ready to say fuck these pieces and go get with a real one, but my time was coming.

"Adelynn, what was that all about?" Ray came in with her brow raised.

"So you remember that man that came here the other day with Keisha? Him and Marco are cool, and he came to tell me that he wanted to get at me. Girl, and that man is fine as hell. I can't do that to my client, though."

Ray was standing there like I was speaking in another language. "What you mean you can't do your client like that? Fuck her ass. Ouu, excuse my language, but you know what I mean. When are you gonna be happy, Adelynn?" she asked me. She did have a point.

"Ray, I am happy. Can't you see? This place makes me happy—"

"No offense," she cut me off, "but when the last time you had a man?"

Her question made my mind wonder, and I immediately thought about Rex's stupid ass.

"And I ain't talking about Rex's childish ass," she continued. "I'm talking about a real man that knew what to do with all your curves."

"To come to think about it, I really never had a man in my life. It has been me, my mom and my daughter so long that I haven't even thought about a man. And as you can tell, this place keeps me busy."

"I know all that, Adelynn, but it's time for you to be happy too. Give that man a shot, and if it don't work, then so be it. But I think it will." She left me with that before walking out my office.

Ray did have a point. What was this gonna hurt? We were just talking. As the day passed by, I was more ready to go home. I was caught up on the day's work, so I guess I could dip out early. Packing my things up, I turned my computer off and walked out my office. When I made it to the front, Ray looked at her wrist like she was checking the time.

"Mind your business, Ray. I'm out for the day. Any important calls, forward them to my cellphone. The rest of the calls, take a message, and I'll get back with them tomorrow. Please make sure you lock up before you leave."

"Got it. Have a great rest of your day!"

When I got outside to my car, there was a note sticking from the windshield wipers. I grabbed the note and read it:

Ever since I saw you the other day, I can't get my mind off your curves. I tried shaking you out of my head, but somehow, you pop right back in that bitch. Join me for dinner at my place tomorrow.

Intriguing! How can this man even have me on his mind, when he got a whole woman at home? As much as I said I wasn't gonna mix business with pleasure, that was just what I was doing. I ain't gonna lie. I love dope boys. Not the fuck boy dope boys. The ones that knew they were the shit and could handle all my curves. Throwing the note in my bag, I proceeded to get into my vehicle. On the way home, I stopped by Walmart and got my Princess some ice cream. On the way out the store, I saw Sticks, or whatever his name was.

"What's up ma?" Sticks asked.

"Oh, nothing. What you doing in my neck of the woods?" I answered his question with a question.

"Shit, I live in this neck of woods. I'm glad that I ran into you, though. When you gonna stop playing and give me some play?" he asked, and I chuckled.

"Stop playing with me. You know that I can't take it there with you. You are my client's man. And I don't mix business with pleasure," I started, and he cut me off.

"I'm trying to mix me and you together to see what it makes," he whispered in my ear.

Lord, this man was breaking me down.

"Sorry, but I gotta run. I'll see you around." I ran off. This man wasn't finna get me tangled in his little web. Even though I wouldn't mind wetting his beard.

I had to make him sweat first. When I made it to the house, I parked the car and headed inside.

"Mama!" Ashlynn screamed as she jumped in my arms.

"Hey, baby!" I picked her up and kissed her all over her little face. "Who's the best mom in the world?" I asked as I tickled her.

"You are, Mama. Enough, I can't breathe." She snorted.

As I put her down, we headed in the kitchen. I wondered where mama was. Usually, she would have greeted me at the front door. As I traveled through the house, I got to the door and pushed it open. She looked like she was sleeping so peacefully. I walked over there and kissed her on her forehead. She stirred a bit.

"Oh, hey, baby. When you get home? I meant to have dinner ready for you by time you got here. Give me just a minute, and I'll get up and cook."

"No, Mom, it's ok. I'll just order some pizza for us. You get some rest. I'll see you when you get up," I assured before leaving out her room and closing the door.

When I made it back in the living room, Ashlynn was laying on the couch watching *Frozen*. I swear she watched it so much, she knew it word for word. Walking in the kitchen, I grabbed two bowls and made us some ice cream. I usually didn't do this, but today was different. Grabbing my phone, I went to my Pizza Hut app and ordered a couple of pizzas. Grabbing the bowls, I walked back in the living room and handed one to her.

"Thank you, Mama!" she said all excited.

"You're welcome, baby. Pizza will be here in a minute. Can Mama watch *Frozen* with you?" I asked, and she nodded.

We sat and watched the movie until the pizza came. When it finally arrived, we ate and went outside to play. I knew I should've been working, but my daughter needed her mother too. When Ash was finished playing, we came back inside, and I ran her some bath water. It was going on eight, and Ash was usually in the bed by 8:30. After getting her situated for bed, I went and took me a nice, hot shower. Today was very eventful, but I wouldn't change anything about it. After checking on my mom again, I went back in my room and grabbed my laptop. I had to make sure I didn't have any important emails from a potential client. I instantly got pissed when I opened an email I received.

Adelynn, I know that it's been some time, but I was hoping that I can see my baby. I know that I should have came before now, but I just didn't know how to step to you.

I see you doing big things, and I hope that we can squash any beef that we may have. Our daughter needs both of us. Please find it in your heart to forgive me. My number is 875-384-4500. Please reach out, and we can set up something.

This man had some nerve to email me about this. This was his choice, not mine. Would I like for Ashlynn to get to know her father and his family? Yes, I would, but I'm not ready for that now. I took a lot of shit from him, and his family never liked me. I think that it was just best to leave him where he was. Ashlynn and I would be fine without him. After wiping the tears from my eyes, I close my laptop and drifted off to sleep. Maybe giving another man a try would keep my mind off Rex. Hell, that didn't sound like a bad idea.

Rex

"Man, naw. I ain't doing that shit. You must dun' fell and bumped your head. I got better shit to be doing than being your fucking dope boy," I vented to West.

West must've thought I was some kind of fool. Hell, I was born at night, but not last night. If I got caught with all the weight that he was trying to send me off with, my ass wouldn't see the light of day. I wanted fast money, but not like this. I had other things to look forward to. Like my daughter who I hadn't met yet. I hoped her mother emailed me back because I couldn't live without them in my life. Yea, y'all heard it right. Let me first introduce myself and then I'd get into how I broke Adelynn's heart. My name is Rex Tyrone Sanders, born in raised in a small town Willacoochee, Georgia. I'm thirty-three, but don't look over the age of twenty-six. When

I was five, my parents split up, and my mom and I moved to Dalton, GA. Dalton was a little bigger than Willacoochee. When I turned sixteen, I bumped into the baddest women I had ever laid eyes on. She was plus-size, so my mother never approved of her. Hell, that didn't stop me from going with what my heart felt. I remember this day oh, so clearly.

The bell rung for school to be out. I was looking forward to this day because Adelynn and I was supposed make things official. "You ready for this?" I asked as I grabbed her hand, and helped her in the car.

"No, the question is, are you ready for this? One dose of this will have you addicted for life."

We laughed together.

The ride to the hotel was quiet and awkward. I kept stealing glances at Adelynn, but no words were spoken. When we get to the hotel, I parked the car and jogged inside to pay for the room. When I got the key, I traveled back outside to get Adelynn. She gave me a faint smile. I could see it all in her face that she was nervous. But I didn't want her to feel that way.

"Look, I won't do anything to you that you don't want me to do. We can go in here and just talk if that's what you want to do," I mustered to out. I hoped that wasn't the case because I had spent a pretty penny on this room.

"Rex, it's fine. Come on and let's get inside. I have to be home in two hours," she stated, and I nodded.

When we made it in the room, Adelynn wasted no time helping me out of my clothes, and I did the same for her. For a big girl, baby girl's body was nice and neat. She looked down at my dick and took a deep breath.

"Adelynn, we don't have to do this," I started, and she cut me off.

"No, we are doing this."

Next thing I knew, she pushed me on the bed. But it wasn't even going down like that, though. I flipped her over and started licking her breasts. I knew that I was doing something right because a moan slipped out of her mouth. I ain't even gonna lie. That moan made my dick stand up. I rubbed on her sweet spot as it gushed out liquid. When the time was right, I inserted two fingers in her tunnel. Her body tensed up as I went in and out of her with my fingers.

"I can't take it anymore. Please put your dick in." She moaned.

Hell, she didn't have to tell me twice. I climbed on top of her and inserted my dick inside her pussy. The feeling was something that I could get used to. Her tunnel was warm and tight. Man, I almost exploded after the second pump. She wasn't lying when she told me I was gonna be hooked. The wetness had a nigga about to lose my mind.

"Oh my God, what are you doing to my body?" She moaned as I was hitting her sweet spot.

"I'm making that body feel good. Isn't that what you wanted?" I asked.

Her body jerked a couple times as she screamed out to the Gods above. I felt some warm liquid slide out of her. Shit, that let me know that she had, indeed, came for a real one. As I sped up my strokes, I couldn't take it any longer. I exploded deep inside her walls. Fuck, that pussy was the truth. As I snatched my dick out, I saw that I wasn't wearing a condom, and I panicked.

"What wrong?" she asked with a weird look on her face.

"Adelynn, please tell me you are on birth control."

"No," she replied as she looked at my limp dick. "Oh my God, you didn't wear a condom. My mother is gonna kill me," she cried as I consoled her.

"Listen, everything is gonna be ok. I will be there for you if you are pregnant. We knew what we were doing when we laid down and started exploring each other bodies. We knew the consequences of all this. Don't worry, I will be there for you," I let her know.

Deep down, I knew my mother was gonna kill me.

"Can you take me home, please?" she asked with her head down.

"Yea, I can do that. Let's take a shower real quick, though," I insisted.

After we showered, I dropped her off at the house. Nothing was said the whole ride there. When we got there, she jumped out and ran inside. After she closed the door, I drove off. Making it home, I pulled into the driveway. I grabbed my phone and texted Adelynn. When she didn't text back, I turned the engine off and headed inside.

"Hey, son. What took you so long to get home?" my mom started as soon as I walked in the house.

"I was with Marvin and Chris playing the game," I lied.

"Well, dinner is almost ready. Go get cleaned up."

On the way to my room, my phone vibrated letting me know that I had a message. Grabbing it out of my pocket, I saw that I had a message from Adelynn.

Ade: Thanks for today. I had fun.

Me: Me too. So does this make us official?

Ade: Yep. If you as much look at another woman, I will end things.

Me: No need for that. You are all the woman I need. ☐

Man, I couldn't take this little stupid smile off my face. I was officially off the market. Putting my phone up, I washed up for dinner. Heading back to the kitchen, my mom had my plate waiting for me. After saying grace, I dug in.

"So tell me how school is going. Any girlfriend that I need to know about?"

"School is good. I mean, as good as it can be, and I do have a girlfriend. Her name is Adelynn. Adelynn is so beautiful," I started.

"Do you have any pictures of Adelynn?" she asked as she took a bite of her cornbread.

"Yes, I do. Let me go get my phone real quick, and I will show you her. Ma, I swear you are gonna love her." I excused myself from the table and went to go get my phone. Jogging back to the table, I handed my mom my phone. I could see that she didn't approve of her the way her nose was turned up.

"So this is the girl that stole my son's heart. I know you can do better than this," she told me in disgust.

"Naw, she is everything to me. I know exactly why you don't like her, and that's ok too. You don't have to like her, but you will respect her." I bossed up at her.

"Oh, so you smelling yourself, huh? She dun' gave you some pussy, and you think she the only one out here for you? There are a lot of skinny women in this world, and you chose her. I am so disappointed in you." She shook her head.

"That could be the case, but I ain't looking for no one else. If you don't like it, I really don't care," I started, and she slapped the fire from my ass.

"You will not disrespect me in my house! If you think you gonna do that, then there is the door! When you leave, leave me the keys for the car I brought!" she screamed.

I didn't need any of this! I called my dad and he came and picked me up. I just couldn't believe that mother of mine. Why couldn't she be happy for me? If it wasn't what she wanted, then it was no way. I couldn't grow up like that. Hell, I was almost grown anyways. I just needed to step up and do what I needed.

Needless to say, neither of my parents liked her. So I had to end things with her. When she told me that she was pregnant, I wanted to be happy, but I knew that we weren't gonna have any support from either of my parents. We lost touch when we ended things, and that was one of the saddest days for me. Here I was a father, and I couldn't enjoy it. There were many days that I wanted to reach out to Adelynn, but my pride wouldn't let me.

Now fast forward to today, I wanted my family, and I would do anything to get them back. I knew that it was gonna take a lot of convincing to get Adelynn back. I wanted to get to know my daughter and to be in her life. I was grown now, and I didn't want my daughter to grow up without me. I knew that Adelyn was doing good for herself. I heard she had a shop, and I decided to pop up there to see if I could get her to talk to me.

After getting myself together, I jumped in my F-150 and headed to the boutique. When I got there, I was impressed. Adelynn was living the dream. Jumping out my truck, I grabbed the flowers and jogged up the steps. When I made it inside, it was breathtaking. She had it decorated beautifully.

"Welcome to Thick Gurlz! What can I do for you today?" the receptionist asked me. She was bad too. Damn!

"I'm here to see Adelynn—" I started, and she cut me off.

"Do you have an appointment?"

"Naw. I was just coming to check on an old friend."

"What's your name? I'll let her know that you are here."

"Rex," I stated.

"Alright, Rex. Have a seat, and I'll be right back."

She walked off, and I watched her ass bounce through the dress she had on. I think she knew I was watching because she put an extra twist in her walk. Women these days were hell. After what seemed like forever, the chick walked back out with a frown on her face.

"She is in with a client, and she wanted me to tell you that she will call you. And are those flowers for her?" she asked.

I nodded and handed them to her.

The bitch smelled the roses and threw them in the trash can that was beside her desk. "You can go now. She will call you when she is done." She gave me an evil look.

I threw my hands up and dipped.

I wasn't worried because I knew that she was gonna call me back. Adelyn couldn't resist me. Hell, if she didn't call me back, I was gonna do some more investigating and find out where she lived. I was ready and wanting to be in my daughter's life. I just didn't understand why she wasn't letting me. Hell, I was young and dumb. Now, I'm ready to be the man she needed. Hell, I wondered if it was too late for that too!

Love

Adelynn

"Ouuu, I can't believe he wanna come in now to play daddy now. After all these years, now he wanna be a father. I believe the hell not," I said as I paced the floor of my office.

I just couldn't believe he had the audacity to come now. Like, Ashlynn was almost four now. Like, why now? At this point, my blood was boiling. I hadn't seen Rex since the day we left the hotel. All of this was too much for me. I sat down at my computer and tried to get my mind right. No matter what I tried to do, Rex popped up in my head. I had too much work to do for that. Turning on some music, I hopped on one of Keisha's pieces. Hell, I was almost done with all her items, and I couldn't wait to see the look on her face when she came to pick them up.

"Ad, I'm headed to lunch. Do you need anything while I'm out?" Ray busted in my office.

"Naw, I'm good. Enjoy your lunch," I rambled off without looking up. "Make sure you lock up when you leave. I don't need no crazies running up in here," I threw out as she closed the door. "Girl, you outdid yourself. This is hot," I mentioned as I twirled the mannequin around.

After I was finished, I walked over to my desk to check my phone and emails. Rex was still trying to contact me, but it wasn't even that kind of party. The next email I clicked on was from Sticks. Like, this man wasn't giving up. Yes, I loved a man that didn't give up easily. Hell, he could've not tried to reach me again, and I would have been cool with it. Opening the email, he insisted on taking me to dinner. I mean, what could it hurt after I finished getting my coins from Keisha? Hell, if you knew me, you knew I didn't play about my coins. After emailing him back, I closed down my computer. It was time to head out of here. It was literally almost six.

"I was wondering if you were gonna sleep here tonight. I almost left you. I got other stuff to do tonight. Jasper is taking me out to this romantic restaurant, and I might lay it down on him. If you know what I mean." Ray winked at me.

"Girl, bye! Listen, take tomorrow off. I won't be coming in. I gotta take mama to the doctor. She hasn't been feeling well."

"Ok, thank you. Keep me posted on what they say. Call me tomorrow if you change your mind and wanna come in. You know I don't mind working."

"Yes, I know. That's why I hired your ass. You remind me so much of myself. Your ambition and drive are out this world. Listen, you are going places," I mentioned, and she nodded.

After locking up the place, I was on the way to my car when I got this bad feeling in my stomach. I tried to ignore it, but something told me not to. When I got to my car, I threw my bag in the passenger seat and slid in. I was just about to crank my car, and there was a knock on my window. Shit scared the shit out of me.

"What do you want, Rex?" I asked, letting down my window.

"I wanna see my daughter. I know I did some fucked up shit, but I want to be in her life." He had some nerve.

"Why?!" I asked, pissed.

"Because I have the right too," he shot back.

"No, you don't. You gave up that right when you left us. All because of your parents. I want you to know that we are doing fine without you. So if you don't mind, move. I got other shit to do," I warned him.

His ass was still standing there as if I wouldn't run his ass over. He knew I was crazy. I don't know why he be trying me. I politely started my engine and drove off. I must've ran over his foot by the way he was jumping up and down. He knew my fat ass didn't have no sense. As I pulled up in the yard, I had an email alert come over. I quickly opened it because I was waiting on a potential client to get back with me. Let's just say it wasn't who I thought it was.

Oh, this ain't over. All you had to do is let me see my child. I'm tired of being nice. Now you gonna make me take it to the court. Call me what you want, but she is just as much as mine. I'll be seeing you around.

I was furious! How the hell could he come in and start demanding shit? Where was his ass when I really needed him?! It would be a cold day in hell if he thought he was gonna come in and take my baby. Nope, not happening. I jumped out the car and headed inside. When I made it inside, Ashlynn looked like she had been crying. I didn't even get to close the door. I ran over to where she was.

"What's wrong baby?" I asked.

"It's Granny, Mama," she cried. That was when I got this feeling in the bottom in my stomach.

"Listen, baby. Stay right here. No matter what I do, I want you to stay right here. Do I make myself clear?" I asked, and she nodded.

I sat her down on the couch and rushed to my mama's room. When I made it to her room, I prepared myself with what I was about to walk into. Taking a deep breath, I push the door open. My mama was laying there like she was sleeping so peaceful. I walked over to her and felt for a pulse, but there wasn't one.

"Mama, no! You are not supposed to leave me now! I need you!" I cried.

From the looks of things, she had been gone for a minute now. I didn't know how I was gonna do this without her. My mama was my rock and biggest supporter. I grabbed her phone and called Ray first. I needed someone to come get Ashlynn; I didn't want her to see this. It took her ass forever to pick up the phone.

"Adelynn, everything ok?" she asked as soon as she picked up the phone.

"Ray, I need you to come get Ash for me. I will t everything when you get here." I sniffed.

"On my way!" she mentioned before ending the call.

I sat on the bed with Mama until she got here. When I heard her talking outside, I ran out to where she was. When she saw me, she ran over to me and hugged me tight. At this point, I couldn't hold it together anymore. I let out an ugly cry. This was for my mother that I couldn't bring back.

"Adelynn, what's wrong boo?" she asked.

"Mama's gone! I need you to take Ash for me. I will come get her when I can get her out of here. I just don't want her to see them wheel her out. Ash saw her like this first. Ray, things aren't gonna be the same without her. What am I gonna do without her?" I cried.

"Adelynn, I'm so sorry. Let me go inside and get Ash while you handle this. Don't worry about coming to get her. You get yourself together, boo." She tried to hold it together for the both of us.

Hell, I wasn't lying. I didn't know what I was gonna do without my mama. I was gonna be lost without her. After Ray left, I went back inside and got close to my mama. This was gonna be the last time I was gonna be with her, so I had to cherish it. I didn't even know she was sick, so this was all a shock to me. Grabbing her phone, I called 911 and waited for them to send somebody.

"Ma'am, can you tell us what happened here?" one of the EMTs asked.

"When I got home from work, I found her like this. Well, my daughter found her like this." I wiped my tears with the back of my hand. "My mother was as healthy as a horse. I was gonna take her to the doctor tomorrow, and now she is gone," I cried. I tried to hold it together, but I couldn't keep the tears from flowing.

After they took her, I laid in her bed and cried. This was one of the hardest days in my life. I felt like it was me and Ash now. I couldn't do this without her. The hardest part was going to pick out a casket for her. Lord, why me? I cried the rest of the night. I just laid in her bed without a care in the world.

Life wasn't gonna be the same.

Hakeem

"Aye, bruh, gone somewhere with that shit. If your ass can't pay, there is no IOU's around this bitch," I told the same crack head that had been around here all week.

"Come on, man. I got this watch that I'll give you. Just give me something—anything," his frail ass started.

"When I give you this, I don't wanna see you around these parts again. Do I make myself clear?" I asked while digging in my pockets.

"Yea, man. You won't see me around here again." He rubbed his hands together.

I knew his ass was lying.

After I gave him the rocks, he tried to run off. I stopped his ass and held out my hand. Wasn't shit in life for free. After he handed me the watch, I looked at it. It was nice as hell. I wondered where his ass got it from. Hell, that shit didn't even matter. Traveling in the house, I took out my phone and checked my messages. It was a bunch from Keisha, but none from thickums from the clothing place. I was the man in these streets, and all the bitches wanted me. Hell, I didn't know what her problem was, but I was gonna be waiting for her fine ass. After checking Keisha's messages, I walked through the house and checked to make sure that everybody was working. Shit, if they weren't, I didn't need their asses. I couldn't stand no leech.

"Alright, Marco. I'm out, my boy. Hold it down while I'm gone." I dapped him up.

"No doubt, my boy! Adelynn hit you back yet?"

"Hell naw. Her ass playing hard to get. I'mma fall back, though. That's one thing I don't do, and that's chase a bitch. When she comes back to her senses, she'll call a nigga. Hell, they always do. Until then, I'm finna head to the crib with Keisha's clingy ass." I shook my head.

"Alright, homie. Be easy."

With that, I hopped in my whip and head to the crib. Shit, I wasn't in no rush to get there, so I rode around my city. When it started getting late, I pulled up to the house. Taking a deep breath, I hoped out the car and went inside.

Once on the inside, it was quiet as hell. That only let me know that Keisha was sleep or her ass wasn't here. Searching the house, there was no Keisha to be found. Shit didn't bother me at all. Just as I was about to dose off, my phone started ringing off the hook. Looking at it, I saw it was Keisha.

"Yo!" I answered.

"Like, I don't know why you put up with Keem's shit. You know he out here fucking other hoes. You can't believe that a man of his caliber ain't out here fucking hoes. Keisha, you can't be that naïve," her friend went on and on in the background.

I pressed the mute button and just listened. This was some real bull.

"Hakeem would never cheat on me. Look at me. Baby, you know I'mma dime. Keem would be dumb as hell to give up a dime for a penny. The fuck you though, bitch?"

"I'm just saying. The way he looks at you, he probably looking at other bitches like that too. Keisha, don't be a fool." She sounded just like a hating bitch. "So what's going on with you and Gerald?" she then asked as soon as I was about to hang up.

Shit, I wanted to know the same thing.

"Shit is good with us. I know that if I can depend on anyone, I can depend on him. And, plus, he got some dope dick." She laughed, and I took the phone from my ear.

I knew she wasn't talking about the Gerald that I was competing with. Oh, yea, that nigga was good and dead. She just signed that nigga's death certificate. Hearing enough, I hung up the phone. Yea, a nigga was thirty-eight hot. I just couldn't believe that I let this hoe play me like this.

After all I did for her ass, and she played me. Naw, she had to go too.

Let me give y'all a back story on Gerald and I. He thought that he was gonna come in and take what I worked so hard to get. I believe the fuck not. From the moment I started getting the streets rocking, Gerald thought that he was gonna come in and take over. Hell naw, it wasn't that kind of party. Gerald would send his niggas to sell on my turf and thought that it was all cool. I knew that they were his people because I'd asked, and they gave his ass up. After I sent a couple body parts of his worker to his doorstep, he fell back. I would see him every now and then, but not as much as usual. I guess his ass got the hint. There was one thing I didn't play about, and that was my money. Get in the way of my money, and I was killing whoever tried to intercept that.

I ran in the room and gathered the little clothes she had and put them in a suitcase. The rest was shit I paid for, and her ass wasn't getting that shit. Call me what the fuck you want to, but I wasn't a dumb nigga. After I got all her things together, I put the suitcase outside the front door. Grabbing my phone, I dialed Marco's line.

"What it do, Keem?"

"Nigga, Gerald's ass got to fucking go. So how about Keisha's ass butt-dialed me and started talking about that nigga. After all I told her ass about this nigga, and she still wants to fuck this nigga. She got life fucked up. After his ass is gone, her ass will be right behind him." I was pissed.

"Nigga, calm the fuck down. We can't do that shit right now. But believe he got it out for his ass. Damn, I can't believe Keisha's ass. I knew that I couldn't stand her trifling ass for something. Nigga, you are too good for her ass anyways. Fuck that hoe," he babbled.

"I think this her ass coming in now. Let me get back with you." I ended the call as her ass strolled in the house.

"Baby, what my bags doing outside?" she asked with a confused look on her face.

"Keisha, you really wanna do this right now?! Get your shit and get ghost before I put my hands on you!" I yelled at her ass.

"Nigga, you ain't gonna do shit! I'll make you ass disappear for a long time. You must don't know I know all your little secrets. You got me fuck up!" she threatened me.

I walked up to her and snatched her ass up. "If you ever in your life threaten me again, I will kill your ass. Do I make myself clear?" She had me all the way fucked to if she thought I wasn't gonna take that threat seriously. "Now get your shit and be gone before you really piss me off." I let her go and she fell to the floor.

I walked away from her ass and went to the room. When I got there, I opened the drawer and pulled out the stuff to make me a blunt. Shit, I needed something to keep me from going to fucking jail. This bitch had shit all fucked up. Then gonna threat me. That shit was a no for me. Just because her ass was fucking around, she wanna throw that shit on me. In the midst of rolling my blunt, my phone dinged letting me know I had a new notification. After sealing the blunt, I walked over and grabbed my phone. When I saw who it was, a nigga was all smiles.

Her: *I haven't been avoiding you. I just got a lot of stuff going on. Maybe we can meet tomorrow for lunch.*

Me: *Shit, name the place, and I'm there. Oh, and before I forget. Cancel that shit that Keisha ordered. Keep the money as a tip.*

Her: *Let's do Mexican tomorrow. Meet me at El Patron at one.*

After reading that message, I heard the door slam. I guess Keisha got the hint. Smoking the blunt, I showered, locked the house and fell into bed. Shit, that was all she wrote from me as soon as my head touched the pillow.

Adelynn

"I'm glad you are getting back on track. Since you buried you mom, I've seen a different you. I think this date is a good thing to get you out of this depression you are in. And don't worry about Ashlynn, We got her." Ray was like an angel from the heaven above.

"Thank you, Ray! I'm really going to see what happened to him and Keisha. The outfits are done, and his ass told me to cancel them. Taking about keep the money as a tip." I laughed. It felt so good to laugh with everything I'd been through.

"Damn! Ain't that about a bitch. Hurry up and get ready. Ya ass gonna be late. And I want all the juicy details when you come back." She winked at me.

Once I was finished dressing, I kissed Ashlynn and headed out the door. I was nervous and excited at the same damn time. This was the first time I was going out with a man in forever. Ever since Rex played my ass, my motto was, niggas wasn't shit. But it was something about Mr. Hakeem that had me intrigued.

When I made it to El Patron, I could tell that it was a lunch time rush. Finally finding a parking spot, I parked and got out. I heard some people on the outside snickering, but I was used to that now. I was a big girl, and I was proud. None of that fazed me anymore. I was comfortable in the skin I was in. Making it on the inside, I spotted Hakeem and walked over to where he was. He got up and hugged me. Lord, the cologne he was wearing almost made me wanna pull his ass in the bathroom and say fuck lunch. Wishful thinking. My ass was hungry.

"Damn, it's about time ya ass got here. I almost left," he stated, and I just stared at his ass.

"Nigga, please. You know ya ass wanted my ass in your presence—" I started, and he cut me off.

"Ass up would be a better view, but we got tome for that. So what's good with you?" He tired to switch the subject. I was gonna let him slide with that.

"Anyways, what's going on witcha'? Tell me what happened with Keisha. I mean, I don't care, but she was my client."

"Shit happens, and people grow away from each other. Enough about her. I'm trying to get to know ya fine ass." He licked his lips.

"I guess, but can you feed me first before you go for home base? A sissy is hungry. Hell, I ain't big for nothing." I let him know what it was.

"I'm trying to do more than feed you. Aye, can we get some service over here?" He flagged the waiter down.

After ordering out food, we made small talk. Our chemistry was out of this world. His ass was as goofy as me, and I could see myself getting tangled up with his ass. As the waiter brought our food out, his phone rang and he excused himself. I mean, I was jealous, and he wasn't even mine to be jealous of. Hell, I started eating without his ass. When he came back, he had this pissed off look on his face.

"What's wrong?" I asked while wiping my mouth.

"Shit, I'm finna have to dip. Some shit happened at the trap. I'mma get up with you." He started taking his burrito.

Shit, I sat my ass right there until I finished. So much for going on a date. It was more like taking myself out. Once I was done, I grabbed my bag and headed out the restaurant. I wanted to call him to see if everything was good, but I didn't wanna look thirsty. Hell, I guess I'd have to wait 'til he called me. Jumping in my ride, I headed to the office. When I got there, Keisha was sitting outside on the stairs. Here we go with this shit. Grabbing my bag, I jumped out the car. Before I could get up the stairs, she started.

"Adelynn, I'm coming by to get my pieces. Are they done yet?" she asked.

"Yep, but I need the rest of my money."

"Keem was supposed to pay you. Let me get my shit so I can go.

"Give me the rest of what you owe, and I'll gladly give you your stuff. If you don't mind, back the hell up so I can get in," I mentioned as she sucked her teeth.

"Fuck you, you fat bitch." She laughed.

Like, this hoe was crazy, but she hadn't met my crazy. She was gonna keep on and she was gonna definitely meet her.

"Shit, I might be fat, but I got Hakeem licking every curve of my fat body. Gon' find you somebody to play with because this ain't what you want. I'll have your ass tasting the bottom of these red bottoms. Keep on fucking with me." This bitch had me pissed.

I unlocked the door and entered the boutique. Lord, have I missed my shop. I hadn't really stepped foot in here since my mom passed. I knew she wouldn't want me neglecting my shop like this, so I came back. I'd reach out to my clients, and everyone was so understanding. After locking the door, I made it back to my office, and I sent Ray a quick message to let her know where I was. Sitting at my desk, Hakeem ran across my mind. That was one fine piece of chocolate. Thinking about him made my mouth water. Just as I was finna get down to work, my phone dinged.

Keem: *I wanna see you. I need a private date. I couldn't do what I wanted to in the public. I plan on getting to know every curve on your body. That's if you allow me to.*

Me: *You think you can handle a woman like me. I'm a big girl that like to do big things. If you can't lift the fupa, maybe you aren't the guy for me.*

Keem: *Man, I can do things to your body that you've never had done before. Let me show you. I'm a man of* *action, not talking. Meet me at the Hilton on Green St. at seven and leave the drawls at home.*

This man had my body reacting in a way that it had never done before. I loved a man that knew how to work me in every way. I got to work so I could leave and get ready. I had to bring my A-game because Keem might give me a run for my money. It was now 5:30, and I was leaving the shop. It took me five minutes to get home. I skipped in the house on this high. I hadn't stepped foot in this house after mama passed. It just wasn't the same without her. That was why I was putting it on the market and getting something smaller. This was just too much house for just us. Grabbing my phone out my purse, I called Ray.

"Yes, girl! Ashlynn is fine. Why don't you go get your back knocked out? We are fine."

"Well, damn. Hey to you, too. I just wanted to let you know where I was just in case this man tries to hold me hostage. With this snapper between my legs, he ain't gonna be able to get enough."

We laughed together. It felt so good to laugh.

"TMI, girl. But text me the address so I'll know where to come looking for you. Put it on him, just don't hurt him. Go enough yourself. We are good." I was so thankful for Ray.

"Let me speak to Ash real quick."

"Can't, she sleep. I'll have her call you when she wakes. Bye, girl." She ended the call.

Just as I was about to get in the shower, the doorbell began to ring. When I made it to the door, I looked and rolled my eyes. What in the hell did he want!

Rex

Adelynn thought everything was peaches and cream. The emails, calls, and the drop-bys went unanswered. So, yea, I followed her ass home. I wanted to see my fucking child. It'd been almost four years, and it was now time to step up to the plate. I needed her in my life just like she needed me. Parking my car, I jumped out and headed up the door. When I made it there, I rang the bell and waited. Peeping on the inside, I saw that Adelynn was doing good for herself. Hell, her ass was doing better than me. The door swung open, and a mad Adelynn closed her robe.

"What, Rex?! Now is not the time—" she started, and I cut her off.

"Now is the time. I want to see my daughter, and I mean right fucking now."

"Rex, now is not the time. Ashlynn ain't even here. I'll call you when we get back," she lied.

"How the hell you gonna call me without my number? Adelynn, stop playing with me!" I boomed, scaring the hell out of her

"I'll email you my number when I get settled," she stated, closing the door in my face.

Like, she was pissing me off. I had something for her ass, though. She was about to lead me right to my daughter, and I was taking her. It was now time for her to get to know me. I ran back to my car and waited for her to leave. That was when I started following her ass. I was not expecting for her to lead me up to the hotel. Hell, it wasn't even that kinda party. I ain't gonna lie. When Adelynn stepped out of her car, her body was looking right. I don't know what made me dip out on her like that. Then to leave my daughter was a bitch move. I would do anything to get my daughter back. Even if that means I gotta kill a nigga. Adelynn would always be mine. As she went inside, I opened the glove box and got my gun. Easing out the car, I put the gun in the waist of my pants. Oh, yes, it was about to go down! I hoped they were ready for this!

My mind told me to go in there, but I didn't wanna walk into whatever that was about to go down in there. I sat there and watched to see if she was gonna come out just as fast as she went in, but that never happened. The thing that pissed me off, though, was she was out here getting her back blown out, but where the hell was my daughter? Her ass was out here hoeing when our daughter needed her the most. Not able to take it anymore, I got out the car and headed inside. *Damn, this hotel nice as fuck,* I thought as I looked around.

"Welcome, Sir. What can I do for you today?"

"Nothing. Thank you for asking," I stated nastily, not meaning too.

As I reached the elevator, I pushed a random floor, praying that it was the right floor. When the elevator dinged, I looked to my right and there went Adelynn. I went back in the elevator and pecked to see if I could see which room she went in. As she went in and shut the door, my mind told me to go in and kill both of their asses. I didn't wanna do that, though, because then our daughter would be without a mother. A mother that was doing God knows what in this room right now. As I made it to the door, I put my ear up against it and listened. From the looks of things, he was about to show her a good time.

Hearing enough, I headed back downstairs and back to my car. I hoped she was having a good time because the jokes were on her. Soon, all this would be over, and I would have my daughter back in my life. Adelynn you dun' fucked with the wrong nigga!

Hakeem

"Damn, lil' baby. All that ass!" I complimented her.

"What you gonna do with all this ass?" she flirted back with me.

Damn, Adelynn had a nigga on rock hard. My shit was trying to bust out my pants. The clothes she was wearing did her body no justice. I couldn't wait to get between them thighs. I pulled her on the bed on top of me. She aggressively kissed me, and my ass kissed her back. Baby girl was nasty just like I liked that shit. When she came up for air, she looked in my eyes, and, Lord, I felt like she was reading my soul. I flipped her ass over and snatched my dick out of my pants. Her eyes bucked, but I saw so much lust inside them.

"You think you can handle all this!" I asked her, jacking my dick.

"I can show you better than I can tell you," she mentioned, giving me full vision of her glistening pussy.

Soon as she gave me the green light, I wasted no time shoving my dick in her pussy. Her shit was like a vacuum as she ate my dick up. No way I was finna let her pussy get the best of me. I snatched out of her and laid on my back.

"Naw, ain't happening like that. Come ride this dick."

Shit, she wasted no time climbing on the top and riding my shit like it was going out of style. Baby girl pussy was so good, it had my eyes rolling in the back of my head.

"Ouuu, shit!" She moaned.

I had to bite my lip in order not to moan. I grabbed her by the waist and held her in place. "Don't cum yet," I said as her pussy muscles started contracting around my dick.

"Too late, baby. Dick shouldn't be so good." She moaned as she licked my ear.

"Naw, I want that pussy to cream again. Toot they ass up," I ordered, and she did just that.

As I entered her, she tightened her muscles up and started throwing that ass back. Hell, you would've thought baby girl was a skinny bitch by the way she was keeping up with a nigga. Not able to take it much longer, I pulled out and came all over her ass.

"Whew, shit! That pussy is seasoned just right. I ain't gonna do like this other nigga. I'mma make a deal with you. Whenever I want the pussy, you meet me, or I'll pull up on you. If I pull up and your ass entertainment another nigga, that nigga's blood is on your hands. Am I clear?"

"And if you gonna keep entertaining this chick, that's her blood on your hands." She threw my phone at me, and headed in the bathroom.

"Man, what, Keisha, damn!" I boomed into the phone.

"You entertaining another bitch is why your ass can't pick up the phone? I don't know why I wasted my time on your dingy ass," she started, and I heard her scream as the called ended.

Shit, I had the plan in motion, and Keisha was about to be a distance memory. I don't know where she got the balls to boss up on me, but her time was up in the world. Fuck she thought! The rest of the night, Adelynn and I chilled. Baby girl was cool as fuck, and I could definitely get used to this shit. But whoever this fuck nigga was calling her phone was about to get dealt with. The fuck he thought? I made a mental note to get Marco to find that nigga and dead his ass. No questions asked.

Keisha

"Marco, what the hell are you doing? And why am I tied up?" I asked with fear in my voice.

"So you were playing my man, and you didn't think we were going to find out? After all his ass did for you, and you still wanted to fuck the enemy!" he boomed.

"Marco, what the hell are you talking about? All I wanted to do was be happy with Keem, but he can't keep his dick in his pants!" I shot back.

"Bullshit!" he banged his hand and the table, scaring the shit out of me. "So you really gonna shit here and lie? You know what? I don't have time for this shit. Let's get down to business. How long have you been fucking Gerald?" he asked me, and I felt my eyes get big. How in the hell could he possibly know this?

"I don't know what the hell you talking 'bout. I would never fuck the enemy," I lied, and that pissed him off.

"Keisha, stop fucking playing with me! How 'bout this? Until you can tell the truth, I'll cut off a body part of Gerald's. Yep, that's right. Right in front of you. Hey, Cleo, bring his ass out." And out walked Gerald, blindfolded and beat up. "So you gonna stop lying or what?" he asked again.

"I don't know what you're talking about," I lied again, with a straight face. There should be some kind of reward for lying this good.

"Alright, you leave me no choice. Cleo, pass me the knife."

That's when he started cutting Gerald's fingers off and threw them at me. Hell, I thought I was gonna be sick from all the blood. Gerald looked weak and seemed like he couldn't take it anymore.

"Alright, enough! Gerald and I fuck from time to time. Nothing more, nothing less. When I felt like Hakeem was fucking around on me, I started fucking Gerald. There! You happy?!" I screamed.

"No, I'm not happy! You just signed both of y'all death's certificate! 'Preciate you for being honest. Watch them. I need to go holla at Keem," he stated, walking out the basement.

"I'm sorry," I mouthed to Gerald.

After what seemed like forever, Marco came walking back in the room. Gerald had passed out from all the blood he had lost. Hell, his ass looked dead to me. Marco walked by him and kicked his ass. He didn't budge. Yea, his ass was good and dead.

"Well, we got the ok. Burn in hell, Keisha!" was the last thing I heard before the cold bullets pierced through my body.

I guess I got what I deserved! I knew what I was doing when I started fucking with Gerald. Hell, I wanted my cake and ice cream too. And I guess that was why I was in the situation I was in now!

 Love

Adelynn

"Dang, somebody got that glow. This is the happiest you've been since your mother passed. I'm so happy for you. I want all the juicy details, though," Ray expressed, and I batted my eyes.

"A good girl never tells." I winked at her. "No, but you remember the guy that came here with Keisha—" I started, and she cut me off.

"Girl, you are talking about the fine, muscular brother! Home boy is fine as hell. He got any brothers?"

I fell out laughing. "Oh, you were serious? My bad." I stopped laughing. "He got a best friend named Marco. He cool as shit. You might like him."

"Negative. You talking about light-bright that came up here a couple days ago. Naw, I'll pass. That nigga looks like he takes all day to get ready. I can't have nobody thinking they look better than me." She was serious as hell.

This girl had my side hurting from laughing at her. She was right. This was the most I'd laughed in a long time, and I had her and Hakeem to thank for that.

"Oh, and I got the autopsy for mom. It stated that she had a heart attack. She never showed signs of having heart problems, though. I just don't understand. She was as healthy as a thirty-year-old."

"Girl, you can't question God. He will have you here one day and gone tomorrow. Nobody knows when it will be their time to go. That's why the time you have on this Earth, you cherish it. That's why I'm living it up now," she stated, and I nodded.

She did have a good point. I just hated how it was my mom that was taken from us. I knew that I shouldn't question God's decision, but I did. My mom was my everything, and it still felt weird that she was gone.

"Mama, I'm hungry," Ashlynn announced, coming out my office.

"Ok, baby girl. Give me a minute to catch up, and we'll go get some food," I mentioned, and she nodded.

Just thinking about Rex trying to take her from me made me sick to my stomach. I'd already lost my mother. I couldn't lose my daughter too. I knew that if I did, I would have to go check into an institute. As I worked on a couple pieces that was due next week, my phone went off.

Keem: *Meet me at my house tonight. I got something to show you.*

Me: *Can't tonight! It's me and baby girl's night. Maybe tomorrow.*

I brushed him off. A man like Hakeem didn't take no for an answer. He kept blowing me up until I decided to turn my phone off. I knew this was a bad idea, but I had work to focus on. I didn't have time for his feelings.

As promised when I finished, Ash and I went and got some food. I felt like I was being watched, so I was constantly looking over my shoulders. This wasn't a good look. Out of nowhere, Ashlynn and I were getting snatched up. We were forced in the back of a truck as a bag went over our heads. To say I was scared was an understatement. I was terrified. Not only for me but for Ashlynn!

As I rode in the car, I prayed that Ashlynn was ok. I couldn't feel or hear her. After what felt like forever, I was led into a place and forced into a chair. The strong smell of piss invaded my nostrils, almost making me vomit.

"What do you want from me? Please don't hurt my daughter," I cried. The bag was still over my head, and I felt like I was tied up to something.

"Why would I hurt my daughter? All you had to do was let me spend some time with her," the one and only, Rex, said.

"Please, Rex. Let's talk about this like two adults. You don't have to do this."

"Oh, so now you wanna talk? I had to kidnap your ass so you would talk. This don't make no sense. Shhh, it's ok, baby. I'm your father." I heard him say to a crying Ashlynn.

I felt defeated, but I knew that he wouldn't hurt her. I was wrong, but I was protecting my daughter. She was now all I had, and I couldn't lose her.

"Rex, listen. How about we set up monitored visitations, and if they go good, then you'll get her on the weekends," I tried to compromise with him.

"So you don't think I can take care of my daughter on my own? Why it got to be monitored? I'm grown as hell—"

"Let her get to know you first and then we can talk about it! Deal?" I cut him off.

From the way it got quiet, the wheels were probably turning in his head.

"You're right. Let's do that. Adelynn, I'm sorry that all this happened. I just wanted you to get where I was coming from. I'm not a bad person. I just made some fucked up decisions. I'm sorry, baby girl."

When he untied me, I slapped the fire from his ass. Like, this nigga took me to be some dumb bitch. I was doing this to protect my child. Fuck what he thought!

"Come on, Ash. Let's go." I grabbed her, and we left out the abandoned house.

"Adelynn, this ain't over! The next time I won't be so gentle!" I heard him hollering behind me.

I stuck up my mind finger and kept it pushing.

I couldn't believe that Rex even did some shit like this. Oh, but you best believe his time was coming. I hoped he was ready for the war that he had caused.

Hakeem

"Thank you for calling Thick Gurlz. This is Ray speaking. How can I assist you today?"

"Aye, Ray, Adelynn in?" I asked.

"I'm sorry, she isn't here. Would you like to leave a message for her?"

"How long has she been gone? Lunch should be over by now," I mentioned, annoyed.

"To think about it, I haven't talked to her since she left for lunch. Every time I call her, it goes straight to voicemail. Something ain't right. I can feel it." She sighed, and it had the wheels turning in my head.

With that, I ended the call. That was all I needed in order to get in the streets. I could find her ass in point-three seconds. I dialed Marco and waited for him to answer. He was my man when I needed someone in the streets.

"YO'!" he answered with the radio loud as hell.

"Aye, turn that shit down real quick. We got some business that need to be handled," I stated seriously.

"What's up?"

"Aye, we got to get in the streets and find Adelynn. Ray said she been missing since lunch. I been blowing her ass up, too, and nothing."

"Shit, say less. I'm already on that shit. Shoot me her cellphone number, and I'll find her ass."

"Bet!" I mentioned before ending the call.

I shot him her cell phone number as I cruised around the city. I was searching high and low and still hadn't found her. Just as I was about to call Marco, he called me.

"Tell me something good!" I answered.

"Mane, her phone was last spotted at this abandoned house on Church St. I'm on my way over to that bitch now."

"Say less. I'm on the way too." I ended the call.

Whoever had her had to deal with me. Once she gave me a taste of that pussy, it was all over. I would do anything to protect her and her daughter, and I haven't even meet baby girl yet. When I made it to Church St., I dimmed the lights and turned the car off. Reaching over in the glove box, I grabbed my piece and put it in my waistband. Oh, yea, it was about to go down. I got out the car and jogged up to the house while still checking my surroundings. I heard two niggas in there talking. Peeking inside, both of them nigga's backs were facing the windows.

"These got to be the two dumbest niggas," I mumbled.

"Mane, these niggas ain't bright. Let's go ahead and do this," Marco commented as I dabbed him up.

"Shit, let's do this...Get your motherfucking hands up, and I mean right fucking now! Where the fuck is Adelynn?!" I boomed as them niggas jumped.

"Who the fuck are you, and what do you want with my baby mama?" this nigga asked, and I chuckled.

"Wrong question. You don't get to ask questions around here. You the one got a gun pointed at your head. The jokes on you, my nigga." Marco and I chuckled together. "I'mma ask you one more fucking time, and I better get the answer that I'm looking for. Either way, you gonna die today. Now where the fuck is

Adelynn?" I asked, hitting him with the butt of my gun.

"Man, I don't know where the fuck she at. I had her out here earlier, but I let her ass go. I just wanted to see my daughter."

"Oh, you the baby daddy. No worries. I will take of your daughter. Because as long as me and Adelynn are together, your daughter will be a part of my life. Thanks for the fuck up, bruh. Mar, handle these niggas. I gotta go find Adelynn." I dapped Marco and dipped.

I knew that Marco was gonna handle them niggas. I jumped in the car and dialed Adelynn again. This time, she answered.

"Hello?" Her angelic voice boomed through the speakers.

"Damn, where you been all day? I been blowing your ass up," I stated, frustrated.

"Long story. Meet me at my place, and I will tell you. I'll text you the address."

"Ade, you good?" I asked.

"I'm fine. Just exhausted. Let me get Ashlynn ready for bed. I'll see you in a bit." She ended the call.

Not even two minutes later, the address came through, and I couldn't take that little stupid smile off my face. I ran by the house real quick and freshened up. Before I could leave back out the door, I got a picture message from Marco letting me know that he handled them niggas for me. I replied back and headed out the door. The drive over to Adelynn's place was short. I parked my car beside her and hoped out. Making it to the door, I knocked and waited for her to answer.

"Who is it?" she asked.

"Keem," I replied as she opened the door.

Damn, she was looking good enough to eat.

"Come in and up here." She snapped me out of my thoughts.

"My bad. Where you been all day?" I asked, jumping right into it.

"Long story short, my baby daddy kidnapped us and scared the shit out of me. I thought that he was about to take my daughter away from me. I need him out of my life for good." She cried, and I didn't like that shit.

"Listen, you don't have to worry about his ass no more. Just know that. His ass is gone for good. Now let's talk about this relationship."

"What relationship? I call you when I want some dick, and you come running," she started, and I cut her ass off.

"Shid, you fucked up when you gave me that pussy. We in a relationship now, whether you like it or not." I raised my brow, and she fell out laughing. "What the fuck is funny?" I was dead ass serious.

"Ok! Damn, but if we gonna do this, then you need to leave all your whores alone too. I will not fight over your ass. I got a daughter to raise, and I will not step out of my character in front of her. Do I make myself clear?" She was talking to me like I was a child or some shit.

"Man, you good. I ain't gonna have you out here looking stupid. Don't worry about nothing. I got y'all." I grabbed her and hugged her.

It didn't matter what you were going through. You just needed the right one to ride for you. From the first time I met Adelynn, I just knew that I had to have her. Love came in different sizes and shapes. To me, it wasn't about the looks. It was about what was in the heart. I ain't going to lie. Baby girl had a heart of gold. I was ready to see where this took us. This ain't the end for us, so stay tuned.

The End!

Khamari & True

A BBW Love Story

 Asia

Synopsis

Always wondering if life would get any better for her, True Hill ends up living with her grand mom and following her dreams. Now at the age of twenty-three, she has a beautiful business that keeps her going daily. But there is one thing missing, and that is the love from a man. Not really thinking anyone would ever want her because of her size, True continues on burying herself in work and not worrying about the opposite sex. That's 'til a dope boy by the name of Khamari Moss enters the picture.

After losing the love of his life and having to raise his baby girl all alone, Khamari doesn't see a happy ending in his future anymore. While combing the streets at night, and trying to be a full-time daddy during the day, life can be trying. But Khamari does it with an "S" on his chest. Never thinking he would ever find love again after his daughter's mother, Khamari just gives up on it until he meets the beautiful True Hill.

When these two worlds collide, things will happen in such a fast pace. Things that these two never thought were coming. Will True let a real man love her instead of believing what society deems? Will Khamari follow his heart and let love rule? Is love in the cards for this couple, or not?

Chapter One

True

This morning, I had woke up in a good mood thanking God for the new life I was living. Business was booming, and I was just enjoying my peace. The sound of the door opening to my little store front I'd just purchased not too long ago bought me out of my thoughts.

"Welcome to True Events!"

"Hello, my name is Taylor McQueen. I would love for y'all to do my daughter's sweet sixteen."

"Ok. What date was you looking to have it on?" I asked her.

"How is October 19th?"

"Erin, can you check and see if we got October 19th available?!" I yelled in the back to get my best friend and business partner's attention.

She came to the front with the calendar. "We only got one time that day available at six PM. Is that ok for you?"

"Yes, that time is great." The customer smiled.

"Ok. Do you have any specific colors you want it to be?" I asked her while writing everything down on a piece of paper.

"I'm not sure. I'm lost, but I do know she's in love with pink, so y'all can do whatever y'all want. Just make sure it's pink in there," she said, making me smile.

I loved when my customers told me to do anything because they trusted me enough to do their party the way I wanted. Whenever I did that, I made sure I hooked shit up. Then, I had my partner/best friend making the treats, plus, helping set up the events.

After me and the lady talked a little longer, she left her name and number if I had any more questions.

"Damn, best friend, we are killing these parties. We booked the whole month of October!" Erin said in excitement.

"Bitch, you lying." I smiled.

"Now why would I lie about some shit like that? LOOK!" she said, making me look down at the calendar.

When I saw she wasn't lying, my big ass jumped up and down like a kid. I thought to myself, *Not me. Not True Hill from Camden, NJ!* And all at the age of twenty-three. Even after the rough life I had growing up with a mama who couldn't stand me because of my weight. I was in complete shock about how good I was doing. I could have gone down the wrong path, but nope. I was strong, and I gave all thanks to my G-Mom.

When I was younger, my mom's boyfriend tried to rape me, and I ran to her to tell her what his disgusting ass attempted to do. To my surprise, she didn't believe me. I thought she would have believed her own daughter, but hell no. She called me a fat bitch and kicked me out of her house. She even told me that she wished I wasn't her child, and she never wanted to see my fat ass again. Good thing my G-Mom took me in. Me and G-Mom always had the best relationship. She never understood why her daughter treated me the way she did. G-Mom would always tell me stories about how my mama was a big girl before she lost all of that weight.

Living with G-Mom changed my life for the better. She started by getting me out of the hood and moving me in the suburbs. New Life, new school, new beginnings. Now I'm an adult doing my thing. I thought G-Mom would be mad about me taking up a trade instead of going to college, but nope. She was fine with what I decided to do. I'd always wanted to be an event planner, so I got a business degree and went ahead to follow my dreams. Here I was today, the founder and owner of *True Events.* Everything that I'd been through with my mom growing up, including almost being raped and being teased at the new school, had me thinking I wasn't going to ever amount to shit. However, being here so young, I was amazed with myself.

"Girl, do you hear me talking to you?" Erin said, taking me from my thoughts.

"I'm sorry, boo. What was you saying?" I asked.

"I was saying we should go to the club to celebrate and find you a man."

Everything she was saying was going in one ear and out the other. The thought of having a man was always a good idea, but my childhood memories always kind of turned me off about it. Whenever I saw a good-looking dude, all that would come to mind was that he didn't want me.

"Girl, you know I don't do clubs, and no man wants my fat ass," I said with a sad face.

"Girl, cut it out. Like my mom always says, 'Big girls need love too.' Love takes time, sissy. Shit, look at me. I still don't have a man."

"Girl, please. You can have any man you want if your ass gives somebody a damn chance."

"I know. I'm just scared to fall in love after Jay's no good ass," she said with tears coming down her face.

I knew that was a reason why she was scared to let anybody in. Her and Jay were supposed to get married but turned out he had a whole family that she didn't know about. My sissy was heartbroken. She didn't eat for months and ended up losing her baby from stress.

"Don't start that crying over that nigga," I said, giving her a hug to calm her down. "Since I'm going to the club with you, I'm going to need something to wear," I added, making her jump up with a smile on her face.

"Ok! I already have an outfit for you and everything!"

All I can do was shake my head and laugh. After we were done with setting up everything for the weekend, we decided to locked up and called it a night. We went to Erin's house to get dressed and ready to go out.

After getting ourselves together, we headed to this club over in Philly. I hated going over there. It was just too much going on out there, and it wasn't never no parking. I just hoped nothing popped off because I didn't want to beat nobody's ass tonight. We parked and walked towards a long ass line.

"I hope we're not waiting in this long ass line. If so, my ass is going home," I fussed.

"Hell no. Girl, I never wait in these long ass lines," Erin said as we walked to the guy that was at the door. "Hey, boo," she greeted, giving the guy a hug.

"What's up, Erin? You and your girl is good to go in. Don't forget to hit me up later. Your ass be hurting a nigga's feelings."

"Boy, please. You got a wife and kids at home. I will see you later, Dee. Come on, girl. Let's go have fun."

"Girl, who was that? He looks familiar."

"That's Dee. His sister, Destiny, went to school with us. He stay trying to fuck when he got a family at home. True you know I'm not that type of girl. I wouldn't want my husband sleeping with other people while I'm at home with his kids."

"Facts. I understand that, sissy. Come on. Let's go and have fun and leave the stress for later," I said, pulling her over to the bar.

"What can I get to drink for you beautiful ladies?" the bartender asked.

"Yeah, can we get two double-shots of Crown Royal?" I replied.

A few minutes later, he came back with our drinks. We then went to sit down at one of the tables that was available.

"Girl, I can't believe we really got the month of October booked, and it's only the end of August." I smiled, still shocked about it.

"Yes, sis! We are doing big things!" I yelled, doing Erin's little crazy dance in my seat, making her laugh. She would always do this dance when she was happy about something.

"Yesss!"

"But, sissy, for real. You need to open up your bakery, and I don't want to hear anything about not wanting to leave me hanging. If you think about it, we can still work with each other, and I know damn well you got the money to open up your own place."

Before she was able to reply, the DJ yelled over the music, "Aye, look who just showed up! My boy Mar and his crew! Won't y'all show them some love!"

Me and Erin looked over to where this big group of girls was headed, and we just shook our heads and continued talking.

Chapter Two

Khamari

"It's fucking lit in here tonight," my cuz Mario said.

"Hell yeah. I need to release some stress messing with Tiara's ass," I said, shaking my head.

"Man, you already know how I feel about that. I never liked her sneaky ass. Shit, I didn't even want you to bring her around my niece, but it was your decision."

"Yeah, I know, but we need a woman in the house. I wish Paris and Moms were here. It's just me, Pops, and of course, her uncles. Shit, I know she don't want to talk about her female shit with us. She scared the hell out of me the other day crying and shit because her period came on. I almost lost it. That shit came too fast. I haven't even had that type of talk with her yet. My baby was scared for her life and thought she was dying and shit." I shook my head.

"Damn, man! Already? That shit is crazy. I didn't even know an eight-year-old could get a period. How did you handle it? Did you get Tiara to talk to her?"

"Yeah. I got her to run it down for me. I was shocked she did it for me, being as though we had just broken up."

"Shit, I'm shocked too, being as though she use to be acting all mean to my niece and shit. I used to be ready to snap her damn head off talking to my niece like she ain't shit." He hissed, making me laugh at his stupid ass.

Mario was crazy as fuck. He was my cousin, but more like my brother, and he gave my baby girl anything she wanted. He didn't play about her at all. It was all love, and I was glad Kera had him and my Pops around to help me raise her. Being twenty-eight years old and raising a little girl all alone got rough. I grew up with both parents until my mom passed from cancer when I was eighteen. So, it was just me and my Pops.

After I graduated high school, I started getting money with my Pops. His name used to ring bells, but now all you heard was Khamari Moss. While being in the streets, I met my first love, Paris Taylor. At first, me and Paris was just fucking until both of us caught feelings. After that, it was always me and her. When you saw me, you seen her. Then she got pregnant with my baby girl. Yeah, we were young, but we knew what we both wanted. So, we began preparing for our little family.

One night, I heard noise coming from downstairs. I got up and saw that Paris wasn't laying down next to me. I went down to the kitchen and found her on the floor crying out in pain while holding the bottom of her stomach. Right then and there, I knew something was wrong with her and the baby, so I rushed her to the hospital. She had the baby that night. But Paris didn't make it due to complications during childbirth. Losing her left me devastated, and from the beginning, I had no idea about being a dad and being the man in the streets, but, shit, I made it work. Me and my Pops raised a smart and beautiful baby girl.

It was still so unbelievable to me how much she'd grown. My baby was about to be nine years old. I knew Paris would be proud of me for stepping up and taking care of our daughter. I knew she was looking down on us daily. She's definitely my angel up above. *Damn, Paris, I miss you so much,* I thought to myself.

"'Cuz, you good?" Mario asked taking me from my thoughts.

"Yeah, man, I'm straight. Just thinking about shit," I said, looking around.

"Damn, who is them fine ass girls over there?" Mario pointed over towards the back of the club.

I looked where he was looking and saw this beautiful chocolate girl. She was thicker than my usual; but, shit, I didn't care. She was beautiful, and she looked like she carried herself well. I signaled the bottle girl to come over to me because I wanted to send them a drink or two.

"What's good, baby girl? You see them ladies over there? Can you get them another drink? It's on me, and can we get a bottle of Henny, Crown, Cîroc, a couple of Coronas." I handed her some money, and she said thank you before walking away.

"Y'all niggas looking lonely as fuck," Trey said, walking into the VIP section with Troy right behind them.

Trey and Troy were Paris' older twin brothers. Trey was a part of my crew, and Troy was a lawyer. He owned his own law firm. Now don't let the suit and tie fool you. His ass got down and dirty, if need be. He also was the family lawyer.

"Nigga, shut the fuck up." I dapped him up.

"Where the rest of the crew at?" Troy asked.

"Bro, you know when they get here, they get pussy-happy in this bitch," Mario said, making us laugh.

Before saying anything else, one of the girls that we were looking at earlier came over.

"I came over here to tell you thank you for the drinks." She smiled. I could tell she was mixed, but I also could tell she had more black in her than anything.

"You're more than welcome, baby girl! Why didn't your home girl come over here with you?" I asked, being curious.

"Damn, you are so damn beautiful," Mario said out loud, making us laugh.

"She scared to come over, especially since it's a group of fine ass men over here. And thanks for the compliment," she said while smiling at Mario.

"What's your name, beautiful?" he asked her.

"My name is Erin, and my best friend's name is True."

"Well, Erin. How about you go get your friend and come join us? Tell her we don't bite." Trey smirked.

She said ok before leaving the table.

"Y'all niggas are foul." Troy laughed, shaking his head.

"Shut the hell up, nigga. We tryna be like you. You got a fiancé and ready to start a family. Shit, we are getting old and still with no wife. We tired of playing with these hoes," Mario said, causing me and Trey to agree with everything he was saying.

The girls were headed back over to us, and seeing True up close really had me eyeing her. Baby girl was so beautiful, and I could tell she wasn't used to all of this by the way she was standing to the side fiddling with her fingers.

"Now, Miss True, why was it so hard for you to come over and talk to us?" Troy asked her.

I didn't say nothing to her yet because I was still looking at how beautiful she was.

"I'm sorry. I didn't mean to be rude or anything. It's just that I'm not used to being around big crowds."

"Lil' mama, we not gon' bite you. We just trying to drink, talk, and enjoy the good vibes," I voiced, trying to make her relax a little.

"Does that mean you will chill with us now? Because I'm tired of these niggas drooling over y'all like they ain't never seen beautiful women," Trey joked.

"Nigga, shut the hell up," Mario said, making us laugh. They always talking shit and going back and forth with each other.

"Sure, I would like that." True smiled.

Damn, for some reason, I wanna get to know True, I thought to myself. Both the ladies sat down next to me and Mario.

"Now that we're seated, what's everyone's name? Except for Mario, since we already exchanged names."

"Well, I'm Khamari, but everybody calls me Mar. These are my brothers, Troy and Trey, and you already met my cousin, Mario," I said.

"Are y'all twins?" True asked Trey and Troy.

"Yup, ma! This my stupid ass twin brother," Troy joked, hitting him in the arm.

"Are y'all having more to drink? If so, y'all can help y'all self to whatever y'all want," I said, letting them know that we had a variety of things to drink. "Where sis at?" I then asked Troy, wondering where his wife was.

"She had to work late; her last photo shoot was at seven, but she should be on her way here."

"Aw, shit. Now I got to find me a hoe to be laid up with because I'm not tryna be third wheeling in this bitch," Trey said, causing all of us to laugh.

"I keep telling you Aliyah is your match, my nigga, and you know she is," I said to him.

"I know, man, but she doesn't want shit to do with me no more. I think I fucked up this time. This has been the longest she's went without talking to me," Trey said with sad eyes.

"Shit, do you blame her? You slept with that girl best friend and kept sleeping with her acting like she wouldn't find out about the shit. If you really love her, you would fight for her and do right by her. That's how I was with your sister. Man, when you meet the right one, you have to be good to her." I was talking some real shit to him. I knew I wasn't able to experience a lifetime with Paris, but I knew when she was living that she was all I wanted. I wanted that good long-lasting love like my parents had.

"She really doesn't want to do talk to his ass now," Troy said, sipping his drink.

"What you mean?" Me and Mario looked at Troy.

"She's pregnant, man," Trey stressed.

"Damnnn," me and Mario said at the same time.

"Yeah, she's not fucking with you," Mario said, not helping with the shit at all.

"True and Erin, can I asked y'all for some advice?" Trey asked them, and they nodded their heads.

"So, I fucked up with my girl, and I need advice to get her back."

"Fucked up, how?" Erin asked.

"I slept with her best friend," Trey said, looking ashamed.

"Y'all niggas ain't shit. You have one good woman in your life and y'all quick to break her heart. I hope she don't get back with your no-good ass," Erin said before storming off.

Damn, what was that about? I thought to myself.

A couple of seconds later, Mario ran after her to see if she was ok.

"I'm sorry for that. She had a fucked up past relationship, and she hasn't been right ever since. Now, Trey I overheard y'all talking a little. Congrats on the baby. Now if you're serious about making it work with her, then go for it so your little family can be complete. But if you're not serious about her, let her go and be happy with someone else. Co-parenting shouldn't be that bad. Think about everything I just said before you go back to her trying to make shit right. You gotta make sure this is what you really want before disturbing her peace."

"Thanks, True. Let me get out of here. I will catch up with y'all later," Trey said, getting up from his seat and dapping us all up.

"Nigga, where you going? You just got here," Troy asked his brother.

"Nigga, I'm going to get my girl back. Ayo, True. Thanks again, and tell Erin I'm sorry. I didn't mean to make her mad."

True smiled while giving him a head nod. I moved a little closer to baby girl, making her a little nervous. I had to push up on her after listening to how she schooled Trey. Her thick ass had me intrigued.

"Ayo, I'm going to meet Natalya at the door," Troy said before leaving the section.

"You don't have to be nervous around me, baby girl," I said to True now that we were alone.

"Is it that obvious?" She smiled.

"Yeah, it is, but you don't have to be timid. Like I told you before, I don't bite. I mean, unless you want me too. Now let's talk, Ms. True. I would love to get to know you. How old are you?"

"I'm twenty-three," she said, still looking a little nervous.

"Oh ok. So you a little young girl." I chuckled.

"Well, if I'm young, then how old are you?"

"I'm twenty-eight, ma."

"Oh, ok. That's now that much older than me." True smiled, starting to get comfortable around me.

We continued to have good conversation, and this was a first time in a long time I just sat down and had a good conversation with a female without fucking them. I loved the way this was going, and I'm hoping for more of this in the future.

Chapter Three

Erin

Hearing what Trey had put his girl through had me furious. I guess my past always knew how to jump back in my present, and it ruined my night. Ever since I went through the terrible breakup, I just couldn't seem to get shit right. I was always telling True she needed to find her a man and stop worrying about her weight, when my ass needed to leave the past in the past and move on with life. I couldn't keep letting what happened to me keep me from being happy.

"Erin, wait up!"

I heard Mario yelling my name from behind me. I stopped and waited for him to get close to me.

"I just wanted to make sure you were ok," he said, causing me to turn and look him in the face. At first, I didn't want him to see my tear-stained face, but then I thought about it. This man hardly knew me, but he ran to make sure I was ok. Him wiping the tears from my face caught me by surprise.

"You shouldn't be crying over that fuck nigga no more. It's his fucking loss, not yours. Whatever he did to you is no longer happening. I know you thinking all men are fuck-ups, but that's not true, beautiful. You just have to wait 'til the right one falls out of the sky," Mario said, causing me to smile.

"I know, and I'm sorry. I didn't mean to snap on Trey like that. I've just been through a lot in my last relationship, and when I hear a similar story, right then and there, I hate all men. I'm scared to give anybody a chance again. Hell, I'm scared of the whole love-thing again. I will be damned if I let another nigga break my heart again."

"You can't do that to yourself, beautiful. I know you scared, but how are you suppose to find what you looking for if you don't want to give anybody a chance?" he asked.

For a second, I stood back and thought about what he said, and he was right about everything.

"Do you want to go for a walk? We can talk about whatever you want," he offered.

"I would love to." We walked to where his car was. "This is your car?!" My eyes lit up, looking at a black 2020 Tesla Model P100D.

"Yeah." He smirked.

"This is my dream car." I smiled.

"Is that right? Maybe I will buy you one day."

After he said that, I didn't say nothing else. After riding for at least a half-hour, we ended up at the park close to my house. We got out of the car and started walking around.

"So tell me about yourself, Ms. Erin," he said with a smile.

"Alright. My name is Erin Collins. I'm twenty-three. I grew up in the house with both parents, Earl and Susan Collins. My mother is white, and my daddy is black. I graduated from Highland Regional High school top of my class. I love baking, I have no kids. Just living my life right now. What about you, Mr. Mario?"

"It's nothing much. My name is Mario Stevens. Born and raised in Camden, NJ. I'm twenty-seven, grew up with my mom, no kids, or no relationships. I own three car dealerships."

I knew he had to have something else going on. Because he was young as hell to be owning three car dealerships. I didn't say anything, though. I just listened to everything he was talking about.

"Oh, that's nice. Now I see where you got my dream car from." I smirked.

"Yeah. Just let me know when you're looking for another car. I can hook you up."

I nodded my head. "So, Mr. Mario, why does a handsome man like yourself not have a family of his own?" I'd been wanting to know this answer ever since I laid eyes on him.

"When I first started making money, I really didn't have time for one. Don't get me wrong, I want a family, but these hoes that be popping up ain't worthy enough to birth my seeds. So, when the right one comes my way, I'mma have a whole bunch of love to give. But until then, I'm chillin'. My mama always tells me don't search, let them find me." He looked me in my eyes, making me blush. "So, when am I gonna get to taste this baking of yours?" He smiled.

"Anytime you want," I flirted.

"Well, since you said that, I need that shit right now. A nigga feeling nice too."

"We can ride to my house and get something. You lucky I made a small cake before I left the house. Are you hungry too?"

"Yeah, I could eat." He smirked.

We walked over to my car and hopped in, then headed to my house. It didn't take us long to get there, being as though I lived close as hell to the Philadelphia bridge. We pulled up to my small apartment. Good thing my house was always clean because I wasn't expecting no body. Especially a man. The only men that ever came here was my dad or my brother. So, I was a little nervous to let him in, but I'm also enjoying his company.

"Your spot is nice. Who did the decorations?"

"True and my mom, but mostly True," I replied.

"That's what's up. I just moved in my house about two weeks ago. Do you think she can hook my house up for me? I don't mind paying her. I would ask my mom, but she don't live out here anymore."

"Yeah, I will ask her. She wouldn't have a problem with doing it. Do you want anything to drink?"

"Yeah, do you have any water?"

"Yes, I do. Let me go get you some. You might as well come on in the kitchen with me. That way I can heat your food up for you. I have a bathroom straight down that hall. Go 'head and wash your hands, and by the time you come back, your food should be in the microwave."

I headed to the kitchen to warm our food up. I had made steak with roasted potatoes and corn. After I was done warming up the food, I grabbed his plate, and a water, then sat them both on the table.

"Thank you. It better be good too." He smirked.

"Boy, whatever. My food is the best to everybody I know that's had my cooking before," I said before walking back over to the microwave to grab my plate. "So, what is your favorite movie?" I asked, trying to spark a conversation.

"I really don't have a favorite movie. Shit, I really don't be having time to watch TV these days. What new movies came out so we can watch something after we finish eating?"

"I don't know any new ones, but one of my favorite movies is *Belly*. That's my shit."

"That's my shit too, but what do you know about that movie?" He chuckled.

"I see you got jokes. Just because I'm part white don't mean I don't got a little hood in me. Besides, my daddy is as black as ya ass." I giggled.

"Trust me, I definitely see where you get that hood from."

"Yeah, so don't be tryna play me," I said with a smile.

"I'm not trying to play you, beautiful. We can watch *Belly*." He smiled, finally taking a bite of his food.

I looked at him waiting for a response. He probably was going to try to be a smart ass about it.

"I see you got some skills, girl," he said, stuffing his face.

"Just wait until you taste one of my cupcakes. You're going to fall in love."

We then headed to the living room with our plates. As I put on the movie, we both ate and continued to talk. About an hour later, we were almost done the movie. He had been talking about the cupcakes for a minute now. So, I decided to take our plates in the kitchen and of course, get him a cupcake. I didn't want any due to the fact that I was already good and full.

"Damn, I feel special." He smirked.

"Why you say that?" I giggled.

"Because a beautiful woman that caught my eyes in the club a few hours ago invited me in her house with a plate of food and dessert. And, yes, I would love to learn more about her if she lets me. I promise I won't do her wrong. She just has to trust me. We can go as slow as you want. All I want is a chance to get to know you more," he said, taking a bite of the cupcake. The facial expression he was giving me with every bite showed me that he was enjoying it. "Damn, baby girl! Where did you learn to cook like this?"

"Well, my mom taught me how to cook, and I taught myself how to bake."

"That's what's up! You should open up your own bakery."

"You sound like my parents and True. I've been working since she started doing what she does, but she told me to do me, and I could work with her if I wanted, too."

"What do she do, if you don't mind me asking?"

"No, it's ok. She's an event planner. I help her set up the parties, and of course, I do the treats and cakes for the parties she do."

"Damn, y'all doing big things out here. True really is good at what she do. She does parties, and she could be doing interior decorating as well. She should really add that to her resume."

"Yeah, that's true. I should put that in her ear. But as for me opening my own spot, I do think about it all the time. I just feel like I'm not ready just yet," I said to him, being truthful.

Mario and I continued to talk about everything under the sun, really getting to know each other. I really was feeling him so far and wanted to see where this could go. I loved how he listened to me and how he was all about me bettering myself for the future. Hell, he even was giving me some ideas for True's business. A good ole' conversation, with no judgement, and with a man that seemed to have a good head on his shoulders. *Would you look at God!* I thought to myself.

Chapter Four
Khamari

I was sitting in my office trying to get some work done but couldn't seem to get True out of my mind. Then I was thinking about Paris as well. I didn't understand why my mind seemed so clouded today. It wasn't like I hadn't dated any chicks after Paris. So, I really was lost to what was going on. A knock on my office door bought me out of my thoughts. Then the sweet sound of my baby's voice boomed through the door.

"Daddy!" Kera yelled, trying to get my attention.

"What's up, Princess! Come on in."

"Can I please go out with Natalya? I finished my homework already! Please, Daddy!" she begged, making that little face that got me every time.

Looking at my daughter, all I saw was Paris in her. More and more every day, she became her twin, and it just made me realize how much I missed her.

"Yes, you can, but remember you better not buy sneakers without getting clothes to match."

Kera was a sneaker head. One of the closets in her room was full of just sneakers. Kera was a little tomboy. Now don't get me wrong. If my baby girl wanted to dress up, she would, but her heart was with sneakers, jeans, and sweats. I really think her tomboy image came from being raised in a house with all men. I loved my baby no matter the way she dressed. I had to stay on her when she went shopping because she was getting out of hand with all them damn sneakers.

"I'm not getting sneakers today. I'm getting some clothes," she said, shocking me.

Before I was about to say something, there was a knock at the door. I was sure it was Natalya, so I hurried to go answer it. Just like I thought, it was her, but I was shocked to see Troy as well. Usually he would be somewhere working.

"Uncle Troy!!" Kera ran to him, jumping in his arms. Kera loved her uncles so much. She'd also took a liking to Natalya over the years.

"What's up, baby girl?!" he said, picking her up. Troy and Trey stayed picking her up. Even though they asses knew she was too damn big for that. But I couldn't tell them shit about their niece.

I walked over to my sis to give her a hug while Troy and Kera had their little moment.

"What's up, bro?" Troy asked, dapping me up.

"Nothing much. Trying to get this paperwork done. Thank y'all so much for taking her out. I really appreciate y'all. She hasn't had an outing since school started back up. I've been so swamped with work. Shit's been crazy."

"Come on now, bro. You know we don't mind taking her. She is my niece, and you know I will keep her anytime. I had a little bit of time off to get our new house together, so she is always welcome," he said.

"Thanks, bro! You know Pop still on vacation."

"Yeah, I heard. He still trying to say it's just for business? Who he with? May's hoe ass?" Troy asked, causing me to laugh.

"Now you know that's exactly who he with." I shook my head.

We all thought it was something sneaky and fishy about Ms. May. But we just couldn't put fingers on it. Shit, we already didn't like her grimy ass son. I think she was using my dad to get what she wanted out of him, but I wasn't letting that shit happen. My dad was so deep up her ass to figure that out. I understand that he was ready for love again, but May's ass was not for him.

Now Ms. Sarah was who I thought my dad would be great with. She's nice, sweet, and she would cook for all of us. She lived up the street from my dad's house. Her and my dad would flirt from time to time, but that was it. I just think Ms. Sarah stayed to herself after her and May got into it over him. Yeah, my dad got a whole love triangle going on right now. Me and Troy talked a little more until Kera ass started rushing us to hurry up.

After they left, I sat back down at my desk to finish my paperwork for about another hour.

Once I was done with all of my shit, I threw on some clothes. Then I was headed to this place that one of the boys from the block told me about. He had just gotten his daughter's party done, and Kera was feeling the decorations. So, I was going to surprise her with a surprise party in November.

It was going to be hard to surprise her little nosey ass, but Trey, Troy, and Natalya were going to play a big part in helping me.

I jumped in my wheels, then put my music on and peeled off. About fifteen minutes later, I was pulling up to the address my home boy gave me. I'm so glad the place wasn't too far from me. I had some other business to tend to, and I didn't need to be going too far out.

I pulled up to this place called True Events Then jumped out of the car and made my way in the door.

"Hello, welcome to True Events," Erin said with her head down.

I was shocked to see that she worked here. That's crazy. I've been thinking about her girl all day, and then I see her.

"What's up, Erin?" I said, making her look up.

"Hey! It's Khamari, right?"

I smiled. "Yes, that's right! You work here?"

"Yup. I'm the co-owner of this place! Oh, and I'm sorry about the other night. I didn't mean to go off like that in front of y'all."

Before I could say anything, True came out looking beautiful as usual. We made eye contact with each other. We stared at each other for a minute until Erin cleared her throat getting our attention.

"Hey, Khamari! What are you doing here?" she asked before walking over and giving me a hug. Shocking me and Erin both.

"I came here to book for my daughter's birthday party. She is turning nine in November. Running into you just made my day, so now can I get that number?"

"Oh, ok. Well, welcome to my place of business. Now let's discuss what services you need from us. Then once we're finished, I guess I can give you my number."

"Alright. I see you, beautiful, doing big things." I smiled.

"Yes, I'm definitely trying. It's a lot sometimes, and it could be very stressful."

"That's what you don't need is stress, baby girl. Why won't you just hire some people to help y'all? You got your business. There is no way in hell you should be stressing. You should be enjoying your life, expanding your business, and getting to the bag."

"Right, Khamari, let her know! I've been trying to tell her no stress, and if we hire some extra hands, we will be better. But she doesn't wanna trust anyone," Erin said.

"It's ok not to trust anybody because people ain't shit these days, but you just got to set their asses straight."

"What date did you want for your daughter, Mar?"

"Is November 12th good for y'all?" I asked.

"Yes, we have that whole day available. Now if you want to book the whole day out and hold that date, it will be $250, but the party will run you about $1000," Erin said.

"Do you want all of it today, or when y'all do the party?" I asked them.

"It doesn't matter how ever you want to do it, but the deposit is required to hold your date," she explained while True went to get something out of the back.

"I can pay all of it today. It's not a problem. I heard about y'all. Plus, I've seen your work. I know y'all about to hook my baby shit up."

"So, what theme do you want to do for her?" True asked, coming from the back.

"Well, I don't know. Her favorite colors are yellow and pink."

"So how about we can do unicorns with yellow and pink? Is this a surprise?" Erin asked.

"Yeah. That's why I'm going to need y'all help."

"I love the unicorn theme. I just never did it before, but I'm going to make it look beautiful. Don't worry. We won't let you down." True smiled.

"I know you won't, beautiful. How much do I owe y'all?"

"It's $1,250.00 all together," True said.

I pulled out a stack of money without counting it and handed it to True. "Here is a little more. I just want my baby girl to enjoy her day, and y'all are definitely invited if y'all want to come."

"Khamari, this is more than enough. You didn't have to give me all of this," True said with a surprised expression on her face.

"It's not a problem, baby girl. You can save it for something else if you don't use all of it for her party," I assured her. No amount of money was too much for my daughter. Plus, I was happy to see two young women from the hood doing big things like this.

"Ok. I guess you're right, and sure, I would love to come to her party. Alright, what is her name?" True asked me.

"Her name is Kera."

"I love that." True smiled.

Baby girl was making me want to take this chance to get to know her. She just didn't know that yet, but it was coming real soon.

"What time are you locking up around here?" I asked her.

"About five. Why?"

"I would love to take you out. Of course, if you let me show you a good time."

"Girl, I think you should go. Stop being a stuck-up bitch and give this man some time. First, you were crying that niggas don't want to talk to you because of your size. Now somebody is practically sweating ya ass and you playing. As you can see, he likes you and all the curves you flaunt. So y'all go out and have some fun, and don't call or text me on your date," Erin sassed before walking to the back, causing us both to laugh at her bossy ass.

"I would love to go out with you." True smiled. I guess Erin putting her in her place helped me out.

"Cool. I will pick you up at eight," I said to her before walking out.

"Wait, you don't have my phone number." She stopped me.

"Baby girl, I got your number already. I was just waiting for an okay to text you," I said, making her blush.

Yeah, I had already gotten her number from Erin. I could tell Erin was going to be alright with me. I made my way out of True Events, so I can go handle some business.

Chapter Five

True

In so much excitement, I had to make my way to my G-Mom's to tell her the good news. I knew Khamari and I weren't a couple or anything like that, but the thought of just going out with a man had me so happy. But nervous at the same time.

"G-Mom, where are you?!" I yelled, walking in the house.

"I'm in the kitchen, baby!" she yelled back.

"G-Mom, what you in here cooking?" I gave her a kiss on the cheek.

"Your favorite," she referred to her famous Lasagna.

"Guess what happened to me, G-Mom?!" I said, not being able to contain my excitement.

"The way you in here acting, you must have met you a boy or something."

"Yup, and I'm so nervous. I don't know what to do," I said being honest.

"Girl, why the hell you nervous? You better put on your big girl panties and have fun on your first date. Now I know you haven't been with anybody, but you can't always be scared of everything."

"I know, G-Mom, but how do I know if he is real or just playing?"

"Baby, you don't know, but that's a part of life. You live and you learn. Every relationship is not going to be a fairytale. Now don't take that the wrong way because this young man right here maybe it for you. But you will never know unless you take a chance on him and yourself. Now what's his name, and how did you meet him?"

"His name is Khamari, and I met him at the club the other night. I wasn't going to give him the time or place, but then he came to my place of business to book his daughter's party. Right then and there, I knew it had to be something with him, so I decided to go ahead and go out with him— after Erin cursed me out for not giving him the time. Not to mention he is so fine, G-Mom." I blushed.

She laughed. "I swear I love me some Erin. That little White Girl sure is a true friend to you."

"G-Mom, would you stop calling her that." I giggled.

My G-Mom loved Erin just like she loved me. She had always called her White Girl as we grew up. At first, I thought Erin would be offended, but she wasn't. She actually laughed at my grandma and called her Old Lady. I loved their relationship, and they both meant so much to me.

"You know I don't mean no harm. Erin is my baby. Now go head and get out of here so you won't be late for your date. Y'all young girls be taking long as hell to get dressed."

"Alright, G-Mom. I have to meet Erin at my house, anyway. She's doing my hair."

"Alright. tell my little White Girl I said hello. And you enjoy yourself. I'll save you some food for when you come over here tomorrow and tell me all about your date."

I kissed my G-Mom on the cheek then left out.

****

I was now home and getting ready for my big night. I had showered already, and my clothes were laying on the bed. All I was waiting for was Erin to style my hair.

"What do you want done to your hair?" she asked when I walked back in the room.

"However you want to do it. You know I trust you with my hair, babes."

"Yes, you're right about that." She giggled.

"So what's going on with you and Mr. Mario?" I smirked.

"I don't know, sissy. He makes me feel like I'm the luckiest girl in the world. True, I'm just scared to give my heart to somebody else. How do I know if he's not going to do me the same way Jamar did?"

"I know how you feel, love, but you can't let that get in the way of your future. I'mma tell you what G-Mom just told me. She said it's a part of life and you live and you learn. Now you can't treat every dude you meet like Jamar's ass. You want me to find love, and I want you find love also, so I want you to make a deal with me. I'll give Khamari a chance, and you have to give Mario a chance."

Erin took to minute to answer. "Ok, I think I can do that."

"So, when are y'all seeing each other again?"

"Tonight. We're going out to eat, then we're having movie night at his house. I'm leaving my car here, though. He is picking me up from here." She smiled.

It'd been a while since I saw my friend like this, and I'm loving every bit of it. I could really get used to the both of us being happy like this.

After she was done with my hair and makeup, I got dressed. Then I stood in front of the mirror falling in love with how good I looked, curves and all. I hadn't felt this beautiful in such a long time, and I knew the way Khamari looked at me had a lot to do with it. I never understood how my mother treated me like I was the ugliest big girl in the world. I thanked my G-Mom every day for putting it in my head that I was beautiful. Her and Erin helped me a lot over the years with my insecurities.

"True, girl, is you ok?" Erin asked, taking me from my thoughts.

"Yeah. Just thinking about shit."

"Don't let none of that get to you. Tonight is your night, so enjoy it BFF. Your beautiful the way you are, and don't let nobody tell you any different," she said, giving me a hug.

"Thank you. I really appreciate you, your parents, and G-Mom for everything." Before she could say anything, my phone started going off. I saw it was a number that I didn't know, so I answered it. "Hello?"

"Hey, ma. I'm outside whenever you ready," Khamari said, causing me to smile.

"Ok. I will be right out."

After I hung up the phone, I couldn't stop smiling. I grabbed my bag and hugged Erin once more.

"That must be Khamari. Go ahead and go. Mario is on his way here to get me now. I'll make sure to lock up, and I'll meet you at G-Mom's tomorrow for dinner. So, that way you won't have to tell the story over again."

"Alright. Have fun and be safe." I told her while walking out of the door.

Khamari was waiting for me at the bottom of my step. He grabbed my hand and lead the way to his car. Right before he opened the door for me, he kissed me on the cheek. Before we had the chance to get in the car and pull off, Mario was pulling up. Of course, Khamari and I had to speak to him.

Chapter Six
Khamari

When I saw True come outside with Erin, all I could think about was how beautiful she was, and I couldn't wait to make her mine. I didn't know what these fuck niggas thought was wrong about her. I knew she was plus-sized, but she was big in the right places, and, shit, I loved it. I'd never messed with a plus-sized girl, but I could now see why Troy was in love with Natalya. Her and True was about the same size.

"Damn, baby girl, you look beautiful as fuck," I said, giving her a hug.

"Yeah, ma, you do look beautiful," Mario agreed.

"Thank y'all." She smiled.

"Thanks to me," Erin said, making us all laugh. "True, remember what we talked about, and Khamari, take care of my sister," she added.

"I got you, E."

"The same goes for you too, Mario," True said, giving Erin a hug.

I opened the door for her and waited until she got in before I did too. I decided to take her to this place called Capital Grille. It was a nice place, and the food was good. I had been there a couple of times myself. It didn't take me long to get there; it took about twenty minutes.

I pulled up to the place, I got out, and paid the guy to park my whip. I then went around to open the door for True and to help her out.

"Oh My God, Khamari, I've been trying to come here but been so swamped with work."

"Well, I'm glad I was able to bring you here." With a smile, I held her hand while we walked into the restaurant. Once we entered the door, the greeter walked our way.

"Hello, welcome to Capital Grille."

"Hey. I have a reservation for Moss."

"Yes, Mr. Moss. Right this way," the waiter said, and True and I followed him to our table.

"So tell me your story, beautiful. I'm all ears tonight."

"Alright. I am twenty-three years old. I lived with my G-Mom growing up because of how my no-good ass mama treated me. Life with her was a nightmare, on top of dealing with how she treated me at home. I went to school and dealt with bullies because of my weight. My mom had men coming in and out of the house. She made me clean up her mess, and she treated me like I wasn't her blood daughter. She really didn't give two fucks about me. When I would get beat up in school about my weight, she didn't do shit about it.

"One day she had a man that was her so called 'boyfriend' over, and while she was sleep, I went downstairs to get me something to eat. When I walked into the kitchen her boyfriend was in there. I always had an uneasy feeling around him, so when I saw him, I turned around to head back upstairs. But when I went to leave the kitchen, of course, he stopped me, and he told me I wasn't going anywhere. He started touching me, and I was fighting and screaming, telling him to stop. That's when my mother came downstairs because she heard me. When she saw what was going on, she immediately got angry. I told her what her boyfriend tried to do, and of course, she didn't believe me and kicked me out of her house.

"At the age of sixteen, my mom didn't care about me. I was glad my G-Mom was still living. She took me in with open arms. She got me in school, and that's where I met Erin at. We started hanging tight. Her parents loved me like I was their own. Just as well as my G-Mom loves her. In twelfth grade was when Erin and I started doing our party stuff. We both took up business in college, and here we are today business owners." She smiled.

"Damn, baby girl. You went through some shit. But I'm glad to see you made it through. And trust me, I know ya mama getting her karma."

"I'm sorry it took me so long. What can I get you guys to drink?" the waitress said while walking over to us.

"You good. Can I get a Long Island iced tea, and a glass of water with lemon?"

"Sure. And for you, beautiful?"

"I will have the same thing," True said.

"Alright. I will be back with the drinks and to take you guys' meal orders."

"So, you know my story. Tell me yours. Where's Kera's mama at?"

"Well, Paris passed away while giving birth to Kera. She was my first love, and it hurt me when she left me all alone to raise a baby. My Pops, Mario, Troy, and Trey were there to help me through.

"Oh, I'm sorry to hear that. Where's your mama, if you don't mind me asking?"

"My mama passed when I was younger. She died from cancer so, it's been me and my Pops ever since. Trey and Troy are Paris' brothers, and we became good friends when Paris and I first got together. And Mario is my first cousin, so he's always been around. Life's been rough for me, but I'm managing."

"Here goes your drinks. Now what can I get you two to eat?" the waitress interrupted again.

"Yes, can I have the Roasted Chicken Breast, Lobster Mac and Cheese, and the creamed spinach?" I asked.

"And can I have the pan-seared Salmon, Sam's mashed potatoes, and Grilled asparagus?" True said.

"Alright, coming right up." She grabbed our menus before walking away.

"I'm sorry to hear about your mom and Paris. That's so sad, and I know it was hard raising your daughter. I would love to meet her one day, if it's ok with you."

Hearing True say that she would love to meet Kera let me know she was a keeper. "So I guessing you love kids?"

"Yes, I do. I want at least two. My grand mom always tells me to stop being so scared and find

me a husband, and make her some grandkids."
She giggled.

"I agree with her. Life is too short to be scared
and not find what's meant for you."

"Why haven't a man like you found what
you're looking for yet?"

"I mean, I've been in a couple things, and I've
tried the relationship thing out but shit just
wasn't right. She wasn't what I needed around
my daughter. And the couple of things I was in
weren't nothing but sex," I said, being honest.

"Oh, ok. I get it. Well, what makes you so
interested in me?"

"I really don't know. Something about you got
me wanting to know more about you."

"Here goes your food." The waiter walked up
and started placing our plates on the table.

After she laid our plates down, True closed her
eyes and started to say her grace. I didn't say
anything, I just followed her lead. This was
definitely what I needed around Kera. This
woman seemed to amaze me every time I saw her.
My phone going off bought me out of my
thoughts. I looked at it to make sure it wasn't
Kera. When I saw Tiara's name pop across the
screen, the shit annoyed me. I had no idea why

she had been calling me lately when she already knew what it is.

"Is, everything ok? Do you need to go take that?" True asked.

"Nah, this is my time with you, baby girl. Anything else has to wait," I said while winking at her.

True and I laughed, ate, and enjoyed each other's company.

Chapter Seven

Mario

I was enjoying my time with Erin. I know it was hard for her to trust anyone. I really did want to change that, but I knew it was going to be hard. I'm willing to do anything to gain her trust. And of course, make her love a nigga. I was already feeling her, and it had been such a little bit of time. Usually, I wasn't like this with chicks, so I didn't know what had gotten into me.

We were watching *21 Bridges.* We both had never seen it before, but so far, it was a good ass movie. These dumb ass niggas were blowing my shit in the movie. I guess because I knew how to move in the streets, and they didn't know what they were doing.

"Can I use your bathroom?" Erin asked.

"Now you know the answer to that question. It's down the hall to your right," I said, right before I paused the movie. I then got up to go get us both something to drink. When she came back, I was going to see was she hungry because I

was getting hungry myself. Plus, we had ate all of
our snacks that we had.

"I still can't believe you got this big ass house
for just you," she said, walking back into the
living room.

"I wasn't thinking about that before I got it,
but then again, I love a lot of space. Plus, I was
thinking about my future when I bought it. I
hope to have a wife and kids one day," I told her,
being honest.

"That's good that you're planning ahead of
time." She smile.

Little did she know, I already had my eye on
her.

"Are you hungry? If so, I can order
something," I asked.

"I can cook if you want me to. What do you
have here I can thaw really fast?"

"Ma, you don't have to do that. You're my
company, and I wouldn't want you to be
cooking."

"No, it's ok. I love cooking, and I don't want
you to order takeout."

"Ok. You lucky I really don't want any
takeout, either. I think I have some party wings
in there. I know they don't take long to thaw,
and everything else you would need is in there."

"Are you allergic to anything?"

"Nah, ma, I'm not allergic to anything." The minute I answered her, my phone started going off. I looked at it and saw it was Jace, so I knew it was about business.

"I need to take this, beautiful. I'll meet you in the kitchen as soon as I'm finished—What's up, man?" I answered the phone.

"Ayo, you and boss man need to get to the trap ASAP!" he said before hanging up.

I knew it was something serious, but I also knew that I didn't wanna leave Erin. I walked into the kitchen to see what she was about to cook for me. The minute I walked in, I guess she could tell by the look on my face something was wrong.

"Go 'head and handle business. I can tell it's serious. Just go handle it. By the time you come back, dinner will be ready, and I will be waiting for you." She smiled.

Yeah, Erin was definitely the one for me.

"Alright. I will be right back, and I appreciate you for being understanding," I said before I headed upstairs to throw on my all-black.

When I came back downstairs, I walked into the kitchen to tell Erin I will be right back again. Of course, she didn't hear me while she was standing in front of the stove. I walked up behind her and wrapped my arms around her waist. "I will be right back," I said, delivering a soft kiss on the side of her neck, causing her to blush.

"Ok. I'll be right here."

I locked the door and the gate when I left out. Then the minute I hopped in my car, I dialed Mar's number. I knew he was probably with True, and I hated to ruin his night, but this was urgent. I dialed his number, and he picked up on the first ring.

"Yo', bro, meet me at the trap. Some shit went down."

"On my way," he said before hanging up.

It took me twenty minutes to get there. Me and Mar pulled up at the same time. We looked at each other shaking our heads. Both of our nights had been ruined, and somebody was going to pay for this shit.

"Sorry I had to call you. Where True at?" I asked.

"I dropped her off at my house. Good thing we were done eating dinner. She didn't want to go home, though." Yeah, my boy was feeling her. He never left chicks at his house. Tiara didn't even know where he laid his head with his daughter. She may have known of one of his jump-off spots, but never where Kera lived.

"I left Erin at the house cooking," I said, shaking my head.

He looked at me with a surprised looked on his face. "Oh, sis doing wifey shit." Mar chuckled.

"Yeah, I'm 'bout ready to wife her ass up. Just like you ready for True."

"You damn right," Mar said, right before we walked in the trap.

"What's up, boss man?" Jace said.

"Don't ask me what the fuck is up. Y'all tell me what the fuck is up!" Mar yelled.

"Man, it's a mess out here."

"What the fuck happened?" I asked, looking at blood everywhere.

"We were at the bar having drinks and chilling with this nigga named Zay. Then this dude from Roc's crew came up to us talking shit. Him and Zay got into it, and them niggas must have followed us to the trap. I was in here playing 2K when I heard a knock at the door. Zay went to get it and said it was Robin. He said he was going to be out front chilling with her on the step. About a half-hour later, I heard gun shots, so I jumped up and ran out front to see what had happen and Robin was laid out on the ground while Zay was emptying his clip on the car that peeled off," Jace explained.

"Fuck! How's Robin?" I asked

"Last time I talked to Zay, she was still in surgery."

"One question: why the fuck was y'all at the bar, anyway? Who the fuck was here watching my fucking work and money?" Mar snapped.

"Since all the work was finished, and Zay had made the drop, we figured we had some down time."

"I don't pay y'all nigga to figure out a damn thing. Next time you need to hit me or Mario up to ask can y'all go the fuck out. Now I'm going to have to shut this trap down because it's going to be hot."

"Boss, we got another problem," Keys, one of our other workers, said. He had come from around back.

"What is it now?" Mar asked.

"Niles and Matt's bag came up short. I think them niggas on Southside rodded us."

"How short?" I asked.

"Ten stacks."

"How the fuck did this happened?" I asked him.

"Y'all motherfuckers really been fucking up lately like I won't blow y'all fucking heads off," Mar said, walking back down to the car.

I knew he was pissed.

"West, you call the cleaning company. Keys, give Trey a call, and y'all go handle them niggas. When y'all done, text me. And for the rest of y'all? Get y'all shit together for now on because next time y'all fuck up, it's not going to be good. Now get back to work!" I headed outside to check on my boy and make sure he was good. He was outside smoking a blunt. "You good man?" I said as he passed me the blunt.

"Man, I'm beginning to think we need to find us a new damn crew," he said, shaking his head.

"I know, but them niggas in there is loyal as fuck. Can't really trust anyone these days. Yeah, they might fuck up sometimes, but we can trust them."

He thought about what I said. "You're right about that. Damn, they need to do better. I run this shit, but I know our pops got a say so about everything," he said, shaking his head.

Before I said something, Trey pulled up. "What the hell happened that fast? I was just here a couple of hours ago."

"Rock and his crew again," Mar said.

"Them niggas really want us to show them our true colors. They really been tripping lately," Trey said.

"We going to handle them soon, though. We gotta come up with a plan," Mar said.

"Well, y'all let me know when and where the meeting is. I gotta get back home. Erin is staying." I smirked.

"Oh, fuck, I forgot all about that. I was so fucking mad. I'm going to get out of here too," Mar said.

"I know what y'all niggas are up to. Y'all ain't slick. True at your house, and Erin is at yours," he said, putting everything together. This nigga was smart as shit when he wanted to be.

"Man, you swear you know shit," I said, making us all laugh.

Me and Mar dapped him up and hopped in or cars and headed back to our girls.

Chapter Eight
True

I woke up in a happy mood. I ended up spending the weekend with Khamari, and I enjoyed every bit of it. He didn't even want me to go to work today, but I told him I had a business to run. He told me he would find some people to work for me so I could work less hours, enjoy the fruits of my labor, and not be at the store all the time. I got up and got my day started. I knew it probably wasn't going to be a long day. I had to do a few center pieces for some of the parties that I had scheduled next month, so I wanted to get some done and over with. Usually when me and Erin were preparing for parties, some people came and asked for our services for other things. And we'd be happy to help. These next two months was going to be busy, so I knew for a fact we were going to need to hire help. But I know me, and Erin couldn't do it alone.

Taking me from my thoughts, my phone started going off.

"What's up, beautiful? Did you get to work yet?"

"Hey, love. No, not yet. I'm getting ready now."

"Your ass sounds like you don't even want to go in." He chuckled.

"I don't, but I have to go. We are booked for the next two months, and I need to get all things I need together for all of the upcoming parties. I already know I'm not going to get all of them finished today like I want."

"Damn, don't worry. It's all going to pay off. How about me and Kera come there and help y'all out for the day? I don't have anything to do, and she don't go back to school until tomorrow."

"I would love that, but only if you want. I don't want Kera to be bored here," I said.

"No, she won't be bored. She loves fixing things. She's not a normal eight-year-old." He chuckled.

"Ok. Well, I will see y'all later."

He said ok before hanging up.

I was a little nervous to meet his daughter. I thought it was a little too soon for me to meet her, but if he didn't see anything wrong with it, then why should I? The only problem was, I hoped she likes me. From what he told me, she didn't like his ex. His ex was mean to her and never wanted her around. All the old stories about his ex, I could tell she wasn't worth shit.

It didn't take me long to get myself together. Good thing I took a shower earlier because I was running late. I threw on something comfortable since I knew I had a work to do. As soon as I walk out of the house, my phone started to ring. When I saw it was Erin, I answered it.

"Hey, sissy!"

"Hey, sissy! I'm at the store already with your coffee and a muffin waiting for you."

"Aww, Erin, you are really a lifesaver."

"Girl, you know I'm ready and prepared to get ready for parties."

"Alright. I'm on my way there."

She said ok before I hung up the phone and hopped in my car. Good thing I wasn't far from the place; I was at least, like, ten, fifteen minutes away. When I got there, it was already somebody in the store, and I thought it was a customer until I saw that it was Mario and Trey.

"What's up, True?" Mario and Trey said at the same time, giving me a small hug.

"Hey. What are y'all doing here?"

"I just came here to bring your girl some lunch. It looks nice as hell in here. True, when you going to decorate my house? I will pay anything," he said.

"Whenever you want me to, but you don't have to pay me. You basically have to pay for the things that have to be put in the house. Does she know that y'all are here?" I asked them.

"Yeah. She said was working on something and she will be up."

"Trey, you are too damn quiet. Have you fixed things with you and your girl?"

"My fault, ma. I was all in my phone and shit. But, yeah, I made shit right with her, and I'm never doing anything to hurt her and my seed again. Thanks for the advice, even though that shit wasn't easy." He hissed, making me laugh.

"Oh, I never told you it would be easy. You fucked up her trust. I might have not been in an actual relationship before, but I know some things from Erin."

"She said if I fuck up again, she's leaving my ass for good. Shit, I don't blame her. I don't deserve her."

"Well, if you fuck up again, I'm not helping your ass, so don't come for help from me. And you know damn well Erin's ass ain't helping, either. She already gave you her ass to kiss when she heard what you did." I giggled.

Erin finally came to the front. She walked up to Mario giving him a kiss, shocking the hell out of all of us.

"Hey, Trey. I've been meaning to apologize to you for a while now. I just haven't seen you since the club."

"It's good. I didn't mean to make you upset."

"It's ok. It wasn't your fault."

"So, are we cool?" Trey asked.

"Yeah, we cool." She smiled.

"Alright, bro. I'mma be waiting outside for you," Trey said, talking to Mario.

I watched them as they loved on each other. They were too cute together. Seeing my friend happy had my heart smiling. I hadn't seen her smile like this in such a long time. I cleared my throat to get their attention. They looked at me with smirks on their face.

"So I am guessing y'all giving this a chance?" I asked.

"Yeah. I just wish your friend opens her heart for a real nigga. Then we can start talking about making this shit official," Mario said, being honest.

"What did you bring me for lunch?" Erin asked him, changing the subject.

"Some spaghetti I made last night, but I gotta handle some business, so make sure you text me when you get off," he said, giving her a hug and kiss on the cheek before leaving out.

"Sounds like you need to make up your mind. Do you want to give this love shit a chance, or do you wanna play with a nigga's feelings? If not, leave Mario alone because I can already see that man likes you a whole lot."

"I made up my mind already. But I know he can tell that I'm still scared. Yet I'm tired of being scared. I want to be happy."

"I understand, but you also can take your time with him. I know if you speak up, he would understand where you're coming from. You just have to talk to him."

"Ok. I will talk to him later."

"Ok. Now let's get to work. We got a lot of shit to do. We also got little helpers today," I said.

She was about to say something until she saw Mar come in store with a beautiful little girl.

"Hey, baby girl," he said, giving me a hug.

"Hey. Who is this beautiful girl?"

"I'm Kera. Thank you, you're beautiful too."

"Aww…thank you. I'm True."

"Are you my dad's girlfriend? If not, can you be his girlfriend? Lord knows he needs one," Kera said, making all of us laugh.

"Damn, Princess! How you going to do your dad like that? You supposed to be on my side. What's up, E! How you, sis?" he asked.

"Hey, Mar. Hey, Miss Kera. I'm Erin, True's best friend."

"So, you must be my uncle Mario girlfriend?" she said to Erin.

"I'm sorry, y'all. She's smart as hell for her age."

"I like her. Come on, Kera. We can have a girl talk in the back while we put stuff together." Erin smiled.

Kera's eyes lit up. Before going in the back, she looked at her dad for an okay to go with Erin. He nodded his head ok before they went to get started.

"She's your twin." I smiled.

"Yeah, that's my Princess, but listen. Something came up before leaving my house, and Troy and Natalya are working, so I didn't have nowhere to take Kera. Can you watch her until I get back? I just have an important meeting with my pops. It's not going to take long."

"You know I don't mind watching her. Go handle your business. I'm sure she would love to hang out with us." I smiled.

"Thank you, baby girl. I owe you one because I know I was supposed to be helping you today. I promised I got you another day this week."

"Ok, and I'mma hold you to that."

"What are you doing when you get off?"

"Nothing, why? What do you have up your sleeve?" I asked.

"Don't worry about it. Just know I will be by to pick you up from here. You can leave your car here."

"Ok," I said, leaving it at that.

I didn't know I was looking at the floor until he lifted my chin up, making me look into his eyes. He knew he made me nervous when I was around him. He then kissed my lips, and all I felt was butterflies moving around in my stomach.

"I will see you later, baby! Kera, I'll be back a little later. Be good for True and Erin!" he yelled to the back.

She said ok.

I knew this day was about to fly by. Me, Erin, and Kera got to working, and I just couldn't help to think about Mar. I couldn't wait to see what this man had up his sleeve."

Chapter Nine

Mario

Life had been straight lately. I had been spending all my time with Erin, along with making money with Mar and the crew. The only thing that bothered me daily was my pops being locked away. For years it had been us against the world since my mama never wanted me. She popped up a couple of years ago when she saw I was making money. But I didn't know what the hell she was showing up for now. I'm twenty-seven years old. What the fuck I looked like needing a mama now?

I cursed her ass out a few good times, and now she knows not to come to my house.

My pops was recently locked up for a drug charge that had him doing ball park numbers. For some reason, I had a feeling my mama had something to do with this because her ass was with him. My pops knew it too, but he wouldn't say shit. See, my dad was a sucker for my mama. And I didn't understand why when my mom didn't give two fucks about us. All she was worried about was money and her other family that she had. My mom was dead to me, and she had been ever since I found out she had another family.

It hurt me to know that she left me and my dad and went off to raise her other kids. The shit hit me hard, which was why I still didn't understand why my pops still loved her. She had a husband and two daughters. But I knew my sisters didn't have shit to do with our mess, and I would love to meet them one day. They were about thirteen and fifteen. I was ready, but I knew since they were young, I would have to deal with my mama to meet them, and I wasn't ready for that.

Right now, I was ready to settle down and get started on my own family. My ass ain't getting no younger. I wanted to make that shit happened with Erin, but it was hard to make somebody that been hurt before love again. I mean, I'm cool with taking my time with her. All I had was time, but the shit was kind of killing me because I'm really feeling her. I hadn't been this into anyone in a while. Like I told her before, she couldn't stay afraid to open up to me because of a fuck boy. Hell, that shit ain't my fault. I'm just trying to love her.

Me and Trey were headed over Unc's crib because he was having a meeting. My phone going off caught my attention. I knew it was a text me message from Erin.

Wifey: *Can we go somewhere and talk later?*

Me: *Cool. Do you just want to come to my place when I'm done working?*

Wifey: *Yeah, that's fine. See you later. I hope everything is alright with your business.*

Me: *Thanks, ma. I'll see you later.*

I wondered what she wanted to talk about, but I couldn't worry about that shit right now. I wanted to know what this damn meeting was about that Unc put together at the last minute. What piqued our interest was that he only wanted to see me, Mar, and Trey. Me and Trey pulled up to the house right behind Mar's car. He was inside smoking a blunt. Me and Trey spoke, then headed in the house.

"What's up, Pops?" Trey said, giving him a hug.

"What's good, Unc?" I said, giving him a head nod before we sat down.

"Alright. I called here today to tell y'all what's about to go down. We got a big ass shipment coming soon. So, if y'all got beef with anybody, y'all need to dead that shit now. We don't need any problems while moving this weight. I also got some of my workers coming to team up with your crew, son. If y'all feel as though y'all can't trust anybody, then don't put them on. I don't need no fuck ups or no grimy ass niggas on the team."

"Well, while you were gone, we got caught up in some shit with them niggas on the Northside starting shit. But trust me, we're definitely going to handle them niggas. As a matter of fact, I'm going to send them a text letting them know the meeting is tomorrow," I said, pulling my phone out and doing just that.

"Any questions, son? This your damn business. You good with this shipment that we got coming in?"

"Yeah, Pop. I have no choice but to be ok with it since you already gave the ok. I'm kinda of upset that you ain't let me know this shit beforehand. I would have loved to feel these niggas out that you got coming to work with my crew." Mar hissed.

"Son, I'm sorry, and I'll make sure next time. I'll come to you before I make any decisions, but your Uncle knows them. Nephew, have you talked to your pops lately?" he asked me, and I shook my head no.

"Well, you should give him a call."

Him saying that had me kind of worried. I hoped everything was ok.

"Alright, that's all I wanted y'all little niggas for. Oh, I almost forgot, make sure y'all keep Troy on standby. We never know when we might need his help. Son, where is my granddaughter at?" he asked Mar.

"She's with your future daughter-in-law," he said, making me and Trey look at him.

Yeah, my boy was deep, but shit I was too. These girls didn't know what they were dealing with.

"Yeah, Pops. They some sucker in love niggas right now." Trey chuckled.

"I know you ain't talking, boy." Unc chuckled.

"I'm just saying. They didn't get the pussy yet, and they all in love," Trey said, talking shit.

"See that's your problem now. You can't keep your dick in your pants. Did Aliyah find out about you and her best friend yet?" Unc chuckled while shaking his head.

"Yeah, and damn near left his ass, and guess what, Unc? She pregnant. So, he went to make shit right with her. But this his last straw. If he fucks up, she is leaving."

"Congrats, son. But let me tell you something. If you going to keep doing that girl wrong, just leave her alone and let her be happy. If you really want to be with her, I'm going to need you to do better. Now when am I going to meet these young ladies?" he asked, looking at me and Mar.

"Soon. We will let you know," Mar said.

"Well, let me know what's going on after y'all have this meeting tomorrow. Now y'all can get out of my house."

"So now your kicking us out?" Mar asked him.

"Hell yeah. Sarah is cooking for a nigga," he said, causing us all of to shake our heads at his dumb ass.

"And your ass talking about me," Trey said.

"Nah, niggas. The thing with me is I'm a single man."

"Oh, so May not your lady no more?" I asked him.

"Nah. It was just something to do; I got needs. Y'all know my heart been with Sarah for a while now, but I don't think she want my ass, though. Y'all know I would not have made May hoe ass my main chick. She got good pussy, but that shit ain't that good to make me want to wife her ass."

"Nah, Pops, you had us scared for a second. I really thought you was loving May," Mar said.

"Y'all know me better than that," he said, and we shook our heads while laughing.

"Alright, let me get out of here. I gotta go get your granddaughter," Mar said, getting up.

We all dapped each other up before leaving out. I dapped Mar and told him to hit me up later and me and Trey hopped in the car and peeled off. I was going to go home so I can get some rest before Erin came over.

****

Waking up to my phone going off, without even looking at it, I answered it.

"Hey, I'm here. I tried to call and tell you that I was on my way, but you didn't answer."

"My bad, ma. I overslept. I will buzz you in."

"I can talk to you another time. I didn't mean to wake you up."

"Nah, you good, ma. I would feel fucked up if you came all the way here for nothing and I told you to come over," I said, opening the gate for her. I threw on some sweats and went to opened the door for her.

"H-h-hey," she stuttered while practically drooling since I had on sweats with no shirt.

"Are you going to stand there and fuck me with your eyes?" I smirked.

"I'm sorry," she said, finally coming inside.

"Make yourself comfortable. Did you want anything to drink."

"Yes. Water, please."

I walked to the kitchen and grabbed two bottles of water, then headed back to the living room where she was at.

"So, tell me what you wanted to talk about."

"I was just going to tell you that I made up my mind, and I think I'm ready to make things official. I'm still a little scared, but I'mma need you to just be patient with me. I still have issues, but I know deep down inside that I wanna be with you. I just have one request, Mario. If you not ready for just me and only me, please leave me alone now. Because I'm not trying to be hurt again."

"Ma, I've been waiting to hear you say this ever since we met. I've been feeling you since day one, and when I told you I wasn't going to hurt you, I meant what I said, shorty. If hurting you were in my plans, I would have never tried to make you mine." I knew she was sitting there battling with her thoughts, so I pulled her to my lap. "Ma, you have nothing to worry about. As long as we're together, I will always do right by you. I mean, everything I say. Erin, I got you, baby," I said, making her look me in my eyes so she could know everything that I was saying was true.

She nodded her head with a single tear falling from her eye. I kissed it off, then I kissed her lips. I was getting excited. I had to calm my ass down. I wanted her bad as fuck, but I needed to see where her head was at first.

"I'm going to use the bathroom," she said, getting up rushing to the bathroom. I hoped she didn't feel embarrassed.

I decided to turn on the TV while I was waiting for her to come back. I didn't know what was taking her so long to come out. As I was looking through the movies, I found *Poetic Justice.* This was my shit. I was so into the movie I didn't hear her come out of the bathroom until she stood in front of the TV ass naked. *Damn!* I thought to myself. Erin was so beautiful. Shit, even better with no clothes on.

I got up to grab her hand, then I pulled her in for a kiss. After we kissed, we headed to my bedroom. Once we made it to my room. I laid her down on the bed, then started kissing on her neck. I stopped to look down at her beautiful face. "Are you sure you want to do this?" I asked before going any further, hoping like hell she said yes. If not, I would have to deal with blue balls.

"Yes, I'm sure," she said.

I began to kiss every inch of her body. Hearing her moan was like music to my ears. I worked my way down to her neatly waxed pussy, then started goin' in on her pussy with my tongue like it was my last meal. I made love to her with my mouth for a little while.

"Baby, I'm cumming! I can't take it no more!" she managed to moan out."

I smirked, going deeper in and out of her pussy with my tongue, making her squirt everywhere. I slurped up all of her juices while watching her body shake. "Damn, baby, you taste good as fuck!" I made sure to compliment her on that sweet pussy.

She wasted no time kissing me back. I told her to sit back and relax. She did as she was told. I snatched my sweats off, and her eyes grew big. I smirked because I knew my ass was working with a monster.

"Don't worry, baby. I'll take my time and go slow," I said, kissing her lips, never taking my eyes off of her.

She nodded her head. When I put the tip inside, this shit felt like heaven. I pulled out, trying not too nut fast. I went back in. This time, I went slowly, and made my way deep inside her pussy. The way her pussy was gripping my dick had me about to cry out her name like a bitch ass nigga. I started going a little faster, looking at her in her eyes. She had a lone tear coming down her face.

"You look so beautiful," I whispered in her ear while kissing her tears away, still going in and out of her pussy with deep slow strokes.

"Babe, I'm cumming!" she cried out.

I felt her juices on my dick as her pussy became wetter. "Fuck, baby, me too." I groaned out loud, falling over to the side of the bed out of breath and sweating hard as hell. I looked down at Erin laying on my chest giggling. "What are you over there giggling about?" I asked her.

"At you because you don't even have to breathe like that," she said, still laughing.

"Shit, it's your fault. That down there is something serious. You trying to kill a nigga," I said, being honest with her.

"So that means no round two?" She smirked, getting on top of me kissing on my neck.

"Shit, we can definitely do that," I said kissing her.

We were at it all night until we both grew tired.

Chapter Ten
True

After working the whole month of October, me and Erin were tired as shit. We started hiring people to work in the store to help us with these parties. We even found somebody to help Erin with the treats. It definitely helped out a lot. Me and Khamari had been kicking it strong. Between me working and him working, we really hadn't had time with each other in a while. Shit, to tell y'all the truth, my ass was nervous to be around him since I knew he was ready to take things to the next level. I thought about losing my virginity to him, but every time it was about to happen, I would stop it from getting any further. I was nervous and scared, but I knew for sure that I was ready.

"Sissy, can I asked you a question?" We were at my place, and I had just finished cooking some fried chicken and making some seafood pasta salad. Something easy and fast. I walked in the living room with two plates in my hand, and I gave her one before sitting down.

"You sure can, love. What's wrong?"

"I'm ready for sex, but I'm nervous and scared," I admitted.

My comment made her put her food down. She looked at me with a smirk on her face. Erin had been waiting to hear this for a long time. "Shit, I bet your ass is with a fine ass nigga like Khamari." She giggled.

I couldn't help but laugh at her crazy ass. When she told me about her night with Mario, from the sound of it, she enjoyed every bit of it. With her nasty ass. "I'm serious, Erin," I whined.

"Ok, ok, girl. If you think about it, it's not that bad. Now your first time is always hard. I'm not going to lie and tell you that it doesn't hurt because that shit is going to hurt like hell, and it also depends on his size."

"Girl, he's got a monster," I said, scared as fuck.

"Damn, that shit must run in the family. Don't be scared. Nine times out of ten, he's going to take his time with you. Hold up, did you see his dick already?" I asked her.

"No, I felt that shit," I said, making her laugh. "Girl, that shit ain't funny. I'm over here scared as fuck, but my vagina telling me to go for it."

"It always be like that," she said, shaking her head.

"Sometimes I feel bad because I know he be having blue balls and shit fucking around with me. I don't know how to tell him that I'm ready."

"Do he know you're a virgin?"

"I mean, I mentioned to him that I never had a boyfriend before."

"Girl, just because you never had a boyfriend don't mean you never had sex. So when he finds out you're still a virgin, he is definitely going to take his time with you. All I can say is just be honest with him. You want the dick, but you scared because you a virgin. Just like that."

"Oh, Lord. You know my scary ass ain't coming straight out like that."

"I have an idea. How about you go get you a sexy ass lingerie piece to go with your heels. I would do your makeup, but you don't need it. Now all you got to do is wet your hair and wear it wild and curly. Cook a nice dinner for him here. Doing all of this for him, he is going to know you want to take it there with him."

"Sounds good, but I'm nervous as fuck. What if he turns me down and don't want to have sex?"

"Then something the fuck is wrong with him," she said, being honest.

"Ok. I'm going to listen to your advice and go for it. I will most likely do it this weekend because this is when Kera is going to spend time with his dad for the weekend."

We talked some more about how I was going to do this night for Khamari. We also talked about our parties we had next week and the week after. I'm glad we had everything set and ready to go. We actually had two events tomorrow: one in the morning, and one in the evening to set up for. One was a small baby shower, and the other one was somebody's mom 60th birthday party. I loved being an event planner, but sometimes it be stressful, and customers could be rude as fuck. I always tried to keep it professional, but Erin on the other hand? She could be a loose cannon.

"I gotta go see G-Mom tomorrow after we set up for the first party. She been calling me talking about, 'What, you don't love me no more?'" I said, rolling my eyes.

"I hate when she does that," Erin said.

"Are you staying the night?"

"Yeah, I should since I got clothes here already."

"Well, my ass about to take a shower and lay it down."

"Alright. Goodnight, sis. Don't worry, I will do the dishes," she said before I went upstairs.

I went in my room and put my stuff down, then headed to my bathroom to take a nice shower. I was in the shower for a minute. The hot water just felt so good on my tired body.

After thirty minutes in, I finally decided to get out. I dried off and put lotion on my body. Then I put on an oversized t-shit before laying in my bed. I decided to send Mar a text telling him I miss him and I couldn't wait to see him before dozing off.

****

Today just wasn't my day, and I just didn't know what was going on. I went to bed early, so I got enough rest. Everything just felt so off about today. I already had a couple of evil ass customers today, on top of a lady calling saying that her cake wasn't what she wanted. I guess it was going to be a full moon or something. Another thing that got me ticked off was when Mar didn't respond to my text message last night.

"What's the matter, bestie?" Erin asked.

"I don't know. I just feel like today isn't my day."

"Go ahead and take a lunch break, and I'll handle everything until you get back."

I was going to take Erin up on her offer, so I headed to the back to get my purse and my shades. The minute I got back up front, I heard someone ask for me.

"Hello, I'm True. How can I help you?" I asked.

"Hey, I'm Tiara, and I was just stopping by to let you know to stay the fuck away from Khamari. We were going through something, but we good now, so it ain't no need for you to keep calling him. And if you think I'm lying, don't. I know you were texting him last night because I saw it. Yeah, I saw you saying you miss my nigga. I came over here woman to woman to let you know the real deal. Now you have a nice day," she had the nerve to say right as she walked out of the door before I could even reply.

Tears started to form in my eyes, but Erin gave me that *I better not* look, and I headed back to the back.

"I know you don't believe that now, True. You need to talk to Mar before you just assume shit."

"If she not telling the truth, how the fuck did she know what I texted him last night? How the fuck did she know where I worked at? He has been acting a little distant lately. Shit, I haven't been giving up the cookie. He does have needs, Erin," I snapped, not wanting to hear what she had to say.

Erin knew I wasn't beat for listening to her, so she headed back up front, and I just sat in the back in my thoughts. I knew a man like Khamari loving me was fake as fuck.

Chapter Ten

Khamari

"Y'all ready to take care of these motherfuckers!" I yelled to my crew.

"I need no fuck ups, or I'm fucking y'all up myself without thinking twice," Trey said with a serious face.

"Y'all better think smart before going out here. This is not a damn video game; this is real shit," Mario said.

We all grabbed our guns, then hopped in our trucks to head to Roc's trap. We'd had our eyes on them for about a month after he had his boys spying on us. We set him up and had one of our own join their crew. After he found out what we needed, it was a piece of cake to get our plan in order. Roc was just a dumb ass nigga that wanted to be like us, but that nigga could never be like us making dumb moves like this. How you gon' just let some nigga on your team that supposedly just moved into town?

When we got there, we pulled up at the corner, then hopped out making sure everything was in place before walking over to where the trap was. I told Tim and Jace to go handle them niggas that was directly in the front. Me, Mario, Trey, and Keys then went right in the front door since them dudes were already laid out. The rest of our crew went to the back. Hearing the gun shots coming from the back of the house, I was sure my men had handled they business. When we walked inside, we started shooting off the rip. After the smoke cleared, all of the men that were downstairs were handled. I was happy about it, but I wanted Roc's ass.

The minute we headed towards the stairs, gunshots started coming our way. Mario was in the front, so he nodded his head to let us know when to come. We both jumped from behind the wall making sure to shoot both niggas in the head. We finally made it to the back room where these niggas tried to run out with a big ass duffel bag, but little did they know, they wasn't going no fucking where. When we walked in, guns were pointed at us, but they were outnumbered, and it was no way they were getting out alive.

"Well, well. If it ain't my arch enemy. To think all I wanted was a spot on your team, but you wouldn't give it to me. So, now here we are beefing for no damn reason."

"Nigga, what makes you think you ever deserved a spot on my team? Not when you don't even move right in these fucking streets. Nobody trusts your grimy ass. Hell, I'm not even the only person that wasn't fucking with you," I spat.

"Man, you don't know shit about me. So, stop acting like you do."

"You hear this dumb ass nigga, Mario?" I asked, causing the whole crew to laugh.

"Yeah, I hear him talking about we don't know him. Shit, we know his ass dumb as fuck for putting one of our men on his team."

We all laughed once more.

"I told my boy, Justin, to tell me y'all every move. It was risky, but hell, y'all made the shit easy for us by not catching on to shit that was happening around y'all. It was foul as fuck what y'all did with my boy's girl. Good thing her and their baby are good. Oh, and your boy Zay is dead." I smirked.

"I told your ass it was something off about this nigga, but you ain't want to listen," Mane said to Roc.

"Sounds like you should've listened to your right-hand man." I smirked.

"Nigga, fuck you," he said, raising his gun, causing me to pull the trigger on mine.

I let off two shots and got him in his head and in the stomach. "Any last words before you join your boy?" Before he could say anything, the crew let off rounds into him and made that nigga look like a piece of swiss cheese. "Damn, y'all wasn't playing." I chuckled while shaking my head.

Justin and Mario grabbed the duffle bags, and we headed out of the door. Before leaving, Keys lit the place on fire and then headed back to our trap. Everybody went inside while me and Mario stayed outside and smoked a blunt.

"I'm glad this shit is finally over," I said.

"Yeah, but you this ain't gon' be the last time some lame ass niggas test us," Mario said.

"Yeah, I know, but we always ready for whatever."

"What you about to get into?" Mario asked me.

"Nothing much. About to go to the condo and hop in the shower, then call True's ass. If she don't answer, I'mma have to pay her ass a visit tomorrow. I heard from Erin that Tiara popped up at her spot."

"Wow. That crazy bitch doesn't know how to stay in her place. Sounds like your ass is in trouble." Mario looked at me.

"I don't know why she just didn't call me and ask me what the deal was. I know Tiara was wrong for what she did, but True shouldn't be listening to people. Kera been asking for her and shit. Enough is enough, though. She gon' tell me what the hell went down."

"Your right about that, but I'm about to head home, hop in the shower, and take my ass to bed."

"No Erin tonight?" I asked him.

"Nah. I talked to her before we came here. Her ass probably sleep now, and she's staying at True's house because they got a party tomorrow morning."

"Damn, nigga, you know more than me."

"Damn, when was the last time you heard from her?"

"Probably about a week now. She doesn't answer my calls or text messages."

"Yeah, nigga, you in trouble."

"Who in trouble?" Trey walked up looking at Mario.

"Nigga, why the fuck are you looking at me? Me and my girl is good," he said, making me laugh.

Trey was always fucking with Mario. The shit was funny.

"What the hell did you do, Mar?"

"Man, I don't know what happened, but whatever it was, Tiara got her not fucking with me."

"Damn, you better make shit right with her. Life too short for that. I learned a lot of shit from fucking up the last time."

"Nigga, I ain't fuck up, though. Tiara and I been over, so whatever she told True is a lie."

"I bet your stupid ass did. You fucked up so many times. Now you want to do right by her because her ass was about to leave you," Mario said, telling the truth.

"Nigga, I know already, but, Mar, don't be like me and keep fucking up. Aliyah deserve better than me, but now I can say I'm in love with her, and I can't live without her and my seed. So, my fucking up days are over."

"That's what I'm talking about. Speaking big things into existence. I see you, nut ass," Mario said.

"Let me get out of here. I will hit y'all up later." I dapped them up, before hopping in my car and heading home.

Chapter Eleven
True

Khamari had been banging on my door for ever, and I was peeking out the window at him. I was pissed and frustrated knowing that I was about to give my all to him and he was still dealing with his ex. Erin had been upset with me because I didn't go to him to talk about it. I didn't see the point, though. Just to think I was about to give my all to this nigga is what hurt me the most. Like, when was I going to find love? When was someone going to truly want a woman of my size? I wasn't that much different than other women. I just had a little more to love, that was it. I was beautiful with my own.

"Come on, True, baby, open the door. I'm not leaving 'til you do. If I have to sit out here all night, then I will."

The way he was tearing my door up, I kind of believed him. So, before my neighbors started to complain, I went ahead to open the door. We would just talk sitting out on the step.

"Khamari, why are you here?" I asked in an annoyed tone.

"Come on, True, don't play with me, ma. You know why I'm here, and it's crazy I had to come here to explain myself after you ignored me for a week. All you had to do was call me and ask me what was going on between Tiara and me. If we gon' be together, ma, you gotta talk to me instead of assuming shit."

Before I got to say anything, I heard banging coming from his car. I looked at him with a strange face, and he didn't say a word. He made his way over to his car and popped the trunk. What I saw caused me to look at Khamari in a different light. This nigga was crazy, and I needed to think about if this is what I really wanted to do. He picked Tiara up out of his trunk and flung her slim frame over his shoulders, then carried her up to me. When he made it over to me, he took the blind fold from over her eyes, and she looked at me with a surprise look on her face.

"Khamari, what the hell?" I said, looking at him with wide eyes.

"I didn't think you were going to believe me, so I bought the lying bitch over here to tell you the truth. True, I told you I wanted you, and I meant what I said. So, whatever it takes to make you mine is what it is."

After he said what he said, it caused the butterflies in my stomach to start back up. I couldn't believe he kidnapped the girl and put her in the trunk of a car. I read that shit before in a book called *Beautiful: The Epitome of a BBW*. This right here reassured me that our feelings were just like a fairytale. Just like all the characters in that book. I was so into my thoughts I didn't even know he had taken the scarf from off of Tiara's mouth.

"You really took it this far, Khamari? You really came into my home and kidnapped me so I can prove to this fat bitch that we don't deal with each other anymore? Oh, you really done with me, and *this* what you left me for?" Tiara giggled.

"Tiara, shut the fuck up! You lucky my pops taught me not to smack a bitch. She is more woman then you'll ever be. So, shut the fuck up and tell her what it is. Or, I'll get some of the chicks that are on my payroll to handle ya ass."

"Alright, damn! Khamari and I been over, and I'm glad, anyway. All he is looking for is somebody to be the mama to that little rug rat he got," Tiara snapped with an attitude. I knew she was lying because if she still didn't want him, she wouldn't have come to my job lying.

"Khamari, please get this hoe from in front of my house before I beat her ass for talking about Kera," I snapped with an attitude.

The smile he gave me showed me that he was pleased with what I had just said. Before he said anything, a Black 2019 Charger with tented windows pulled up. A fine ass light skin dude with a long, full-beard and two French braids in his hair walked over to us.

"What's up, boss?"

"What's good with you Jace? I need you to take Tiara back to her crib for me, and before you get there, take her by the trap where Troya and 'dem be. I want them to see her face in case she tries some bullshit with my girl. I might need them to kick her ass."

Tiara didn't do shit but suck her teeth and roll her eyes, then got her ass in the car. The minute they pulled off, Khamari walked up the steps and stood right in my face. The smell of his Savage by Dior danced in my nose while his eyes pierced into mine. The way he was looking at me was doing something to me.

"Khamari! Why are you in my space?" I said, knowing damn well I was enjoying him in my face.

He didn't say anything, though. He just kissed my lips making sure to use his tongue to pry my lips apart. I was nervous, but I made sure to kiss him back. After we kissed for what seemed like forever, I grabbed his hand and led the way into my house. I was nervous and scared, but I wanted Khamari more than I'd ever wanted anyone in my entire twenty years of living. The way he treated me and talked to me had me wanting him since day one. Not to mention the way he came over here with Tiara making her tell me the truth. I definitely was wanting him even more.

Once we made it all the way into my house, I pulled Khamari all the way to my room. When we got inside, we stood in front of my bed with him standing in front of me. I was a nervous wreck, and my palms were all sweaty, but I pulled him in here for a reason. I guess he noticed the look in my eyes because he kissed me on my forehead before he spoke.

"You don't have to do this if you don't want to, beautiful."

"But I want too," I said just above a whisper while pulling my t-shirt over my head. Then I dropped my shorts that I was wearing to the floor. I was now standing in front of Khamari in my panties and bra covering myself the best way I could.

That's until he walked over to me and pulled my arms from around my body so he can look at me in a lustful manner. "Why you covering your body, ma? You look so damn good. It ain't nothing wrong with a little more to love," he said while pulling my almost naked body close to his.

He then started to kiss me hungrily while coming out of his clothes. Once he was completely naked, the sight of his toned body had me feeling shit from my pussy I never felt before. I looked down at his dick and almost fainted. Thinking about that big ass thing going inside of me had me terrified.

"I'm not gon' hurt you, lil' mama. It's definitely going to hurt from the beginning, but I'mma be gentle with you."

"Please do because this is my first time, Mar," I said just above a whisper.

"I already knew that, and I got you, baby," he said while beginning to kiss me hungrily. At the same time, he eased me down on the bed while climbing on top of me.

I still wasn't completely naked, so when Mar pulled my bra off letting my D-cup breasts out, I gasped the minute he took one in his mouth. He began to lick, suck, and squeeze, turning me all the way on.

"True!"

"Yes." I breathed out, licking my lips watching him have his way with my boobs.

"You know after this you're mine and ain't no turning back. Whenever you feeling some type away, make sure you talk to me instead of running."

Not saying anything, I just gave him a head nod letting him know I got it so he could hurry up our session.

The feeling of Khamari poking at my center caused me to instantly claw into his back. The shit was hurting, but he was definitely being gentle to me. The shit hurt so bad casing my body to tense up. Khamari kissed me softly letting me know it will feel ok in a little bit, but first it was going to hurt. He gave me study and short strokes until he made it all the way into my opening. Once he broke all the way in, I didn't even know I was crying until he kissed my tears away.

"Shhhh… baby, don't cry. Do you want me to stop?" Khamari asked while now kissing my tears away. The pain was starting to subside, and his deep strokes were making me wonder why the fuck I had waited so long.

"Oh My God! Khamari…" I moaned out in pleasure.

"See, baby, I told you I wasn't going to hurt you. This pussy feels good, ma. I don't know how long I can last," he managed to get out in between strokes.

This crazy feeling was taking over my body, and I wasn't sure what it was, but I was for sure that I didn't want this shit to end. A few minutes later, after I decided to move the same way Khamari was moving, meeting him stroke from stroke, he was pumping in and out of me while he continued to stare in my eyes. The faster he moved, for some reason, had me feeling like this was coming to an end. I cried out and gripped the sheets tightly while he moved in and out of me in a fast motion. After a couple more strokes, Khamari's body began to jerk, and I knew right then and there he was cummin'.

The minute he finished, he kissed my forehead and laid on the side of me. My first time wasn't a fairytale, but it was with the person I wanted it to be with. While we were in the mix, the pain subsided, but now that we were done and just lying on the bed, I wasn't even going to lie. My pussy was sore as fuck.

"Will sex get better than this? Not saying that it was bad, but I know you're used to women more experienced than me. Not to mention this damn pain."

"It won't always be pain, and me being with more experienced women doesn't mean anything, baby. I want you, and I'm willing to teach you all the tricks in the bedroom. So, don't worry about that. We gon' be good. I'm gon' definitely show you how to be my little freak," he said while kissing me once more.

Khamari and I laid in each other's arms and discussed everything under the sun until we drifted off to sleep.

Chapter Twelve
True

Life was great, my business was doing great, and I ended up hiring two more people to help out. Mar and I were finally together after fixing the situation with that bitch Tiara. I thought I was never going to see him again, but he had other plans. So, I was low-key happy that he came over and told me how he really felt. Today was Kera's birthday, and I was excited. I knew Kera would be surprised and happy.

Me and Kera had the best relationship. She was like my lil' best friend. We did everything together. I was shocked that we hit it off the way we did. Now I was loving her just as much as I loved her daddy in such little time.

I felt strong arms wrap around my waist.

"Damn, baby, y'all did this shit?" Mar said while wrapping his arms around my waist.

"Yeah, sis, this is nice as fuck. Kera is going to love it," Mario said while giving a complement.

"I mean, y'all act like I'm not standing here. I mean, I did help her put everything together," Erin sassed, making us laugh at her simple ass.

"I'm sorry, beautiful. You did help do a great job," Mario said, pulling her in for a kiss.

I was really happy for my friend. Mario was just what she needed in a man. I was happy that Mario got my friend a place to start her own Bakery too. I knew that meant a lot to her. Erin's parents loved Mario. She was scared that they wouldn't like him because of who he was, but, shit, they proved her wrong. I couldn't wait until my G-Mom met Mar. She really couldn't wait to meet the man that was finally putting a smile on her granddaughter's face. All she said was, 'When I'm going to meet this boy that you fell in love with?'" G- mom was a piece of work sometimes.

I had finally met Mar's dad. The boys invited me and Erin over for dinner one night at his dad's house. We sat down, and we got to know each other, and from there, he grew to love us like his own.

"We're going to go get dressed while y'all smoking," I said to them.

"Don't be taking all day neither." Mar frowned.

"That goes for you too, Erin," Mario said.

We walked away not paying their asses any mind. We had already taken our showers earlier, so all we had to do was freshen up a little, then put our clothes on. We both put on a two-piece sweater outfit that we got off Fashion Nova. I had a the black one on and Erin had the green one. I unwrapped my hair that I had straightened the night before. Erin wore her hair in a long ponytail.

"Girl, you ready? I don't want to hear their mouths," Erin said.

Before I could say anything, my phone started ringing. I looked at it and it was G-Mom calling. "Hey G-Mom. Are you out front?" I answered.

"Yes, baby. I'm hope I'm at the right spot. All these big ass houses and shit," she said.

"Ok, I'm coming down now," I told her before hanging up. We went downstairs to let her in. I opened the door for her, then me and Erin gave her hugs.

"Ok, I'm here. Where are these men that y'all been telling me about?" she said.

"Damn, G-Mom. You don't miss a beat," I said, messing with her.

"No. I see y'all asses damn near every day. Now it's time to meet my soon-to-be grandson-in-laws."

"Damn, G-Mom, that's cold you not messing with us," Erin said, laughing.

"Mar, Mario, I have somebody that wants to meet you!" I yelled. I knew they were in the mancave.

They came upstairs and walked to the living room where we were at.

"Damn, y'all got lucky with these fine ass men," she said, making them laugh.

"G-Mom, this is Khamari and Mario."

"Do y'all mind if we have a talk fellas? Y'all may think these is y'all women, but they not until I get to know you two. I need to know where y'all heads are at and if y'all are good matches for my babies. Come on, let's go!" G-mom said while pulling them outside.

An hour later

Everybody was having a great time. Me, Erin, Natalya, Ms. Sarah, and G-Mom were sitting in the living room having a good conversation waiting for Kera to come. Trey and Aliyah were bringing her. They were on their way.

"Babe, come on. Turn the lights out. They're pulling up now," Mar said to me.

I didn't know why my ass was so damn nervous. I guess I was hoping she loved everything. We heard them unlocked the door, then Kera turned the lights.

"Surprise!!!!!!!" we all yelled in union.

The smile on her face was priceless. I knew right then and there that we had did an amazing job.

"Happy Birthday, Princess!" Mar smiled, walking up and pulling her in for a hug.

"Thanks, Daddy, but you didn't have to do all of this," she said, giving him a hug.

"I know, baby, but you know I'll do anything for you. Now go say thank you to True and Erin. They hooked this up for you."

Her eyes lit up when she saw me and Erin. She ran over to us and gave us a big hug before she went to say hi to everybody else.

We ate having a good time. Seeing her having so much fun made me the happiest person ever. I walked around to make sure everything and everyone was ok. I saw Aliyah and Erin over in the corner talking.

"Hey, love! How are you? I love your little belly, Aliyah," I said.

"Girl, I will be glad when this shit is over. I love my son and everything, but I want my body back. Shit, I can't even take the dick like I want to." She frowned, making us laugh.

"Is it that bad?" Erin asked, amused.

"Girl, to me, yeah, but everybody is different. When you guys have kids, y'all will understand."

"I was pregnant before, but I didn't get a chance to get big. The morning sickness was the worst, though," Erin said.

"What happened, if you don't mind me asking?" Aliyah asked.

"I lost the baby due to stress and depression," she said.

"I was the same way, but I'm good this time around," Natalya said, making us look at her.

"Yes, I'm pregnant, but I didn't tell Troy yet. So, Aliyah, keep it to yourself," she said, making us giggle.

"How the hell I'm going to hide some shit like that?" Aliyah frowned, making us laugh.

"Y'all can have all the kids y'all want. My ass don't mind babysitting," I said.

"You don't want kids?" they said at the same time.

"Yes, but, shit, I just started getting the dick. I'm still young, and I got a lot of time to think about kids," I said, and they agreed.

"Just don't wait until Kera is eighteen years old to have a damn baby," Natalya said, causing me to nod my head.

I was about to say something else but Kera walked in the kitchen.

"True, Daddy told me to come get you. He has a surprise for you." Kera smiled.

I smiled and held her hand as I let her lead the way. The girls followed us in the living room. I didn't know what the hell was going on.

"Mar, baby, what is going on?" I asked, standing in front of him not knowing what was going on.

"What I knew I was going to do since the first day I met you," he said getting on his knee.

Nah, this man was not about to propose to me.

"I been looking for someone like you for a long time. I know we just met and still getting to know each other, but I'm ready for everything that's coming our way. We don't have to get married tomorrow, but I want you to know that's the next step for us. You love my daughter like she's your own. You're all she talks about when you're not around. Our families love each other. Baby, I see my future with you and only you. Will you marry me, beautiful?" he said, opening the box showing a 14k princess-cut diamond ring.

With tears coming down my face, I nodded my head yes. Everyone cheered us on. He put the ring on my finger, and I pulled him off the floor giving him a huge kiss. Kera ran to us hugging us both. I ended up having a fucked-up life in the beginning, just because of my weight, to me finding a man that loved me and my curves. I swear I loved it here.

The End!

Disclaimer:

Genesys & Adonis story isn't your average BBW story. Yes, it's a love story, but it involves a newly turned vampire. Yesss, your sexy and lovely Genesys Cullman, is a vampire with a heart filled with gold and her eyes on a human, Adonis Villin. So, if you're not scared of a little neck biting, a few splatters of blood here and there, feel free to place your eyes on TN Jones first BBW paranormal love story.

Genesys & Adonis:

A BBW Love Story

TN Jones

Acknowledgment

First, thanks must go out to the Higher Being for providing me with a sound body and mind, in addition to having the natural talent of writing and blessing me with the ability to tap into such an amazing part of life.

Second, thanks most definitely go out to my Prin Pretty; you mean the world to me. Without you, I wouldn't be anything. Mommy loves you, yes, I do!

Third, to my lovely readers and supporters who have been rocking with me since day one, and to the lovely new readers for giving me a chance.

Fourth, to Tyanna Coston and Tyanna Presents. The best team to ever rock with. I love you amazing ladies to the moon and back!

Like always, I wouldn't have made it this far without anyone. I genuinely thank everyone for rocking with me. Muah! I want to thank everyone from the bottom of my heart for always keeping it real with the novelist kid from Alabama no matter what I drop. Y'all make this writing journey enjoyable and have once again trusted me to provide all of you with quality entertainment.

I hope all of you enjoy my loves!

Chapter One

Genesys Cullman

Ah, you got this. You can handle anything that comes your way, I thought as I checked my makeup for the final time.

Clearing my throat, I continued looking at my face while running my hands down the front of the black, off-shoulder, cocktail dress.

Ring. Ring. Ring.

Reaching into my small, black, clutch purse, I retrieved my device. I answered the call from one of my best friends, Gemini, with a smile on my face.

"Where are you, heifer?" she excitedly exclaimed.

"I'm in the gym's bathroom," I told her, stepped away from the clean sink.

"Well, get your ass out here. We haven't seen you since you returned from Prague, and you know it's time for us to show out," Gemini spoke in a high-pitched tone.

Giggling, I replied, "I'm on my way. Hold up, where is Venus?"

"Chile, taking a million pictures with Adonis, Hunt, and Gabe."

Tripping over my feet, I responded, "As in Adonis Villin, Hunter Wells, and Gabriel Mackrel, right? They are here? Like in this damn gym with us?"

Laughing, Gemini replied, "Yep. Yep and yep."

"Oh. Okay. Um, in that case, I'm going to pray I don't make an ass out of myself, and then I will be on my way," I nervously stated.

"I know damn well you ain't acting shy, Genesys? Baby, we are older now ... that shy shit is for the birds. Girl, bring your ass out that bathroom. I'm ready to hit the dance floor."

"All right. All right, I'm on my way." I tried to speak calmly.

After ending the call, I wanted to run for the hills. I had the biggest crush on the sexy and kind Adonis Villin, and I was sure he knew it. Many memories of our teenage school days surfaced, resulting in me growling as I became overly hot. Now wasn't the right time to be in Adonis' presence. Still, I had some things to iron out within myself. I wouldn't say that I wasn't confident within my body because I had no choice but to be, but I was a different type of person at the end of the day.

Since my ten-day vacation in Prague, a lot of things had changed. Even though I possessed the same qualities as before, I still wasn't the same; I fought myself a lot more. I was more aware of people's thoughts and perceptions of me. Still, I was afraid of what people would say or think upon placing their eyes on my full-figured and well-trained body.

Fuck these people and enjoy those that love to be around you. You don't owe these people shit, I thought as I inhaled and exhaled several times before exiting the bathroom.

As the crisp air slapped me against my face, the speakers within the gym blasted The Magic One "The Baddest". Feeling myself more than I should've, I bobbed along to the beat as I walked towards my friends, who were standing beside Adonis and his best friends.

My, oh my. Nothing has changed with those handsome males. None of them look a day over thirty, I thought as

Amena Golden squealed my name, a few inches to the right of me.

With bucked eyes, I blushed as I placed my dark-brown, medium beaded eyes on the kind, sweetheart of a biracial woman.

At the same time, Gemini yelled, "Look at my girl. Yasss! Show up and show out!"

"Oh my goodness, Genesys. You are so beautiful. I love your dress, hair, and shoes," Amena voiced as everyone placed their eyes on me.

Blushing harder than ever, I politely responded, "Thank you, Amena. You are beautiful as well. Like always, your attire is splendid."

"Thank you." She smiled before continuing, "Um, Genesys, before you leave the reunion, please let's exchange numbers. I would love to take a few pictures of you for my blog."

"Sure. Sure. I would love to participate," I responded, feeling warm and bubbly.

After Amena and I hugged, I sashayed my scary behind towards my friends. My heart raced like crazy. I tried to keep my eyes off Adonis, but they had a mind of their own.

Shit, he's looking at me, I thought as I nervously looked into each of their eyes and said, "Well, hello everyone. How have y'all been?"

Everyone spoke at once, minus Adonis. He was the last to reply as he sexily strolled towards me. Instantly, I felt like running away. As always, being too close to him caused me to perspire more than I wanted to. My words would clam up before he told me to calm down. I didn't want to seem like the clumsy girl I was in high school. I refused to be seen in that light, especially by Adonis.

"I see you are still nervous when I'm in your presence, Gen," he spoke, flashing the bottom gold grill in his mouth.

Staring into his eyes, I couldn't think of a thing to say. Therefore, I didn't. I simply smiled and moved away. The second I did, I felt his eyes roaming over my mind before my annoying ability to read his mind kicked in.

Shit, she smells good as fuck. My Gen still lookin' good than a motherfucka. I want her. I wonder does she have a man. If she does, that nigga gotta get gone, Adonis thought.

Shocked, I turned to look at him. The expression on his face didn't match his thoughts.

"What's wrong, Gen?" he asked with a crooked smile on his handsome face before licking his thick lips.

Seeing that I was acting weird, I hurried away from him, all the while cursing myself out. If anything went wrong tonight because of my paranormal abilities, I would hide under a rock for as long as possible.

On my heels, my best friends asked in unison, "Why did you look at Adonis like that before storming away?"

Stuttering for what seemed like forever, I finally said, "No reason."

"Yes, there was a reason, and we want to know?" Venus giggled.

Feeling flustered and super-hot, I began to fan myself. I had lost my damn mind thinking I could handle the pressure of being around people. All at once, I began to hear what others were thinking. Becoming overwhelmed and thinking of the worst, I scanned the gymnasium; I needed a way out of the tenth class reunion without being spotted by Adonis. To no avail, there wasn't a way to escape without people stopping me for whatever odd reason.

"Gen," Adonis whispered in my ear.

When did he walk behind me?

"Huh?" I shouted louder than I intended to as I turned to face him.

"You good?" he asked, wrapping his arms around my waist.

I wanted to enjoy the moment of my crush's body pressed against mine. I wanted to relish in his long and muscular arms wrapped around my thick frame. I wanted to have fun, but I couldn't. My thoughts, that of others, and their beating hearts frightened me. Too much was going on around me that no one could understand; hell, I barely understood.

Rapidly, I shook my head and voiced, "No, I'm not good. It was nice to see you, Adonis. I have to go."

As I turned to walk away, Adonis grabbed my wrist and pulled me towards him, close. Before I could push away, his tongue parted my lips. Shocked out of this world, I had no idea what to do other than to move my tongue around his weed and liquor-filled, warm, and wet mouth.

Upon his head turning one way, and my head turning the other way, my thoughts and those of others—minus Adonis'—and their beating hearts, ceased. While my body became increasingly hot and pussy moist than ever, Adonis thought process had me shaking.

Finally, I'm kissing my crush with her sexy ass. Her tongue tastes better than I could've ever imagined. Damn, Gen, got a nigga bricked in this place.

Urgently, I broke the kiss and stared into his light-brown, medium-beaded eyes. Immediately, I rehashed the many times I had been around Adonis. None of those times ever indicated he had a crush on me.

Placing his mouth to my ear, Adonis whispered, "I want you, Genesys Cullman. I've always wanted to be yo' nigga. Please stop runnin' away from me. I've been lettin' you know what's up since ninth grade."

No, you didn't, or did I not receive the message because of my insecurities and the bullying?

Granted, I still had a crush on him. It would've been great to hear those words back then, but now I was a different being. I wasn't even classified as human. I had to be careful around people, especially those I cared deeply for.

Adonis was the last person I needed to be involved with. My feelings for him ran more resonant than the oceans. He was a fearless, top-notch, dope boy with plenty of unworthy, spiteful bitches trying to hang on his coattail. The same bitches who treated me like shit during our school days. Whereas, I was a beautiful, plus-sized model and a newly turned vampire with minimal self-control.

Gazing into his light-brown eyes, I said, "Adonis, I would've loved to hear those words when we were younger. Now is not the best time for me to indulge in a relationship. I'm just not a good candidate to be your woman. I hope you understand."

With a displeased expression on his fine ass face, Adonis chuckled for a while before shoving our bodies together and sticking his tongue into my mouth.

Fuck me, I thought as my legs grew weak.

As he lifted me off the ground, he broke off the kiss. Adonis seriously stated, "Back in high school, I always told you that you were beautiful an' not let those angry, messy bitches get to you. Also, I remember tellin' you that a nigga was going to give you the world one day because you deserved it. Well, Genesys Cullman, I'm that motherfuckin' nigga, an' I don't give a fuck who don't like what they are seein' or will see from us in the future. I suggest yo' ass start not givin' a fuck either. 'Cause a nigga ain't going no-damn-where, an' I mean that shit."

But I'm a whole ass vampire roaming the streets, Adonis. What you want from me, I can't give it to you, I thought as everyone's thoughts and beating hearts returned tenfold.

Chapter Two

Adonis Villin

"Die For You" by The Weeknd played from the speakers within the gymnasium. As all eyes were on Genesys and me, I strolled out to the gym with a rapid heartbeat, a massive smile was on my face, and so was the need to shove my tongue back into her sweet, juicy mouth. Since she was nervous and fidgety, I refrained from doing so.

Along the way towards the short distance to my vehicle, I thought about our school days and how I badly wanted to date Genesys. At night, I would masturbate to the previous year yearbook picture of her. Genesys was the perfect female. Always, she was thankful, kind, sweet, and beautiful. Her smile was captivating; it saved me from many troubles. Whenever I was having a bad day, I would seek Genesys. She was the only female capable of clearing my mind, all by the flash of her perfectly aligned white teeth.

However, since her weight was always in people's mouths, I stayed away from asking her to be my girlfriend. I didn't want those evil, vindictive people to put her down any more than they had. There were only so many niggas asses I could beat on a given day. I had received plenty of disciplinary actions for popping niggas in the mouth for disrespecting her. The females were a no-touch zone until I found other ways to make them pay.

Junior high and high school was too overwhelming for Genesys. Our classmates were cruel for no reason. They didn't take the time to get to know the loving, funny female, as I did. Simply, their parents didn't instill any type of morals into those bastards.

As I arrived at my vehicle, I unlocked the passenger door. Genesys sighed heavily as she tried her best to avoid glaring into my face.

Chuckling, I asked, "What's that sigh fo', an' why you avoidin' lookin' at me, beautiful lady?"

Sexily, she bit her bottom lip before saying, "Like ... we've always been cool or whatever, but um ... what's making you step out the way you did?"

As I placed her on the ground, I wrapped my arms around her waist and said, "I've always wanted you. I didn't want you to deal wit' the stupidity from our peers. Either way, I'm doin' what I should've done all those years ago. I'm seekin' what I need in my life."

"Oh," she nervously announced before blushing and looking at the ground.

I was expecting more of a response than what she gave me, but I had to understand I did spring things on her out of the midst of nowhere.

To break the awkwardness, I asked, "So, I think it's best to play catch up. Where shall we start?"

"With ... how are you, Adonis?"

Smiling, I replied, "I was all over the place, but now I'm good."

"Would you care to explain the phrase 'all over the place'?" she inquired with a raised eyebrow.

I'd never been shy to share my issues with Genesys. Half of the materialistic things I'd accrued were because of Genesys, little did she know. Every relationship I'd been in was influenced by Genesys. Once unwanted drama arrived in said relationship, it was Genesys who told me how to get out of it.

"I think we need to sit in the car for this one," I replied, shaking my head.

"Okay," she voiced, big beautiful eyes glaring into mine.

After I gazed into her peepers for a while, I aided her inside my vehicle and closed the door. While making my way towards the driver's side, one of my best friends, Gabe, called my name as he ran towards me. The sternness in his voice informed me he would tell me something that would have me highly pissed off.

"Let me start the car before you tell me anythin'," I told him as Genesys opened the driver's door.

"A'ight," he replied, inches away from me.

"I'm going to see what Gabe wants. I won't be long," I quickly told Genesys as I started the engine and turned on the air conditioner.

"Okay," she responded, softly smiling.

While closing the door, I said, "What's up?"

"Hunt overheard a convo that seeks our attention ... now," Gabe spoke clearly yet lowly.

"An' what's that?"

"We know exactly where that fucka Bryant layin' low?"

Becoming angry, I spoke through clenched teeth, "Where Bryant fuck ass at?"

"Don't know. Bryant's partner in crime, Skeebo, was escorted out the back by Hunt. Hunt's takin' him to the torture chambers," Gabe replied as Layla loudly but nastily called my name.

Fuck, here this bitch go, I thought as I looked into Gabe's eyes and said, "I'm finna chat wit' Genesys. In ten minutes, we headin' out."

"A'ight," he replied as Layla strolled beside him, giving me the evil eye.

"Well, hello, to you too, Layla," Gabe chuckled while backing away.

While flipping him off, Layla asked, "What in the fuck is that big bitch doing in your car?"

As I stepped closer to the gorgeous yet ugly person, I cleared my throat and said, "I drop my dick in every hole in yo' body. What you are not going to do is question me nor disrespect Genesys. She hasn't done anything to you. Now, the best thing you can do is go find someone else to torture. We are done, Layla."

Stunned, she glared at me before saying, "What in the hell do you mean 'we are done'? You and I have been a thing for as long as I can remember."

Chuckling, I replied, "Correction, my dick has been slidin' in an' out yo' holes fo' as long as you can remember. You were never my girlfriend. Don't get shit twisted. Anyways, you've taken up enough of my time. I'll see you 'round."

As I opened my door, Layla grabbed my arm. She angrily spat, "Oh, you are going to regret putting me to the side for a bitch that can't do shit but flatten your tires, eat up all of your money, and damn near break your spine for trying to ride you."

Shaking my head, I glared into Layla's eyes and said, "You are so motherfuckin' fine. You know that, right?"

"I sure the fuck do," she replied, placing her hands on her hips.

"Yet, you have the nastiest and ugliest persona. Yo' spirit is nasty as hell. You, as a person, is rotten to the core. You wonder why shit never goes right in yo' life; it's because of the fucked up person that you are. You will down talk the next if they don't look as society wants them to or work at a job paying top-notch dollars. You have a lot to learn, Layla. Like this fo' instance, I only chose to deal wit' you because of how you treated Genesys. So, all those nights I fucked you in the ass, dropped my nut all over yo' expensive hairdo, in yo' eyes, an' called you out the house when you weren't feelin' good; it wasn't because I was into som' freaky shit. I was into som' get back shit fo' one of the realist women I know. Have a good one," I sternly voiced before shoving her stunned as out of my way.

While taking a seat in my car, I locked the door, all the while looking at an unpleasant Genesys. As I grabbed her hand, I placed a kiss on the back and asked, "I'm sure you heard that conversation. So, I'm going to ask you ... how are you feelin' 'bout that convo?"

"Truthfully?" she asked, not looking at me.

Turning her to face me, I said, "Yes."

"I feel like I will always be judged because of my weight. Not because of how much money I make or what I do for a living or how smart or nice I am. People will always see me as 'a big bitch', and I'm sick of it. Like damn, what did I do to people for them to have so much hatred for me because of my weight," she spoke in a saddened tone.

Sternly, I said, "If you let one damn tear slide from yo' beautiful eyes, I swear we are going to the pet store."

Busting out laughing, Genesys squealed, "You wouldn't dare!"

"Shid, try me," I replied in a matter-of-fact tone.

Shaking her head as she continued to laugh, I stated, "I will go buy the biggest gotdamn hamster in there, an' have its ass sittin' in the console."

"Adonis, shit will be all over your damn seats and my dress. You know I can't stomach the sight of rodents," she giggled.

Becoming serious again, I sincerely voiced, "What I told you all of those years ago still apply to this day, Genesys. No, I'm not sayin' box every bitch out, but all it takes is to knock a bitch out once an' the rest will stir clear. You have to stand yo' ground."

As she nodded, I kissed the back of her hand. Genesys breathing became erratic. For the life of me, I wanted to reverse out of the parking lot and head to my crib. I wanted to do everything to her body I envisioned for years. I wanted Genesys' body to yearn for me when we were afar and together. I needed her spirit to connect with mine. I wanted my virgin mouth to suck on her until she begged me to stop.

Looking at me in a sex-crazed manner, Genesys moaned, "Oh my God."

"What's wrong?" I inquired in a confused manner.

While clearing her throat, Genesys shook her head several times before saying, "Shit, I'm so sorry. Um, I need to go. Maybe we can chat later."

"I have seven minutes befo' I'm to leave this reunion. I don't want you to cheat me out of my time wit' you, especially since you've been gone from the States fo' over a year. Now, the reason we hopped in the car was because of a question you asked. I didn't get the chance to respond to why I was all over the place. So, let me tell you … I have been through the motions on whether or not to shoot a nigga in the face fo' runnin' off wit' my dope. I want to flatline his entire bloodline fo' his actions. I'm dealin' wit' the fact my mother has Multiple Sclerosis an' it's incredibly aggressive. My dad can't handle the love of his life being so depressed an' down 'bout life. With all that going on, I still find myself wondering why I let you get away—the one female who can calm me down by simply smiling. Ever since you left a year ago, to travel the world … I've found myself wantin' to start a family; yet, there's only one person I want to create a family wit'. I'm sexually frustrated because no one is satisfyin' me the way I need them to. Now, I'm one track. I want to have a relationship wit' you, but you will give me one hell of a time. I'm cool wit' that. I'm all fo' provin' myself an' to help you along the way wit' being comfortable wit' us. So ... um, you have made my life just that much more straightforward. With you home, I feel I can tackle any an' everything."

Once I finished talking, I analyzed the shocked expression on Genesys' face. I knew I threw a lot of information at her. It wasn't like she was used to be me being blunt about my illegal actions or my family matters. I didn't want to waste any more time.

As a few knocks sounded at my driver's window, Genesys said, "Oh, wow."

Glancing at the window, I saw Gabe. His facial expression informed me it was time to go.

Clearing my throat, I turned to look at Genesys and asked, "Is that 'oh, wow' was meant fo' my statement or Gabe?"

"For your comment."

Knowing I had somewhere to be, I began to end our conversation.

"Genesys, I have to handle som' shit. When it's over, I really want to be wit' you. Later tonight, I need to pick things up where I left them. My number is still the same, granted you hadn't deleted any of my messages from yo' Messenger."

Blushing, she replied, "No, I haven't."

"So, when I send you a message to call me, you will?" I asked, unlocking the doors.

With a small, cute smile on her face, Genesys slowly nodded her head and replied, "Yes."

"Good," I happily replied before saying, "Don't you open that door. From here on out, when I'm present, you will not open a single door. That's my job. Understand?"

"Yes, sir," she voiced, saluting me.

Laughing, I replied, "I see you are still silly."

"Just like my weight, that will never change," she spoke in a vibrant mood.

That's the attitude I always wanted her to have. Being confident was the best thing anyone could be. In my eyes, confidence in oneself was one of the keys to success.

Upon ensuring Genesys made it inside of the gym safely and bestowing a magnificent kiss to her plump lips, I hurriedly walked towards my vehicle, all the while smiling.

As I opened the door and sat in the driver's seat, I placed the gearshift in reverse. I glanced at

Gabe before saying, "Oh yeah, you know we finna send a grand message to anyone that thinks they can fuck us over. Whatever we gotta do, we get in an' get that shit done. Tonight 'til the early mornin', I got somethin' I been itchin' to do."

With a massive smile on his light-skinned face, Gabe asked, "Oh, yeah? An' what's that nigga?"

"Have my face ridden fo' the first time an' make love to Genesys," I spoke in a matter-of-fact timbre as I sped away from the gym.

Hype as hell, Gabe replied, "Shid, nigga you better do som' practice on eatin' pussy wit' a piece of fruit or somethin'. Don't get yo' amateur ass embarrassed because you don't know what to do."

"Nigga, I been watchin' porn. I know what to do."

"Nigga!" he hollered before continuing, "Just because you watch porn doesn't mean you can eat pussy, dude."

Shit, I thought as he continued, "I tell you what … befo' you have yo' time wit' Genesys. I'll ask my guhs to let you watch them go at it. They'll give you pointers while they are doing the do."

Looking at Gabe, I replied, "Are you serious, nigga?"

"Yep. Females are the best to ask 'bout pussy eatin'. They know what they like. I wouldn't advise you to ask Genesys; after all, you are supposed to be the nigga of all niggas in the bedroom. So, you know she knows 'bout yo' reputation."

"True. True. Go 'head an' set that shit up," I stated before saying, "Thank you. I owe you one."

With his phone in his hands, Gabe shook his head and replied, "Nigga, we have been boys since pamper days. You don't owe me nothin' fo' this. Let's say it's one of my many gifts to the soon to be Villins."

Loving the sound of 'soon-to-be-Villins', I had a grin on my face as I dapped up my partner.

While Gabe was on the phone with his girlfriends of two years, I thought, *tonight is the night my mother's dreams of her son getting married an' livin' a happy life wit' one woman is on the way of comin' true.*

Chapter Three

Genesys

Later that night

Adonis: Will you meet me at my house, love?

As I stared at Adonis' message, I shook my head and sighed heavily. Badly, I wanted to be underneath him, but in my current condition, it wasn't the best. I wasn't comfortable being around my friends, much less be around someone I'd secretly loved for quite some time.

My worst fear was for Adonis to catch me out on a late-night, feeding off the very people he knew all too well. I didn't want to be responsible for countless more deaths.

Ding.

As I held a martini glass in my hand, I slowly swirled it around as I placed my eyes on my phone. The radio station's DJ must've known what was on my mind. The perfect song played as I grabbed my phone. While bobbing my head to Erykah Badu's "Next Lifetime", I outstretched on my black suede couch and unlocked my phone. Shortly afterward, I opened the messenger to one of the most annoying apps of all time, Facebook.

A huge smile appeared on my face as I glared at Adonis's name and profile picture.

He's so damn handsome and sweet to me, I thought as I didn't open the message.

Instead, I read the first few words of his statement. Instantly, I wanted to read what he had sent.

Ding. Dong.

Looking at the door, I hollered, "I'm coming."

There was no need in me asking who it was. Venus and Gemini had informed me before I left the reunion that they would stop by. Once the reunion ended, they had called to see if I wanted to attend the after-party. Of course, I declined. I didn't stay at the reunion long; there wasn't a way in hell I was going to an after-party. It would've been a massacre.

"Hurry up, girl. I have to pee," Venus loudly spat, causing me to laugh.

By the loudness of her voice, I knew she had one too many drinks. After the reunion, the girls decided to go to a party. Out of the crew, she was the one who would plop her ass on a toilet quick.

As I strolled towards the door, I ran my hands through my soft, jet black tresses. My nails sensually dug in my scalp, resulting in a moan. At that moment, I wished I could felt Adonis' gentle touch on my scalp and body. With every fiber in me, I wanted to feel his lips pressed against mine as he took my breath away.

The moment I opened the door, Venus ran beside me, all the while chanting, "I'm almost there. I'm almost there."

Drunkenly sashaying across the door's threshold, Gemini looked around my home with a pleasant smile on her face.

"You have it looking and smelling good in here, Genesys. I'm loving this vibed."

"Thank you. I decided to redecorate ... making it more vibrant and ghoulish," I blushed as I closed and locked the door.

While "Do Me Ri" by Blackbear played, Gemini swung her hips to the beat as she replied, "I dig it."

As we sat the long black sectional sofa, Gemini asked, "So, have you talked to Adonis since he left the reunion?"

"No."

"He hasn't reached out?"

"He has, but I haven't responded."

"Heifer, why?" she inquired, shaking her head.

Shrugging my shoulders, I lied, "Because I'm nervous. I don't think we should date. We have a good friendship, and I don't want it ruined if we don't work out."

As she rolled her eyes, Venus sauntered into the living room and said, "I want to know one thing, Genesys. Why are you holding back with him? He made it perfectly clear he wants you. Stop being shy and see where y'all end up."

"I'm not going to waste my time," I voiced as Gemini's phone chimed several times.

"You've been secretly in love with him for ages. Now that he put his heart out there, you are going to stomp on it. Wow, Genesys. Wow," Venus voiced, taking a seat next to me.

"Can we change the subject please?" I asked, looking at my best friends.

"Sure," they replied as Gemini rapidly texted on her phone.

"So, tell us about your trip. Why did you stay so long after we left? Did you finish soul searching ... as you called it?"

Nope, I took souls, I thought, taking a long gulp of the delicious martini.

"Yes, I did," I lied before telling them about the remainder of my trip.

I made sure not to tell them what happened the last night we were destined to leave together. I refrained from telling them my DNA had been altered by a fine and tall, handsome pale-looking male whom I had the pleasure of having a one-night stand. I didn't tell them I had the best orgasm of my life while being bitten on the neck as if I was a freshly baked sour cream pound cake. I ensured I didn't tell them I had an issue with draining people of their blood, morning, noon, and night while I was on the extended stay.

"Show us some pictures. I'm sure you took some," Venus voiced as Gemini cleared her throat several times.

Placing my eyes on her, I asked, "Are you okay?"

Nodding, she replied, "Yeah. Now, show us those pictures, woman. Prague was truly a beautiful place. We didn't get a chance to see it all, but I'm sure you did."

Yes, the good, bad, and ugly, I thought, retrieving my phone.

While my friends looked at the pictures, I rehashed my time there with Jakub. A day after being turned into a vampire and the fourth feeding, I never saw Jakub again. I had many questions that needed answers. For days, I looked for the man who had changed me. He was nowhere to be found, which sadden me. I regretted I didn't have a photo to show people. After two days of being unsuccessful in locating him, I became emotionally--for the worse. Every word bullies had ever spoken to and about me, flooding my mind. I wanted to kill myself; yet, the effects of being a human for so long took over. I couldn't take myself out or hurt anyone over a situation I could adapt to by learning more about my new found DNA.

After learning all I could, I decided to avoid drinking from humans. Any animal would suffice, so I thought. I was wrong, horribly wrong. My body rejected animal blood. Since I refused to indulge in human blood, my body became weary. In need of feeling better, I did the unthinkable--drained the blood of innocent beings lurking in the alleyways or dark areas within the downtown area.

I told myself I would take enough to restore my strength and rid the sickness. I was out of my mind thinking I could control when to stop feeding. Upon draining the bodies of ten people, I was at full potential and loving the enhanced abilities. I could've stopped feeding, but I didn't. Before I hopped on a plane, aiming for the United States, I had voided a total of four dozen individuals of their lives.

"Earth to Genesys," my girls voiced as they swayed from side to side.

Snapped into reality, one of my favorite jams played, Ballgreezy "That's What I Like". Falling in sync with my girls' body movements, I replied, "Sorry, I dipped off into memory lane."

"We have to go back there. I want to see these places," Gemini voiced as her phone chimed.

I'm heading back soon enough. I have to find Jakub, I thought as I replied, "Yes, we should."

"Girl, if you don't reach out to Adonis, I know something. Gabe is getting on my damn nerves." Gemini laughed before biting her bottom lip.

Damn, I can't wait to leave here. I need that fine black ass nigga in between my legs. Tonight is the night of all nights, especially by the way he's talking, Gemini thought, causing me to gasp.

My friends looked at me crazy before giggling, "What's wrong with you?"

Shocked, I lied, "I have no idea."

Needing her to cease her thoughts immediately, I asked, "So, what's been going on with y'all?"

"Well, I'm fucking around with Hunt," Venus replied with a smile on her face.

Gemini and I hollered, "Say what?"

Laughing, Venus began to tell us how she and Hunt became a thing. The more she talked, the more I felt terrible for my friend. She was too beautiful, kind, and loving to be dealing with Hunt, who suggested she acted a certain way in public towards him. Basically, he didn't want people to know about them. Being a loyal friend I'd always been, I spoke my mind. By her facial expression, she didn't like how honest I had been.

Seriously looking at me, Venus sternly replied, "Until you put your big girl draws on and talk to Adonis, you will not express your feelings about my relationship with Hunt. Okay?"

"Venus, my dealings with Adonis has nothing to do with the fact Hunt is treating you like a booty call. You are so much more than that. If he can't be seen with you, then you should rethink spreading your legs for him. We, as big beautiful women, shouldn't be hidden as if we are creatures. We are fine women who are on their shit, and if a nigga can't respect our weight, then they can kick fucking rocks. Simple as that."

"I agree," Gemini stated as my phone rang, thanks to Facebook Messenger.

As Venus tried to argue with us about the bullshit, I placed my eyes on my phone. Curiosity consumed me as I pondered why Gabe was calling me. For a few seconds, I thought of whether I should answer the call. After inhaling and exhaling several times, I answered the call.

"Hello," I stated while sitting upright.

"Woman, you got us niggas on a damn goose hunt," Gabe's rich, deep, and sultry voice spoke before he laughed.

Feeling warm, I smiled. "My fault. What's up?"

"Yo' ass know what's up," he chuckled before continuing, "This nigga 'bout to lose his mind. You ain't answerin' his calls. Will you please call or text his ass back? He's 'bout to drive us crazy. I would love to lay up with Gemini, woman."

Stunned, I replied, "Say that last part again, please?"

"Guh, you heard me the first time," he chuckled.

"Oh well, damn, when that started?"

"When her sexy ass returned from Prague. Now, enough 'bout yo' girl an' me. Will you call my homie, please?"

GQ "I Do Love You" sounded from the speakers as a warm sensation overcame me. The song brought back memories of the most special day; Adonis and I were sitting on my parents' front porch. We were completing a science project flooded. Out the midst of nowhere, Adonis looked into my eyes and sang the song, all the while grabbing my hands and engaging me to slow dance. I didn't think much about it that day. I thought he was trying to put a smile on my face since the bitches of bullying did a number on my mind. The way he looked and smiled at me should've caused me to realized he harbored feelings for me. If I would've paid attention to how close our bodies were as he sang those words wholeheartedly, I would've known for sure Adonis Villin had a thing for me.

"I will do that." I smiled, feeling bubbly.

"Like right now?" Adonis hollered on the phone.

"What the hell? Y'all are still childish as hell."
I giggled as Gabe busted out laughing.

"That ain't gon' change. Now, call me, please,"
Adonis gently stated as Gabe talked in the
background. Gemini and Venus had an
interesting conversation going. I wanted to place
my four cents but felt I shouldn't entertain it.

"Okay," I blushed as I ended the Facebook
call.

With shaky hands, I dialed Adonis' number.
He didn't let the phone ring one full time before
he answered.

"So, why are you dodgin' me, Genesys? You
never did that before. Are you afraid I will hurt
you? Are you worried 'bout what people are
going to say 'bout us or you?"

"No, it's nothing like that," I replied as I
stood and stretched.

"Then, pack a bag, come outside, an' hop in
my ride," he voiced seriously.

Giggling, I replied, "It would be dumb as hell
for me to do all of that granted you don't know
where I live."

"You still underestimate me, huh? I'm the
hottest nigga in town. You really think I can't
find anyone or anything I want—money talk. I
knew yo' address a few minutes after I left the

school's ground. So, what do you say 'bout packin' a bag an' hoppin' in my whip?"

"Um," I stated as I nervously looked around my one-bedroom apartment.

"Or should I ask, is it okay if I bring my bag inside?"

"Huh?" I asked as my knees grew weak.

"You heard me," he laughed as my girls told me they were going to leave.

While nodding my head at my girls, I didn't know what to say to him; thus, I stood in the middle of my living room floor with several emotions and a super heightened sexual sense.

"You not going to answer, so I'mma grab my bag an' make my way towards yo' door," Adonis voiced in a thuggish manner.

"Okay."

"You better tell that nigga hold on and give us our hugs and farewells, trick," Gemini jokingly stated, smiling.

After completing the norms with my best friends, I said, "Call me when y'all make it to your destinations."

In the sexiest voice ever, Adonis said, "I'm at the door."

"Oh Jesus," I lowly replied, causing him to laugh.

"Girl, why does it seem like you just saw a ghost?" Venus inquired as Gemini opened the door.

Standing at the door holding a small, expensive black bag, Adonis had the most powerful and sexiest posture. The expression on his face was priceless as he licked his full lips, all the while gazing at me.

"Oh, this is why." My friends laughed as I bit my bottom lip and ended the call.

"May I come in?" he asked softly.

As I nodded my head, my friends joked, "Oh, this nigga brought his spend da night bag."

While laughing at the known jokesters, Adonis entered my humble abode. Turning to look at Venus and Gemini, he sternly yet politely said, "Y'all will call her once. That's to let her know y'all made it safely. After that phone call, Genesys will be unavailable, just like you will be unavailable, Gemini."

Silence overcame us as Gemini and Adonis stared at one another.

"So, you know about us?" she inquired with a huge grin on her face.

"I have been known. You forget that we don't keep anythin' from one another. I'm going to tell you like I told him ... don't hurt each other an' think I will be in the middle," Adonis genuinely voiced.

At the same time he spoke, I noticed a peculiar expression on Venus' face.

Say something to me about Hunt. Place me in a better mindset with him, Venus thought, her eyes didn't leave Adonis' body.

Smiling from ear to ear, Gemini stated, "You have my word that I won't hurt him nor put you in the middle of our relationship."

"Good. Y'all be safe. I can't really start my night wit' Genesys 'til y'all call. So, get to yo' places fast."

"Aye, aye, Captain." Gemini saluted while laughing and walking further out of the door.

With a weird expression on her face, Venus said, "You said you know everything ... what do you know about Hunt and me?"

"Say what now?" Gemini loudly said, walking back into my apartment.

You really don't want to know what I know, Venus. I promise you don't, Adonis thought before saying, "Um, I don't know anything. So, what's going on wit' y'all?"

Oh God, Hunt's going to hurt her. I have to prevent him from destroying my friend like the others he has done. I'm going to drain his pathetic ass of every ounce of blood in his body, I thought as Venus shook her head and sadly said, "Nothing. Just good friends as we always have been. Um, goodnight. Love y'all."

Rapidly, Venus exited my apartment. Gemini blew me an air kiss before darting behind our friend. Instantly, I felt my fangs growing. With bucked eyes, I cupped my mouth and ran towards the bathroom.

"What's wrong?" Adonis voiced loudly.

As I escaped inside of the bathroom, I lied, "Nothing. I have to use the bathroom."

While Adonis talked to me about my stylish décor, I tried to calm my mind so my fangs would go back up. Closing my eyes, I slowly inhaled and exhaled several times. I focused on the calming moments of my life. Shortly afterward, my fangs disappeared. In need of feeling more relaxed and to cease the thoughts of Hunt hurting Venus, I stripped out of my clothes and announced to Adonis I was going to take a shower.

Close to the door, he said, "Open the door an' let me bathe you."

Stunned and scared, I shook my head. I had never experienced a man bathing me. My eyes were liable to change colors. Low growls to purring noises would escape my mouth. At the moment, I couldn't allow Adonis to be close to me in my current state. Simply, I just couldn't afford it.

"No, I can bathe myself," I replied, turning on the water.

Adonis chuckled for a while. When he stopped, the bathroom door opened.

With bucked eyes, I shouted, "Really?"

Stepping into the bathroom, naked in all of his damn fine ass glory, Adonis seriously yet sexily replied, "Baby, I can pick a lock easily. I can break into any type of house. You are done runnin' from me. You have no need to hid all of that sexiness from me. I'm ready fo' you, Genesys. Give in an' give me all of you because you really have all of me."

I've waited so long to be in this predicament with him. I've imagined him saying those words to me, yet I can't enjoy and relish in those words or this situation. What am I supposed to do? How can I be with him with my vampire ways? How can I hide the truth from him?

Strolling closer to me with a long and fat dick, Adonis softly said, "Stop thinkin' an' feel. Feel every word I've told you since I've known you. Feel every sensual touch I've blessed upon yo' gorgeous body. Let me in. Don't hide from me, please don't. All I want to do is love you, all of you."

A few tears slid down my face as I slowly nodded my head. If I couldn't have him for a lifetime, I surely would have him for a few months, and then I would disappear. It was the only way to prevent him from knowing what I truly was.

As Curtis Mayfield's "The Makings of You" played, Adonis' face held the most beautiful smile. Never wanting to forget this moment or his face, I slowly etched the memory into my brain. When the times would get hard from being away from him, I would think of this particular moment. The moment I had finally said yes to Adonis Villin as we were butt naked in my bathroom.

Wrapping his arms around my chocolate body, he said, "Thank you so much fo' givin' me a chance, Genesys. I will always honor, respect, an' love you. Oh, I should add in annoy you because I won't want to leave yo' side. You gon' be my wife. Know that."

No, I won't, love. No, I won't.

Chapter Four

Adonis

A Week Later

"Adonissss! Oh, my God! Pleaasseee stop!" Genesys whimpered as she pulled her hair and tried to run from my mouth.

With a mouthful of her delicious pussy, I shook my head, growled like a pit bull, and continued to diving my tongue in and out of her precious jewelry box.

"Why are you doing me like this? Why Adonis?" she cried as her body shook.

Inserting two fingers into her juicy pot, I surfed through her tight, pink walls as if I was an explorer of a newly found city. I took my time learning what areas in her pussy made her weak to her knees. While she continued asking questions, I continued claiming the pussy I needed in my life, forever.

"Ooouu," she cooed, arching her back.

A few more taps on her G-Spot while I sucked on her clit, Genesys screams were loud as her body locked. My sexy baby's juices ran out of her like water out of a fire hydrant. Being the thirsty motherfucker I was, I lapped every ounce of her sweetness.

"Mm, you taste you so fuckin' good, Genesys," I praised.

"Adonnisss, why are you doing this to me?" she voiced in a shaky yet strained tone.

"Because I love you," I sincerely replied, removing my fingers from her gushy insides.

As I placed kisses from her abdomen region until I reached her lips, Genesys softly cried. I wanted her to stop, but I knew there wasn't anything I could do about it. I continued loving on her because she deserved it.

Glaring into her eyes, I rubbed the sides of her face and said, "You own me. Since you've allowed me to be in yo' life, I feed off you. I do everything because of you. I strive hard in these streets fo' you. I ensure I make it back to you. I've cut down my appearances in the hot zones because of you. I worship the ground you walk on, Genesys. You have no idea how long I've been waitin' to have you the way I do."

"Oh, Adonis Villin." She smiled, tears seeping down her beautiful face.

Gripping my man, I slowly rubbed him up and down her juicy folds. Moaning, Genesys shook her head and said, "Don't go any further."

"Okay," I voiced before sucking her bottom lip into my mouth.

As we engaged in a fiery kiss, Genesys placed her soft hands on my chest and began to push it while sitting up. Slowly, I turned over. Lying on my back, I watched the motion of our lips and tongues dancing wonderfully. Genesys massaged my chest before sliding her perfectly designed, long nails down my torso.

"My turn to please you," she provocatively, softly spoke as she licked my lips before dragging her tongue towards my chest.

Succulent kisses were placed on every inch of my body. When she arrived at my navel, Genesys gripped my man and started to stroke him.

"Damn," I groaned, pumping into her hand.

"Can I be honest?" she asked, glaring into my eyes.

"Always be honest wit' me," I told her, rubbing her cheek.

"I'm a newbie at a lot of this sex stuff."

Chuckling, I replied, "I know, an' I'm okay wit' it."

"Okay," she voiced, nodding her head.

Resuming to pleasing my body, Genesys took her time learning what areas caused me to groan. She found the right stroke motion that had me squirming. After exploring the do's and don'ts of what I liked, Genesys licked the head of my dick. The wetness of her tongue and the heat from her mouth sent a ripple of chills through my body. When she looked into my eyes and enveloped her mouth around the head of my dick, my spirit left me.

The sensation and the realization of being pleased by Genesys were better than being the man of the streets or fucking plenty of broads at my leisure. Her loving and attention were better than having every materialistic thing I owned.

Eyes locked onto mine, Genesys slowly slid the rest of my tool into her mouth. The moment she gagged, she laughed.

"Goofy self," I chuckled as she continued gagging on my dick.

Seeing how wet her mouth became from that action, Genesys continued. As she became used to my girth and length, I enjoyed watching her take her time tasting and using different techniques.

After all, it felt damn good. I had never dealt with a female who chose to figure out how I really liked my dick sucked. Genesys was on the path of mastering it. That was one of the many things I loved about her. She didn't mind observing to ensure she fully understood anything.

"I think I'm ready to try this dick sucking thing," she goofily voiced, nervously looking at me.

"Have at it. You got this," I coached before blowing her a kiss.

Blushing, she winked and said, "I hope you will enjoy this."

"I know I will."

Shortly afterward, Genesys got down to business. That damn woman sucked my dick in the most passionately, beautiful way. I was in awe. I had never moaned the way I did, and I wasn't ashamed.

While she gobbled the dick, Genesys massaged my balls before inhaling them into her warm, wet mouth. Genesys put me on a different cloud when she licked and sucked in between my thighs before blowing on my dick as if it was a spoonful of hot rice.

"Gotdamn it," I groaned, watching her sloppily and happily eat up my dick.

Within a matter of seconds, I was ready to bust. I didn't want her to swallow my kids. I wasn't ready to have my sperm in her stomach; I wanted it in her pussy.

"Come up from down there," I weakly stated as she sucked my dick as if her life depended on it.

Shaking her head, she growled on my man while giving me dumb yet intelligent head.

"Oh, shiii," I voiced as I tried to push her off my tool.

"Mmmgrrmhhph," she hummed as more of my dick slide into her mouth.

Feeling helpless, my body flopped and jerked on the bed as I tried to tell her I was cumming. The second my body locked, my mouth dropped open. I had never had a woman lock my body, and I didn't know how to feel about it. Yet, one thing I knew, Genesys had a nigga on another level.

"Fuccckkk," I moaned as I felt my soldiers rising from their resting places.

As Genesys looked into my eyes, she had a smirk on her face, all the while giving me a run for my money. She gave my man the best talk he could ever have. With my white soldiers on the brink of slipping into her mouth, tears streamed down my face. I wasn't sure if it was because of the glorious feeling I experienced or because I was vulnerable and in love with a woman I always needed.

Weakly, I replied, "Genesys, I love you. I swear, I do. Be mine fo'eva. Please."

A few seconds later, I gripped the back of Genesys' head and groaned, "Oh fuck. I'm cummin'."

"Mmhm," she cooed as my warm liquid filed into her mouth.

Genesys didn't stop sucking and massaging my balls until she was sure every ounce of sperm was out of me. Satisfied, she glared into my face and asked, "Should I even ask did you enjoy?"

Shaking my head, I breathlessly replied, "That should never be a question. So, don't even ask.

I'm sure my body's reaction told you whether or not I enjoyed it."

Blushing, she replied, "True."

Nervously, she looked around the room. I was sure she was thinking about what to do next. Thus, I helped her out.

"My dick is still hard, Genesys. He doesn't only do that when I'm on liquor. That's him sober as well. So, what we are going to do is make love. I'm going to kick things off. When you are comfortable, you can take over. Deal?"

Nodding, she said, "Deal."

Pulling her towards me, I said, "Never be afraid to initiate intimacy wit' me. I'm down, anywhere, anyplace, or time. I'm always up fo' pleasin' you. Understand?"

Biting her bottom lip, she replied, "Understood."

"Get on this pole," I told her as I held my dick in my hand.

Nervously, she said, "Oh no. That's not happening."

Growling, I said, "Get ... on ... this ... dick, Genesys."

"No, I'm too big to be on you."

"No, you ain't now get on this dick, woman," I sternly announced.

Rolling her eyes, she shook her head and climbed on top of me. She was shaking and not from being horny but from fear. Still, she wasn't comfortable with her weight. I had no idea what it would take to free her mind of that, but I was going to try everything in the book to get her one-hundred percent confident about her body on top of mine.

As I inserted my man inside of her, Genesys' eyes fluttered. Soft yet beautiful coos escaped her mouth. Large breasts perfectly bounced as I slowly thrust inside of exclusive pink walls.

"Adonniiss," she whined, closing her eyes.

"Open yo' eyes, Genesys," I hissed as I gripped a fistful of her hair.

Taking her time, Genesys opened her eyes. Once I had her undivided attention, I began to drop good, dope dick inside of Genesys, savagely.

"Fuck me!" she hollered, rubbing her clit.

"An' I intend to do just that." I smiled as I pressed her breasts together.

The wetness inside of Genesys sounded off as I licked one nipple and pinched the other. Since the first night, I had been making love to her. I needed her to become comfortable with us, naked. Today was the first time she'd ever told me to fuck her; Genesys was going to see the beast in my sexual skills. She was going to get what no other female could ever get out of me.

Sliding towards the edge of the bed, I delivered long, deep dick strokes into her starving pussy.

"Adoniiss," she whimpered as she began to meet my thrusts.

"I see you, baby. I feel you. Get that dick. Get yo' dick, baby," I coached as her body relaxed.

"I … I…." she stated before saying, "I'm cummin', Adonis!"

With a crooked smile on my face, I gripped her hair tighter and shoved her face close to mine. Working my waist, I gave Genesys the business all the while thuggishly saying, "When I say get on this dick, I mean it. I don't want to hear shit 'bout yo' weight. When I say bend that ass over, you better toot that motherfucka high. When I say I want to eat that pussy in the car while you drivin', you better get comfortable in the driver's seat an' let me eat. When I say sit on my face, I fuckin' mean it. Drop that fat, pretty pussy on my face. I don't give a fuck 'bout suffocatin'. All my fucks are given to pleasin' you. Do I makin' my-fuckin'-self clear, Genesys Cullman?"

Loudly, she hollered, "Yesss!"

For the next hour and a half, my baby and I rocked my bed until we fell asleep, soaked in each other's sweat and juices.

Besides the wonderfully powerful lovemaking, I wanted to show my heart off to the world. Every night, we went out on a date. Tonight was no different. It was her turn to pick the restaurant and the activity. To my damn surprise, she wanted to go skating. I hadn't participated in skating since we were in high school. I wasn't worried about busting my ass because the kid had excellent coordination skills.

After I wined my beauty at an expensive five-star restaurant, we made our way to the only skating rink in the city. The loud, popular music from within the establishment had us bobbing our heads. The crowd was at an all-time high. There weren't any teenagers or kids, strictly grown people, just the way I liked it.

As I looked around the vibrant-hued place, I saw Layla, who was pointing my way with an ugly expression on her face. The bitches around her had to have said something smart because they busted out laughing. I didn't give a damn what was said, but I knew not a soul was going to make Genesys feel less than, or it was going to be hell to pay.

After we retrieved our shoes, we found a small table to house our bodies while we put on the skates. Genesys and I made small talk until she had her skates laced tightly. Standing, I maneuvered about on the carpet.

"Hey, Adonis," a group of females stated as they strolled by me.

"What's up," I replied as I really didn't pay them any mind.

After all, there was no need for me to be rude to them when all they did was speak.

"You ready, handsome?" Genesys asked, standing.

"I sure am," I replied as she skated towards me.

As I held out my hand, she blushed. I loved it when she blushed. To me, it highlighted her eyes.

While placing her hand into mine, a well-known twerking song from a female rapper in the city blasted from the skating rink's speakers. Feeling the music, Genesys began to roll her ass and skate towards the floor. With a smile on my face, I looked around us; all eyes were on her. The females had their noses turned up as the males eyed what was mine and mine alone.

Planting our feet on the official skating area floor, Genesys danced as I wasn't far behind her. I wanted to see that ass shake, wobble, and jiggle. Being the suave nigga I knew how to be, I cruised towards her wobbling rump shaker and danced with my girl—just as I did when we were younger.

From that moment until she wanted to rest, I was behind Genesys like flies on shit.

"Okay. These knees of mine need to rest, and my throat needs a nice amount of quality H2O," she giggled, stepping off the skating zone.

"Cool wit' me," I replied as I saw my homies stepping through the door.

As we chunked the deuces, they went their way as Genesys and I waltzed towards the concession stand.

"Here comes Godzilla! Watch out, or she might fall if her knees aren't as strong as those ankles of hers!" Layla shouted, causing people around us to laugh.

Anger consumed me immediately. I was on the verge of saying something, but Genesys's action prevented me from stopping the bullying.

Facing me with a naughty expression on her face, Genesys glared into my eyes and slowly bent at the knees and pulled me closer to her.

"Woman, what are you doing?" I asked as those who laughed at Layla's joke eyed on us.

"Oooh, I can't wait to get back to one of our cribs' so I can be in this position to rock you after you've been down my throat," Genesys confidently replied before kissing my clothed dick.

Busting out laughing, I replied, "Get yo' ass up, woman."

Genesys rose slowly from the ground, all the while running her nails up my torso before planting them on my chest. As she wrapped her arms around my neck, she stood on the brakes of the skates and licked my lips.

With a raised eyebrow, I wrapped my arms around her waist and asked, "So, it's like that, or is this fo' show?"

"Both," she responded before parting my lips with her tongue.

As the crowd did what they did best, egg shit on, my dick was hard. After breaking off the kiss,

Genesys stepped into Layla's face. Sweetly, my lady said, "You have one more time to disrespect me before I drain the blood flowing through your skinny ass body. If you don't mind, I'm done entertaining you. I'm on a date with the man who's been itching to be between these thick ass thighs. I'm on a date with someone who knows what a real chick looks and feels like. A chick with walls for years to come. Have a good one, sweetie."

Genesys strolled away with her head held high. I was impressed and turned on by her standing up for herself. She was surely going to drive my whip from this place because I had a need to reward her behavior.

After we rested for a while and talked shit, the fellas pulled me away. Usually, when either of us was on a date, we weren't to disturbed the other. For them to disrupt the norm, some shit had gone down.

Ducked off in a corner with my partners, I asked, "What's wrong?"

"Just got word that twelve pulled over our trucks. Shit don't look good at all," Gabe voiced, shaking his head.

"Say motherfuckin' what?" I hollered, stuck to the wall.

"How? It wasn't random inspection time," I voiced as I knew it was time to end my date.

"We called Wesley, but he didn't answer the phone. We need all hands on deck fo' this one," Hunt stated.

"A'ight. Let me get Genesys home safely," I told them before we dapped.

As I departed, I thought, fuck, fuck, fuck.

With a scowl on my face, I looked at the table we were sitting at; I didn't see Genesys. Quickly, I scanned the area. She was nowhere in sight. Sighing sharply, I slowly rescanned the area. This time, when I looked towards the bathroom, I saw her smiling as her hair and titties bounced. Upon approaching me, Genesys' eyes were lighter than before. I never knew or noticed that her eyes change from dark brown to a golden brown; Instantly, I was intrigued about how I never noticed before.

"Is everything okay?" she inquired, grabbing my wrists.

Shaking my head, I replied, "Nawl. We need to leave. I have som' business to take care of."

"All right. I hope everything is okay," she softly said as Layla wobbled away from the bathroom area, drawing a crowd.

"That fat bitch is a vampire!" Layla hollered, pointing at Genesys.

As eyes fell on Genesys, she smiled and shook her head.

"Bitches will do anythin' fo' attention," I voiced, embarrassed for the hysterical drama queen.

"Yes, they do," Genesys chuckled as I placed our skates on the counter.

Chapter Five

Genesys

Later that night

After Adonis dropped me off at home, I sent him on his way with a safe prayer. Along the path towards my apartment, I dreaded going inside my living quarters, alone and staring at the same walls. All sorts of things would consume my mind, turning me into someone I didn't want to be, making me one powerful, bloodthirsty female.

Furthermore, I needed to feed. Having a small amount of Layla's blood running through my veins had heightened my senses and increased my strength. My heart pounded faster, the fastest it had ever been beating. My mental wasn't insecure; it was more confident and mischievous. I felt invincible. Thus, I patiently waited until Adonis was out of sight before I hopped in my car.

While driving towards the skating rink, I decided I would forever feed on people who bullied me in school. Each of those misguided souls would have the pleasure of seeing me puncture their necks and suck the blood out of their bodies.

As Jakub had told me the first night of my feeding, "There's nothing wrong with crippling someone just to be stronger or rid them from the world. Me, I don't care who I drain dry or suckle from as long as I'm powerful than I was before."

I wasn't into being cruel for the hell of it. I wouldn't kill anyone; it's damaging to my soul. I was still recovering from the small pile of bodies in Prague. However, I would take pleasure in seeing fear in my bullies' eyes. The fear would disappear once I swiped their memory. I would happily prance around daily, knowing what I did to them. The only reason I didn't hypnotize Layla because I wanted her to tell people I was a vampire. Quite a few of the human species didn't believe in something that was deemed folklore fiction. I needed those around her to think she was losing her mind.

The way she terrorized me for years was unacceptable. Her recent actions at the skating rink were too much for me; thus, it was time for me to put the bitch in the mental institution for the rest of her natural life.

When I arrived at the skating rink, I saw a heavy presence of police officers. Clearing my throat, I shook my head and drove past. With a dire need to torment those that hated me for no reason, I made it my business to find them—one by one.

Three hours later, I pulled into a well-frequented service station on the boulevard. I was sure one of my targets would be present. I didn't have a single strategy as to how I would get my chosen target away from the crowd. All I knew was that I wasn't going home without having my fangs sunk into the skin of those who bullied me.

As I stepped inside the chilly establishment, my eyes landed on Sheena. She was one of the three females who were good friends of Layla. The others, Melanie and Janae, weren't with the tall, pretty, and dark-skinned bully. While approaching Sheena, her eyes landed on me. A wicked smile spread across her face as she shook her head. She opened her petite lips to say something, but a handsome guy ceased her actions.

An assortment of feelings flooded my body. I froze. I had no idea what I should do with a large crowd, hooting and hollering as if they were wild animals. Exhaling, I turned around, aiming for the door.

Oh, I'm going to cripple you, Sheena. Just wait and see.

Once I arrived inside of my car, I took several deep breaths. Immediately, I thought of what Jakub told me about waiting for someone. Upon knowing what I had to do, I continued sitting in my car, all the while thinking of the grandest masterplan.

Ten minutes later, the broad exited the store with a bag in her hand. I prayed she was going to leave the place by herself. To my disappointment, she didn't. The handsome guy she was talking to hopped in the passenger seat of her car.

"Fuck," I spat, starting the engine in my car.

Ring. Ring. Ring.

As I reversed my vehicle, I grabbed my cell phone and glared at the screen. Quickly, I answered the call.

"What are you doing?" Adonis sexily asked.

"Nothing," I lied as I sped away from the store, two cars away from Sheena's vehicle.

"Can I come over when I'm done?"

"Yes," I replied as I watched the direction Sheena's car had gone.

"Okay. I'll be there in thirty minutes or so."

"All right. I'll be waiting."

"I'm going to make it up fo' endin' our date. Okay?"

"Okay," I voiced as I followed Sheena.

A brief silence overcame us as I was eager to get my hand around Sheena's neck and glare into her eyes as my fangs descended. I was so into my thoughts that I forgot I was on the phone.

Chuckling, Adonis asked, "Why are you growlin'?"

With bucked eyes, I stuttered, "Uh. Uh. I'm reading something that has my blood boiling."

"Well, you need to stop readin' that. I don't need you pissed off when I arrive. I need you ready to receive all this lovin' I must give to you," he softly said as I heard Gabe calling his name.

"All right," I replied as Sheena turned into a quiet neighborhood, filled with mostly elderly and middle-class persons.

"So, I'll call you when I'm close," he quickly said.

"Cool with me," I responded, zoned on Sheena's car, which stopped at a house with no front porch light on.

"I love you, Genesys," Adonis spoke, causing me to gasp for air.

Pulling in front of a house, several houses away from Sheena, I was elated yet sad upon hearing Adonis' words. I didn't know what to say, or how I should've reacted.

Chuckling, he rapidly spoke, "You better get used to hearin' me say that, woman."

"Uh."

"I'll see you soon, beautiful."

"Okay," I voiced in a shaky tone as I was a bundled of nerves.

Ending the call, I didn't know which matter was more critical—trying to comprehend Adonis' words or sucking two ounces of blood from Sheena's petite body.

Ring. Ring. Ring.

Placing my eyes on my device, I stared at Gemini's name, contemplating whether I should answer. After sighing a few times heavily, I responded to my phone, all the while keeping my eyes on the prize.

"Hello," I stated in an upbeat tone.

"Get to Venus' house now!" she screamed, panicked.

There was no if's, and's, or but's if I needed to be there. I didn't give a damn about my current mission. My friend was in need; therefore, I zoomed away from the curb of the unknown person's give property.

As I did so, I asked, "What's going on?"

"She's talking crazy. Her rants about has Hunt's name written all over it," she spoke angrily as I heard Venus smashing things.

"I'm on my way. In the meantime, tell me what happened."

"I have no idea. She won't talk to me. She's just smashing shit and saying she's going to kill him for playing with her feelings."

Growling, I replied, "Lord, what has he done to her."

"Answer the phone, bitch ass nigga!" Venus yelled.

"Venus, please calm down. Put your phone down. The best way to handle a nigga like that is to not give two fucks about him. You deserve so much more than whatever he's put you through. He doesn't deserve to have you reacting to his foolishness like this," Gemini softly stated to our friend.

"I'm a good fucking woman. I'm nice. I'm sweet. I love wholeheartedly. I have my head on right. Why does he think he can walk over someone who simply just wants to love him?" my friend cried.

Hearing the conversation between them, I felt my heartbreaking. Never had I ever seen Venus act up about a man. She was the type to be picky with who she gives her love to; she took her time getting to know a man before opening her legs. She was so kind-hearted and loving; whereas, Hunt was ruthless and heartless. I didn't understand how she became smitten with him. Hunt was handsome as ever, but he wasn't the type of man any woman should deal with. He didn't mind disrespecting women. Outside of the streets, disrespecting women was his full-time hobby.

When I arrived at Venus' house, every light was on. I was sure she tore the place up, and I wasn't in the mood to clean up. Yet, since she was one of my best friends who had a bad moment, I had to do what I had too.

As I stepped through the door, my eyes damn near bucked out of the sockets. Glass, whatnots, tables, and etc. were smashed. Different sized holes were in the walls. The cotton in her sofas was lying about on the floor. In the middle of the kitchen floor, Venus was lying across Gemini's lap, crying her soul out.

"How can he use me like he's been doing? Why would he want to hurt me? I haven't done anything to receive this karma. I'm one of the good ones; yet, I'm getting treated as if I strut around town dogging men," she sobbed.

Forty minutes later, Venus was all cried out. She retired to her room. From her looks and outrage, I ensured she didn't have anything in her room or bathroom that she would use to harm herself. Venus had a problem with chronic depression. Any little thing would set her off. Given her condition, I couldn't begin to comprehend why she would place herself in the likes of Hunt.

After we ensured the safety of our friend, Gemini and I began to clean Venus' home. While we did so, we didn't say a single word. Honestly, it was for the best. We had to keep a lookout for her. I needed to hear her thoughts. As I picked up large pieces of glass, I was thankful for my vampire abilities. Being able to listen to others' thinking was really going to come in handy until Venus was better.

The front screen door opened, followed by Adonis saying, "What in the hell happened here, Genesys? I've been tryin' to call you fo' the past ten minutes? Are y'all right?"

Nodding, I replied, "Yeah, I'm fine."

Curiously, I asked, "How did you know I was here?"

"When you didn't answer yo' phone Hunt told me you were probably over here. So, I hightailed it this way."

Growling, I asked, "Where is he?"

Walking closer to me, Adonis looked at me oddly and said, "He just pulled up. Why what's going on?"

"Good," I replied as I felt my fangs descending.

"What's going on, Genesys?" Adonis voiced as I shook my head.

Eager to place my eyes on Hunt, I was ready to rip Hunt's throat out for how he was treating my friend. The moment he walked through the door, I was going to pounce on his ass, and there wasn't a soul that would stop me.

Grabbing my wrists, Adonis gazed into my eyes and said, "It's apparent they have somethin'

going on, Genesys. We, as in you an' me,
will *not* get in the middle of it. Okay?"

As I pulled my wrists out of Adonis' grasp,
Hunt and the others sauntered through the door.
Quickly, I made my way towards Hunt.

"Genesys!" Adonis hollered.

Ignoring him, I jacked Hunt against the wall
and glared into his eyes.

"Gotdamn it, Genesys!" Adonis loudly spat
from behind me.

I didn't have to say anything as I peered into
the eyes of a man who wasn't shit. While I glared
into his peepers, I took the pleasure of listening
to his thoughts.

*I hope my baby is okay. Lord, please let her be okay.
Please don't let my ways pushed her over the edge because I
would really have nothin' to lose. All I want to do is protect
her from this cruel world. That's it. I swear that's it,* he
thought.

Contentment softened my heart, which
allowed my fangs to retract. Slowly, I began to
release the collar of Hunt's shirt.

While clearing my throat, I pointed my finger
in his face and said, "You better get your shit
together with my friend. I don't give a damn
about my relationship or situation or

whatever Adonis and I have going on ... I will fucking hurt you about Venus, bitch!"

Nodding his head, Hunt couldn't look me in the eyes. After he walked away, I dropped my head and closed my eyes. A part of me was relieved he truly cared about Venus, but another part of me didn't like it. He wanted to shield her from the world, yet he hurt her by not fully being the man she needed.

As I thought about Venus and Hunt's relationship, I thought of the situation I was in with Adonis. Mostly, I thought about myself. Just like Venus deserved a good and pure person in her life, so did Adonis. I was never going to be refined. I was a blood-sucking vampire who couldn't control herself. There was no way Adonis and I would have a happy life together. It wasn't possible.

With tears forming in my eyes, I turned to stare at the handsome male.

"What's wrong?" he questioned worriedly, grabbing my wrists.

"Us. We are wrong. There's no way we can do this. It's going to be too much drama. I don't do drama, Adonis, and you know this. I'm simply not stable enough to deal with you and the world. I'm just not. I enjoyed our time together.

Thank you for telling and showing me how you really feel, but I can't do this anymore. I just can't," I softly cried as I pulled away from him.

"I be damned if you are going to leave me because of som' bullshit. I have never done anythin' to harm or disrespect you. You just can't end us like this, Genesys. I've waited a long time to find the courage to tell you how I feel," he sincerely spoke as he never broke his gaze.

"We can be friends, but we can't be what we were trying to be, Adonis," I spoke, voice cracking.

"Yes, we can. We can do whatever the fuck we want because we are grown. I love you, an' I know like hell you love me," he spoke firmly.

Nodding, I replied, "I do, and that's why I'm choosing to leave you alone."

Confused, he asked, "What have I done fo' you to chunk the deuces at me?"

"Nothing, Adonis. You haven't done anything. I'm not comfortable being with you. Please don't debate me on this. Just don't. Let's just be friends. Please."

Seeing the hurt in his eyes nearly broke me. Yet, I had to stand firm on what I believed.

As he stood tall, Adonis said, "Genesys, I can't be yo' friend after all I've experienced wit' you. I just can't an' I won't."

After stepping closer to him, I rubbed his face and planted a kiss on his lips.

Glaring into his eyes, I replied, "Then, I guess I should say good luck in life, and I wish you nothing but the best. Goodbye, Adonis."

Chapter Six

Adonis

Four Days Later

Several large quantities of dope were in police custody. Millions of dollars were lost because of that traffic stop involving the eighteen-wheeler. My crew was exhausted because I had them working overtime since the bust. My partners were mentally exhausted and ready to shoot everyone who knew about the drugs arriving at the pickup spot. Until we had a clear understanding of what happened, we couldn't drop any bodies. The time was ticking for us to do so; yet, I wasn't sure if I should since my emotions weren't in check.

I was on another level of frustration, confusion, and sadness. I hadn't slept well since Genesys told me goodbye and hadn't responded to any of my calls and texts. I didn't understand what happened between us. In my opinion, we were on the right track. She had built up the confidence to stand up for herself. She was smiling more than I'd ever seen. There wasn't any indication that something was going on that would cause her to end us.

For the past four days, I racked my brain and that of my homies to see what could've been the issue. It surely wasn't the streets because I was barely in them. It wasn't the fact I was a dope dealer; she knew that shit in high school. There wasn't a single bitch that could say I was with them. My time was split between the illegal activities and Genesys; honestly, Genesys received more time than the illegal shit I had going on.

Standing away from the desk, I snatched my keys and cell phone off the edge of the newly polished object. As I looked around the furniture warehouse, I was proud of my best friends and my accomplishments. Even though we did what we did, we still looked out for our people. We were equipped with quality, low-cost furniture. Every second weekend, we purchased a large amount of food and did a giveaway. On the third weekend, we raffled furniture to those in need.

"Where are you going, woe?" Hunt inquired, snapping me into reality

"To talk to Genesys."

Throwing his keys at me, he said, "In that case, you might want to take my car. It'll get you to Atlanta a lot faster than that whip of yours. You don't want to miss her flight out of the country."

"What?" I hollered as I threw my keys at him.

"Just get in the car an' I'll call you to fill you in," he stated as he pointed towards the entrance/exit door.

"Why are you just now sayin' somethin'?" I questioned loudly as I ran towards the door.

"I wasn't supposed to have said anythin' to you! Venus made me promise, but I can't stand to see you lookin' the way that you have been!" he yelled as my right foot stepped across the threshold of the door.

"I'mma beat yo' ass when I get back nigga!"

Laughing, he replied, "I'll be lookin' forward to it!"

Upon arriving in the driver's seat of Hunt's custom painted Ferrari, I didn't worry about calling his phone. The only person I wanted to talk to was leaving the country for whatever reason. As I reversed Hunt's vehicle, I dialed Genesys' number. She sent my call to voicemail; therefore, I called her until she answered.

"Hello," she sighed.

At the same time, a female said, "Here is your drink. Enjoy."

"Why didn't you tell me you were leavin'?" I questioned, hopping onto the narrow road within the country parts of Montgomery County.

"Things would be easier this way."

"Genesys, baby, tell me what I did wrong?"

"You did nothing wrong, Adonis. This is on me."

"Then, tell me what's on you that have you leavin' the country."

The line grew quiet.

"Genesys, what time does your flight leave?"

"In two hours."

Shaking my head, I voiced, "Hunt lied to me. I won't make it to Atlanta to keep you from gettin' on that damn plane. So, I guess I will have to try my damnedest to do it as I pull over at this gas station. Genesys, please don't leave me. I've been through enough. I need love in my life, an' I need it from the right person … you. I've never experienced joy the way I have when I'm wit' you.

You complete me. I'm sure you've always known that. Whatever is going on, please, can we talk 'bout it? There is no issue we can't face together. I meant what I said when I told you I'm here, an' I'm not going anywhere."

"I wish we could've had what we tried to build. Adonis, I'm not the right woman for you. Hell, I'm not the right woman for any man. I'm not the type of female who can settle down and have a family. I wasn't placed on this earth to be that type of woman. I will not hold up your life for something you deserve. Just let me go, Adonis. We will always remain friends. I promise."

"I can't be your fuckin' friend anymore, Genesys. Why can't you understand that? Since we've been together, I've slept like a baby. My heart is content. I don't let tedious shit get to me. I see a future, an' it doesn't involve me sellin' dope fo' the rest of my life. I see a bright future, a beautiful wife, an' three kids, maybe four. I see a lifetime of happiness, commitment, an' love. I see us. The Villins."

"Adonis, I meant what I said. I don't want a relationship with you. I just want to remain friends. If you can't respect that … then, I guess this is goodbye. So, before I end this call … what is it going to be? Friends or no friends?"

Shaking my head as I beat on the steering wheel, I tried to remain calm as I said, "The best of luck to you. If you need anythin', an' I mean anythin' … please don't hesitate to call me. I love you, Genesys, but I can't be your friend."

I didn't give her a chance to end the call because I did it for her.

Hours after hours, I thought of the last thing I said to Genesys. Wanting to kick my ass for not going harder than I did, I cursed myself out something awful when night fell. My thoughts wouldn't let me rest. So, the best thing going for me was to pull up at Gabe's crib. Every Thursday night, he and Gemini had a date night at his place.

I thought Gemini was going to give me hell about Genesys' whereabouts, but she didn't. I was relieved when she told me where Genesys was headed and where she would be staying. As I sat on my partner's sofa, I surfed the internet for flights and a hotel. After I secured the flight, I informed them not to say a single word of my arrival in Prague. Shortly afterward, I zoomed away from Gabe's crib with a racing heart, a smile, and warm wishes from the best friends anyone could be blessed to have.

I was determined and passionate about having Genesys in my life. I wasn't going to leave that place until we were on good terms, and I wasn't aiming for us to be friends. I didn't give a damn how long it took her to realize I needed her. My ass was going to stay put. If she wanted me to uproot my life for her, I would do it without a moment's hesitation.

"Would you like anything to drink?" the petite and friendly flight attendant asked with a small smile on her face.

"Yes, a Hennesy on the rocks," I told her.

After I received my drink, I gulped it down before sighing heavily. The long-distance trip wasn't my first. I had the pleasure of visiting a few must-visit places over the world. After college, the fellas and I had a hell of time bouncing from country to country seeking the best quality of drugs. In the meantime, we explored different cultures. I must say Prague wasn't on our list. Now, I was elated to be arriving in another section of the world.

I need to get som' sleep, I thought as I opened my photo gallery.

As I stared at a picture of a sleeping Genesys, a huge smile crept across my face.

I'm on my way to you, girl.

Closing the app, I placed my phone in my lap and closed my eyes. I didn't intend to go to sleep, but my body got the best of me. When I opened my eyes again, it was because of the pilot. He was thanking the passengers for allowing him to safely bring them to their destinations.

Upon gathering my small bag, I exited the plane along with others. Eager to feel the air of the largest city in the European Union, I walked as if I was in a marathon. My time was of the essence. I couldn't wait to see the shocked expression on Genesys' beautiful face. I couldn't wait to hold her in my arms as I professed my love for her.

While catching a ride to the grandest hotel, which Genesys was staying at, I prepared a gut-wrenching speech. As I thought of it, tears formed in my eyes. What I had come up with was meant to be spoken as wedding vows. That's just how powerful they were.

"We have reached your destination, sir," the thick accented man spoke as I looked at the fare costs.

"Thank you," I replied as I paid and tipped him.

"Enjoy your time here."

"I most definitely will," I voiced, grabbing my small bag and opened the door.

Go time, I thought as I retrieved my cell phone.

While I texted my partners, I was in awe of the hotel. It reeked of elegance. I understood why Genesys chose to the establishment. The outside view was indescribable. Excitement coursed through me as I was eager to wine, dine, and enjoy Genesys in the beautiful land.

It didn't take me long to check-in and arrive inside of my luxurious room. I didn't waste any time starting on my mission. I retrieved the only outfit I brought with me before taking a shower. Upon the completion of my task, I called Genesys. My call was sent to voicemail. For thirty minutes, I called her. She wouldn't answer; therefore, I texted her. From the delivery report, I knew she read my messages.

I was close to her, and she didn't know it. I surely didn't want to tell her. I was afraid she was going to run away from me. I needed her to see me in the flesh.

Unsuccessful in hearing Genesys' voice, I threw my phone on the bed. Staring out of the window, I pondered how I was going to find her. For hours, I critically thought of the best way to bring her into my line of vision. Tired of thinking about finding Genesys, I decided to step into the beautiful night's atmosphere. While exploring the city, I was sure to bump into someone who has placed their eyes on my beauty.

An hour into roaming the short perimeter around the hotel, my stomach growled. In the proximity of a bistro with a friendly crowd, I dashed inside. My dinnertime was horrible. The food was great, but I couldn't stop thinking about Genesys and her safety. I was disappointed I hadn't found her.

In between taking bites of an exquisitely made sandwich, I dialed Genesys number several times. Like the other times I called, my calls were forwarded to voicemail.

"Gotdamn it, Genesys. Where are you?" I questioned as I eyed my waitress.

Seeing that she was needed at my table, the smiling individual sauntered towards me. In the proximity of me, I informed her I needed my meal ticket. Within a decent amount of time, she arrived with a slip. While placing it on the table, I told her to stay put until I placed money in her hand. After I had done so, I exited the bistro, praying I would bump into Genesys.

Even with all the excitement, smiling, and chatty people near me, I couldn't shake the blue emotions. It seemed as if I was the only person on the sidewalk; thus, making the walk back to the hotel a lonely one. The closer I arrived towards the hotel, the fewer people I was around.

As I crept towards a dark alley, a chill ran through my body. I had never felt anything like the unusual sensation coursing through my core. Intrigued as to why I felt the tingling sensation, I walked faster. The closer I arrived at the alleyway, the more clearly I heard soft moans. The moans weren't sexual; it was more of a pained type of sound.

Stepping closer to the bricked wall, I peeked around it.

"Please stop," a soft cry escaped from the mouth of a woman.

Heart racing, I held my breath, continued to listen, and focused where the voice had come from.

"Pleasee," the woman begged.

That's not Genesys. Go on 'bout your business, I thought as I tried focusing my eyes on the dark figures as best as possible.

Within a blink of an eye, as gurgling noises and a thud sounded, heels clinked against the cement, and the one person I was looking for stood inches away from me, wiping her mouth.

What the fuck? Genesys? I thought as I glared at the red-eyed, stunned woman I flew halfway around the world to profess my love to.

Chapter Seven

Genesys

Before I left the United States, I was angry. When I arrived in Prague, I was still infuriated and super hateful. I was nothing like the person I was when I arrived in Prague for the first time. I was no longer considered a human. I was a fucking monster thanks to the one handsome bastard who decided it was in his best interest to turn me into the same thing he was.

At first, I arrived back in Prague in hopes of freeing Adonis from my potential madness. I wanted to live my life where people didn't know me, and I didn't owe them anything. Yet, upon me stepping foot back into the known territory, I sought after Jakub. I wanted to crush his spirits, just as he had crushed mine.

While I searched high and low for the creep, my mind wouldn't rest from thinking about Adonis. The more I thought about the kind-hearted and loving man, the more I was eager to find Jakub and end his life to my best ability. Jakub had taken a lot from me. I always dreamed of being a wife and bearing my husband's children. I dreamed of the day I would be worshipped by a man who loved me more than anything in this world. Jakub stripped that from me, and I hated him for that.

It took me a while to track Jakub's family members, granted I didn't know his last name. I remembered key things he told me about himself before he turned me into a blood-sucking creature.

In a short amount of time, I was standing in front of his mother's door, inquiring about her son. The snobby look and sarcastic tone didn't sit well with me; thus, I snatched the bitch out of her home. I had no intention of bringing harm to her; yet, she brought her life to an end by being like those ratchet bitches in the States. She was cruel to me for no reason. Hateful words spilled out of her mouth. I didn't feel any remorse as I dropped Jakub's mother's deceased body on the ground.

I felt powerful as ever. My mind was settled as it seemed like every part of my body was being rejuvenated and strengthened. With a calm mind, I welcomed the sensations coursing through my full-figured core.

As I stepped into the light, my body resumed normal, well vampire normal that was. Wiping my mouth, I felt odd. As I felt that emotion, my ability to hear the thoughts of someone dear to me consumed me. My heart raced as Adonis saw me for who I was. I never wanted him to see me in my current state. I knew he wouldn't judge me, but I needed who I had become to be a secret. I wanted to bear that burden by myself.

Slowly stepping away from the bricked wall, Adonis crept towards me and softly said, "Is this the reason you cut us short?"

Nodding, I replied, "You shouldn't have come."

Approaching closer, he gazed into my eyes and sternly said, "Yes, I did. You need me now mo' than ever. Don't say a single word 'til we arrive inside of my hotel room. When we come in the comforts of those fo' walls, you will tell me what happened, who did it, an' how can I fuckin' find him."

As I nodded, he grabbed my hand and connected it between his. While walking in silence, I carefully listened to Adonis' thoughts. He was furious at the person who turned me into a vampire. He was upset that I didn't trust him enough to tell him what had happened to me. He was happy he found me and hopeful we could start a life together.

I was content with his way of thinking; yet, I had to think about him. He was human. I was going to outlive him, and I didn't like that one bit. I didn't like the fact I was going to survive everyone I loved, especially my parents. Having superhuman abilities was terrific, but it was nothing if I didn't have those I cared about partaking in the journey of my everlasting life.

When we arrived inside his hotel room, Adonis sat beside me on his bed and said, "Now, tell me everythin'."

"The last night of our family/friend vacation here, I met this guy named Jakub; no, I don't know his last name. He was handsome, intrigued with me as I was with him. We had sex. On the brink of me having an orgasm hit bit me. When I woke the next morning, I was not the same person I was when I arrived ten days prior. Upon realizing what happened, Jakub took the pleasure of telling me everything he wanted me to know. While doing so, he presented a scared hotel worker so I could drain her dry. No matter how many times I asked him why he did this to me, he never responded. Frightened out of my mind, the only thing I could do was learn how to survive as the new person I had become. I extended my stay here so I could learn about who and what I was. I needed to gather as much information I could get to rid the world of Jakub. Badly, I wanted to end the man who changed me. I didn't get the chance to end him because he disappeared before I was due back in the States from my extended vacation."

"Are you afraid you will hurt me or those you love?"

Shaking my head, I replied, "No. I have self-control over my loved ones. Now, that Hunt … that's a whole different story."

Chuckling, he replied, "Yeah, I kind of figured that. He's better now. Trust me, he is. Now, since I know 'bout you … are you still eager not to be wit' me?"

Clearing my throat, I asked, "Why weren't you afraid of me?"

"Because I know you. You are kind, sweet, an' loving. Why should I be afraid of you just because your fangs are longer than mine? I have som' skills that'll cripple you," he replied in a goofy manner.

Laughing, I said, "True, but it wouldn't cripple me if I sink my fangs into your neck, sir."

Leaning his head over, Adonis said, "Then bite me. Turn me into a vampire. I'm not afraid of you, Genesys. I'm afraid of not havin' you in my life."

Silence overcame us as I glared at him. His words were too much, which was a great thing. I couldn't tolerate how they captivated my mind, body, and soul; yet, I loved that captivation feeling. I couldn't handle not having him in my life. I didn't want to be on a journey with someone else because I was afraid of being uniquely remade.

Sensually running my nails down the side of his neck, I climbed on top of him. Turning his face to stare into mine, we gazed into each other's eyes. No amount of words could explain the way he looked at me. With tears streaming down my face, Adonis laid me on the bed, snuggling in between my thighs.

While rubbing my thick thighs, he sincerely said, "I don't care 'bout yo' superhuman ways. My human behind will always protect an' love you. There's no one I rather be wit'. No one completes me mo' than you do, Genesys. Through anything, as long as we are a team, we will be the best an' get through any obstacle placed in our way. Allow me to take som' of the burden off you. Allow me to be the man you come runnin' to after a long day of workin'. Let me be the man to sweep you off your feet 'til the last day I'm on this earth. Allow me to be the happiest an' most humble man to ever roam the world wit' billions of people livin' on it."

As my tears seeped onto the soft covers on the bed, I planted my hands on the sides of his face, nodded my head, and replied, "Okay."

"No mo' runnin', Genesys?" he questioned as he began to unbutton my denim jeans.

"Yes, Adonis, no more running," I purred as I lifted up so he could take off my bottoms and underwear.

Our breathing became heavy and erratic as we savagely took off the other's clothes. Our tongues connected with such passion, it scared me. From that moment on, Adonis and I made love, all the while making promises we weren't going to break.

"I love you, Genesys Cullman," he breathed, slow stroking my pretty kitty.

"As I love you, Adonis Villin," I moaned with an arch in my back and sweet juices cascading down his lengthy member.

Chapter Eight

Adonis

Three Months Later

"You don't suppose to be in here!" the smiling ladies within the large room of my parents' home shouted.

"Get out now!" I barked, eyeing each of the beautifully dressed women.

"Adonis Villin, you do not belong in here!" they squealed.

"If I have to say get the fuck out one mo' time, all hell is surely going to break the fuck loose! Now, get out!" I hollered sternly.

A confusion expression was written on their faces as they looked between Genesys and me.

Shaking her head and sighing sharply, she nodded her head. Soon after, the ladies left, puzzled and worried.

Sitting at the dresser, stunned and confused, Genesys shook her head and said, "I knew you were going to do this to me. I just fucking knew it. How dumb of me to think you were sincere about everything you spoke?"

I didn't say a word until the last female was out of the room.

Slowly walking towards Genesys, I held a mean poker face. In the proximity of her, I sternly said, "Stand up an' face me, Genesys."

"You don't have to say a word, Adonis. I understand," she replied, kicking off her heels.

I didn't have the time to go back and forth with Genesys about looking at me. Therefore, I roughly handled her by placing her on top of the very dresser she was hell-bent on staring at. As she looked at her trembling hands, fearing the worst, I had a wicked smile on my face.

Quickly, I shoved my face towards hers, parted her lips with my tongue, and snaked my hand underneath her gorgeous dress. Instantly, Genesys glared at me. Shortly afterward, she got with the program and reciprocated the kiss I bestowed upon her.

"Oouu," she cooed in my mouth as I worked her middle.

Unzipping my tuxedo pants, I aggressively pulled out my man. Dropping to my knees, I glared into my soon-to-be wife's face and said, "You crazy as hell to think I was comin' in her fo' anythin' other than to get a taste an' feel of you. It's been a long as week without yo' lovin' an' I couldn't wait another damn second, Genesys. I promise our weddin' will start on time. A nigga just needs a lil' quickie or som'."

Cupping her mouth, she laughed and shook her head, "Oh Adonis. You are awful. You really had me worried. Don't you ever do that shit again."

Winking, I replied, "I promise I won't do it again. You like how I blocked you from readin' my mind upon enterin', huh?"

"How in the hell did you do that?" she inquired with a raised eyebrow.

"I focused really hard. I'll teach you while we are on our honeymoon."

"Okay."

Resuming to our sexual matters, I indulged in my baby's pussy as I heard my mother inquiring about the reason for the ladies being in the hallway. I ignored everything they said as I took

my time sucking and licking on my lovely
fiancée.

"I love youuu," Genesys cooed as she rode my
face.

I spelled my name all over her goodies before I
drove my hammer into its own toolbox. I wanted
to make love to Genesys, but she wouldn't allow
it. That woman fucked me, resulting in me
blowing out her back.

"Adonniisss!" she loudly stated, causing me to
laugh.

"That's motherfuckin' me," I stated, drilling
the only pussy I ever wanted to be in.

"Oh, no wonder he got y'all in the hallway.
Well, we can go downstairs," my mother said,
inches away from the door.

"Shit, I forgot where we were," Genesys voiced
as she stopped thrusting her precious pussy on
me.

"Focus," I growled as I slowed my pace and
aimed for her G-spot.

As she did so, we glared into each other's eyes.
The sounds of wetness turned us on more. I held
my nut, which I knew was a bad idea. I never
wanted to have a quickie with Genesys. I always
wanted her to be fulfilled beyond relief.

"Even though I'm a vampire. I still ovulate. Like I'm ovulating now," she smiled wickedly.

"Really?" I voiced as I found the will to come inside of her splendid pussy.

Nodding, she moaned, "Yesss."

"In that case, let me bust so we can be on our way towards me being yo' husband."

As I sucked her bottom lip into my mouth, I served my woman extraordinary dick action until we came together. Afterward, we struggled to catch our breaths. When we did, we scrambled to get on with the show. I washed off her lady parts before I took care of my guy and brush my teeth.

Placing a loving kiss on her lips, I'll see you out there, beautiful."

Grabbing my hand, Genesys said, "I so love you, Adonis. You have no idea just how much I do."

Smiling, I replied, "Oh, I know. Come on so we can seal the deal on being partners of love fo' ever."

"Okay."

Skipping out of the room, I cleared my throat and descended the stairs of my parents' elegant home. I thought with a smile on my face; *finally, I get to have what my parents have. The one thing that's mo' precious than any riches in the world. A lovin', kind woman*

*fo' a wife. The one who's going to bear us children an'
solidify our home mo'. Finally, I get to have a happy endin'
wit' a woman who was made just fo' me.*

Yes, you do, Genesys stated before giggling.

*Woman, get out of my head. Hurry up an' get yo' fine
ass down here. I can't wait another second 'til you become
my wife.*

Okay, she giggled.

As I stepped into the sunny, beautiful day, I
had a lot to be thankful for. Not only was I
going to live a gloriously long time with Genesys,
but I was also going to enjoy having superhuman
abilities. There was no peace like the one I
found, knowing I could protect Genesys from
any and everything.

When we arrived back from Prague, Genesys
didn't hesitate to turn me into a blood-sucking
creature. I couldn't believe the rush I received as I
welcomed the heightened senses. I thought about
leaving the dope game behind but quickly
decided against it. I was good at it, and now I
would be spectacular at providing users with the
best dope they would ever encounter. The threats
made upon my illegal operation were surely going
to cease. I had an advantage over everyone; I was
able to read mines, move superfast, hypnotize
people, and so much more. I would know who

was on the fuck shit before a single clue or action was committed, and have those killed for moving against me. I would be fucking untouchable!

Within a few months, Genesys and I would be permanent residents of Prague. Upon her decision to move away, I had begun to put my lifestyle together. To keep a low profile, I had lined up a few building owners to show me a few buildings. One of those buildings would be a furniture store; another would be for Genesys to take her modeling pictures. The furniture store would be the place I would traffic my drugs out of. With the large estate I'd purchased for us to live on, there wasn't any need to have another building to make drugs. I had an entire lower level, made just for that. While I took over the drug game in Prague, my partners would have the territory we built together. We surely were going to be a force to reckon with.

As I stood at the altar patiently waiting on my beautiful soon-to-be bride, I overlooked the large estate. Family and friends had no idea what Genesys and I were, and we planned to keep it that way. We weren't going to age; thus, we decided it was best to move away. We didn't iron out many things, but we had time to figure out the small stuff—such as coming home to visit and people noticing we didn't age. In the end, we knew everything would be okay.

As the classic wedding song began to play, our guests stood and looked towards the open terrace doors. As Genesys walked down the aisle, my heart fluttered.

You are so beautiful. I've imagined this day a thousand times, an' it doesn't compare to experiencin'. I love you so much, my vampire woman, I thought, causing her to blush.

You better stop talking to me. You know I can't control certain things, Adonis, she playfully responded while continuing to strut down the aisle with her father holding onto her arm.

I'm going to strip that fuckin' dress off you the moment I get a chance. I'm sure our guests won't mind us missin' in action fo' a few minutes. I didn't get the opportunity to eat you right, I smiled.

Adonniiisss!

What?

I'm wet wet! Ayyyeeee!

As I tried to stifle my laughter, I looked at the preacher. With a raised eyebrow, I opened my mouth, but Genesys nipped it in the bud.

You better not do anything stupid, Adonis, she thought, closing in on our standing spot.

I was just going to tell him to skip a lot of the words an' get straight to the 'I do's. I smiled.

Sir, really?

As a heart attack, my vampire woman.

You better not say a word to that man, Adonis.

Stepping in front of me, I smiled and thought, *Okay.*

The music ceased. Genesys and I focused on each other. One stern look from her, I shut off the ability to read her mind as I was sure she did the same. Our vows were lovely, sweet, and warm. Genesys shed a few tears as I held mine in. Her eyes turned a light blue color, resulting in me bucking my eyes.

I'm overwhelmed, anxious, and happy, baby. I know my eye color isn't brown. Hopefully, I will be able to control my emotions. The last thing I need is for anyone to notice my eyes.

Okay, I thought as the preacher wrapped up our wedding ceremony.

"You may now kiss your bride," he announced with a smile on his face.

And I did just that. Since there were kids in the crowd, I didn't go overboard as I badly wanted to.

"I now pronounce, Mr. and Mrs. Adonis Villin," the preacher happily yelled as I scooped my wife into my arms.

Placing my mouth to her ear, I provocatively said, "Oh, how I love you, woman. You have really made me a better man. I thank you fo' that."

With a massive grin on her face, Genesys said, "As you've made me a better woman. Together we will thrive. Together we can beat any obstacle. I'm truly honored to be loved by you and having your love. Now, I need you to calm down because your eyes are orange."

"Fuck. They've been orange fo' a whole week now," I lowly said in an annoyed tone.

With a raised eyebrow, Genesys quickly laughed, "Then, we need to jump the damn broom and find the room far away from our guests. We will deal with the pictures and stuff later."

Smiling wickedly, I hollered as we jumped the broom. Our guests applauded us as they stood. Yes, entertaining our guests was highly significant, but I had to break free of them for a minute. I needed at least thirty minutes with my wife, so my eyes color would resume their natural hue.

While walking down the aisle, I turned to face my partners. I cocked my head to the right. That was the cue we needed to talk. Once we made it inside, I held tightly to Genesys' hand as I poorly looked at my guys.

Bae, if they see my eyes. They will question me. I need you to tell them to hold the fort down 'til we return.

Okay, she replied.

"Bruh, it's okay if you wanna cry," they joked.

As I laughed and avoided looking into their eyes, Genesys said, "Adonis and I need a huge favor."

"What's that?" they asked in unison.

"To cover for us. We need at least forty minutes."

Thirty minutes woman.

"Go handle the deed. This nigga here been actin' weird fo' a week. Please take that pressure off him," Hunt chuckled.

"And that I will do," she giggled.

As she squeezed my hand, I said, "I owe y'all big time."

"No, you don't, orange-eyed ass nigga," Gabe stated in a hushed tone.

Stunned, I didn't look his way.

"Boy, we are bros fo' life. You think we don't know somethin' strange is going on wit' you?

Apparently, orange eyes mean you are horny. You need to get that shit under control—all of it. When you come back from yo' honeymoon, you got shit you need to explain," Hunt softly said.

"Yep, because I want in," my partners replied in unison.

Without a moment's hesitation, I glared into their faces. Nodding, I said, "I trust y'all will keep shit quiet."

Looking at me with smirks on their faces, Hunt hollered, "Nigga if you don't get the fuck on wit' that bullshit! Look at what we do fo' a livin'. If we ain't on no fuck shit on that front, what makes you think we on som' fuck shit wit' the new show?"

As I looked at Genesys, her face was calm and serene. She nodded her head and thought, *we will talk about it later. Before you ask, I'm cool with you turning them if they want to be turned.*

Placing my eyes on my partners, I said, "The moment we step back into the States, we will discuss the new front. Genesys and I have to disappear fo' a minute."

"A'ight. We got y'all backs," they replied as we started to walk off.

As I wasn't far from them, I read their thoughts. I had a smile on my face huge than the Pacific Ocean.

"They are very loyal. They will do right by being a vampire," Genesys softly said as we arrived inside a room far away from the wedding guests.

"Yes, they will." I smiled as I unzipped my wife's wedding dress.

Naked as the day we were born, Genesys and I got it on like we never did before. Loud music boomed from the speakers outside. Thankful, my partners kicked off some entertainment; Genesys could be as loud as she wanted.

With her legs wrapped around my waist, she squealed, "Fuck me, Adonis! Fuckk meee!"

"Say no mo', my beautiful wife," I growled as I gave her the business up against the wall.

New beginnings. New places. New people. A dynasty. A bond. A love like no other. Many nights an' days of pure love an' pleasure. A reign like no other thanks to you, Genesys Villin. You are the G.O.A.T, babe, an' you always will be. I love you, woman.

As I love you, man. Now flip me over and pound this pussy and pull my hair. Slap my ass and make me weak, she sexily thought.

Bet, I thought as I did just what she demanded of me.

About the Novelist

TN Jones was born and raised in Alabama, which she resides in her home state with her daughter. Growing up, TN Jones always had a passion for reading and writing, which led her to create short stories during her teenage years.

In 2015, TN Jones began working on her first

book, *Disloyal: Revenge of a Broken Heart*, which was previously titled, *Passionate Betrayals*.

TN Jones writes in the following Urban/Interracial fictional genres: Women's/Romance, Chick Lit, Mystery/Suspense, Dark Erotica/Erotica, and Paranormal.

Published novels by TN Jones: *By Any Means: Going Against the Grain 1-2, The Sins of Love: Finessing the Enemies 1-3, Caught Up In a D-Boy's Illest Love 1-3, Choosing To Love A Lady Thug 1-4, Is This Your Man, Sis: Side Piece Chronicles, Just You and Me: A Magical Love Story, Jonesin' For A Boss Chick: A Montgomery Love Story, That Young Hood Love 1-2, Give Me What I Want, If My Walls Could Talk, A Sucka for a Thug's Love, Her Mattress Buddy, Chocolate Enchantress, I Now Pronounce You Mr. and Mrs. Thug 1-3, Disloyal 1-3, Hood Lovin': Santa Sent me a Hoodlum, Santa Sauce: A Kinky Christmas Tale, Baby Be Mine: Lovin' on My Hoodlum, Do Me Baby*, and *Barcoded Pu**y*.

Collaboration novel: Dating a Female Goon with Ms. Biggz (Paperback can be purchase via authors.)

Re-releases: If You'll Give Me Your Heart 1-3. Dates TBA.

Works in Progress by TN Jones: The Goddess of Ghosts, Soulless: An Infatuation with Love, *and* The Lost Dhampir Princess *(trilogy)*.

Thank you for reading the short story, *Genesys & Adonis: A BBW Love Story*. Please leave an honest review under the book title on Amazon and Goodreads.

For future book details, please visit any of the links below:

Amazon Author page:
https://www.amazon.com/tnjones666

Black Junction:
https://blackjunction.com/TNJones

Black Junction Fan Page:
https://blackjunction.com/novelisttnjones

Bookfam (formerly called Bookstagram): @Novelist TN Jones

Facebook:
https://www.facebook.com/novelisttnjones/

Goodreads:
https://www.goodreads.com/author/show/149 18893.TN_Jones:

Goodreads Creative Writing Blog:
bit.ly/37Sz5Po

Instagram:
https://www.instagram.com/tnjones666
Pinterest:
https://www.pinterest.com/tnjones666/
Twitter: https://twitter.com/TNJones666
Wattpad: @TNJones6
You are welcome to *email* her:
tnjones666@gmail.com
Chat with her daily in the *Facebook* group:
It's Just Me... TN Jones,
https://www.facebook.com/groups/itsjustmetnj
ones/

Did You Enjoy This Short Story?

Leaving an honest review is beneficial for me as an author. It is one of the most potent tools used as I seek attention for my books. Receiving feedback from readers will increase my chances of reaching other readers that haven't read a book by me. Word of mouth is a great way to spread the news of a book that you've enjoyed.

With that being said, once you reach this page, please scroll to the review section and leave an honest review. Be sure to click the boxes for Goodreads and Amazon. As always, thank you for taking a chance on allowing me to provide you with quality entertainment.

Peace and Blessings, Loves!

Nasir & Kenyan

A BBW Love Story

Tyanna

Synopsis

The daughter of a lieutenant, Kenyan Moore, is no stranger to the loyalty of the men in blue. On top of struggling to find the beauty in the extra pounds she handles with grace, Kenyan is trapped in an unhappy relationship with someone she doesn't want to be with. To escape the displeasure of her relationship, Kenyan finds solace in her job. Little does Kenyan know, her real escape happens the moment she becomes intrigued by Nasir.

Nasir Baker is the type of dope boy your parents warned you about—sexy and thuggish with a no tolerance attitude. After a devastating accident, Nasir becomes a clueless single-father. That is until Kenyan steps into their lives. Knowing that Kenyan is in a relationship doesn't deter him from wanting her; however, if Kenyan's father finds out about the pair, Nasir's empire could start to crumble.

Nasir has already chosen Kenyan, but will she choose his love over the acceptance of her family? Find out what happens in this short story *Big Girls Love Dope Boys...*

Chapter One

Nasir

"You always got work to do. When are you goin' to make time for me? What you gon' do when this baby gets here, Nas?" Terri bitched.

"Come on, ma... don't start. You know everything I do is for y'all. Shit, you knew what I was into when we started out. Now all the sudden you are bitching. You good when you got on them Gucci sneaks or you pushing that new 2019 Charger that's out front. So, don't start, Terri, 'cause if I wasn't able to keep you laced with the finer shit, ya ass would leave me. Go ahead and take ya hormonal ass to bed 'cause I got work to do."

"You know what, Nas... I ain't goin' to bed. I'm goin' to my mother's house. Whenever you feel like you ready to be the man I want you to be, call me."

I loved Terri, but I wasn't goin' to change who I was. Especially when this was who I'd always been from day one. All of a sudden, she was having a problem with how I ran things. I knew it wasn't nothing but her being pregnant. She became one evil ass arguing crybaby. If she wanted to go to her mama's house, that was fine with me. 'Cause if she thought I was gon' go chase her ass, she had another thing coming.

"Yo', what's wrong with Terri? I just saw her storm out of here. I spoke, but she flipped me the bird."

"Man, fuck her spoiled ass. I'll deal with her tomorrow. What kind of news you got for me?"

"That ain't nothing but that baby. I told you how Meek was when she was pregnant with CJ."

"Well, the good thing about this is we don't have long to go."

"I hear that... now let's get down to business. We have to fly out in a couple of weeks to meet with a new connect. Now I know you don't wanna go anywhere 'cause Terri almost due. So, Khalif and I are goin' to make the run for you."

"Alright, cool. 'Cause that's the last thing I need for her to trip about. She keeps threatening to leave my black ass, and at this point, I don't care. But she ain't taking my baby no damn where. Shit, I ain't no different, Cody, so I don't know what the hell her problem is. I'm hoping it's the baby like you keep saying."

"Man, I'm telling you it's the baby making her that way. After she drops that load, y'all will be back loving each other. So, just chill. Everything gon' be straight. What's good with Big Norm?"

"He good. Just keep getting on my damn nerves about how I run shit. He could have kept his empire if he gon' keep fucking with me," I snapped while Cody laughed at me.

Cody Boyd and I go way back. You might as well call us brothers. He knew everything about me and vice versa. So, when my pops, Norman Baker, known as Big Norm to the streets, passed me the throne, of course Cody was goin' to be my right hand.

"Nigga, you need a drink or something. Do you wanna go to the strip joint?"

"Nah... I'm good. I'll just go sit at my bar for a little bit."

"Ok... cool. I'll chill with you for a little bit since Meek at her mama house, anyway."

We headed out of my office and down to the little bar I had in my basement for me and my niggas to chill. I didn't play the streets too much due to who I was. Every once and a while, I'd head out to go see strippers, but not to hit up a regular bar. It was really no need for that when I had my own with top shelf liquor.

"So, what are you drinking tonight, bro?" I asked Cody before I sat at the bar.

"Let me get a double shot of Jack Daniels."

"I can't believe you drink that shit."

"Yes, you can, nigga. That's why you got it behind that bar." Cody chuckled.

"Remember we use to steal it from ya dad's bar when we were fourteen?" I laughed while shaking my head.

"Yeah, I remember. I swear I miss my old man so much."

"Yeah, I miss him too. How's the bar goin'?"

"It's doing good. Money still rolling in. You know everybody respects that old place just like they did my pops."

I poured me a double shot of Henny as Cody and I went down memory lane for a little while. Then my phone rang bringing me out of my thoughts.

"Hello, Ms. Patrice. What's goin' on?"

"Nas, get to Cooper Hospital now. Terri was in a car accident. I'm on my way there now."

"Ok... I'm on my way right now. Come on, Cody. Let's go. Something happened with Terri."

We both jumped up so fast and ran out the door. I didn't know what the fuck happened or if her and my seed was ok, but my mind was all over the fucking place. Cody told me to hop in his truck and he would drive. I was glad 'cause I was too fucked up to be driving.

After Cody broke every traffic violation I could think of, we were now pulling up to the hospital. I jumped right out before he even parked good. I ran straight into the emergency room. Ms. Patrice was standing there pacing the floor. I ran over to her to see what happened.

"How is she? Where is she?" I started raddling off questions.

"They had her in surgery, Nas... They had to hurry and get the baby out 'cause her heart rate was dropping. Then Terri had to go back into surgery. She was on the phone with me when she got into the accident. I kept telling her to hang the phone up, but she wouldn't listen." Ms. Patrice cried while I pulled her in for a hug.

"Everything is goin' to be ok. Can we go up to check on my baby while we wait for Terri to get out of surgery?"

"Yes... they said we can go right up to labor and delivery when you got here."

I grabbed Ms. Patrice's hand and we headed to the elevator. "Why she come to this hospital?"

"They said we needed to come here 'cause they have the best trauma unit. It's not sounding good for Terri, Nas."

"Ms. Patrice, don't talk like that. She's goin' to be fine."

Once we made it off the elevator, I ran right up to the desk and explained to them what had happen. They knew exactly which baby I was here for.

"Hello, I'm Nurse Moore. I'll be the nurse taking care of your little princess while she's here. She's fine, but she's not out of danger yet 'cause of her being born early. She will have to stay here until she reaches her birth weight and starts eating on her own."

"Ok... well, can I go see her?"

"Yes, you may. Just follow me."

When we made it to the window where she was, I looked in at her, and she was hooked up to all these different tubes. She was so fucking small. "She's extremely small. How much does she weigh?" I asked in a sad tone.

"She's 2 pounds and three ounces, but she's a little fighter."

The sadness in my heart wouldn't keep the tears from falling. I felt like shit 'cause the only reason she left the house was 'cause she was mad at me. I looked around to see if Ms. Patrice was still standing next to me, but she was talking to a doctor down the hall. So, I headed that way to see if there was any news on Terri. Right before I made it down to her, she let out a gut-wrenching scream, which caused me to run up to her. She fell to the floor, and I had to help her up.

"She's gone, Nas. My baby is gone."

I snatched away from her and jumped up so fast. "What the fuck are you talking about? She is not gone... stop lying! She is not gone!" I barked, causing the doctor to nearly jump out of his pants.

"Come on, bro. Calm down," Cody said while walking off the elevator.

"Don't tell me to calm down! What the fuck did y'all do to her?! Why didn't y'all save her?! We have a baby to take care of! My daughter need's her mama, Cody!"

I broke down and cried like a little bitch in my boys' arms. This was some devastating shit; my girl was gone, and my baby girl was hooked up to all these tubes and shit. How the fuck was I goin' to make it raising her alone?

Chapter Two

Kenyan

Today was a long and sad day for me at work. I usually did a double, but after the sad shit I saw today, I just couldn't do it. To see a man cry was some deep shit for me. Especially when it was Nasir Baker himself. I didn't know him personally, but I knew of him from my best friend, Mysti. She knew all the big-time niggas in the city. I actually only saw him a couple of times at the club, but he was so sexy that he was one of them dope boys you'd never forget.

"What the hell you sitting there thinking about? I thought you were doing a double?"

"Jerome, don't come in here bothering me, please?"

I couldn't stand his ass. I hated that I was engaged to his stupid ass. I used to have some love for him, which was why I agreed to marry him, but now I was unhappy. He did nothing but talk shit and put me down about my weight.

"Ain't nobody bothering you. I just asked you a question. Since ya ass ain't doing a double, why I don't smell no food cooking?"

"You don't smell no food cooking 'cause you didn't start cooking yet," I snapped while rolling my eyes.

"Whatever, Kenyan, but I bet ya fat ass ate something already."

"Nigga, fuck you!" I fussed and stormed off to my bedroom.

While I was on my way to my bedroom, my phone rung. I looked down and saw that it was Mysti calling.

"Hey, suga! What are you doing?" she greeted.

"Nothing. Just got home not too long ago and already got into an argument with Rome's sorry ass. I'm so sick of him."

"I know you are, and that's why you need to stand up to your daddy and tell him that you ain't beat for ole' shrimp dick."

"Not shrimp dick, Mysti. I ain't about to play with you tonight." I laughed while shaking my head.

"Yup... and I only know that 'cause you told me. I can't wait until you go out there and find you some good Mandingo so you'll definitely leave his fucking rent-a-cop ass alone."

My stomach was hurting laughing at Mysti. My best friend hated Jerome with a passion, and vice versa. But they kept it cordial for the sake of me.

"Girl you so stupid. What did you call for, anyway?"

"I wanted to head out for a little bit. Are you down?"

"Shit...why not? I ain't doing shit, and I don't have to be to work until eleven tomorrow. Where you tryna go?"

"I wanna shoot over Philly to the Clock Bar. I need me a seafood platter and a Cîroc punch. You don't drink when you gotta work the next day, so you can be my designated driver."

"Ok, cool. Give me an hour to get ready. What you wearing tonight? 'Cause I ain't tryin' to be over or under dressed."

"Some jeans, a brown V-neck t-shirt, a crop jean jacket, and my Louis Vuitton flats. Just simple tonight. I don't feel like being extra."

"Good 'cause if you were in one of your extra moods, I wasn't beat."

"Be quiet, hoe, and hurry up! I'll be there in a half-hour."

I looked at my phone and saw the hoe had hung up. I shook my head and jumped off my bed, then headed to get myself together. Deciding on a white graphic tee with red lips on the front that said *Flawless,* a pair of ripped white jeans, and a pair of high-top Vans, I was satisfied with the look I chose.

After taking care of my hygiene and applying a little makeup, I slipped on my clothes. My hair was still on point being as though I'd just gotten it done a couple of days ago.

"Where the fuck you think you goin'."

"Out… now move out of my way, please?"

Rome grabbed my chin and squeezed it as tight as he could. I really wasn't beat for his shit today, but I knew if I resisted I would never get out of here.

"Keep playing with me, Ken, and one of these days, I'mma fuck you clean up. You think shits a game all the time."

"Nobody is playing with you. I told you I was goin' out. Mysti will be here to get me in a couple of minutes."

Rome let my face go then walked off. I couldn't stand his simple ass.

I grabbed my bag and phone, then headed out of the door. The minute I walked out, Mysti was just pulling up.

"You riding with me, or are you driving?" she asked.

"I'm riding with you. I need to drink my ass off tonight."

"Bitch…you don't even drink like that."

"I know, but I am tonight."

"Lil' ugly must dun' pissed you off."

I didn't say a word. I just jumped in the passenger seat and waited for her to pull off. Before she had the chance to do so, Rome was standing at the window of the car.

"Make sure you bring ya ass home at a decent hour."

"Nigga, bye! She grown as hell!" Mysti snapped.

"Mind ya business, hoe."

"Nigga, she is my business, and has been since before ya time. Now beat it… don't you have to play cops and robbers?"

Rome mean mugged Mysti then walked away. I wasn't goin' to let them two ruin my night. So, I didn't bother to say anything, and I was praying she didn't bring it up. I knew that prayer was un answered 'cause Mysti just couldn't leave shit alone when it came to Rome. I knew she hated him, but damn did they have to keep the argument goin' all the time?

"I can't wait until you see the day that nigga ain't worth shit." She sucked her teeth and rolled her eyes.

I didn't say shit, though. I just turned the music up and began to bop my head. Me turning the music up must have pissed her off 'cause she peeled off driving like she had no sense. I couldn't do nothing but roll my eyes. *She better hope we don't get pulled over,* was what I was saying to myself. Welp… that thought went out of the window when I saw those flashing lights in the rearview. Mysti pulled over and rolled the window down. I knew by the look on her face that she was about to give this cop word for word.

"License and registration, please?"

I looked up and saw that it was one of Rome's dick head ass boys, Officer Davis. He looked at me and smiled. I couldn't even be mad 'cause it wasn't like Mysti wasn't speeding.

"Here you go, officer. Everything is straight. Just give me my damn speeding ticket and let me be on my way."

"Ms. Lewis, let me run your name, and I'll be back."

I wondered what was really goin' on 'cause when one of my daddy's or Rome's cop buddies saw me in the car, they would warn us and let us go our way. Something just didn't seem right to me.

"Ms. Lewis, I'mma need you to get out of the car. I have it in my system that there is a warrant out for your arrest for unpaid speeding tickets."

"That's a fucking lie unless someone has been using my name. I don't play about my license. If anything is fucked up, I fix it right away."

"Come on, Officer Davis. You know my dad and Rome. They'll handle this. Just let me give them a call."

"Sorry, Kenyan. Can't let you out of this one. I was given strict orders to bring her in. If you want, you can follow us to the station in her car."

"Ain't no 'I can follow y'all.' I was doing that anyway."

Mysti stepped out of the car. He placed the handcuffs on her, then placed her in the back of the squad car. I didn't wanna bother my daddy with this 'cause Mysti *was* speeding. So, I decided to give Rome a call. I wasn't feeling him at the moment, and I knew he hated Mysti, but it didn't hurt to give it a try. Of course, he didn't answer. I banged my hand on the steering wheel in anger right before starting up the engine and following behind the cop car.

Chapter Three

Rome

"Thanks, bro. I owe you one. I'll be there in a half-hour," I assured Davis.

"No problem. You know I got you," was the last thing he said before we disconnected our phone call.

Kenyan and her side kick thought they were goin' out. Not if I had anything to do with it. Ken knew how I felt about her hanging with Mysti's hoe ass. I knew all about her, and the last thing I wanted was my fiancé to be hanging with her. Not only that, but Mysti was bad as fuck, and I knew she drew a lot of attention. Lately she been having Kenyan change her whole appearance as far as makeup, weave, and certain clothing. It took me a minute to make Kenyan think no one would want her cause of her size. But Mysti changed that shit completely. I still say shit to her to try and fuck up her self-esteem, but lately she'd been givin' me a fucked-up attitude.

A half-hour went by, and I was pulling up to the police station. Kenyan tried to call me a couple of times, but I sent her ass straight to voicemail. I jumped out of my truck and headed straight inside of the police station.

"Yo', Officer Myers. They just took your fiancé to the back."

"I know. That's why I'm here."

Bob's ass was so fucking nosey. I swear that's why they kept his ass at the desk up front. He didn't miss anything coming in or going out. When I walked in, Kenyan was sitting in the chair looking at me like she had an attitude.

"I been calling you like crazy. Your friend locked Mysti up. He knew damn well he could have let her go like they always do," she fussed.

I walked over to her and sat close to making sure no one heard me. "You should have stayed ya ass in the house today and you wouldn't have to worry about this shit," I snapped.

"What you want me to do with Ms. Lewis?" Davis asked.

"You can cut her loose, and ain't no need to do no report." I stood up and pulled Kenyan's arm signaling her to bring her ass along. She tried to snatch away from me, but I gave her the look letting her know not to fuck with me.

"Rome, I need to talk to Mysti and make sure she gets to her car safe."

"She'll be fine. The officer will walk her to her car. Now let's go. I'm sure you don't wanna make a scene in here. You know you don't want the lieutenant to hear about this, now do you? Plus, I'm sure she gon' call or text you as soon as she gets in the house."

Kenyan snatched away and stormed off, but I didn't give a damn about her attitude, and, of course, I didn't give a shit. I wanted her night to be ruined, and I did just that. Now that my mission was accomplished, I was gon' go home and sleep good tonight.

Once I made it to the car, Kenyan was standing there waiting for me to open the door. I opened it and made sure she was straight before I closed it. I hopped in the driver's seat and turned to her before I started the car up. "Are you gon' keep this attitude for the rest of the night?"

"Rome, I know good and damn well that you had everything to do with this. I just can't believe you'd stoop this fucking low just to make sure I didn't go out tonight. What is your problem?

Why don't you ever want me to go out? All I do is work and take care of home. Why can't I go out and enjoy myself sometimes?"

"I don't mind you going out at all. I just don't want you out with her, and I didn't have shit to do with y'all getting pulled over. You should tell your best friend to stop speeding then she would be good."

"Yeah right, Rome. This had you written all over it, and I don't know why you always think negative about Mysti. She's not what you think she is. I don't know where you get your information from, but we've been friends way before you and I even started out. She's my best friend, Rome, and if you're going to be my husband, y'all need to keep it cordial."

"I'll try, but only 'cause I love ya spoiled ass. Now give me a kiss." I leaned over and kissed her, and to my surprise she returned the favor. I smiled at her then started the car up and peeled off. I lied to her about trying with the Mysti situation. I didn't want her hanging with her, and I meant what I said.

We were now home, and Kenyan had showered and taken her mad ass to bed. I decided to head in my office for a second to look through some of my paper work I had on an upcoming case. I was shocked that Kenyan's dad put in a good word for me to get this case. I wish the old fart retired from the force. He swore he ran shit and it pissed me off. But his name did ring bells, and I'd been needing him to keep my name on top. Which was why I even considered dealing with his daughter. Don't get me wrong, I loved Kenyan, but she wasn't what I was used to messing with.

My phone vibrating on my desk brought me out of my thoughts. I looked down at it and when I saw who it was, I started to shake my head. She knew better then to text me when I was in the crib with Kenyan.

Detective: *What you did today was foul.*

Me: *You know not to contact me when I'm in my crib.*

I guess she got the picture 'cause she didn't respond back. After looking through a couple more files, I headed to shower and climbed in the bed with Kenyan.

Chapter Four
Nasir

It had been exactly a week since everything went down with Terri. I had already taken care of the funeral arrangements. Her mother only wanted a small private ceremony, and I gave her exactly what she wanted. I had been up to the hospital all day, every day since the accident happened. I finally was able to name my baby, so we decided on Treasure Monae' Baker. Treasure had some complications due to her being born a little early. So, she needed to be here just a little while longer. She was just now starting to drink out of the bottle, so now they could remove the tube that they were feeding her through. They didn't wanna remove it right away in case she started not eating again. But I knew my baby girl was a trooper, and she would continue to eat from her bottle.

"Hello, Mr. Baker. How are you today?"

"Hello, Nurse Moore, right?"

"Yes, you're right. I see little lady is drinking from the bottle."

"Yes, she is, and I'm so proud of her."

"Your daughter seems to be doing well with in this short time. If she keeps eating, when she reaches the date of her actual due date, she will be released. They usually want baby's to be at least five pounds before they allow them to go home. If you don't mind me asking. Will you be able to handle a new born baby?"

"I know it's going to be a hard job, but she's my world, and I will do anything for her. Even if I have to die doing it."

"Well, when she is released, I'll give you my number, so you can keep me updated on her progress."

"No problem. . . I'll make sure you give it to me. So, her actual birth date is in two months. She really has to stay here that long?"

"I mean, if she reaches her weight and everything else is good, she will be able to go before then."

"Oh ok...I just can't wait until I get her home inside of her nursery. I have been chilling in there sitting in the rocking chair, when I'm at home. Terri and I did her nursery together a week before the accident," I said in a low tone.

"Mr. Baker, everything is going to be ok. Little Miss Treasure is going to help you get through the hard days," Nurse Moore assured me.

Shit had been going crazy, and I couldn't help but to blame myself for what happened to Terri. If it wasn't for us arguing, she would have never left out the house in anger. She drove me crazy with her spoiled ways, but I had mad love for her.

"Yo', bro, what's good with you? How's my niece doing?" Cody walked up bringing me out of my thoughts.

"What's good, bro?" I asked while pulling him in for a one-arm hug.

"She good. My princess is drinking from the bottle, finally. So, soon, they can take the feeding tube out. When she reaches her normal birth weight she can get out of here."

"That's what's up."

"Oh, my bad...Ms. Moore, this is Cody. Cody, this is Treasure's Nurse."

"You're fine, Mr. Baker. I was just leaving to go on break. I just wanted to check on Treasure. I'll be back by once my lunch is over. Nice to meet you, Cody."

"Nice to meet you, ma," Cody said, walking away.

"So, what's been going on? How was the trip? Did you and Khalif handle everything?" I asked Cody.

"Yeah, you know I got you. Hell, I didn't even wanna go, but Meek was on my ass telling me how much you needed me to handle the business. So, I sucked it up and took my ass out of town."

"I swear I love my sis. How's my nephew doing?"

"His terrible-two ass is doing good. Oh, and Meek brought Treasure all this shit. I'mma take it by the house later. Has Big Norm been up here?"

"Yeah...you know he hates hospitals, but Ms. Crystal made him bring his ass up here."

"Ms. C be on Norm's ass, and he do whatever she says." Cody chuckled.

Ms. Crystal was my pop's wife. I never thought I would except him with anyone after my mama passed, but Ms. C came in and stole his heart and took care of me like I was her own. For that, she'd always be good with me.

"You already know how that goes. How's Ms. Patrice holding up?"

"Man, she's fucked up. I was talking to her this morning. I've been trying to convince her to come up here to see Treasure, but she won't. She says it's going to make her think about Terri. I feel so bad bro. If it wasn't for me, none of this shit would have happened."

"Come on, bro...don't do that shit. You can't blame a fucking car accident on yourself. I know y'all were arguing, but it still isn't your fault."

I wasn't trying to hear Cody right now. I was going to always feel like I played a part in Terri's death.

"Mr. Baker, Treasure has been fed and changed. Do you wanna come back in and do your bonding time with her?" one of the nurses asked.

"Yeah. Give me a couple of minutes and I'll be right back in."

"Alright, take your time."

"These nurses are fine as shit, and they look young as fuck. That nurse Moore is the cutest one, even though she a little chunky," Cody said, causing me to laugh.

"Nigga, you ain't right. Let me get back in here and feed my shawty. I'll hit you up later on. I'm thinking about going home to get some rest. Then again, I don't wanna leave my baby here."

"I feel that. Well, just hit me when you get comfortable. I'mma go check on ya crib and drop Treasure's stuff off."

"Ok, cool, bro, and tell sis I said thanks for all she does for the baby."

"You know it's no thanks needed. We always got little mama."

After dapping Cody up, I headed back in the room to hold my baby. Looking at her put me in a different mindset. All I wanted to do was raise her and be happy.

Chapter Five
Kenyan

I hadn't talked to Mysti since Rome did that bullshit. I didn't understand why, though, since we talked all the time. I hoped her simple ass wasn't mad at me when I didn't have shit to do with what went down. If she wasn't speeding, we wouldn't have gotten pulled over. I had gotten off work early today, so I decided to pop up on her ass. After parking my car, I jumped out and made my way up the steps of Mysti's townhouse. I banged on the door about four times before she even answered it.

"What are you doing here, Kenyan?" Mysti said dryly as she walked away from the door.

"Well, damn, hoe. It took you long enough to open the damn door."

"Look, I don't feel like arguing with you. What the hell do you want?"

"What the fuck is wrong with you? I just came over here to check on you since you haven't been answering my phone calls."

"Oh, so today you wanna be a friend and make sure I'm good? The other night you just left my ass there and left with that asshole fiancé of yours."

"Come on, Mysti. Don't be like that. I asked Davis to make sure you got to your car safe. Besides if you weren't speeding, we wouldn't even had been in that situation," I said while rolling my eyes.

"Yeah, whatever, Kenyan. Go ahead home with ya punk ass fiancé 'cause I'm really not beat for any company."

Mysti didn't have to tell me twice. I got my big ass up and made my way out of her house. She always got in her moods like this, and today I wasn't feeling it. I just wanted to make sure she was good since she wasn't paying me any fucking mind. I just hopped in my car and peeled off.

Since I knew today was my daddy's on-call day, I decided to go pay him a visit. A half-hour went by, and I was now pulling up in my parents' driveway. I was a straight up daddy's girl. Me and my mama were cool, but my daddy was who I always stayed attached to. I hurried and parked my car and made my way into the house that I grew up in.

"Daddy and Mama, where y'all at?!" I yelled, walking in the door.

"Girl, what the hell I tell you about yelling in my damn house?" my mama snapped.

"Darlene, leave my baby alone. We in the kitchen, Princess." My daddy beamed while calling me one of his many pet names.

"Sorry, Mama," I said while walking right past her and heading over to hug and kiss my daddy. Once I was finished acknowledging him, I made my way back over to hug and kiss my mama.

"Don't bring ya spoiled ass over here and hug me now," she sassed.

"Darlene, there you go with that ole' jealous shit."

"Keenan, shut the hell up before you be cooking ya own damn dinner tonight. Better yet, ya Princess could cook it for you," my mama fussed while my daddy chuckled.

"If I wanted my Princess to cook, she would do it."

"Mama, cut it out. You know I love you and daddy the same way," I lied.

"Yeah, whatever...child, tell me anything."

"So, what brings you by, baby?"

"Oh…nothing really. I just knew today was your on-call day. I figured I'd stop by to see what y'all old people doing. Mama, what you cooking for dinner?" I asked, being nosey.

"Fried chicken, garlic mashed potatoes, string beans and smoked turkey butts, and honey butter biscuits. Why, you staying for dinner?"

"Yeah, I guess I could do that. Let me call Rome so he can come over here when he gets off. 'Cause I won't be cooking if I'm eating here."

"What if your fiancé wants to go home after work?"

"He can if he wants to, Mama, but I'm still going to let him know that I'm eating dinner here. If he doesn't wanna come, then he doesn't have to," I said while rolling my eyes.

"I don't know how you gon' keep that man happy when y'all get married if you can't do it while y'all engaged."

I hated when my mama started her shit. Everybody didn't have to be the way she was with my daddy. I wished she would just understand that my relationship was really none of her damn business. Sometimes I be feeling like telling her that shit, but I know my dad would have a fit if I did that.

"Darlene, leave her alone. I don't know why you stay in their relationship. Worry about keeping ya own man happy," my daddy snapped while leaving out the kitchen.

I followed right behind him not wanting to hear my mama fuss.

"Don't mind ya mama, sweetheart. You know how she is."

"Yeah, I know. That's why I wasn't paying her any mind."

"How's Mysti doing? I heard about y'all the other night."

I knew Bob's big ass mouth wasn't going to stay shut. I swear his fat ass gets on my damn nerves. That was exactly why they kept him sitting up front. He didn't miss a beat.

"She's fine, but right now she has an attitude with me. You already know how she is, with her stubborn ass. This time she mad at me for something stupid, and I refuse to entertain her foolishness."

My daddy looked at me and started laughing. "You two still go at it like when y'all were younger. She'll come around. You both get like that every now and then. Tell her little ass she better stop speeding before I tell them to stop calling in favors."

"Ok, Daddy. I'll deliver the message when she starts talking to me again."

"So, how's work been going?"

"It's been fine. Right now I have a little baby whose mother died in a car accident, and they had to deliver her via an emergency c-section. I think I'm starting to get close to her." I looked at my daddy with sad eyes.

"Kenyan, baby...I've told you before to switch floors. Why do you continue to put yourself through this?" my daddy scolded me.

"Daddy...I promise you I'm fine. I enjoy working with babies."

Years ago, I was told I couldn't have any babies, and my parents always tried to talk me out of working on the maternity wing at the hospital. Some days it bothered me, but other days I enjoyed taking care of the precious bundles of joy.

"Alright, baby. I'mma take your word for it now. I need you to promise me that if it starts to bother you, you'll change floors."

"Ok, Daddy. Bet."

I agreed with what he was saying. My daddy and I continued to chill and talk some more until dinner was ready.

Chapter Six
Rome

Last night, Kenyan and I had dinner with her parents. They were great people, but I just wasn't happy with their daughter. I pretended the best way I knew how to get where I was in the department. Now I was about to crack one of the biggest cases in the city, and after that, I would be done with this fake ass shit.

"Hey, Jerome. Are you ready for this briefing?" Lieutenant Moore asked while walking over to my desk.

"Of course. I've been ready for this." I got up and walked into the conference room.

"Alright, people...this has been an on-going case for many years. We have not been able to take Big Norm down. Word on the street is that Nasir Baker is now the man in charge, with his right-hand, Cody Boyd, by his side. They also have Khalif Reynolds on board. These three young men run with each other just like their old men used too. Clancy, who is Cody's father, is deceased. He lost his life in a bar brawl a couple years back. Kyle, Khalif's pops, is doing Fed time, and Norm is chilling while his youngin' runs the throne." Moore did the break down and everyone was just listening.

"Well, if we have one in custody doing ballpark numbers, why we can't offer him something to talk?" I asked.

"Man...they don't snitch on each other. That's how they were able to hang so strong for many years," Dale said.

"Yeah, Dale is right. Numerous people dun' tried to cut Kyle a deal. I even went up there to try and work my magic, but he wasn't trying to hear that shit. So, since we couldn't take their asses down, we gon' take their boys down. Alright, for this case, I'm going to pair certain people together. You may not like who your partner is, but I'mma need y'all to make it work. This case is something big for this department. It also will look good for everyone who's involved. Jerome, I'mma need you with Dale. Carlos, I'mma need you with Tom.

"In the folder that sits in front of y'all, it will tell you what all you need to do. I also placed pictures in there of everyone. It seems they keep their families tucked away tight. So, we don't know who their mates are. The minute you find anything out, keep me posted. This all starts tomorrow, so go on home and get a good night's rest. Cater to your wife and kids 'cause y'all getting ready to have some late nights until this case is closed."

Once Moore got finished with briefing, I ran my ass up out of there. I hated that he put me with Dale, but fuck it. We were going to put in this work. I jumped up and grabbed my folder and headed out of the room. Dale jumped up and began to follow me.

"Yo', bro, what time we getting on this tomorrow?"

"I'll hit you in the morning," I said while walking in a fast motion.

I could tell this shit was going to get on my nerves, but I couldn't really let it get in the way. I needed this job to get done the right way since my future was based on it. I didn't feel like heading home, so I hit up a friend of mine and told her I was on my way. I wanted my dick sucked and my balls licked, and nobody did that shit better then Shonna's nasty ass. She was one of my little shawties I fucked with from time to time.

After I shot her a text and told her I was on my way, I peeled off and sped down the highway. Once I made it in the front of her crib, I noticed there was two cars in her driveway. I looked down at my phone and noticed she never texted back. I hopped out my whip and pulled my gun out of my holster. I dun' told this bitch many times before if she wanted company, make that nigga take her to the motel.

When I made it on the porch, I grabbed the brick that sat on the side of her step and broke the glass. Then I slid my arm through to unlock the door. Either they were in here sleeping, or fucking, but I didn't give a fuck. These bitches never listened to shit. I made my way into the house, and just as I suspected, this bitch's moans and screams could be heard from upstairs. I walked up the steps and stood in the door way of her bedroom for a couple of minutes watching her getting her back blown out. I laughed right before I walked into the room and put a bullet right in that nigga's head.

All that could be heard were her cries and screams, but I didn't give a fuck. I walked closer to her and grabbed a handful of her hair. I wanted her to look directly into my eyes while I said what I said.

"I told you I didn't want nobody in here, and you seem to test my gangster. If you ever pull some shit like this again, the same thing will happen. Only, *you'll* be pulling the trigger. Now get the fuck up and go shower while I come up with a plan. I'mma call this shit in as soon as you get dressed. I'mma need you to act like you just came back from the store or something. You gon' call it in, and I'mma act like I was in the area. If you fuck this up, you'll be next."

Shonna did as she was told and made her way to the bathroom. I wiped everything down that I may have come in contact with, which wasn't much. Then I walked to the bathroom to make sure Shonna was good. She was staring off in to space like I had fucked her head up. Maybe I over reacted, but somebody needed to let these bitches know who was in charge.

"You good, ma?" I asked.

"Why did you have to do that, Rome?"

"Why don't you fucking listen, Shonna? If I'mma be breaking you off and paying bills in this muthafucka, shouldn't nobody come in here but me. I didn't say you couldn't fuck that nigga, but you shouldn't have fucked him here."

Shit, I wouldn't say my bitches couldn't deal with other people 'cause, hell, I had a whole fiancé at home. All I asked them was to respect me. Now besides Kenyan, Shonna was the only one that really got my money.

"I know, and I'm sorry, but you still didn't have to kill him, Rome."

I walked in front of her and pulled her face to mine and kissed her lips passionately. Once we finished kissing, I slapped her ass and pulled away.

"Well, now you know I ain't playing. Now hurry up and get dressed so we can get this over with. I came over here to get my dick sucked, and you over here on some other shit," I said while leaving out of the bathroom.

Twenty minutes later, she came out of the bathroom fully dressed. I gave her the phone, and she called the police station and put on a whole act. I hurried and walked out to my car, picked up the walkie, and told the dispatcher I was in the area. After that, I walked into the house and made my way upstairs to where the incident took place. I then called for backup and waited until they arrived. Shonna was putting on a great seen crying and everything while falling to the floor. The sirens were heard, and I knew back up was on the way.

"Make sure you keep that same energy when them other cops come in here. Remember you ran to the super market to get something to cook for him while he slept, and you walked into this."

I briefed her real quick right before a couple of police officers walked in. After this shit, I was taking my ass home to my fiancé. All this bullshit, and all I wanted was my dick sucked.

Chapter Seven

Cody

"Baby, how is Nas holding up?" Meeka asked while walking into our bedroom.

"He fucked up, but he maintaining. He told me to tell you thanks for the stuff you brought Treasure."

"Tell him I said no problem. We got his back, always. I wanted to talk to you about something."

"What's good, beautiful? You know you can talk to me about anything."

"I have a life insurance policy, and I wanted you to know that you and CJ are the beneficiaries."

"Meek, what the hell are you talking about?"

"I'm just saying, Cody, if something was to happen to me, I want to leave y'all with something. See, you have money, so in the event that something happens to you, me and the baby will be good."

"Meek, ain't shit going to happen to neither one of us, so end of discussion," I snapped, not meaning to. But I knew I didn't wanna talk to her about this crazy shit. If something was to happen to her, I would be fucked up out here. Shit, I feel like Nas taking this shit really well.

Meek climbing on my lap brought me out of my thoughts. She grabbed my face and looked into my eyes with a serious look on her face. "I'm sorry. I didn't mean to get you all upset, but the shit that happened to Terri got me thinking ahead, baby. I'll leave it alone for now, but I'mma bring it up again later. You should still get one too 'cause God forbid if something happens to you street wise. They been dun' took everything, and CJ and I will be left with nothing. Ok…now I'm done with it until next time. I see ya face getting red." Meek laughed and pulled me in for a kiss.

Meek and I go way back. Other than Nas, she'd been my best friend from day one. We'd been in this shit forever. I fucked up a couple of times along the way, but today I valued her and my son and would never do anything to mess up our relationship. Which is why I planned on asking her to marry me on her birthday this year. I thought it would be a perfect time since Nas and I were talking about cleaning this street money up. I mean, I was a street nigga at heart, but it didn't hurt to invest some of this big money we making.

"Girl, don't be kissing me like that. You know CJ still up, and you can't handle this right now," I said while pushing her center down on my hard ass dick.

Meek looked at me and smiled. "I got you all night long, though. Don't even worry," she said while getting up off of me and making sure to wink right before she walked out of the room.

My phone started to vibrate on my night stand. I picked it up and saw that it was Khalif.

"Yo', Kha, what's good, bro?"

"Nothing much, my boy. I wanted to know how Nas was doing. I didn't wanna bother him. I wasn't sure if he was up at the hospital with princess."

"He ok…that nigga holding up better than I would be if it happened to Meek."

"Shit, I feel you, man, 'cause if some shit happened to Lee-Lee, I would lose my fucking mind out here. I would be looking for the car she hit and everything. You know I ain't wrapped too tight."

"Hell, you and Lee-Lee ain't wrapped too tight." I chuckled.

Him and his girl were crazy as fuck, but they were a part of the family. His girl, Charlee, and Meeka were cool as fuck. They tried getting along with Terri when she was living, but she was to bougie for our girls. We had bosses. They were actually female versions of us when it came to this street shit. I mean, we didn't let them in the street shit, but they could run this shit if need be.

"Nigga, I'm the only one that could call my bitch crazy."

"My bad, but you know I was only telling the truth."

"Yeah, whatever...I'm gon' come around tomorrow so we can discuss business. Norm hit me up last night, and I told him we had shit under control. Nas better get his pops before I beat his old ass. He always coming at me wrong. I told him he lucky my pops was locked down. 'Cause if he was out, I would get him to fuck him up like he used to."

"Now you know how Norm be acting. He doesn't mean shit by it."

"Yeah, I know, but he needs to remember we learned from the best. Shit, I ain't trying to fuck shit up. I need all my bank."

"You and me both, but check this. Meek was thinking of doing something at Nas crib when he brings little mama home from the hospital."

"Alright. You know I'm down with whatever. Just keep me posted. And Lee-Lee could decorate, so tell Meek to get at her."

"Oh, and, yeah, I'mma need to discuss some numbers with Lee for our wedding. I'm thinking about popping the question on Meek's birthday."

"That's what's up, bro. I'm happy for y'all."

"Yeah, I feel like it's about that time. I ain't going nowhere and neither is she, so we might as well make it happen."

"I feel you, but let me go. Lee-Lee's dumb ass coming in here hollering. I'll stop by tomorrow so we can really get into details about work."

I hung the phone up and headed to see where my family was. I made my way to the kitchen, and CJ was in his highchair eating some fruit while Meek was at the stove cooking.

"What you in here cooking?"

"Jerk salmon alfredo, tossed salad, and garlic bread."

"That sound so good, baby," I said, walking up behind Meek and wrapping my arms around her waist.

"It is good. Wait 'til you taste it. Who were you on the phone with?"

"Khalif hit me up checking on Nas and complaining about Big Norm."

"What Norm old ass doing now? I don't understand why he agreed to let y'all take over, but he always gotta be in the business. They raised y'all up in this shit, so y'all got it."

"I think he just worried because of all the shit Nas is going through right now. I'mma go talk to him tomorrow. I need him to know that we got shit covered."

✧✧✧✧✧✧

A couple days had went by since I talked to Khalif, and I was finally able to meet up with Big Norm. Usually, I would have let Nas know that I was visiting his pops, but I didn't wanna bother him when it really wasn't nothing wrong. I just wanted Norm to know that we were taught by the best. Khalif and I were doing our best running shit while Nas was down.

"Hello, baby. How you been?" Ms. C asked while walking into the living room.

"I'm good, Ms. Crystal. How about yourself?" I asked while standing to pull her in for a hug.

"You know I'm great, baby. Norm said come on back to his office."

After hugging and kissing her on the cheek, I made my way into the office.

"Hey, there, youngin'." Big Norm got up from his seat the minute I walked in. He walked over to me and pulled me in for a one-arm hug.

"What's good, OG?" I asked.

"Nothing much. Just been relaxing and enjoying my retirement. How about you? What brings you here?"

"I came to sit and have a talk with you. I just wanted you to know that we got this. Y'all taught us well. Nas is going through a lot and for you to worry him about what we got going on is not cool. You, my pops, and Unc had shit popping. Just sit back and chill with ya wife. We got this."

Big Norm didn't say shit. He just sat down in the chair and stared at me for a second before he spoke. I knew he wasn't feeling the way I just told him to chill, but we really had this thing straight.

"I'm not doubting that y'all got this, but I heard that the police have been cracking down in areas near here. So, I know that they making their rounds. One specific detective has been coming at my neck for years, and he knows I've been out of the game for some time now. So, I know he's going to be gunning for my boy. Nasir's head is not in the game right now, and that's all I need is a fuck up. Before I let what I worked hard for crumble, I'll come up out of retirement. Now I know we taught y'all well, but I also know how hard this detective goes. I'll stay out of your way for now, but if I sense some shit going wrong, I'mma be all up in your way."

"I promise we got shit covered, OG," I assured Big Norm.

"Alright... you interrupted me and my wife's time together. So, go ahead and see yourself out, and tell Khalif's bitch ass don't be snitching on me. I'm still the muthafucking boss." Big Norm chuckled, causing me to do the same.

"Alright, OG. I'mma head out, and if you have any questions about anything, just hit me up instead of Nas since you know his head is not in the game. I told you we got this," I said while heading out of the door.

I knew Big Norm was serious about everything he had just said, but I wished he would just let us handle this shit our way. Khalif and I were already up on the shit with the cops. That was why we were being extra careful. We all had already done our research on detective Keenan Moore. The same way our Old Heads got pass all these years was the same way we were going to get pass. Nasir, Khalif, and I had already started getting shit cleaned up. That way when we had to leave it alone, that was exactly what we were going to do. Terri dying may have slowed shit up just a little, but we had shit under control.

Chapter Eight

Nasir

I was sitting in Treasure's nursery just looking at the wall. My baby was doing well and gaining her weight the way she needed to. So, it looked like she would be coming home real soon. It had been about three weeks, and I was still in my feelings about losing Terri. I didn't care what my Pops or Cody said. This shit was my fault. If I wasn't fussing with her that night, she would still be here.

"Son!" My dad's yelling brought me out of my thoughts.

"I'm in the nursery, Pops!" I yelled back while wiping the lonely tear that fell down my cheek.

"I've been knocking on the door for a minute. That's why I let myself in," my pops said when he entered the room.

"My bad, Pops. Just in here thinking about Terri."

My dad placed his hand on my shoulder and took a deep breath before he sat down. I knew right then and there he was about to get into one of his serious conversations. Once he was seated, I turned towards him giving him all my attention.

"Son, I know you're going through a lot right now, and it's understandable. You don't have to play the tough roll in front of me. I know you loved Terri, and I know the minute she got pregnant with our little princess, your feelings got stronger for her. When your mama got pregnant with you, I fell for her even more everyday watching her belly grow. So I know this is hard for you."

"Pops, I'm hurting, but I'll be ok. I think what hurts me the most is that my baby will never have a mommy, and it's all my fault, Pops," I cried out while finally breaking down.

This shit was fucking a nigga up. It seemed like it got harder knowing that Treasure would be coming home soon. My Pops jumped up and walked over to me and pulled me in his arms.

"Son, Treasure will always have a piece of Terri in her heart. Make sure while she grows you let her know how great of a woman her mama was. That way she'll always have good memories of her. As far as a woman-figure in her life goes, she has Patrice, Crystal, Meek, and Lee-Lee. She will be just fine, son. Do you want Me and Crystal to come stay with you for a while when my grandbaby gets home?"

I knew Ms. C and my Pops would do anything for me and the baby, but I couldn't let them put their lives on the line. Treasure and I would be just fine. I had planned on hiring a nanny, on top of an at-home nurse, to come by and check on her for the first couple of weeks when she got here.

"No, Pops. I couldn't ask y'all to do that. You both are welcome to come over as much as you want, but I wouldn't ask you to leave ya crib. I have a couple of things lined up, so me and the baby will be just fine."

"Alright, son, but the offer always stands. Now on another note, how's business going? I know Cody and Khalif been handling everything. Have they been reporting to you?"

I knew this question was coming. My pops wouldn't be him if he didn't stay in our business. I looked at him and started to shake my head while I made my way out of the nursery. He knew I hated to discuss business with him, especially when he left it to me. Cody and Khalif had been putting me up to speed. I knew how my pops had been treating them, and I wasn't feeling it. I been wanted to say something, but I was waiting 'til the time was right.

"Pop, I don't know how many times I have to tell you I got this. Me and my crew learned from the best, so why won't you just trust us?"

"Son, Keenan Moore and his dickhead ass workers are coming for y'all. Keenan been trying to get at us for years, so I know he is coming with vengeance this time around. Son, you not on your game right now, and I don't need you slipping up. Just like I told Cody. Before I let y'all lose my empire, I'll come out of retirement."

I hated that he felt like this. I often wondered why he even bothered passing me the torch. I knew what I was doing and didn't need him in my face every five minutes.

"Pops, why did you give me your empire?" I asked in an angry tone, not really wanting to get into this with him today.

"Son, I know why I handed you the empire. I'm just trying to make sure everything I worked hard for doesn't come crumbling down. I know your head is not all the way in the game right now, and times like this is when people really come for your shit. Keenan is pissed because he could never catch us, so I know he is coming harder than he's ever come before."

My team and I were already ahead of the game when it came to Keenan Moore and the rest of them dickhead cops. Which is why Cody, Khalif, and I had already started moving money around and was starting all types of businesses. We already knew about them last year when he first handed over the throne. I knew I couldn't do this forever, anyway. I had plans on stepping down and working from behind the scenes when my daughter was born. Now since Terri's not here, it was forcing me to move a little faster with my plans.

"Pops, I get what you are saying. Just know I got this. Even when you think I don't, I do," I said in a serious tone.

Right after I said what I said and before my dad got to respond, my phone started to ring. When I noticed it was the hospital, I hurried and answered the call.

"Hello, may I speak to Mr. Baker?"

"Yes, you may. This is him speaking. May I ask what this call is referring to?"

"Hello, my name is Doctor Taylor. I'm calling to let you know that Treasure's progress is incredible, and it looks like she can be released this weekend. Usually, we would wait 'til her birth date, but according to her weight, how she eats, and how alert she is, it tells us that she's ready."

A big smile crept up on my face, and I was the happiest man in the world. I had tears of joy rolling down my face. Today was Thursday, and I couldn't wait 'til I was able to bring my little princess home.

"Thanks, so much, Doc. I'm so grateful to hear this good news. Do you know what time I'll be able to bring her home Saturday?"

"Well, the paperwork is already finished, and we already got clearance, as soon as you come in Saturday morning, she can be released. Just make sure you have a car seat for her."

"Ok, cool! Now when she comes home, I would like to have the same nurse that took care of her to come out to my house. Is there a way you can give me her number? I'll also make a huge donation to the hospital so you can hire someone else to cover her spot."

"Unfortunately, I won't be able to get her number, but I'll call her to my office when she gets to work and let her know. That's very generous of you, Mr. Baker, and I'm sure Nurse

Moore would be thrilled since she's gotten close to Treasure."

"No problem at all, Doctor Taylor. You guys were great with my baby, and I appreciate each and every one of you," I said right before hanging the phone up.

"That princess making ya ass soft already." My pops chuckled.

"So what? And I'm good with that." I chuckled while wiping the tears from my eyes.

My dad didn't lie. Treasure had me wrapped around her tiny fingers already. I would do anything for her. She was my pride and joy.

"My grandbaby coming home this weekend. Are we having a party?" Pops asked with a huge smile on his face.

"Yeah. I have to call everybody and let them know what's going down. Then I'll invite everyone over Sunday."

I was so happy about my baby coming home that I couldn't hide my excitement if I tried. I knew this was going to be a hard road for me and my family, but I also knew we would get the job finished.

Chapter Nine
Kenyan

I had been arguing with Rome for the past couple of days, and I was just about over it. He had been working late nights and was coming home with an attitude, just to take that shit out on me. Not only was he giving me his ass to kiss, but Mysti was still being a bitch. I couldn't believe she was still on one from the night she got pulled over.

"Hello, Mrs. Moore. Dr. Taylor wants to speak to you in her office." My supervisor had just walked up to the desk to let me know.

Lawd knows I wasn't in the mood today, so I hoped I didn't do anything wrong. "What, does she want me for?" I asked with an attitude.

"Girl, let me tell you what I heard," one of the nosiest nurses on the floor said, butting into our conversation. I mean, she knew everyone's business, and it was sickening.

"Ms. Latrell, do you ever mind your business?" my supervisor asked.

"Don't act like y'all don't be wanting to know the tea. Now come on, Kenyan. Let me walk you to her office and put you up on game."

Candace Latrell was nosey, but she was right. We all be trying to listen to the tea. Me and her had went to nursing school together and had been at the hospital for a couple of years now. We were cool, but we really didn't hang out much.

"Ok, so what's the tea?" I asked.

"Girl, Nasir Baker wants you to take care of his baby at home. So instead of you coming in here in the morning, you have to go to his house and stay there all day with the baby like it's your regular shift. He gave a big donation to the hospital and is doubling your pay."

"Say what now?" I said in a surprising tone.

The idea didn't sound bad, and the mentioning of my pay being doubled sounded even better. But I didn't know if I could do it. I had already gotten close to the baby.

"Bitch, if you don't wanna do it, I will. Shit," Candace said while swinging her ponytail.

"Bye, girl. Now go cover my wing until I'm finished here," I sassed while knocking on Dr. Taylor's door.

"Come on in!" she yelled from the other side.

I walked in, and she was sitting at her desk looking on her computer. Dr. Taylor was the Chief of Staff at the hospital, so she handled a lot of different things. The opportunity didn't sound bad, but I wished they would have asked me first before just taking Mr. Baker's money without finding out if I wanted to do it.

"Hello, Kenyan! Please have a seat."

I sat down and looked around her office like always. I was never really called in here unless it was a problem, and I hadn't had any of them in a while.

"Ok. I called you in here today to let you know that for the next month or so, you'll be going straight to Nasir Baker's home. He requested that you take care of his baby girl. He wanted no one but you. He even doubled your pay and gave the hospital a big chunk of change. So, I'mma need you to do this and do your best. You will keep the same hours you have for your regular schedule. You have to call me in the morning when you arrive, and call me when you leave. This is how we keep track of your hours.

Mr. Baker will also have a log sheet for you to sign in and out, and that's how you'll be getting paid from him. Once the baby is out of the woods, you'll be back at the hospital in your same place, so you have nothing to worry about."

I sat and listened to everything she said. I really couldn't believe they just knew I was doing this. That was the problem with this hospital. They were some greedy asses, and whatever worked for them, worked for them. No matter what the other person wanted.

"So, I guess I have no choice but to do this, being as though I didn't get asked. I just got told what I was going to be doing. He must have paid y'all real damn good," I snapped.

"Ms. Moore, it's no need for the foul language. This was above me when I bought it to my boss' attention. She said I had to do what I had to do to get the donation he was giving. Hell, both our jobs were on the line. At least your pay gets doubled. I actually didn't think you would mind since you had gotten close to the baby. At the rate she was going, you probably won't be there no longer than two weeks."

"When do I start?"

"Treasure was released today, so you'll start in the morning. Mr. Baker said if you want, you can stop by on your way home from work today to get acquainted. I just sent an email to you with his address and your new pay rates. As long as you work there, that's how much you'll be getting paid."

I didn't have anything else to say to Dr. Taylor, so I just got up and left out of her office. I really didn't know how to feel about being in Nasir Baker's house. But I was pissed about how the hospital was just using me so they could get some money. My daddy or Rome could never know about this. Nasir's name rung bells in the streets, and I knew that from Mysti. I didn't exactly know what he did for a living, but I also knew with all the money he had, there was no way it was legal. It really shouldn't be hard to keep away from them since I leave for work and return home around the same time. I just had to continue to wear my uniform and everything would be just right. Hell, at a time like this, Rome wasn't fucking with me, anyway.

✿✿✿✿✿✿

I was pulling up to this big ass house that sat in the middle of the street. Nasir lived in Delair, New Jersey. Not too far from me. There were several cars in the parking lot, so I assumed he was entertaining company. I didn't even wanna bother getting out, but I knew I needed to get the run-down of my job description. I sat for a couple of minutes while I got my mind straight. A tap on the window brought me out of my thoughts. I looked up, and it was a beautiful older woman standing there. She looked to be about my parents' age, or maybe a little older, but she wore it well.

"Hello. My name is Ms. C. May I be of assistance?" she asked in a pleasant tone.

"Hello. My name is Kenyan, and I'm the nurse that will be coming in to take care of Treasure. I was asked to come over this evening by Mr. Baker."

"Ok. Well, come on in. I'm his stepmother, and I want to thank you for all you did for our princess when she was in the hospital. Please get out and come in. You must be something special for him to want to hire you to work with her at home."

I was flattered by what she said, but at the same time, it was numerous cars out here, and I didn't want to bother them if they had guests. Besides, I was still in my uniform and ready to head home to relax.

"It looks like so many people are in there. I
don't want to take him away from his guests. I'll
just wait 'til the morning when I come in for
work."

"Nonsense, Kenyan. Come on in. Today is
Treasure's Sip and See we planned for her.
You're one of the reasons she is home. So, please
come in and celebrate with us. Plus, I'm sure you
can use a glass of wine or something after
working in the hospital all day."

She didn't lie about that. I damn sure could
use a glass of wine. Hell, maybe two, and I knew
for sure that Rome was at work, so I wasn't
going to bother him. I unlocked my car, rolled all
the windows up, then jumped out. I decided to
go ahead and go in. If I felt uncomfortable in any
way, I would just leave and go home. Nasir's
stepmother seemed like a very nice lady. I just
hoped that everyone else in his family were nice
people. If they were like her, that meant I would
probably have a wonderful time. Once I locked
up my car, I followed her in the house, and the
minute I hit the front door, I was in awe about
how big his living room was. Everyone was
talking, so no one knew I had walked in yet.

"Hey, y'all! Meet, Kenyan. This is Treasure's
nurse that took care of her when she was in the

hospital. I ran into her out front, so I invited her in to meet everyone," Ms. C said while introducing me to everyone.

Nasir got up and made his way over to me. This man was fine as fuck! *Kenyan, now you know better. You have a whole fiancé at home.*

"Hey, Kenyan! I meant to call your job to let them know that you didn't have to come today. My family surprised me when Treasure and I got home from the hospital. Since you're here, I'll give you a tour of the house and then if you want, you can have something to eat and drink. But, first, let me introduce you to everyone. These are my brothers from another mother, Cody and Khalif."

"Hello, Ms. Kenyan! It's nice to see you again. This is my soon-to-be wife, Meeka," Cody said while introducing me to his girl.

She waved while smiling from ear to ear.

I wished Rome would introduce me like that. I thought to myself.

"It's nice to meet you, Cody and Meeka," I said while shaking both their hands.

Then I was faced with his other friend. This chick didn't look as friendly as the other one, but I could tell she would keep it cordial.

"It's nice to meet you, Kenyan! This is my girl, Charlee, and we call her Lee-Lee," Khalif said while holding his hand out to shake mine.

When I tried to shake Lee-Lee's hand, she looked at me like I was crazy. I didn't say shit. I just walked over to the older man that looked a lot like Nasir, so I assumed that was his daddy.

"Last, but not least, this is my pops, Big Norm, Kenyan," Nasir said.

"Hello, young lady! I heard you were doing your job up at that hospital, and we all really appreciate you. You are always welcome here. We can't never thank you enough for all you've done and will continue to do for my grandbaby."

"Thank you so much for all the kind words. But Treasure is a very strong lil' mama, and her support system is awesome. So she's destined to be great, and as long as you all stay around, everything will be just fine. She'll be a hundred percent real soon," I said truthfully.

All of these people seemed extremely nice. Charlee was the only one that seemed iffy, but she wasn't my friend, and I didn't have to deal with her.

"Come on, Kenyan. Come this way," Nasir said while walking towards what I assumed to be the kitchen. "Ok, this is the kitchen. While you're here, you're welcome to whatever you want in here. If there is anything special you'll need, just have a list ready for me in the morning, and I'll make sure it's here for you. I want you to be as comfortable as possible while you're here."

"Alright, but before we go any further, I wanna ask you something. Why me? You could have paid for a nanny, then gotten a nurse to come out since she has medical insurance," I said, being honest.

"First of all, I didn't wanna just hire anyone. Secondly, out of everybody in the hospital that worked on the floor where you worked at, they just seemed like they were there for a paycheck, but you were different. You put your all into your work. I sat and watched you with my baby, and I could tell you fell in love with her. I haven't known you that long, but I trust you around her. And I know you're not a nanny, which is why I doubled your pay. Treasure is still small, and I'mma need a lot of help with her. I just believe you're the right person for the job."

Hearing everything Nasir said touched my heart. He was right. I loved my job and cared a lot about each patient I took care of. Which was why my daddy hated for me to work on the same floor with babies. Just because he knew sometimes it bothered me that I couldn't have children of my own, I could never tell him I was coming over here to take care of a baby.

"Thank you for all your kind words, Mr. Baker, and at first, I wasn't feeling coming over here. I actually was coming over here because the hospital was giving me no choice. Now that I'm here and listening to you, I feel better about taking the job. I really did get attached to Treasure, and I would have missed her so much. So, I'm glad I was given the opportunity, and I hope after she's well enough to not need care, I'll still be able to visit her."

"You can visit her anytime you want, and please call me, Nasir. You ain't at the hospital anymore. Now don't forget to let me know what your list is for groceries. Come on. Let me show you the rest of the house. Then we can go to my office, and I can show you the sign in and out sheet," Nasir said while finishing up the tour of the house.

I didn't know how long this was going to go on for, but I was now more comfortable about doing the job. Since I knew his reasons, I actually liked everything he said, and now I was intrigued about who Nasir Baker really was.

Chapter Ten

Rome

This case had been one of the hardest cases I had ever worked in my entire career. I just couldn't believe we couldn't find shit on these dudes. It was like nothing they did was wrong. Usually, when drug dealers started making bank, they started getting stupid and fucked up, but not this family. I was starting to think this family was invincible.

"Baby, what's going on with you?"

"Nothing. Work has been kicking my ass, that's all. What's been up with you? I haven't heard from you in a minute? You good?" I asked.

"I'm good. Just needed sometime to myself. You know I be getting all in my feelings because we not together yet. How long I gotta wait, baby?"

"After I crack this case and get the position I want. I told you this shit takes time. Just chill. Our time is coming, sweetheart. Now get over here and make me feel good. It's been a minute since I felt your insides."

I had been messing with Mysti for a long time now. She was where my heart was, but I had to put on a show so Kenyan would never find out. Mysti knew from day one that I was getting with Kenyan so I could get her pop's spot. All I needed to do was win this case that his ass could never win.

Mysti crawled over to me and ended up right in between my legs. The look I gave her told her exactly what I wanted her to do. She started rubbing on my dick through my pants. The sensation from the friction of the fabric running across my dick was turning me on. It had been a minute since I got my dick sucked, and I was all for this. When Mysti saw how turned on I was, she unzipped my pants. Then eased her little hand inside and unleashed the beast. My dick was standing at attention.

She looked me in my eyes and smiled while licking her lips before she kissed the tip and took me into her mouth.

"Make that shit really sloppy for me, ma. Just the way I like it."

"I got you, baby!" Mysti said between sucks and slurps.

She began to rub on my balls right before placing each one in her mouth, making sure not to forget to show them just as much attention as she was showing my dick. Mysti licked and sucked some more on my balls right before she deep throated my dick. My girl even gagged on purpose a couple times knowing that was the shit I liked.

Baby girl must have missed me just as much as I missed getting my dick sucked. She bobbed her head in a fast motion—making sure to put her all in it. Mysti was on some Superhead shit, and I was enjoying every bit of it. After kissing, licking, sucking, and slurping Mysti took me all the way in the back of her throat once more causing me to reach my peak. My body began to jerk, and there I was releasing all my seeds down her throat. Mysti swallowed every bit of it, then got up off the floor while wiping her mouth off.

"You want me to make you something to eat before you go home?"

"Yeah, make me something good, and I don't think I wanna go home tonight," I said, being truthful. All I wanted to do was eat, shower and climb in the bed next to her.

"Well, you know you always welcome to stay here. Go ahead and shower, and I'll bring your food up to the room when I'm finished."

Mysti didn't have to tell me twice. I was tired as fuck, and all I wanted to do was shower, eat and get comfortable. I had been working this case for about a week, and it was like we were still where we started. Early mornings and late nights for no fucking reason. I was truthfully over this to the point I wanted to just kill these dudes just to wipe them off the face of the earth. But they were indeed better alive and breathing.

☆☆☆☆☆☆

Damn... I thought to myself as I pulled up in the driveway and Kenyan's car was still there. I was hoping I missed her this morning so I wouldn't have to explain shit to her. This was one of the main things I hated about a relationship. I hated telling people where and what I was doing. I was a grown ass man, and I shouldn't have to tell a damn soul what I was doing. I hurried and made my way into the house, and Kenyan was sitting at the dining room table having a cup of coffee.

"Good morning, beautiful!" I said while kissing her on her cheek.

"So, we back to this bullshit, Rome?"

"Kenyan, what are you talking about? I just got in from work. I'm about to shower and head back out. This is one of the hardest cases to crack, and I don't need a nagging fiancé to add to the stress. Now excuse me so I can get my shit together."

"Tell that bitch, or that nigga, which ever you doing these days, that you don't use Irish Spring. You smell like soap but you going to shower. Nigga, you swear I'm a dummy. It's cool though, Rome. One day you gon' be alone in the bed while I'm pulling an all-nighter in somebody's damn face," Kenyan sassed while grabbing her things and heading out of the door.

"Yeah, whatever! You ain't crazy, ma! I'll kill anything that fucks with what's mine!" I yelled while making my way upstairs to change my clothes.

Kenyan knew who and how the fuck I was, and being a cop made the shit so much better. I knew how to do shit, then cover it up at the same time. I hurried up and changed my clothes, then made my way out of the door. I didn't need to stop for breakfast because Mysti made sure she fed me before I left. She always made sure to take care of me when I was in her presence. I just didn't like when she hung with Kenyan, which was why I would treat her like shit when she did. I knew they'd been friends, but I didn't give a damn. I couldn't chance Kenyan finding out anything about Mysti and I.

Plus, I could tell Mysti was jealous of Kenyan. I didn't understand why. Mysti was bad as hell with body for days versus Kenyan having a pretty face for a big girl. She really had nothing on Mysti but being educated and having a great job. Which was fine with me. I loved bitches that just stayed home and let the man work. I liked my bitches to be home cooking and cleaning.

Once I was dressed and on my way to the car, I got an alert from the job telling me to come in because they had some news about Nasir Baker. I hurried and jumped in my car, turned my siren on, then peeled off.

After speeding through traffic, I was now pulling into the parking lot. I parked my vehicle, then jumped out and made my way inside. I wasn't in the mood to speak or talk to anyone today, so I walked in and headed straight to the meeting room, where I was sure everyone was seated.

"So, we've been investigating these guys for years, and no one knew about Baker's girlfriend dying in a car accident. How the hell could this be? Moore, if you don't get a handle on this case, I'mma have no other choice but to hand it over to someone else. Now from my understanding, his baby just was released from the hospital. Look into it. His mind is elsewhere, which means he's not all in the game. I want to hear some news by the end of the week. Moore, get your best men on the job, and I mean it!" the Chief, McNeilly, yelled right before heading out of the door.

Hearing him talking to Moore like that had me smiling on the inside. All I needed was for them to know I cracked this case, and his job would be right in my lap.

"So, you want me to look into that for you, boss man?" I asked, now taking a seat in the chair right next to Moore.

"I want everybody on the job, Rome. Y'all go ahead and head out to get y'all day started. Rome, I need to speak to you before you go."

Everybody headed out, and when we were left alone, I closed the door and locked it. "What's up, sir?" I asked while giving him all of my attention.

"I remember Kenyan saying it was a new baby in the NICU a couple of weeks ago. How much you wanna bet that was Baker's baby?"

What the lieutenant said was rolling around in my head. What if he was right? This baby was possibly the key to getting these niggas off the streets.

"Ok, so what do you want me to do?" I asked curious.

"I need you to go talk to the Chief of Staff and find out if Baker's baby was there and when was it released."

"You know they not gon' talk to us without some type of warrant or something, but I may have an idea. I got a little friend up there that wouldn't mind telling me what I need to know."

"Ok, do what you have to do, but try not to run into Kenyan. You know she would be mad if she found out we were snooping around her job when we could have just asked her."

"I got this. I'mma make sure she doesn't even see me. I'mma do all my talking from the parking lot."

I had this little baddie that worked at the hospital. I had to cut it off a while back because she ran her mouth too much, and I didn't need them problems in my life. I already had enough going on, and a leaky faucet just wasn't cutting it for me. It had been a minute since I saw her, and when I shot her the text, I knew she was going to be excited to see me. Even if I needed to break her off, then I would do so just to get all I needed to get out of her.

"Rome, make sure you keep this between us in case Kenyan does know something."

"I got you, boss. I'll have some information for you by the end of the day." I smirked while making my way out of the door. Not having my partner with me was like music to my ears.

Chapter Eleven

Nasir

The cops were on our ass, but we had shit under control. Khalif's pops had let us know that they were back up there asking questions. He also had put us on to some personal bank accounts that he had overseas that they didn't know about, and since he was already doing a life sentence, he made it so that whatever funds the came in contact with would lead all evidence to him. At first, we didn't wanna do it, but like he said, he was never coming home, and we had our families to raise. He also brought to our attention that he was already living like a king in there, so he was cool. They were pissed off, but it wasn't really anything they could do. When ya money was as long as ours, you could do anything you wanna do.

Treasure was down for a nap, so I was going to go find Kenyan so we could chat. I noticed for a couple of days she'd been looking a little down, and somebody as fine as her shouldn't be moping around. I went down to the kitchen and she wasn't there, so I made my way out back near the pool, and that was exactly where she was.

"It's beautiful out here, isn't it?" I asked, sitting down in the lawn chair that was right next to her.

She looked up at me and smiled like she always did. I wasn't even going to lie. I'd been interested in Kenyan since I watched her with my daughter at the hospital. Usually, I would have thought that she was only doing this for work, but when she called and checked on me the days I went home from the hospital, I knew she was a special lady. Then a couple days ago when she asked could she still visit my baby once she was out of the storm, that shit spoke volumes. Now I just wanted to get to know her.

"Yeah, it really is nice and peaceful. I hope you don't mind me coming out here. I made sure Treasure was fed, bathed, and down for her first nap of the day. She should be waking up for her next feeding in exactly two hours," Kenyan rattled off.

"You good, ma! I told you to make yourself at home, so I don't mind you coming back here to clear your mind. I actually came back here to find out what's going on. I noticed you haven't been yourself."

Kenyan looked at me with a raised eyebrow. I didn't know what that look was about, but I was getting ready to find out.

"You noticed I haven't been myself?" Kenyan repeated what I said in a surprised tone.

"Of course. Today and yesterday you weren't your usually bubbly self. What's going on? If you don't mind me asking."

She looked at me strange at first, but then she gave me the what the hell look and started talking.

"Have you ever been in a relationship with someone and you do just about everything? But no matter how much you do the person is just never happy? Like, actually bend over backwards but the shit just ain't enough, I guess? I mean, I work, I clean, I fuck him when he wants, I even try to be romantic, sometimes. Like, what makes him not happy if I'm doing all I'm supposed to do?" Kenyan ran down not even realizing that she was crying.

I moved closer to her and pulled her in for a hug. Baby girl had all that built up inside and needed to get that shit out. "Shhh, ma, stop crying. That just mean that nigga ain't ready for what you ready for. You shouldn't be crying. You should be happy and living your best life. Now to answer your question, yes, I've been in a relationship like that. I actually was in one with Treasure's mama. I knew she loved me, but I just felt like love was never enough for her. The day of the accident, we had gotten into a big argument, and she stormed out of here with an attitude. Which is why I blame myself every day. If we weren't arguing, this wouldn't have happened. I shouldn't have let her go," I said in a sad tone.

Kenyan pulled out of my arms and placed both her hands on each side of my face then looked me straight in my eyes.

"Don't do that! Don't blame yourself. You can't help that she got into an accident. Baby, God don't make no mistakes. It's crazy, but maybe this happened for a reason. Maybe God knows you need Treasure for whatever reason," Kenyan said, causing me to want her even more.

I just couldn't help myself. I leaned in to kiss her lips, and to my surprise, she kissed me back.

We engaged in a passionate kiss for what seemed like forever.

"Waaaah, Waaaah, Waaaah!" The sound of Treasure crying through the baby monitor interrupted our kiss.

"Mmm, let me go get her," Kenyan said while pulling away from me.

I could tell she was feeling some type of way about the kiss. Which was understandable, since I knew she was in a complicated situation. But while she was here, I was going to start making her feel right at home. If that no-good ass nigga didn't wanna treat her like she needed to be treated, then I would kindly take her off his hands. I didn't wanna snoop around in her life, but I was curious to know who her duded was. When I realized Kenyan was taking too long to come back, I was about to go up to talk to her, but my phone alerted me that I had a message. When I looked, it was Cody telling me he was out front. Usually, he would call first, so I knew this must have been business related. I hurried to go answer the door. I would just have to find Kenyan when Cody and I were finished.

"Yo', bro! What brings you here unannounced?" I asked while pulling him in for a hug.

"Can we go talk in your office?" Cody asked while looking around.

"Sure, and why are you looking around like you looking for somebody?" I chuckled.

"No particular reason. Just come on to your office so we can talk."

Once we made it into my office, Cody hurried and closed, then locked the door. I could tell something was on his mind. I hated the way he was looking all suspicious, so I wished his ass would hurry up and tell me what the fuck is going on.

"Man, what's up because you starting to worry me the way you are acting."

"Where's Kenyan at?" Cody asked.

"She's upstairs taking care of Treasure. Why, what's wrong?"

"Did you do a background check on her? Do you think it's safe having her in here taking care of the baby?"

"She's cool, bro! If I thought she wasn't, I wouldn't have her in my crib. Now tell me what this is all about."

"Khalif said Lee-Lee been asking questions about ole' girl. You know how Lee be, so he asked me to come and talk to you. You know it's a heavy investigation going on right now to end us. I just wanna make sure you know what you are doing and you're being safe," Cody explained.

"Man, she's good people, and I can't believe y'all going off of what Lee-Lee's crazy ass said." I chuckled.

"Alright. I'm just checking, and you right. Lee-Lee's ass is a little off."

I looked at Cody trying to figure out if I wanted to tell him about how I was feeling. After what they'd been talking about, I didn't want them to really start tripping. So, I decided to keep it to myself until I decided to make shit official between Kenyan and I. Because that was definitely in my plans.

"Which is why y'all shouldn't be listening to her. Now you already know if I felt like I was putting Treasure in any danger I wouldn't have put up all this money for her to work in my home to help take care of her. I got this, man, and we good. Now did y'all handle all of the accounts that Unc told us about?"

"Yes. Everything's straight, and everyone has been paid that's involved so shit should work out just fine. One more thing. They finally found out about Terri, so don't be surprised if they pop up here snooping. You know, since they know they gon' think they got one up on you. They about to test ya gangster to see if you off your game."

"They ain't got shit on me, and they better know that Treasure got me more on my game than I've ever been before. I have her to live for, so I'm gon' make sure shit is straight, and I mean that shit."

"I believe you, man! Now let me be out. I have to pick CJ up from daycare. I'll holler at you a little later. Meek wanna know when she can come see the baby."

"Now sis knows damn well she's welcome anytime she wants. Just tell her shoot me a text."

"Ok, cool. Let me go, and I'll talk to you later. Kiss the princess for me, and I'll make sure everything else is taken care of. After this last thing we need to do, the cops should be thrown off there square, and we should be fine," Cody assured me right before he dapped me up.

I walked him to the door, then watched him hop in his truck. Once he peeled off, I made my way upstairs to see what Kenyan and Treasure were doing.

Chapter Twelve
Cody

It had been days since we got the last thing in motion, but there was still buzz out in these streets that this dickhead ass cop, Rome, was still out questioning people. They had ran into all type of dead ends, so I had no clue what this asshole was still in these streets looking for.

"Hey, baby. What you in here doing?" Meek asked when she walked in.

"Just sitting here trying to figure some shit out about this one cop that's still snooping around."

"Well, you know if can't find shit, don't worry about his ass. Now give me a kiss," Meek said while climbing on my lap.

"Where are you coming from?"

"I just came from having a lunch date with Kenyan and Treasure."

I looked at her with a raised brow hearing her say lunch date with Kenyan. I knew she was going to see Treasure, but I didn't know she was having a date with Kenyan.

"So, how did that work out?"

"It was nice, and I like her for Nas. She's a very beautiful person, and I think that's exactly what he needs."

"Wait, what? Exactly what he needs? What you talking 'bout, baby? She's just the nurse taking care of the baby, right?" I asked, curious.

"I know damn well you can tell he has a thing for her. I peeped that the first day we met her. You know damn well Nas don't be letting nobody in his crib. Truth be told, we could have helped him with niecey pooh, but, no. He chose to hire someone that none of us knew. I been on to him." Meek giggled.

When Meek finished talking, I just thought about what she was saying. This was why when I said something to him about what Lee-Lee said, he was taking up for her ass. Now I see exactly why.

"Yo', it's all making sense now. So, you think she good peoples?"

"Yeah, I actually do, and she's great with the baby."

"That's good to hear. I have noticed my boy been having a smile on his face lately. I thought the shit with Terri was going to break him. Especially being home with Treasure alone, but I guess Kenyan is there to help him get through it. I guess that's why he didn't want us to check her out."

"Y'all know damn well Nas got shit straight. Ain't no need to be spying. If he trusted her enough to come in his home, then she good. Just pray that it all will work out in his favor. I love to see him happy. Now enough about him. I need you to get me right before we have to pick CJ up from daycare," Meek said while kissing my neck.

She began to pull at my shirt. After helping her take it off, she then started unbuttoning my jeans. I stood up with her still wrapped around my body. Once we walked over to our California king-size bed, I threw her sexy ass on the bed and finished taking my clothes off while she came out of hers. Once we both were completely naked, I climbed on top of her, then started to kiss all over her body. I made my way to her boobs making sure to show them both some attention. Then I eased my way down her entire body.

"Shit, baby, just liked that!" Meek moaned out in pleasure as I began to enjoy the sweet taste and scent of her neatly shaved pussy. The way I attacked her clit I had her moving like a snake all over the bed. As usual, she was trying to get away from me, but I wasn't going to let that happen.

I began to flick my tongue in a fast motion determined to get the first nut of the day out of her.

"Come on, beautiful. I need you to let that nut out for me," I said in a husky tone, continuing to devour her sweet spot. On demand, Meek's body reacted to me, and baby girl came all over my face.

Once I finished, I let her get herself together, then I kissed her lips hungrily while I made my way back on top of her. I began to poke at her entrance before I entered her. I slid in her nice and slow giving her nice, long deep strokes. Meek always felt the same when I entered her, just like our first time. I swear she was tight and wet. I was never a man of many words during sex. I loved to do all the talking with my eyes. We would give each other intense stares while we made love to each other's soul. I swear Meek was my soul mate, and I was so ready to marry her sexy ass.

I continued to dick her down, and she continued to match me stroke from stroke from underneath. WE both were giving each other the business. I felt her tightening up on my dick, which was causing me to move at a faster motion.

"Mmm...baby, just like that. Come on, fuck me back," I said while moving in and out of her faster.

Meek started moving just as fast as me causing my nut to build up. "I'm about to cum, Cody!" Meek yelled out in pleasure.

As soon as she yelled out, it was like my body moved on command, and we both came together.

Once we both came long and hard, I signaled Meek to climb on top of me. I just wanted to hold her while we took a nap before we had to get CJ from daycare.

☆☆☆☆☆

Me, Khalif, and Cody were sitting at the bar down in Nasir's basement. We were celebrating finally being able to chill. Treasure was doing great, Nasir was happy, and our legal business ventures were finally starting. Things were finally looking up for three young niggas that grew up in the drug game.

"So, wait. Unc's lawyer said the investigation is closed?" Nasir asked.

"Yes, that's what he said. So, there shouldn't be no one poking around anymore."

"Good, because I'm getting tired of that Rome dude. I'm supposed to have the paperwork on him tomorrow. I wanna know what's this nigga's vendetta against us. If the case is closed, why is he still sneaking the fuck around."

"Don't worry. We gon' find out tomorrow. Right now, let's just chill and drink to our future."

"I heard that! Now let me ask y'all something, and be real with me," Nasir said.

"You know I'm always real with you. Now what's up?" I asked.

"Yeah, what Cody said! Since when we not real with you?" Khalif asked, giving me all his attention.

"I just wanna know what y'all think of Kenyan?"

I knew we were coming to this soon. I knew they had already been talking, but I was just waiting until when he brought it to my attention.

"I think if you are feeling her, then I'm cool with it," I said, being honest.

"Yeah, baby girl straight with me. Plus, Charlee met up with her and said she cool," Khalif said, causing us both to laugh.

"Wait, when did sis meet with her?" Nasir asked, curious.

"I couple days ago. Shit, Meek met with her first," Khalif said, running his mouth.

"Yeah, our girls were worried about you, so they decided to meet up with her on their own time to feel her out. They both seem to be feeling her just as much as you are, so do you." I chuckled.

"Yo', I can't believe them. They both are a trip. But I can dig it. They just trying to make sure Treasure and I are good, and I appreciate them both for that."

"Yeah, because, first, Lee-Lee wasn't feeling her, but she cool now. So, as long as you feeling her and she good to my niece, she'll be good," Khalif said.

"That's what got me hooked from the beginning is the way she is with my baby. But she got a dude that haven't been treating her right. I'm waiting on some paperwork on his ass too. I'm dying to see who this fuck boy is. The other day, she was here crying and shit. I don't know who this cat is, but I wanted to go kill his ass."

"Damn, dawg. So she got you open like that, already? Did you even hit yet?" I asked, being curious.

"Nah, I'm waiting 'til she ready. I know she's in a complicated situation, so I'm good with waiting 'til the time is right. Hell, I've been months without getting pussy. I'm good with waiting a little longer."

"Yeah, that nigga is open!" Khalif chuckled.

I was shocked at everything I was hearing, but I was sure glad to see my bro happy. These past few months have been torture on him, and to see him light up over someone made me proud. Everything was starting to look up for us all, and soon, we all would have our happily ever after.

Chapter Thirteen
Kenyan

For the past week, I had been going crazy with my feelings, and I just couldn't help myself. I had to see what the fuck Rome was up to. Granted, I already knew what it was, but I had to see it with my own eyes. I was now sitting in my car with a face full of tears. I had followed this nigga to my best friend's house. He had been in there for hours already; and, I was hurt, I was furious, and I wanted to kill them both.

Nasir had been texting me all day, and I had yet to answer him. My feelings for him had been spiraling out of control. I wanted him so bad, but I didn't wanna pursue anything with him knowing I was already in a relationship. Since I discovered this, I guess I could go ahead to the next level with someone that really acted like he cared for me.

The sound of Rome coming out of the house brought me out of my thoughts. I hurried and leaned down in my seat so he didn't see me. What type of cop was he? I followed this nigga here and sat here half the night? His stupid ass didn't even realize he was being followed. I waited awhile, then I pulled out my phone to call him to make sure he wasn't coming back. I dialed his number, and surprisingly, he answered on the second ring.

"Hey, baby! What's up?"

"Hey, you! I was checking to see of you were home yet. You've been working late nights, and I've been missing you like crazy."

"Aww, I've been missing you too, beautiful, and I'm pulling up to the house right now. Where are you?"

"I'll be there shortly. I promised my boss I would stay for another hour. I'll see you later.

"Ok, baby. I'll be waiting."

No other words were spoken. I just hung my phone up, jumped out of my car and walked up to Mysti's front door. I knocked three times before she opened it. When she saw it was me, she stood there like a deer stuck in head lights.

"K-K-Kenyan? What you doing here, girl?" she stuttered.

"I was wondering why I haven't seen you in so long. That's all. I've been missing you. Can I come in so we can talk?" I lied.

Truth be told, I had been gave up on Mysti ever since she had been acting crazy about the night we got pulled over. Now I understood what she was mad at. She was mad her man set her up to be locked up. His crazy ass must have told her to stay away from me, and her stupid ass listened. Mysti moved to the side and let me in. As soon as I made it all the way in the house, I turned to her and looked her right in the face.

"So, what do we need to talk about?"

"For starters, I wanna know how long you been fucking Rome's stupid ass? The 'little dick bastard' that you don't care for. The one you always arguing with."

She stood there looking at me in shock like she didn't know what to say. Then she just started laughing out of nowhere. "You don't know what to do with a man like Rome. Plus, he was my man first. He only was using you to get your daddy's position, and it looks like he going to get the spot after all since he's about to lock up Nasir Baker. Yeah, he knows you've been working in that house taking care of that baby. He didn't say anything yet because he was going to use you to take Nasir down—"

Before she even got a chance to finish, I punched her dead in the face causing her to fall right on the floor. Once I saw her about to get up, I kicked her right in the side.

"You stupid, bitch! I'm not beating ya ass over Rome. I'm beating ya ass for disrespecting me. All these years you smiled in my face acting like you were my friend and using me as a barbie doll dressing me up just so I can make your man jealous and mad. You are foul for that shit! You and Rome's sick asses are made for each other, and for the record, bitch, you ain't the only one. It's a few bitches that Rome fucking. So, I guess the joke's on you, and for your information, he ain't smart enough to take down Nasir Baker," I snapped while delivering another kick to her side.

Hearing her screaming didn't seem to faze me, but I knew sooner or later, I had to stop before I killed her. After getting a couple more hits in, I decided to head on out the door. I jumped in my car and banged my hands on the steering wheel in anger. I then pulled off with a heavy flow of tears streaming down my face. I didn't wanna go home, and I couldn't go to my parents. I headed to the only place I knew I was wanted. To the one person that I knew liked me for me. I hated that I had to tell him about Rome. I hated that I had to tell him that I was a detective's daughter. I wasn't no dummy. I knew what Nasir Baker was about, but I couldn't help that I had already practically fallen in love with him.

After driving like a crazy person and breaking every traffic violation known of, I was now pulling in front of Nasir's house. I was glad to see that only one car was there. I parked my car and hopped out. I then walked up to his front door and knocked on it. I stood there for what seemed like forever. As soon as I was about to walk away, he opened the door. As soon as he saw me, no words were spoken. He just pulled me in his arms.

We stood in the doorway in each other's arms. I cried while he held me. I was so hurt, and I don't think it was because of Rome. It was the fact that someone I knew for so many years had betrayed me like this. Finally breaking apart from each other, Nasir grabbed my hand and pulled me into the house.

"Go ahead out back and sit by the pool while I run to get us something to drink from the bar."

He didn't have to tell me twice. I made my way out back and sat down waiting for him to come back. Now that I'd gotten the chance to see what the fuck Rome was up to, I could let that part of my life go and move on. The sound of Nasir coming out bought me out of my thoughts.

"I'm sorry I came over here like this. I just needed someone to talk to, you know?"

"You don't have to be sorry. Just tell me what happened," Nasir said while handing me a glass of red wine.

"I found him with my best friend of fifteen years. She ran it down to me tonight. Oh, and your name came up in this too. When I tell you this, please don't get mad at me. Believe me when I tell you I didn't know, and I also didn't plan to fall for you."

"I believe you, baby! Just tell me what happened."

"Well, for starters, my ex is Jerome Myers, and he's a cop. My daddy is Lieutenant Moore, and they've been on the case against you for years. Well, I just heard it from her right after watching Rome leave her house. She also went on to say, after I kicked her ass, that the only reason he was with me was to take my daddy's spot, and it was about to happen soon because he was about to bring you down. He knows about me working here, but he didn't say anything because he has plans on using me to set you up.

"Now that his whole plan is going to backfire, I don't have a clue what he's going to do. I would go to my daddy, but he's not going to believe me. He just going to see you as a drug dealer and wanna come take you down. I don't want that, Nasir. I want you, and it's killing me knowing that we may not be able to be together because you live a totally different life then me," I said in a sad tone.

"If we meant to be, then that's what it is, ma. As for the life I live, it's soon going to be all legal. I'm not trying to put Treasure in any danger. Your daddy and the whole team, we have them taken care of. That case has been closed for a week now. Your little boyfriend must be looking for shit so he could try to catch me out there because he mad because I'm about to steal his girl." Nasir chuckled while pulling me closer to him.

"This is just too much. I don't wanna talk about this any longer. I know we eventually going to have to figure this out, but tonight I just want you to take my mind off of everything," I said just above a whisper.

No more words were spoken. Nasir grabbed my hand and lead me inside the house. We were going to the living room, but I didn't wanna go there. I wanted to go to his bedroom, so I grabbed his hand and led the way.

Chapter Fourteen

Nasir

Some would say Kenyan and I were moving too fast, but I didn't care what people thought. I wanted what I wanted, and that was what it was going to be. Even if I had to kill her crazy ass dude. I had been up half the night watching her sleep. After we made love to each other, and she cried some more, she drifted off to sleep. Me, on the other hand, I couldn't sleep. So, many different things were going around in my head. I was worried about her father tripping, my father tripping and not to mention her ex. Killing his ass would be easy, but the after math would be crazy. We'd just got off with the police. The last thing we needed was for them to think I killed Kenyan's fiancé.

"Good morning! What are you doing up so early?" Kenyan asked.

"Nothing. I'm just used to being up this early when Treasure is here," I lied, not wanting to alarm her.

"Oh, ok! When is she coming back?"

I had let my dad and Ms. C keep her for the night. Of course, I was kind of scared about letting her go, but I knew they had it. Hell, they raised me. Plus, Ms. C figured I needed some time to myself. I didn't expect for the night to turn out the way it did, but I was truly grateful.

"They said whenever I call them. So, it looks like you have a free day today. What you wanna do?"

"Whatever you wanna do."

Hearing her say that caused a smile to creep up on my face. I turned to face her, then pulled her close to me. An uneasy look on her face had a nigga wondering what was going on in her head. "What's on ya mind beautiful? Talk to me!"

"You can have any woman you want. I mean, you're Nasir Baker. Your name ring bells out here in these streets. So, what do you want with a woman like me? I'm not the next model chick, you know!"

"Kenyan, I know we are moving fast, and I know you may not be used to a man like me. But your beauty, kindness, and how you are with my baby, and now that good loving you put on me last night, sealed the deal." I chuckled, but she didn't look like she was too happy about what I said.

"Sike, baby, I'm just kidding. Definitely your beauty and kindness. The rest I'm still trying to feel out. Is it wrong that I wanna get too know you better while we're together?"

"I mean, that's different for me, but I don't mind trying it out. But you still didn't comment about the model chick part. I bet you never been with a big girl before, so why now?"

I knew what she meant when she said something about a model chick, and I blocked that shit right out of my head. Kenyan may have been a big girl, but it didn't take away from her beauty or who she was. Hell, it ain't shit wrong with a little more to love.

"To be honest with you, I have been with a big girl before, but it's been a minute. But trust me, baby girl. Your size doesn't stop how you got me feeling, and this is a discussion you never have to bring up again. I want you, curves and all! Don't never forget that shit, either. Now can we continue to get to know each other inside and out?" I asked while pulling her close to me.

"You so fresh, boy!" Kenyan cooed.

"I know you ain't talking the way you pulled me to this room last night and pushed me on the bed. I wasn't ready at all." I chuckled.

"Are you ready now?" Kenyan asked while climbing on top of me.

As Kenyan slowly slid down on my erection, I made sure to grab ahold of all her ass while I bit down on my bottom lip. The feeling of her tight, wet, gushy insides had a nigga's mind gone. I'd been with plenty of women, but it was something about Kenyan that had a nigga ready to risk it all in such a little time. Kenyan was moving in a slow motion making sure she felt every inch of my dick drilling in and out of her. She was moving just the way I liked, which was a plus for me because if she was moving any faster, my ass would probably be cummin'.

I tried to refrain from letting out a moan, but I couldn't contain myself any longer. I felt when she started to contract her muscles, and I knew right then and there I needed to take over before I nutted. I was ready to show her how it was when I took control. I let her get her shit off last night; now it was my turn.

Grabbing Kenyan by her waist and lifting her from on top of me, I could see all confusion in her face. Before she had the chance to say anything, I kissed her lips aggressively while grinding at her opening to keep her in the mood. After kissing her lips, I made my way down to her big breasts making sure to kiss, lick, and suck on then while I entered her nice and slow. When she began to let out soft moans while digging her nails into my back, I knew it was time for me to go all in. I sped up the pace giving her faster, long, deep strokes making sure to hit her spot.

"OH, NAS! What are you doing to me?!" Kenyan yelled out in pleasure.

"I'm making you feel good, baby! You like that, don't you?" I asked in a husky tone.

"Yesssss! Just like that."

I placed kisses on Kenyan's soft lips, once again, and she used her tongue to part my lips. So, I followed her lead. French kissing Kenyan did something to me causing me to hit her with soft, deep strokes, hittin' spots that I don't think she knew she had. I was never a big kisser, but since the first day Kenyan and I kissed, it felt so right. I could tell from her wetness that her body was reacting well to everything I was doing to her.

Kenyan used her hand to push me back, and I moved, but then she sat up on the bed. She eased to the side of it and looked at me with seductive eyes, while signaling for me to get up and come to where she was.

"I want you to hit it from the back," Kenyan said with a wink of an eye.

Baby girl didn't have to tell me twice. I did as she demanded and moved behind. The sight of all that ass up in the air sent chills up my spine.

Damn girl! I thought to myself as I got positioned behind Kenyan. Once I got my footing in order, I drilled inside of her from the back in a swift motion. I began to give her fast, long, deep strokes. Knowing damn well hitting from the back was a weakness for me. No matter how many times I slowed up to keep from nutting, it wasn't working. Watching that ass bounce, and the feeling of her wet, gushy walls just wouldn't let me live. I tried to pull out because we were so into the moment, and I realized I didn't put a condom on, but it was too late. Watching her ass had me in a trance, and ya boy got caught up.

"Fuck, ma! I'm about to nut!" I said while I released inside of Kenyan.

She fell on the bed, and I fell on the side of her. The moment was quiet, but I had to ask.

"Are you on birth control?" I felt ashamed that my old ass didn't ask this from the beginning. I know last night we used a condom. So, why were we so quick to not use one today?

"Don't worry, Nasir. I'm not trying to get you caught up if you think that."

I looked at her with my face all turned up because I couldn't believe she said that shit to me.

"Woooah, baby girl. It ain't even nothing like that. I just was asking because I didn't know if you were ready for all of that if it happened. I know we should have established that from the beginning, but we both got caught up. Kenyan, if it ever came down to that, baby, I'll take care of mine, so this shouldn't even had come out of your mouth."

She looked at me with said eyes before she spoke. "I'm sorry about that. It's just that, when the talk about birth control comes up, I start to feel some kind of way. See, I can't have any kids, Nasir."

I didn't know how to address a conversation like this, so I had to think quick of something to say right quick. "I'm sorry to hear that, and we can talk about that if you want. If not, I'll just leave it alone, and we can come back to it later," I said truthfully.

"We can discuss it later. Right now, can we just take a nap? You got me tired," Kenyan said with a smile on her face.

"Whatever you wanna do, beautiful!" I said while pulling her closer to me and kissing her forehead.

Kenyan and I laid in each other's arms until we drifted off to sleep.

Chapter Fifteen
Rome

When I learned that Mysti had told Kenyan everything, I was furious. I had been over here arguing with her stupid ass ever since. She kept fussing about us being together, and I was sick of hearing it. I had been sitting in my own thoughts to figure out how to get Kenyan up out of Nasir's crib.

I didn't wanna cause a scene since the case was now closed. Everyone was walking around the office with sad faces. This had been the biggest case we had for the past couple of years, and it all got thrown out. I wasn't dealing with it well at all. I figured if I found some evidence on Baker, I could take him down on my own. So, when I learned that Kenyan was working for him privately, I didn't say shit to her or her pops. I just continued to follow her and watch her and old boys' activity. The shit had pissed me off so bad because she seemed to be happy in such a little time when my life felt like it was going from sugar to shit with the snap of a finger.

My job didn't seem like it was going to happen, Kenyan wasn't going to be fucking with me anymore, and last but not least, Nasir Baker was still going to be a free man. At this point, I just wanted his ass dead and gone. And he was big time, so it shouldn't be hard to do and cover it up.

"Rome, what you in here doing? I know you heard me ask what we going to do about this baby?" Mysti had said, pissing me off once again.

We had learned that she was pregnant when she was rushed to the hospital after Kenyan beat her ass. I didn't understand how she still was pregnant after the beating she took. I wanted kids, but not right now, so she was going to have to get rid of that shit.

"I don't want no babies, Mysti. Not right now. It's too much going on."

"You know what? You always acting like this with me! You say you don't love Kenyan and she ain't ya type, but yet and still, you wanna stay in that fat bitch's presence! She was pregnant by you *twice!* If her big ass could carry a baby, y'all would have kids, Rome! I been around for years playing second to a man that was supposed to be mine! I'm sick of this shit, Rome! You say you don't care for her, but you still trying to fight this case that's closed! I ain't no dummy, Rome! I know you jealous! Now you see she not worried about ya ass because she knows the truth, and you can't deal with it! You mad because your dear old stuck up fat bitch snagged her a baller and left ya raggedy ass!" Mysti yelled, causing my anger to build up.

Whap...Whap...Whap...

I jumped up so fast and was now on top of Mysti delivering slap after slap to her face.

"You always were jealous of Kenyan! To be honest, you'll never be half the woman she is! Fat this fat, but other than, that you ain't got shit on her! So, that's why you so mad! Kenyan may be fat, but she beautiful, got a good head on her shoulders, and she make her own money! Unlike you! She never stayed home and waited for me to come give her money! She got her own!" I yelled while still hitting Mysti. I didn't know what the fuck came over me.

"Rome, please stop hitting me! The baby, Rome, the baby!" Mysti yelled, and it caused me to stop.

I didn't even realize I had blacked out for a second and continued to hit her. Mysti was curled up on the floor crying, and I didn't like the sight of what I just did. So, I hurried and gathered my things. I knew she was going to call the police, so I decided to call to let them know a call was going to come through so they'd fix it. After I made a couple of phone calls, I decided to head over to the Baker estate to find out what exactly was going on between Kenyan and Nasir. For some reason, the shit was bothering me. I thought I wasn't in love with Kenyan, but now I'm having mix feelings.

☆☆☆☆☆

I was hiding in the woods behind Nasir's house watching him and Kenyan. This had been what I was doing ever since I found out she was here. Watching them kiss and hug and be all lovey-dovey had me fucked up. I was starting to wonder where the hell that baby been at. It was like she hadn't been home for the past couple of days unless they just kept her inside the house. Nasir leaned over and kissed Kenyan on the lips before going into the house. Since he had gone, I used this for a chance to make a move. I sat and watched Kenyan a little longer, looking around making sure I didn't see anyone else, then I walked around the bush's and entered the yard. This nigga needed a better system out here. Got all this money and this weak gate.

"So, this is what it is, huh?" I asked while walking in front of Kenyan what my gun pointed to her.

"Rome! What are you doing here?!"

I could tell from the surprised look on her face that she wasn't expecting me. "Hmm...I should be asking you that question. My fiancé has been working with a drug dealer for the past couple of months, and I'm just now finding out about it. Then I started following you, and guess what I've been seeing? My bitch kissing all over this nigga! Tell me, Kenyan, has he fucked yet?" I asked, mean mugging her ass.

Kenyan looked at me like I had lost my damn mind before she spoke. "Nigga, please! You don't want me, so why does it matter to you who I'm dealing with? You already got you a bitch, and a bad one too. Ain't that right Jerome?"

"Baby, what are you talking about?" I asked like I didn't know.

"Don't play with me, Rome. Ya girl told me everything, which kind of made me understand better. I was shocked and hurt, but then I thought about it. I haven't been feeling ya ass for some time now, and it's about time I moved on. What really had me pissed off was the fact that the other woman was supposed to be my best friend. The other thing that had me wanting to kill you was the part about you trying to get my daddy's job! Like, you really went this far to move up in the department. Now ya stupid ass is going to get fired because you're trespassing and not following direct orders to stand down. This is a closed case no matter if what you think is right or not. Nasir is innocent, and you have no way of finding out anything different. So if you were smart, you would walk away now."

"I'm not going a damn place! I'm waiting for your Superman to come out. So, that way I can save you from the notorious Nasir Baker. See, you found out some things while being here with him, and you called me so I can take him in. But when I got here, he had already found out that you were the daughter of a lieutenant. He also found out your fiancé was a detective, and you were in on taking him down. So, when he found out, he shot you, and then his self to keep from going to jail."

Pow...Pow...Pow...

I let off three shots into Kenyan while heading into the house to get Nasir. As soon as I made it into the house, I was met by a gun being placed at the back of my head.

"You had a nice little plan home boy, but too bad it didn't fall through," Nasir said from behind.

The minute I was about to turn to him to grab his gun, I was met by Lieutenant Moore facing me. "Rome you're a disgrace to the field. I can't believe you did all of this just for my job that you weren't even sure you were going to get. Just because you move up doesn't mean you would have been in my spot. Not to mention there has been so many complaints over the years about you. I'm the reason you even still had a job. Then you around here playing with my baby's heart.

"I've been keeping a close eye on you because I've noticed how you've been acting since the case was closed. My daughter had even called me and told me what was going on. Then Davis came an told me what happened to Mysti. When she told him that you beat her up because she was pregnant, he felt bad and took her to the hospital and called me. He said he's sick of covering for you."

"You're so fucking weak, which is why you'll never get anywhere in the department!" I snapped at Lieutenant Moore.

He chuckled, right before he spoke. "You're right, Rome, because after this case, I decided it was time for me to retire, and guess who was next to sit in my seat? You until they started reporting ya dumb ass. I had put in a year ago to retire, and it was happening after this case. Since the case was closed, I decided to retire earlier. So, the jokes on you, young man. Boys, take his ass away."

Davis began to read me my rights while he placed the hand cuffs on me. Right before I went to walk out of the door, Kenyan was walking in with another officer.

"You ok, baby girl!"

"Yes, daddy. I'm just glad the vest helped. The power from the bullet just made me fall back, and I figured that was good for the show." Kenyan giggled, while running over to Nasir.

"Thanks for calling me, son. I know we have been enemies for years, but I was just doing my job. I don't know how to feel about you dating my baby, but she's assured me that you're a good person, and I'mma just hold you to that. It's going to take me some getting used to, but I'll try for her. Just, please. If you have any illegal activity going on, keep her away from it. I may be a retired cop, but I'll come out of retirement for my baby," Lieutenant Moore said to Nasir.

Chapter Sixteen

Kenyan

Four months later

It had been an amazing four months being in a relationship with Nasir. At first, I was battling with myself about moving in with him, so I just ended up getting my own apartment. Which lead to me not staying for two months, so I just decided to move in with Nasir and Treasure. I just couldn't deal with not waking up to the both of them. So, I stopped playing and made the big move. My dad wasn't too happy. He still felt like we were moving too fast, but I assured him I was ok. Nasir's dad couldn't get past me being his arch enemy's daughter, but he still respected me for how I care for Treasure.

I don't know what they gon' do, but Nasir and I don't feel like we should slow down for anybody. They may not love our relationship, but they damn sure gon' respect it.

"Hey, baby. Hold her for a second. I have to go finish setting up the tables in the back room," Nasir said while handing me Treasure.

We were getting ready for her half-year party. Treasure was now six months. She was sitting up, saying mom-mom and dad-dad, giggling and slobbering. She had become a precious gem in my life. Not only was I attached to her, but my parents were as well. My daddy wasn't sure how to feel about us being together, but he sure loved Treasure. I knew eventually she would bring us all together.

"Baby, I don't know why you just didn't hire someone to do that," I said truthfully.

"This is one of the milestones I wanted to help with. We already hired Charlee to decorate and someone to cook. The least I could do is set up the tables and chairs."

Nasir was serious about everything for Treasure, and it was so cute to me. She was definitely his pride and joy. Treasure was loved by so many. Her grandmom had even started to visit in the past couple of months. It was hard for her, but we sat and had a long talk, and I convinced her to come and see her. I also told her that Terri was smiling down on how much everyone loved Treasure.

"Alright, baby. I guess you're right."

Today we had all of the family coming over to help celebrate. We had all went out last night to Meek and Cody's engagement party. Everything was so beautiful, and I was so happy for the both of them. Meek and Charlee had become my good friends. At first, it was kind of awkward since I had just gone through all of that with Mysti. But then when I thought about it, these were different kind of friends. For starters, they both were in relationships. So, I was now hanging with women that were on my level. Being with them made me realize half of the arguments Mysti and I had gotten into were because she was jealous of me. I had heard from hospital staff that she was still pregnant with Rome's baby, while he was serving time. I heard even though he still talks to her like shit, she still makes sure to visit him every chance she got. They both deserved each other, and I'm glad their bullshit came to the light before it was too late.

As far as the hospital, I went back to work a couple of weeks ago. I decided to keep a per diem schedule. Even though Nasir said I didn't need to work, I still did a couple of days a week.

Shit, I didn't work my ass off to go to school to be a nurse to just give it all up.

Treasure was doing great, and Nasir was cool with being home with her the two days I worked. If he had things to do, either my parents or his parents would keep her.

Nasir, Khalif, and Cody had business booming. Since they had gotten off the cop's radar, it was easy for them to really get in position to clean all of their money and businesses up.

Their girls continued to do different types of things they enjoyed doing too. Meek had a hair boutique online, while Charlee was getting booked for plenty of different events.

We all were happy and living life to the fullest. I never had intentions of things falling into place like this, but I wasn't against it at all. When I look back on how Nasir Baker used to be one of them fine ass dope boys me and the girls used to rant and rave about, I never in a million years thought I would be in love with him today. Hell, I didn't think he would be interested in me, but guess what! Just like big girls love dope boys, dope boys love big girls too!

The End!